HOWLING SHADOW

CORRUPTED REALMS – BOOK TWO

T. B. PHILLIPS

Howling Shadow
Corrupted Realms, Book Two

Published by Andalon Press
Copyright © 2022 by T.B. Phillips

Cover design by Lynnette Bonner of Indie Cover Design, images ©
  depositphotos.com, File: # 308011538 – background
  depositphotos.com, File: # 113498914 – wolf
  depositphotos.com, File: # 237166398 – wolf 2
Map artwork by Cary Beshel
Book interior design by Stewart Design, https://StewartDesign.studio

ISBN 979-8-9872191-1-9

Books by T.B. Phillips

Chilling Tales
Ferryman (October 2022)
Don't Pay the Ferryman (Expected June 2023)

Corrupted Realms
Wailing Tempest (May 2021)
Howling Shadow (September 2021)

Andalon Saga

Andalon Origins
Andalon Project (April 2022)
Andalon Paradox (Epected Winter 2022)

Dreamers of Andalon
Andalon Awakens (June 2019)
Andalon Arises (July 2020)
Andalon Attacks (December 2020)

Children of Andalon
Andalon Legacy (September 2022)

Helpful Tidbits

CAST OF FAE CHARACTERS
Alistaria – Queen of the Fae
Betarian – (Deceased) King of the Fainne and general of the Kern
Brechan – A Fainnen root tender
Clíodhna – (Deceased) Banshee Queen and ruler of the Deamhan/
Biological mother of Alistaria
Girtrán – Former Fainnen King. Enchanted the Deamhan to appear
as Banshee
Kern – Elite Fainnen military force
Korl – A Fainnen root tender and teacher
Maerlin – Deamhanen Skygate Sentry
Nastauria – (Deceased) Daughter of King Betarian/Mother of Alistaria.
Stripped of title
Palathia – Former root tender and member of Tuatha
Restarian – Grandson of King Betarian/A root tender
Sìth Morkur – (Shē Morkur) – Master of beasts
Torian – Kern general of Fainnotheria
Tuatha – Elite combination of Kern and mages

CAST OF HUMAN CHARACTERS
Boyd – A thief (and not a very good one)
Conner Liam – General of the Storm Riders
Markey O'Malley – King of Enatherr
Niamh – A former Searcher loyal to Lord Radviken
Lord Nodrick – Exiled Storm Warden loyal to Lord Radviken
Piotr – A thief (and not a very good one either)
Lord Radviken – (Deceased) King of the human realm/Betrayer
of Nastauria

THE PLACES
Fainnotherr – Fairy Realm
Enatherr – Human Realm
Luchorpár – Gnome Realm

THE RELICS
The Bláth de Saol – Blossom of Life
Healing – Rose/Ruby
Resurrection – White Lily/Pearl
Corruption – Black Iris/Onyx
Sight – Hydrangea/Emerald
Fire – Begonia/Garnet
Water – Hyacinth/Aquamarine
Air – Aster/Lapis
Power –Morning Glory/Diamond

Bláth de Eolas – Blossom of Knowledge
Blossom Gifted to Humans (Currently Owned by the Luchorpán)
Powers and Description Unknown to our Characters

The Bláth de Cumhacht – Blossom of Power
Blossom Gifted to Luchorpán (Currently Owned by the Luchorpán)
Powers and Description Unknown to our Characters

N
W
E
S
NORGAARD
MIDLANDIS
BAY of WINDS
DUNE SEA
CROSSTON
PORT of ENAT
RIVANIA
ENATHERR

N
W
E
S
Deamhan Palace
Fainnotheria
FAINNOTHERR

Part One
Tuatha

Chapter One

"They came to us aboard a gleaming ship, slipping through the fog as if settling from the sky itself. They were warriors, clad in shining armor and bearing weapons equipped with powers unbelieved if not recorded in these tomes. Each and every Tuatha de Dannan was a god to us, truly people descended from the spirit Danu."
– The Annals of History Book III, Passage 12

The sun dipped below the horizon, casting perpetual shadow over a darkening forest. Not a single star shone in the sky and chilling breezes cut through the branches overhead. In the distance, animals screeched into the blackness—a sign either of life or one ending. Shivers ran down the arms of every fae gathered around the ring. Nervous eyes darted amongst the soldiers, betraying distrust and lack of unity. The shriek meant something different to each.

Not long before, that sound would have warned some in these ranks of approaching Banshee, hell-bent on destroying peace. To the others it bellowed defiance of oppression and bias against their visage. But the corruption marring the Banshee had been lifted by their new queen, Alistaria—a girl raised within the very walls of Fainnotheria as the granddaughter of the Fainnen King. She had issued a single command during her coronation, that both races must work together under a common name. Gone were the kingdoms of Fainne and Deamhan, for they were finally united as fae.

No longer at war, they discovered a new threat lurking beyond the portals in the Shadow Realm. Alistaria ordered immediate integration of both the root tender ranks and the newly formed military. Despite quiet grumblings by those with the most closed of minds, the unification had proved effective as both sides brought talent of equal measure. Former Deamhan demonstrated powerful abilities not only to heal and wield fairy spark, but also with swinging swords and spears. Though odd to see former Banshees wearing golden armor, these gathered comprised the first of the unified Kern—warriors of legend and the best fighters Fainnotheria had to offer.

Torian's mind raced with his own anxiety, but battle waited on the other side of the portal, and it cared not about race. Even now, as their general leading the charge, Torian was far different than his soldiers. He was a changeling, a human raised among the fae, but none cared as long as he proved the bravest and most capable leader. Besides, soldiers had a way of overcoming bias simply by sharing the dangers of a lurking threat—with trust won by teamwork and respect earned by selfless deeds.

He stepped forward, a signal to the men their attention was needed elsewhere, and they adjusted ranks around him. Under the late King Betarian, the Kern had been an elite force of single units whose best tactic was swarming their enemy with speed and agility. But this general had a new tactic to try—one better suited to fighting in the other realms. In Enatherr, flight would be a wanton dream, so he lined shoulder to shoulder to fight on the ground.

In this formation, their golden armor and glistening shields formed a wall ten soldiers wide by three deep with spears outstretched. If one fell, another could step forward into the phalanx and replace him. Likewise, each shield position could move in unison providing protection to any threatened side. More importantly, simple facing movements could redirect their attack with a single command, allowing them to outflank their enemy as quickly as they could retreat.

Though eager to test his army's recent training, he hesitated before committing them forward, one rank at a time, into the Fainnen Ring. He drew in a soothing breath of calm. Letting it out slowly, the general nodded to companions who signaled they were also ready.

He commanded their advance, and the first line fae stepped through the portal.

The blinding flash of light muddled his senses on the other side, but it was surely better than before. The first time he had crossed over, Torian had passed out from pain, awakening with muscles contorted and trembling against wanton spasm. But now, with Radviken's curses gone, the experience only mildly affected the travelers as they emerged in a melee of violence. He had expected the battle had already begun, but failed to anticipate the enemy's numbers.

Here, the entire forest crawled with Draugars who moved with greater speed than one would expect from the dead—a sure sign little was actually known about the Shadow Realm. The reeking bodies passed around his position while avoiding the ring, heavy with decay or advanced enough in their rot to resemble loosely constructed skeletal beings.

They had pinned down a small group of human Storm Riders in a clearing up ahead. Knowing the dead couldn't step inside its boundary, his squad took a moment to acclimate before taking up stances. He wished again for flight, but focused instead on the new tactics. The other line would emerge soon, so he looked around quickly to determine his action and a way to step out of the ring.

The Storm Riders stood shoulder to shoulder, forced to dismount, and backed into a line along the forest edge. Each a master swordsman, they cut down the advancing spirits as they came, pushed back by their numbers but clearly overwhelmed. There were only six against the horde, and Torian frowned at the small number sent by Markey O'Malley. Either the king underestimated the enemy's strength, or he had fewer men to spare. He had no time to waste.

"Shields! Ready!" He commanded, locking his with the fae on his left and each soldier doing the same. "Spears! Ready!" Their silvery weapons reflected the moonlight as they were raised, ringing a metallic resonance as they fell into place upon their shields. "Forward! Charge!"

The squad ran in unison toward the skirmish, crashing into the Draugar focused entirely on the Riders and pressing them into the backs of their kind pressing ahead. This enraged the spirits, and many turned to face the newcomers head on. The move split the enemy force, catching them squarely between the allies. Torian frowned at the iron weapons in their hands, surely meant to harm the fae with the metal's poisonous properties. *But not me*, he thought, *because I'm not fae.*

The dead suddenly parted, inviting his squad deeper into their mass of gnashing teeth, but his men had prepared for the move and held position.

They expected us, he realized, suddenly suspecting a trap. "Spearhead! Adjust!" His own line folded slightly, resembling the point of an arrow and facing the two fronts with an angular defense.

He didn't have to wait long for the second wave. More Draugar leapt from the underbrush and moved to flank. His eyes flashed to the Fainnen Ring as he wondered what delayed the second squad. Moments later the ring flashed and he breathed a sigh of relief. "Rank! Close!" he shouted, adding with urgency, "Shields! Turtle!"

The fae in his line moved as a single unit, pivoting, and placed shields all around the squad. Each soldier took advantage of the brief respite and waited, breathing in each other's body heat. The odor of battle was a mixture of metallic and musk as they listened for the signal to lower their shields and resume fighting.

"Squad two! Flanking! Break!" came the shout from the second squad, signaling they had emerged and were in position.

"Broken squad! Ranks!" cried Torian, and his squad broke into two rows of five, each facing a different direction and enemy. His line faced their attackers, now turned against the reinforcements. "Thrust!" Five spears attacked in unison while the line of Kern reinforcements did the same. The Draugar screamed into the night as they died. "Phalanx! Fall in!" he commanded, and his line turned to rejoin their original foe. The reinforcements fell into a line behind his and the two squads became one. He felt the reassuring heat of comrades behind him as they marched slowly forward, thrusting and stabbing over his shoulder at the animated dead. Soon, the third and final rank had emerged, bolstering his unit. After a few short minutes, his front line stared at six very thankful Riders with the fallen remains of Draugar beneath the feet of the phalanx.

"You came just in time," one of the humans grumbled.

"It appears so." Torian stepped forward with an outstretched hand which the Rider eyed suspiciously. *At least the* humans *view me as fae,* he thought, putting it away unshaken. "I'm called Torian, General of the Kern."

"I'm O'Donnel, Rider of the Riders." He must have made a joke because the other five Storm Riders laughed. None of them seemed happy to be fighting alongside fae, even if they *had* just saved them in battle.

Torian turned his head and eyed the carnage all around. Something was off. He looked down at the closest Draugar, a mere skeleton with decaying flesh stretched over bones. One of its eyes was long rotted out, and the other was a ghostly white. The long beard was coated with blood, but had been bright blonde at some point. The armor it wore was unlike any he had ever seen on either human or fae. It was beaten bronze and ancient in make. Whoever these dead men were, they were not recently passed. He pulled a vial of yellow paint from his tunic and splashed it on the chestplate.

"What are you doing?" one of the humans asked.

"Marking him in case he rises again."

The man's eyes grew wide with fear and he asked, "You think he will?"

"I have a theory, that's all." Torian looked around. "I know the Tempest hasn't returned this month, but what of Ganshee? Have you seen any since Radviken fell?"

The Riders exchanged more looks of worry, and one of them spoke while pointing upward into the trees. "The pixies are around, but they won't touch these bodies."

He pointed upward, and Torian spied several Ganshee hovering in the trees overhead, chittering and gnashing teeth with displeasure over the offered meal. *Odd,* he thought, as they were usually quick to devour decaying flesh. "Where do they go, the Draugar after they're killed?"

"We don't know. About an hour after, they simply disappear."

Torian nodded. He'd had the same experience with the other's he'd dispatched before. "Tell me why there're only six of you. Their numbers have obviously grown, and would've wiped you all if we hadn't arrived when we did."

"We haven't men to spare, fairy boy. We're spread out covering each city as well as these damned portals."

Torian ignored the edge to the man's voice. "Have you figured out how they're getting inside your realm?"

"How can we? By the time dark falls, it's as if they're here already! Tonight they popped up all around our camp as early as dusk!"

"Here?" Torian asked, pointing to the spot on which he stood.

"Yes." The Rider replied. "Well, not exactly. We were over there." He pointed to a small escarpment in the woods. It was devoid of trees but not of fauna. Through the dense brush Torian could tell the ground was higher here, a rounded mound, but nothing appeared supernatural or out of sorts. There were no caves or entrances he could find. He fanned out his squad to finish searching while he talked to Rider O'Donnel.

An animal howled in the distance—too guttural to be a wolf and lacking the high pitched whine for which that animal was known. The hairs all over Torian's body stood atop chilled bumps on his skin. The human standing with him laughed.

"You've never heard a hellhound's howl, have you?" the human asked.

"No," Torian shook his head. He'd heard of the beasts, but only in legend.

"Neither had we, until our Riders reported hearing one or two near the Port of Enat. It's said they're moving farther north each night, but those sounded close."

"Too close," Torian agreed. When he turned from scanning the tree line, he found the man staring questioningly as if he'd something more to say. "What is it?" he demanded.

"You're the human changeling, aren't you? The one they're sayin' was swapped for a fairy."

Torian flinched. Markey had told him he'd become a celebrity—the fae-trained warrior who had bested the greatest swordsman to ever serve among the Storm Riders. He tried to push by, hoping to avoid the usual questions, but the man stepped to block his exit. They were always the same—wanting to know how it was living among the fae, but failing to realize he couldn't compare this life to one he'd been denied. He knew nothing about being human. "What do you want?" he asked in a low growl.

"I heard something about Markey," the man said. "Maybe you can tell me if it's true."

Torian paused, suddenly aware all six pairs of human eyes stared while awaiting his response.

"I barely know your king," he lied, pushing past. He wanted to search the bodies of the Draugar. For what, he did not know, but even rifling through the pockets of the dead beat having conversation with humans.

"But you did spend several days traveling with him," one of the others pointed out, "and you *were* there when he killed Radviken."

"He didn't kill Radviken," Torian corrected, "the Sith claimed him as part of their deal."

"But you were there," O'Donnel insisted, "so you can answer to the truth."

"What truth?" Torian whirled around to face him. "Which truth do you want to know? Every time I save a group of you Riders from the Draugars, I get the same questions: 'Are the Banshees coming back?' or 'Is Radviken really dead?' Well, he's gone and the fae are your allies now." He pointed to a squad of his Kern gathered around a flat stone. "They're fae, and look no different than you in this realm."

"What I wanted to ask," the Rider said intently, "is Markey really one of them?"

Torian felt his breath leave him at once and paused. He'd worried this question would emerge. "He's human by all accounts," he said, "and the son of Radviken. He passed every test your Storm Warden gave him."

"Then who's his mother?" one of the Riders asked. "We're hearing tales Radviken bedded the Banshee Queen."

That was a question the Kern general hadn't been prepared to answer. His eyes flicked back and forth between the men, each awaiting his answer.

"Is it true then?" O'Donnel asked. "Is our new king the brother of your Queen? Is he really a Banshee?"

Torian suddenly realized he had no answer. It was true, but the knowledge would damn his friend and ruin relations between the realms—at a time they needed to work together to push back the Shadow Realm. He finally found words and hoped they'd be enough.

"You all served with Markey O'Malley, rode and trained beside him for more than a decade. What difference would it make if he *were*?" In the distance another howl caused the men to perk their ears. It sounded closer than the first. "He's the son of Radviken, and therefore, your king. And right now your realm is under constant attack from dark forces and you need help from fae to fight." Another guttural bray was followed by distant barking. Torian felt his skin welt up with goosebumps and added, "At this point, what difference would it make if your king were a *hellhound*?"

Before the men could answer, a shout of excitement came from the escarpment and several Kern beckoned furiously. Thankfully, Torian broke away and hurried over.

They stood around a flat stone, partially uncovered from an ancient burial. He could tell it was longer than it was wide and still mostly buried in the earth. It was taller than a man and as wide across as one's shoulders, and probably had stood erect at some point in its distant past.

"There's writing," one of the Kern pointed out.

Torian saw it too, deeply inscribed with strange runes he couldn't make out. "We need to study these," Torian realized. "It's too heavy to take with us, and we've nothing to take a rubbing." Then he remembered the vial of paint. Laying down his shield, he took out the vial and dipped the tip of a branch into it, transcribing the yellow letters onto the silvery metal.

"The Draugar have disappeared," O'Donnel said from beside him.

Torian only nodded, too focused on copying down the runes. "You'll need to make a rubbing of this and get it to Markey," he told the Rider.

"I will."

After he finished, he waved the shield around in the air, hastening the paint to dry, then led his Kern toward the Fainnen Ring. "We'll send another squad tomorrow evening, and every night thereafter," he told O'Donnel. "Just remember we're your allies in this, and your king is a better option than Radviken." He did not wait for an answer and stepped through with the first squad. With a flash of light, he was gone. Back to the only realm he ever truly considered home.

CHAPTER TWO

The roots of the great trees thrummed with vibrant life. Overhead the flapping of wings broke the gentle rushing of wind through leaves, and Alistaria looked up from her work. Where her eyes would have once found wailing Banshees among the lush canopy, she smiled to find birds had returned to the forest and their sweet chorus settled the girl's heart. The period of warfare between the fae had ended, replaced instead by uncertain peace. She would enjoy it as long as it lasted.

It had been several weeks since her tenders had removed the beetles hiding in the bark, and new growth had sprouted near ancient stumps and fallen trunks where much of the forest had recently died off. It wouldn't be long, she hoped, for rejuvenation to reach the ancient ruin in the far Northeast (the once home of her birth mother's refuge) called simply the Deamhan Palace.

It turned out Alistaria had two mothers, one she loved and missed dearly and the other she knew not at all. That she did not love Clíodhna did not mean she was incapable of bonding with her late memory. She yearned to learn more about the woman from who's womb she had been stolen at birth. She would stop at nothing to understand and unite both her people—those who shared her blood and also those belonging to the culture in which she was raised.

She returned brown eyes to the forest floor, pausing to watch tenders going about their work. Three young women were nearby, demonstrating to a boy how he should feel along the roots for life-force. She recognized these four as once being Fainne, and noticed how they made a point to avoid two other women listening from a distance. She shook her head with disgust and rose into the air with the barest vibration of wings.

"Do you have any questions?" Alistaria asked of the women listening on. They no longer resembled Deamhan, the once sworn enemy of the tenders. She spoke loud enough to shame the others who had shunned them. All eyes dropped to the forest floor, some with embarrassment and the others in reverence. Alistaria was barely a young woman, but bore herself with grace and dignity of a queen—an attribute learned from the late Nastauria. She addressed the entire gathering with gentle rebuke.

"We'll never recover our livelihood unless everyone works together and forgives the past," she warned. To the two women she said, "And you must not tolerate even the quietest slight, whether intentional or not." She quickly added, "But do so lovingly, as we must treat others with example. You cannot live in ignorance simply because they avoid your company. They only do so because their ignorance of you is greater than yours for their ways. They fear the future and can't let go of the past. *All* of us should look past who we once were and accept who we are together."

"Yes, Queen Alistaria," all six woman replied with eyes down. Only the boy looked upon his queen directly, seeming to fully accept the changes she had brought. *Of course the children understand,* she thought. *It will be the elders of our people who are slow to accept the new way of life. Change is easier for the youngest.* She knew she should end their rebuke there, the lesson taught by what she had already said, but added more for measure. "We are all fae now as we've always been. You've seen the tapestries I brought back. Are they not displayed in the Chamber of Life for all to view?"

"Yes, your highness," they each agreed.

"The true history of our people dates back even further than those, when we were of one people before splitting off to find their equal way. Though we may never know much before recorded times, I hope our kind are never fractured again. That is our future, for which we must strive."

Upon that she left them, wings beating and bearing her away to tend another darkness in the form of a damaged trunk. As she stole a glance over her shoulder she smiled, observing the larger group had accepted the women with newfound welcome. Busying herself with a burl, she continued to listen to their distant conversation with hope. She smiled inwardly after detecting quiet laughter and a lifting of their previous discomfort. It would take time, she knew, but full unity *would* someday be reality.

She suddenly frowned.

The cancerous knot bulging the bark was not of the usual kind. Though it appeared similar to the eye, the thrumming lifeforce rang with a resonance that failed to match the rest of the tree. She leaned in close and listened, waiting for the distinct off-beat vibration. There it was. Faint but surely present. Drawing upon the strength of both the healing rose and the morning glory of power at the same time, she tried to realign the thrum. It refused to respond to her ministrations, and so she called another tender over. The man she beckoned was named Korl, one of the most adept of tenders. He hurried to her side, his magnificent wings gracefully pushing against the air with the slightest of effort.

"What is it, Alistaria?" he asked, using her given name. She understood when some of the elders had left off her title, and it didn't bother her when some of the others skipped the formality. She was, after all, the same girl she had been before the adventure that resulted in her crowning. But it came as a surprise when one of the teachers, one she had herself been lucky enough to train under, dropped the honorific in front of young tenders. The slight almost sounded intentional and worried the young queen.

She pushed her insecurities aside and drew his attention to the problem. "Take a look at this burl and tell me why I can't heal it," she commanded.

Korl leaned in, placing one hand on the tumor and the other against the healthy portion of the trunk. "It seems the usual malady," he assured her. "You must simply realign the passage of lifeforce to work out the kink that is blocking flow. Now that we have access to power," he said, "you can force it into place like a broken bone if need be."

"I tried that," she explained. "But something is off and I can't explain it."

Distant shouting drowned out what he said next, and she flew off immediately to investigate. Leaving him to work, she made haste toward the Skygate. There, she found a group of male tenders had surrounded one of the sentries. He stood alone as his companions idled off to avoid getting involved.

"You don't deserve the silver," one of the tenders said mere inches from his face, slapping at the sword at his side and daring him to push back. But the sentry resisted, staring stoically ahead while the tender continued. "Just a few weeks ago you were attacking this entrance, you don't deserve to guard it now!"

"How do we know you won't let the enemy inside when they come again?" another asked.

"Yeah!" Agreed the other. "How do we know you don't have more Banshee hanging around the old palace?"

"Is there a problem here?" a commanding voice interrupted. The idle soldiers saw the newcomer right away and snapped to attention, but the others did not. Torian landed beside the guard and used his silver spear to push the tenders away. "I asked if there's a problem here. Is there?"

"No, sir," one of the tenders admitted, stepping away and leaving his friend to stand alone against the general.

A general, Alistaria mused. *My general,* she thought proudly. He had worked hard to rebuild the Kern to their glory, but also commanded the Skygate—the place he had once protected without regard for his own life. She was curious to see how he handled this problem.

Torian addressed the remaining heckler. "Is this how it is, then?" he demanded. "I selected this fae myself for this detail, do you challenge *his* validity or *my* authority?"

"Fae?" the tender sneered. "We both know what he is, even if our eyes are enchanted to see otherwise. He's a Banshee and doesn't deserve to guard the Skygate." He spat his disdain, leaving the spittle to roll down the silver armor of the sentry's chestplate.

Alistaria had heard enough and stepped forward. "Your name is Brechan, is it not?"

"Yes," the tender replied without taking his eyes from Torian. When the commander bowed deeply before her, the tender turned with surprise, not expecting to find the queen standing beside him. "I mean yes, *your highness*," he corrected.

With a wave of her hand she sent a cloud to wash over the tender. He shuddered under the cold touch of the cloud, then cried out in fear—unsure what magic she had wielded or the damage she may have done. Everyone gathered took a step backward, including Torian. She had worked the gift of sight and altered his appearance.

Brechan looked down at his hands, once slender and smooth, now coarsely heavy with thick hues of dark grey. He reached up his hands and touched his cheeks, once graceful and rounded, now bulging with bony protrusions beneath the skin. He touched a fingertip to an orange tooth and recoiled from the sharp tip of the incisor. His once bright green eyes stared up at Alistaria like two voids—dark pools swimming with corruption and as seemingly endless where his soul had once resided.

"It seems," she said calmly to the root tender, "you now have something in common with this Skygate sentry. Like him, you have worn a false veil of corruption which has blinded others to your true form. I could grant this gift forever, by using corruption instead of sight, so you may feel how it is to have ignorance hurled back, when your only transgression was to walk among others."

Brechan opened his mouth to plead the queen's mercy, but his voice had left him. In its place was the mournful wail of sorrow and pain. He swallowed and tried once more to speak, but his voice was rendered a screeching cry as Banshee wails poured forth instead of audible words. He wheeled on his friend, the other tender who had jeered the sentry. That Fainne fell backward trying to scramble away, shrieking and whimpering and wanting nothing to do with his friend.

Alistaria snapped her fingers. Abruptly the root tender stood as before, the veil lifted and looking once more like himself. His friends laughed at the look on his face, mocking and jeering as he fell to his knees and begged his queen for mercy. But she noticed the stoic sentry responded differently. His eyes held pity for the Fainne sniveling before him, and Alistaria immediately realized her mistake. She should never have publicly shamed the tender. In her attempt to sow empathy, she had inadvertently sparked fear. Brechan would blame the sentry and take it out on him if he ever had him alone—or was forced to heal him in battle.

"Go about your business," she commanded suddenly, and all in attendance scurried off except Torian and the sentry. "I'm sorry," she said. "I followed my instinct and let emotion guide my actions. I may have worsened the situation."

To her chagrin the sentry nodded agreement. "It is getting worse, not better," he said. "Though you've brought us together, a simple desire for unity is never enough. Many of the Deamhan feel entitled now to receive more than promises, and the Fainne fear they will be put under the boot if we are granted too much control over key positions."

"There's no more Fainne or Deamhan," Alistaria corrected. "We are all the same as we once were and are only fae."

The sentry shook his head sadly. "No. I'm afraid that kind of thinking is the problem. We've been forced to sleep in a nest, piled upon one another and huddled for warmth for so long. We are unable to vocalize our true needs and desires to those with power. The worse crime King Girtrán committed upon us was theft."

"Of your dignity?" she asked.

"No, my queen. He stole our voice. Without a voice, no group of people is ever equal to those in charge. We were judged by appearance, but our lack of voice further reduced us to savages in the eyes of the Fainne—even to you, I recall."

"You... recall?" she asked. She was confused. *Have I met him before?* He was not familiar in this form. "You saw *us* as savages, as well!"

"Yes, we saw you as blind, deaf, and dumb to our hearts and souls," he said. "I know because I came across you in the human realm. You were frightened, running from the Ganshee when you became tangled in the burial pyres."

"You spoke to me."

"I spoke to you *and* you understood, replying back in our language and begging for help."

"I remember," she said. "You were cruel with your words, claiming all Fainne deserved the fate they'd receive."

"That was not me," he replied, "I was the other. I said your pleas were in vain and left you to face your sins."

"Had we not wrought so much suffering on you, would I have received your mercy? I doubt that very much. But I *did* turn out a Deamhan. Do you still believe I should've been denied your aid?"

"Your blood turned out Deamhan, but you truly know nothing about living as one. You've been pampered here in Fainnotheria. True, it was no fault of your own, but you know nothing of our plight. Your hopes of instant and lasting peace are those of a child, foolish and blind to what goes on when you are not around."

Alistaria stiffened at his honesty. "You challenge my authority, then?"

"Not at all," he replied. "You are my queen. I merely worry you will take too long to discover the best path to this peace and unity you preach."

"What's your name?" she asked.

"I am called Maerlin."

"Torian," she said to the general standing by, "I want Maerlin to continue to guard the Skygate, but also to serve on my personal guard. Ensure he rotates several times a week, so we may continue this candor with more depth. And more often."

Maerlin seemed confused. "I've spoken openly. I don't understand why you'd seek to place me closer to your person."

"I need to surround myself with truth at *all* times, but especially now. It's your council and company I seek. Especially your wisdom."

He opened his mouth to speak, but shouts from the forest floor caused her to turn with sudden alarm. Several root tenders were racing upward with someone draped limply in their arms.

"Who is it?" Torian asked.

She strained her eyes to identify the fallen healer, but couldn't tell from this height. When they stumbled onto the platform, she recognized Korl. Kneeling beside him, she demanded, "What happened?"

"We don't know. We came upon him just as he is, lying next to a tree and unmoving."

Alistaria placed a hand on the teacher and felt for his lifeforce. It beat slowly, but there was an odd rhythm thrumming out of sync with the rest of him. Whatever had corrupted the great tree had worked its way into Korl.

"Should we have left him for the Sìth?" one of the tenders asked anxiously.

"No," Alistaria replied, "at least I don't believe so. He's alive, but something's terribly wrong with his spirit. Take him to Chamber of Life, but for observation. Until we understand exactly what happened, I won't risk any more healers."

She suddenly wished Nastauria could give her council and felt starkly alone beneath her crown.

CHAPTER THREE

"Every god has a dark side, and we learned to keep always in their light. It took many generations to learn they weren't to be worshipped."
– Annals of History Book III, Passage 30

Alistaria ordered Korl moved closer to the Bláth de Saol. His hidden injuries were very real, and she hoped the healing power of the Blossom would speed recovery. The soft pulse of the bloom seemed to have no effect on his body, and full recovery remained a distant hope. Something about his lifeforce felt foreign, just as she detected within the tumor of the great tree. She stood beside him, helplessly watching as the shimmering glow-stones cast shadows upon his skin. She was unsure how to proceed.

The elders gathered, looming behind their young queen and silently watching her every move. *No doubt they judge me, deciding if I'm worthy of this crown or if my actions will destroy our people.* She wanted to run away and hide, wishing this nightmare would end with a gasp of sudden awakening. *If only this* were *a dream,* she thought, *Nastauria would still be alive.* Another thought gripped her stomach and squeezed hard as she watched the elders staring wordlessly. *And they would no longer see Clíodhna's face when they look upon* me.

Erania, the eldest, cleared her throat and tried to calm the young queen's fears. "We're doing what we can for him, but you mustn't blame yourself, dear."

The words echoed in Alistaria's mind, braiding anxiety with new fears. *Is that how they view this?* she wondered. *Did I bring a curse upon my people?* She decided to confront the woman as Nastauria would have.

"But do *they*, I wonder? Will my people blame me? Or do your words reflect only the elder's thoughts?"

Erania's long pause confirmed Alistaria's suspicion.

"You're divided, then?" She turned to face them fully. "Speak to me directly of your fears and let's have it out. If our wisest can't agree on unification, then our people never will."

Erania cleared her throat and spoke for the assembly. "We don't disagree over unification, rather the alliance with the humans."

Do they fear Markey O'Malley has ambition of his own? Her twin brother was the first Banshee male born whole and without corruption, the herald of the lifted curse. "Their king is one of us and has no intention of stealing back the Blossom."

"We don't believe he'll betray you, nor that he'd seek to steal our source of power."

"Why then do you worry?" Alistaria asked.

"The fight against the Shadow Realm is his alone to undertake, yet you send our strongest through the portal each night. You aid his fight and soon will do more," the elder advised.

Alistaria disagreed. "His hold over Enatherr is weak, and there are many who oppose him. If he falls, our borders will echo with the sounds of a new enemy—one who *will* seek our gifts."

"You speak with wisdom," the older fae agreed, "but the people of Fainnotheria have worries at home, and won't enjoy watching their resources diverted to humans. Not while our times are still uncertain. We're also hungry and cannot spare anything for them."

"He *is* my brother and so I'll provide aid," Alistaria said sternly. The old woman was correct, and the elders spoke with wisdom as usual. But the queen had given promises and would find a way to honor them.

Erania nodded and the rest of the elders bowed slightly.

Changing the subject, the queen turned back to Korl's sleeping form. "What do you think afflicts him?"

"We don't know for certain."

"Then I want you to guess. Even the most experienced of healers couldn't identify the source, but I believe it passed from the tree. A strange resonance beats out of phase with his lifeforce."

Erania let out a sigh. "I felt it too, but it's a sensation I've never experienced." Waving her hand to indicate the assembly, she added, "none of us have."

Whatever it was, Alistaria knew the strange pulse loomed as an echo—a murmur of something sinister on her people's horizon. "When Radviken controlled the Blossom, he brought false balance to our worlds, claiming he kept the shadow realm at bay and saving both of us from its stain. What if this variation is imbalance showing through?"

"That is one possibility. That it passed from the great tree into his body would suggest their roots already feel the darkness."

"Then we must continue to aid O'Malley and the humans in their fight, because it may already be ours. Help me by spreading urgency to our people. I *will* find balance, for both our realms and not just ours."

The clearing of a throat announced Torian's arrival. Relief filled her instantly. She was so thankful for this man. *Odd,* she thought, *how Nastauria warned me never to trust a human, but she herself had placed her own daughter's safety in the hands of this one.* She winced with sudden remembrance. *Not* her *daughter.*

"You sent for me?" he asked dutifully.

"I did," she answered. "Walk with me." Taking his hand, she led her friend away from the chamber and the watchful eyes of the elders. She liked the feel of his hand in hers and wished he would someday offer it on his own. But even he failed to recognize how lonely she had become as ruler. *If only I could stop being queen for a day,* she thought, *but even then, he may never notice me.*

Once they had emerged from beneath the Tree of Life, she let go and explained, "I must know more about the control Radviken had over the realms. I need his notes, his journals. His own words."

"I can speak with Markey," Torian agreed. "I'm to meet his new general on the morrow to discuss a shared training program. I'm proposing his Storm Riders learn our new tactics and also train here with flight."

She nodded, agreeing to his wisdom. Torian certainly had a mind for warfare, if not for women. "He may not part with them. He already gave us the tapestries but may not part with the private notes of Radviken. If he could agree to merely lend them, that would be enough, but a transcription would be best if we had the time to make one. Let him know we'll offer to make the copies."

Torian frowned. "And the reason I should give for the urgency?"

"The truth. The Shadow Realm began spilling into his realm almost immediately after we recovered the Blossom, and he must know we see subtle signs of it here."

"How so? Do you mean the injured root tender?"

"I do. I believe the shadow has reached the roots of the Great Trees."

The general nodded. She could tell something bothered him by the way he held his jaw.

"What is it?" she asked.

"I want to train some of your root tenders to fight, and I'd like you to learn as well."

"I know how to fight," she replied.

"No, you don't. You know nothing about a real fight, much less a battle, and..." He broke off, leaving something unsaid.

"What?" she demanded. "Say it."

"You have all this power now, but it wasn't meant for only tending roots or healing the fallen. We'll need you and the others who can wield it against the Shadow Realm when it comes."

"No." She stepped back from her friend—aghast he had asked for something so brazen. "Radviken used the gift to harm others, but I won't... I can't allow it. The Great Spirit gave it to us for good, and there's no good in killing."

"Alistaria," he pleaded, "it would be foolish not to train other ways to use the gift. When the time comes and you actually have to use it in a violent way, you'll need it to feel second nature."

She bristled. "So you're calling me foolish?"

"Not at all," he said softly. "I'm a soldier," he explained, "and our lives revolve around preparedness."

"I *do* understand." She said the words and meant them. To use the gift while harming others bothered her deeply and she knew why. *I don't want to use it like Clíodhna had planned. She wanted a weapon, whereas Nastauria hoped for healing.* Thinking of healing brought another problem to mind. Changing the subject, she asked, "What of Restarian?"

"Still no sign nor word. No one's seen him after the final Tempest."

Tempest. That was another issue she must urgently solve. It served a purpose before Radviken bent it to his will, raging only over the Deamhan Palace and surrounding lands. It should have reemerged already but had not. Markey had reported it ceased raging in his realm as well. Turning her mind to her missing cousin, she said, "He's here and watching us, no doubt. He wasn't happy to learn I'm Deamhan, so he certainly won't be accepting of our unified kingdom."

"He *is* the rightful king of the Fainne." Torian's words carried a darker foreboding, and she noticed he absently touched his hand to the hilt of his blade as he spoke. "He's no longer your friend *or* your cousin, Alistaria. He's dangerous."

"Or *wretched*," she corrected. "You saw what those Searchers did. You saw what they did to his *wings*." She shuddered. The monsters had flayed every bit of flesh and sinew until only the jointed bones remained. Restarian was certainly no threat, not politically or physically, as he would never fly again. He suffered so terribly under their ministrations.

"He also killed Nastauria," Torian crassly pointed out.

"You think I don't know that?" she snapped. "She was my mother—the woman who raised me! I shouldn't be able to forgive him, and I can't. Not yet. But he was Radviken's victim, a mere weapon wielded against her. I'm not ready to damn or cast Restarian aside. There may be something remaining in his mind. There may be something we can repair."

"I'm sorry," Torian said with tenderness. "I know he was tortured, but I must still caution against seeking him as an ally. You remember what he said before he left. He wants to *kill* all Deamhan."

"There *are* no Deamhan. Only fae, Torian. Besides, he's broken. They *killed* him—sent him to the Shadow Realm where he must have witnessed horrors. Then they *revived* him and tortured his body more. His mind is broken, but I can hopefully heal him. I believe I can."

"And if you cannot? If he's as lost as Korl?"

"Then at least I can say I tried," she said with finality. She was done discussing her cousin, and apparently so was Torian. A bit of tension lurked beneath the surface as they walked, and she could tell he hadn't finished addressing the topic weighing so heavily on his mind. "What is it?" she demanded.

He swallowed hard before speaking. "I've trained my entire life to rise to Kern. That's all I know. I wield every weapon in our arsenal with adept mastery, can recite the proper tactic for any threat which approaches with conventional threat. But I don't know how to fully prepare for what is coming."

"You mean you studied war against the Banshee and nothing else?"

"Meaning I can fight man, or beast, or fae, but only with traditional weapons. I don't know what to expect from the Shadow Realm. Fighting a foreign concept is both frightening and strange. I fear I'll unwittingly lead our fighters to their death. I need to train your root tenders."

She rolled her eyes. "I thought we were finished with this topic."

"I'm not. You unlocked all the elements for your people to use, but even *they're* unsure how to use them."

She finally understood. "I gave it all to them except corruption and resurrection."

"Exactly. Unlike Radviken, who chose to share his power with only his most trusted, you bled on the Blossom for all who could wield it and only gave one restriction—do no harm. But now they can wield fire, water, air, or sight, as well as heal."

"They won't misuse it."

"Not intentionally, no. But a weapon is only dangerous to a user who's untrained. You *must* teach them."

Finding herself unable to look at her friend, Alistaria scanned the ledge near a row of living quarters. Brechan was there, huddled over a mixed group of tenders and Kern, and deep in a fiery conversation. He was animated, using hands to convey his frustration. In the midst of telling, his eyes caught hers and glared menacingly. She turned away.

"What do you propose?" she asked Torian cautiously, afraid she knew the answer.

"We must further explore the uses of the blossoms, both in peacetime as well as in battle. Let me recruit a new class of warrior from among your root tenders."

"I can't," she protested. "I won't spare anyone. We're too busy restoring the forest."

"They can serve both duties," he suggested. "Both as fighters and healers."

Alistaria laughed. "Restarian yearned for that opportunity," she said. "But he's proof the healers can't also fight. They aren't built for combat. It would be too dangerous mixing the two roles."

"They needn't be on the front lines. They would serve as support behind the line of Kern. Imagine a soldier who avoids close proximity during battle! I watched Radviken's Searchers fight, and they used the elements to attack from behind the palace guard's shields. If I'm correct, this new corps could both deal damage and heal from safety!"

She felt excitement in his voice and couldn't remember any other time he'd spoken with such exuberance. This idea was certainly filled with passion.

"Killing from a distance isn't a new concept," she pointed out. "Humans also have bows with which they can send projectiles long range. Look into those."

"I have, but archers are limited by how many you can carry in a quiver, and they're less effective against a flying target. That's why the Kern and Skyguard have never used them. Our chief weapon is agility in the air."

"Maybe you *should* use bows," she suggested. "Imagine how powerful archers could be shooting downward. Your mobile squads would get a better angle of attack."

Torian smiled back very pleased. "Your idea makes sense," he agreed. "But can I try a few volunteers and see if my plan has merit? I promise I won't make it public. We'll train in the mountains."

She frowned, chewing on her lip in the least regal way. "I suppose, but keep the first squad small, say ten members?"

"I was hoping for twenty," he said with a smile.

Alistaria sighed and agreed. "Fine, take twenty. Erania has a list of names showing most progress, but recruit quietly. And try to balance the ranks with both Fainne and former Deamhan."

"I will do my best," he promised.

"One other thing," she added. "I've decided to come with you to see Markey on the morrow."

"What? No. Absolutely not. We can't risk our queen leaving the realm, not when Enatherr is so dangerous."

"I *will* come with you, Torian. My mind's made up. Besides, I need to speak with Markey regarding the texts. And, since we'll have to pass through the Deamhan Palace, I'd like to poke around for a library—anything that can provide a glimpse into our history. Don't you agree those are reasons enough for your *queen* to come along?"

"I suppose it's worth a look. What do you think, Queen Alistaria? Would you like to journey to the Deamhan Palace and help me search through old books?"

"Old books? Why General Torian, did you not know books are the most romantic gesture you could offer a young woman?" She smiled up with brown eyes that dared him to gaze back. He didn't, of course. He was utterly confused.

"Are they?" He asked with a frown. "It seems like picking flowers would have more effect."

"Not at all! Flowers wither and die," she explained with a sigh. "But books provide access to knowledge never dreamed. They're portals to other worlds and journeys into the past—dangerous weapons to place in a woman's hands, especially one you wish to conquer." She offered him another smile, this one revealing her most flirtatious attempt.

"Who said anything about conquering?" Torian asked, completely lost.

"Must you always be the soldier?" she muttered with just the right amount of irritation. "Can't you *ever* just be a man? We'll travel in the morning if you don't mind. I'd rather not walk around those ruins like a clueless *man* always in the dark." *For such an intelligent man,* she thought, *you really don't know anything about women.*

His confusion darkened more, and he said seriously, "I'll be both, whatever it takes to protect my queen." As he bowed to take his leave, she quickly pulled him in for a hug.

"Don't be so formal with me when we're alone," she whispered. "You're one of the only friends I have!"

"I'll try," he promised, "but I'll always be a soldier first."

"That's what bothers me the most," she muttered. And he looked the part, marching away and looking splendid in his golden uniform. As she watched him depart, a voice called her name. She turned to find Erania motioning to return under the Tree of Life.

"He's awake," the old woman informed, and Alistaria hurried her pace, nearly running to join the ring of elders gathered around a dazed and very confused Korl.

"What happened?" she asked the teacher.

"I... I don't know," was his honest reply. "I took over tending the burl after you left, thinking it was a normal tumor. When it didn't respond, I overpoured power into it, thinking to reroute the flow of lifeforce around instead of through the bulge by force."

"But that didn't work?" She would've tried the same had he not taken over.

"It was... different," was all he could say.

"Besides the thrum?"

He nodded but said nothing in response.

She placed a hand on his chest to gauge whether that off beat thrum had subsided. It still beat out of phase just as subtly as before. "What happened when you poured in the power?"

"It felt like... like I'd opened a river I couldn't shut again. So much of me poured in, I'm surprised I'm still alive."

"I am too," she replied honestly, "but I'm glad you are. I need your help, Korl."

"Do I not serve you already, Alistaria?"

"You serve *Alistaria,* but not your queen." She paused, allowing him time to understand her meaning. "You're a teacher to others who watch your behavior. Despite once my mentor, it's vital you appear obedient in front of the tenders. If you disagree, do so privately. And don't hold back."

Confusion clouded Korl's face. "I've never disobeyed, Alis..." He paused, catching himself midst slight. He cleared his throat before continuing, "... your highness."

"No, you haven't. But at the tree you treated me like the young tender you taught long ago. I couldn't do something, and you nearly killed yourself proving it was my method that failed."

"I'm sorry," he said. "I didn't mean..."

"No, you didn't mean to," she interrupted, "but the damage was done all the same. The Blossom responds to me, and the power you wield is a gift from me. Work with me and teach me if I'm wrong, but do not correct me again in public."

He nodded, rendered speechless by her chastisement.

"Work *with* me to master these powers of the Blossom. I'm giving you full authority to train *all* fae, but ensure there's no division or lack of unity among them. Neither Fainne nor Deamhan has advantage in your school, is that clear?"

"Yes, your highness."

"Good," she said. "Then rest up and we'll talk later." She stood to leave but he called her back.

"Alistaria," he said, "you *are* my queen, even if the habit of familiarity is difficult to overcome. I *will* show you respect." He smiled and added, "you are so much like her."

"Who?"

"Nastauria. I am sorry she turned out not to be your mother."

"Not my mother?" she asked. "She was the *only* mother I had and I'll not hear otherwise." She spun on her heal and left the Chamber of Life, ignoring the stares of the watching elders. But in her mind she wondered. *Could a woman who stole another's child truly be called a mother?*

Chapter Four

"The Dannan arrived on an island, ripe with life and brimming with opportunity. Tired of flight, they chose a point high upon a hill composed of rock and iron and built a splendid palace with stone hewn by their magnificent tools. Upon completion, they rested - pleased with their work and ready to settle forever into their new home. When the inhabitants came calling, they brought with them gifts of sacrifice. The Dannan found these offerings pleasing and allowed them to settle nearby. They later learned the inhabitants called the site, Sliábh an Iarainn."
– The Legends of the Tuatha, Chronicle I, First Passage

The corruption surrounding Deamhan Palace had not lifted, and the air seemed to shimmer with decay. It had a putrid odor of rot and foulness, and everything in the palace was wretched and wrong, even the young Fainne digging through the ancient gardens. Starving, he scavenged for food left behind after the Banshee departed. He heard a sound in a far distant corner of the grand hall and lifted his head to listen. His mouth dripped with dirt and the half-eaten remains of a shriveled root.

Restarian cocked his head to one side to listen more intently. His ears, once long and pointed in true fae fashion, were gone—mutilated and carved down to nubs. Despite their appearance, they detected tiny nails scratching stone nearby. Peering into the darkness, he stared blankly trying to pinpoint the source of the sound. He avoided the light now, and his large eyes saw easily in the shadows. Fully dilated, the whites were stained forever crimson by the torture. The light made them burn, drawing forth harsh reminders of Radviken's interrogation.

As he turned his body to follow the sound, he passed through a glimmer of sunlight squeezing through a crack in the wall. The brightness revealed the skeletal remains of what had been grand wings upon his back. Once full of flesh and able to catch the air with grace, these hung as useless as he—a reminder Restarian was the lowest life form in the palace.

The sound of scurrying became clearer, and he crawled carefully along the floor, avoiding the rubble and moving toward a better meal than roots and dirt. Meat, he knew, offered strength for his sunken ribs and gaunt cheeks. With his father's sword in his hand, he prepared to thrust, pulling scrawny legs underneath his body and willing them energy to pounce. He watched a pile of animal bones discarded by the Deamhan—the cursed Banshee and bane of his kingdom. *It should have been mine,* he mused, *but no more.*

Movement drew his focus and he perched like predator seeking its prey. Antlers moved in the corner as the skeletal head of a hart shifted upon the pile, revealing a long whisker-covered snout. He leapt, swinging the blade downward deep into the rodent and breaking its back. It squealed its protest into the echoing hall, writhing beneath the Fainnen silver until it could protest no longer. Its will had departed, just as Restarian's had fled under the Searcher's blades.

With no means to build a fire, he cracked the rodent's neck, slicing it open to devour the raw meat within. As he chewed, he sobbed, pulling hairs from his teeth and wiping tears with a filthy hand. His fingers reeked constantly of death these days, a reminder of his visit to the Shadow Realm. Living in filth, his entire body carried the odor of carrion and disease and he wondered what kept him alive. *Alistaria did this to me,* he knew, *when she healed my body but not my mind.*

"She could have left me alone to die," he said to the parts of the rat he couldn't eat, twisting it around like a puppet to stare back with beady eyes as red as his. "But she wanted me alive so she could lord her victory over my defeat." She'd have enslaved the Fainne, by now—the evil part of her heart being Banshee. He roared his anger at the remains of his meal and dashed the head in a fit of rage.

Belly full but protesting the raw meat, he leaned back onto the pile of bones and closed his eyes, yearning for the courage to end his own life. He raised his father's sword and turned it upward toward that spot where ribs met and the heart beat within. But he froze. With tears he lowered it again, always a coward and never a fighter. *Pathetic and useless,* he scorned himself. *You were a root tender, not suited for killing.*

A loud creaking interrupted his thoughts and sent him scrambling for safety, slipping in the pile and falling hard to the ground. Across the hall an ancient door opened at ground level. Light flooded in through the opening, sending every sort of crawler to its den. He counted five shadows on the marble floor. As he tried once more to stand and run away, he slipped on the femur of what had once been a forest cat. Nausea rushed in as a bone of his own snapped with startling pain.

His right arm had broken in his stumble. Cradling it with his left, he hurried toward the rooms just off the hall. Whoever had entered were not his friends, and he knew he must escape or hide. Down the hall he scurried as fast as he could, searching out the best room in which to hide. But it was too late. They had spotted him and gave chase through the passages. Soon they over took him, backing him against a heavy door that had once hidden the private lives of queens. He pressed his bony wings against it and wept, desperate for death and hoping they'd show him mercy by granting its release.

"It's him," a woman said quietly, leaving the others waiting as she crept forward. "Restarian," she said. "Can you hear me?"

That voice! He cringed, remembering her sweet and awful lies. *Trust her not!* he pleaded. *So beautiful,* another part of him argued, and reached a ragged finger upward to touch the orangeness of her hair. She smiled down at him sweetly.

"He's completely lost his senses," a male voice said. "Surely he's no use to us now!"

"Shh!" she warned. To Restarian she asked, "Can you understand me? We're here to help you, to set things right."

He raised his eyes, trying to focus on her face as it swam into view. But she shifted weight and moved, the blinding light behind her burned his orbs like Radviken's poker had once marked his cheek. He shied away, whimpering and fearful.

The woman stood and motioned to the others. "He's only frightened," she said, "and he'll come around. Be gentle, but bind him for his own safety. I want to search these rooms for the library the Storm Warden said we'd find."

Two of the men grabbed Restarian heaving him to his feet from both sides. As they did, he finally focused on her face, smiling warmly at the prince. Niamh was just as beautiful as the day they'd met. And she was just as deadly and full of lies.

"We're not here to hurt you," Niamh said to Restarian once they were near the Fainnen Ring.

"I'd rather you killed me," he replied sullenly.

She noticed his arm, broken when they'd found him, had somehow completely healed by the time they reached camp. "Why do you say that?" she asked, but she knew the answer. The boy she'd flirted with and fawned over at Radviken's palace was gone, replaced by this wretched husk.

"Why can't you leave me be?" he begged. "It's over. I've nothing to offer you, and your king is probably dead."

"He is."

"Then what could you possibly gain by taking me away from my misery? Just let me die in peace."

"How did your arm heal?" she asked, changing the subject and sick of his self-pity.

He shrugged, then avoided a few more of her questions.

She suddenly whirled on him with dagger drawn and pointed at his cheek.

He didn't even flinch, only begged. "Please do. I was serious when I asked you to kill me."

"I won't kill you," she said, dragging the tip deep enough to pass through. She reached out with her other hand and grabbed a handful of his stark white hair, holding him steady while removing a neat circle of flesh. When she pulled back, she could see right into his mouth. He gritted his teeth and averted his eyes from hers. *Good,* she thought, *he's still broken to our whims.*

"How long will it take?" she asked.

He shrugged again.

"I'll figure it out eventually," she said. "Either you'll tell me or you'll wear a hole in your nasty little cheek long enough for me to guess. Either way I'll have my answers. But by remaining silent, we'll have to endure each other's company longer."

"How big is the hole?" he finally asked.

"Only a robin's egg."

"Then tonight. It'll be healed by tonight, but I'll have a hideous little scar."

She scooted closer, leaning her lips close to the nubs that once were ears, and whispered, "*You're* a hideous little scar, Prince Restarian."

He shied further away, eyes down and focused on the fire. "You don't bother me anymore," he said. "You've already done everything you can do to me."

"How do you have a connection to the Blossom?" she asked.

He shrugged. "I don't know."

"I think you do."

"Alistaria must have allowed it somehow."

"Can you connect to any others? Or just to the healing rose?"

"Only the rose," he replied. "Look, I don't have any gifts, if that's what you're after. She's feeding me healing, probably out of pity, but that's all—I can't control it. And you've already done all you can to me. You've killed me. I've *seen* the Shadow Realm, so why do you keep pestering me?"

She smiled and winked before answering, "*Because* you've seen the Shadow Realm." She touched the tip of her blade to her own cheek and added, "We have so many questions... things we'll ask in ways Radviken never considered."

This time he shuddered, and she knew he truly was her hideous little scar. She hefted a satchel of books and placed it before her. Reaching in a hand, she drew one out and began to read.

"Those are abominations," Restarian said.

"What are?" she asked, gnawing on a piece of jerky as she read.

"Those texts. They're full of Banshee lies," he said.

"You read them?"

"I looked over a few, flipped some pages while I was looking for anything useful in the palace."

"Well, they're true, you know. Every single word, but they weren't written by the Banshees. That palace wasn't originally theirs, and these were left by the ancient ones."

"Who?" he asked.

"The ancient ones. They recorded their histories in these volumes, leaving a complete saga of each of the realms."

He sat up, suddenly interested. "Were the ancient ones fae or human?"

She shrugged. "I don't know. These were authored long before humans drove the Fainne from Enatherr."

"Then why do you need them?" he asked.

"If my master is to make a deal with the Shadow Lords, the answer of *how* is in these pages."

"Why would I care if your master makes a deal?"

"Because he'll reward your assistance—maybe even by granting the revenge you seek against the Deamhan." The fae prince sulked as she picked up the books. By the way he fidgeted, she could tell he wouldn't stay quiet for long. "Get some sleep," she suggested.

"I can't. I haven't for some time."

"Here," she pulled out a satchel and drew out some leaves. Chew on these and you'll settle down pretty quick."

"What is it?"

"An herb. Perfectly safe if you don't eat too much." Eyeing them suspiciously, he eventually took them in hand and sniffed their aroma.

"Smells minty," he said. "Will it settle my stomach?"

"It may, but it mostly relaxes. Chew slowly, and never more than a pinch." He sniffed the leaves one final time and popped them into his mouth. She nodded approval. "Now be quiet and let me read."

He remained silent while she went through each one carefully, documenting a brief description each passage in her journal. After she had finished, she frowned up at her companions. "How many books were in the annals?" she asked.

"Twenty, ma'am," one of them replied.

"And how many in the legends?"

"Ten in all."

Her frown deepened, the furrows of her brow deep and her eyes full of worry.

"Did you lose something?" Restarian asked with a hint of sarcasm. He already knew. He must have seen her brute drop it in the library.

"Just a volume of annals." Checking her notes, she added, "First century Dannan – the third volume." She turned her to escorts. "Which of you will go back?"

They each blanched at the thought of returning alone, and one protested. "The palace is too far to go back, especially when we're expected in Midlandis tomorrow night."

"I can fetch it, ma'am," one of the guards said dutifully. "I don't mind, really. I could catch up with you on the road."

She shot a glance at Restarian, measuring his threat. Once the herbs kicked in, he'd be asleep anyways, and she decided, "Go ahead, Seth. Take Reynaldo at first light, but hurry. Meet us at either Midlandis or the Bay–in whichever you find us."

Restarian grunted when she checked his bindings. "What happened to him?" he asked.

"To whom?"

"To Radviken," he said.

"Shut up," she commanded. "I don't want to talk about him."

"After I killed Nastauria, I felt connected to him somehow. But Tempest ended and I was swept away immediately to the Deamhan Palace. But that feeling never left, so I want to know. What happened to Radviken?"

"The Sìth stole him away, and your cousin claimed his power as her own. Morkur took him into the Shadow Realm."

He said nothing else for a while, just stared at Niamh as she studied each tome and scribbled notes into a journal. After a while she closed the book and smiled warmly. "What's it like?"

"What was *what* like?" he replied with indifference.

"The Shadow Realm." She watched with satisfaction as his entire body shuddered at the mention.

"The worst thoughts imaginable," he finally said drowsily. The leaves were finally kicking in.

"That's what I figured," she said, slamming the book and causing him to jump. "And why I'm glad *you* get to go back there, Little Scar." She leaned in close. "You deserve the worst thoughts imaginable."

Chapter Five

"I'm not keeping a damned journal; I'm writing down everything we tried that didn't work, and when I'm done with that, I'll write down everything that did. It's the least I can do for Germaine. I can leave my son a legacy."
– Journal of King Markey O'Malley, First of his Name

Markey O'Malley wanted a quiet life alone with his wife and son, out of the limelight and working a job that wouldn't require tough decisions or wear his body out too early. Those hopes ended the day he killed a Storm Rider, and vanished completely when he helped overthrow his king. The king? His father. It didn't matter. Radviken the Wizard was dead. All hail King O'Malley.

Markey laughed at the thought each time it took him. Jaana had too when he told her what had happened. The last she had seen him, her husband had left home in the middle of Tempest with a young man he suspected was half Deamhan like him—a secret which would destroy him if the people of Enatherr found out. He had kissed her goodbye, meaning to see her after the storm. But fate was cruel, and a blurry series of events swept him into the most confusing several days he'd ever experienced. He wound up summoning her north to the palace to watch her face when he broke the news.

The truth sounded like a tall tale. Before Radviken had become king, he journeyed through a fairy ring with the rightful heir to the throne. He murdered the true king and sought out the source of the fae magic, stealing it away along with the innocence and hearts of two fairy princesses. He planted children in each, and sneaked his way home to claim Enatherr as his kingdom.

"But that was more than a hundred years ago," she had protested. "How can you be his son?"

This was the rich part of the story—the outrageous introduction of a spirit, the Sìth Lord of Beasts. Sìth Morkur brought Markey as an infant through a portal and transcended both time and space to arrive at a moment in the future. He arrived at the precise moment fate would bring him together with his siblings. Jaana had not only laughed at the foolery Markey had spouted, she demanded to see the king and hear it all from him, but it was too late, the Sìth had carried away both the body and soul. Part of him thought his wife still had doubts, but she settled into the role of queen quite easily by ordering about servants and getting the household in order. He asked her to begin with the privies, by demanding tighter security and iron bars installed at various levels. Again she thought him daft, but he had his reasons. On her own, she went to work improving every aspect of the castle.

Gaining control of the kingdom had proven easy for Markey. Governing it was a much more difficult endeavor. Right away, at the end of Tempest, the townspeople and farmers emerged and resumed their business—shocked to learn they had a new king, but shrugging it off when the new ruler claimed to be the former's son. They went to work as they always did following Tempest, planting seed and moving livestock to graze the fresh grass. But that's when the problems emerged.

Something had changed following the death of the king. Usually, crops were planted on the first day following the storm, and they would sprout, green up, mature, and bear fruit within the first few days. They would be harvestable most of the thirty days leading up to the next Tempest. But this time, after the storm moved on, the harsh cold and wintry conditions did not. Snow remained on the ground in the north, creeping southward and chilling the ground all the way to the Port of Enat. As weeks went by, it became clear to all that planting wouldn't occur for quite some time. If ever.

Markey gathered the historians, but no record remained of the weather before Radviken, when growing seasons were longer and famine loomed every year. If only they hadn't been so spoiled with abundance and had stored up for emergencies instead. A period of starving soon set in, and many questions plagued his first weeks as king: When will rains return? Will it *ever* rain? Will we have floods? How long will each plant take to produce vegetables or fruit? Why can't this new king intervene?

Soon, everyone blamed King Markey, calling him Markey the Incompetent, the Powerless, the Tempest Killer, and (his least favorite) Markey O'Malley the Impotent. Boyd had begun that nickname, and he planned to box his friend's ears when he returned. Thankfully he had support of most of the Storm Riders, and those who hadn't deserted swore loyalty to him over the exiled Storm Warden. That silver lining gave him brief respite—until the monsters of the Shadow Realm began appearing in Enatherr.

He spread a map out for his newly appointed general to study, pointing out locations of every portal in his kingdom. "Torian will bring his army over in squads, rotating them weekly to augment our Riders. The portals will be the rally points, so we should set about building gatehouses above each. Those will also prevent humans from stumbling into the fae realm."

The new general, Conner Liam, was a good friend of Markey's and also served a Storm Rider. The two had ridden together many times and had also studied blades under Markey's fallen partner, Blayse. Like the new king, he had avoided elevation to Searcher, the rank by which Radviken had bestowed magical powers upon his private army.

He studied the map and placed a finger atop a spot near the Bay of Winds. "This is close to the first few sightings of Draugar. Farmers here and here reported them in the woods. I want to send two pairs of Riders to scout and confirm."

"Threes," Markey corrected.

"Beg pardon?"

"We used pairs when we had Searchers to aid us, Conner. I think we'd be wise to send groups of three instead of pairs for two reasons. One, there's a better chance of surviving, and two, we're throwing off any lingering disloyalty. Crooked Riders usually gravitate to each other, and two's company but three's a crowd when mutiny is whispered."

Conner nodded. "A third wheel *would* urge them to caution, since their crimes would be harder to hide. But surely you don't think disloyalty remains?"

"We'd be fools to assume otherwise." Thinking of the two he killed in the woods while escorting Torian, he added, "Every now and again we get a criminal among our ranks."

"Not your ranks anymore, your highness. You're no longer a Rider."

Markey stiffened at the title. He doubted he'd ever get used to that. Personally, he hoped he never would.

"Seems weird, don't it?" Conner asked.

"What does?"

"Joining forces with the fae to save our world. Radviken was a lot of things, but he brought balance by putting Enatherr first. The people will blame you if things get worse, and I hope you have a plan when it does."

"Just a goal, not yet a plan." Markey cleared his throat and sat up taller in his seat. "Call together the ministers and guild representatives. It's past time we put our heads together."

"What is it, exactly?" Conner asked. "What's your goal?"

"Simple," Markey said, "I'll steal our magic bush back from the luchorpán."

Conner roared with laughter. "You realize you need an army to take them on, don't you? But you only have a handful of Storm Riders."

"I'm working on that, too."

"How's that going for you?"

"Well, so far I have *you*, help from the fae, and a handful of Riders. But my secret weapon is a pair of thieves."

"I was afraid that was all." Conner abruptly ceased laughing and suddenly frowned. "Please tell me you're not talking about Piotr and Boyd!"

Nectar of the Gods Tavern was the seedy sort, avoided by people with upstanding reputations, fortunes to keep, or who are generally honest. A law abiding type wouldn't be caught dead in this particular establishment, nor would a priest, persons of nobility, or anyone seeking upward mobility. You might say this bar was a cesspool of crime or a den of ill repute. You would be correct in that assumption, and, as you can guess, this is where our story finds Piotr and Boyd.

Markey had sent the pair on a special mission to Midlandis (to spy rather than thieve) and to listen for and investigate any plots to overthrow his rule. Specifically, he sought out former Searchers and Storm Riders still loyal to Radviken and any clues leading to the whereabouts of the Storm Warden. After dropping a bit of coin around the street urchins, they discovered this was the place to begin. Several Riders had recently been seen passing through and staying here.

The duo reclined near the fire with feet on the hearth, and a one-eyed dog lounged on the floor between them. His mange improved but not entirely gone, Lucky was slightly better to look at than when they first found him. All three had their backs to the door, pretending to ignore the riffraff and the comings and goings of the night. To rent a room here had been Boyd's idea, since they could afford a bit of luxury while using Markey's coin. He perked up when the door opened and several new guests arrived.

"What about them?" he asked.

"Nope, not them either," Piotr replied, tossing Lucky a sausage. As the door slammed behind the newcomers, the men settled.

This was the easy part of their new job, their thieving days replaced by service to the crown. It split the difference for the duo, providing honest work for Piotr while satisfying Boyd's need to perform reckless acts of unsavory business. They were never actually that good at thieving, but recently discovered they fared better when focused on a good cause. It almost felt like their luck depended on the nobility of the act. For Boyd, the luckiest moment had been when he narrowly managed to perform an acrobatic move inside a palace privy. Had it not been for a bit of luck and a sudden burst of brute strength, that mission would have ended the same as all their others—in dismal defeat.

The door opened once more, held wide to reveal gentle snowfall. A gust of wind chilled every tavern-goer's skin, and cries of protest erupted from those already inside. The group of men entering offered no apology and strode directly to the tavern keeper.

"Them." Piotr suddenly said without turning to look. "Most certainly them."

"You sure?" Boyd asked, feigning a big yawn and stretching his arms. He turned his body to get an innocent peek at the party that entered. The newcomers wore dark hoods to hide their faces, each a dark brown which may have once been black. Acid washed, he presumed.

"Certain."

Boyd rose and picked up his mug, sauntering toward the bar for a refill. He did his best to appear drunken, despite a clear head and steady feet. He loved acting drunk. It was the best way to avoid or gain attention depending on one's goal. Moving as close as he could to the newcomers, he slammed down the empty tankard.

"All be havin' sum more..." he slurred, interrupting their conversation with the bartender.

The man behind the bar instinctively grabbed the mug and refilled it while the newcomers were forced to wait. Without making it obvious, Boyd studied their faces and quickly assessed the three visitors. They were the dangerous sort with chiseled and stern faces.

The tavern keeper pushed the refilled mug toward Boyd and asked one of the men, "So just the one room? Will you be taking dinner down here or in your rooms? It's extra if we have to haul the pot to you."

"The common area will be fine," the man replied. "But we're expecting more in our party, and we'd like to reserve two more rooms in a couple of days. One will need to be private."

Boyd took a deep draw from the mug. This ale was heavy on the barley and a little tart, but he palated the liquid well. He lingered near the men, merely a drunk settling into a new perch at the bar and ready for his next drink.

"How many nights do you need?" the tavern keeper asked.

"Not quite a fortnight, but maybe sooner. Do you have a meeting room where we can conduct business during the day? We'll pay extra for privacy."

"You can have the barrel room in the basement if you wish. It's kind of dusty, but I can promise no one will interrupt. I just changed out kegs yesterday, and you'll need to help roll some out every three days if you want privacy."

"How many keys do you have for the storeroom?"

"Just this one." The tavern keep patted one dangling from a string around his neck.

"We'll rent that as well, then," the hooded man said, slamming a satchel of coins on the bar. The bartender grabbed it quickly and handed over the keys. To one of his traveling companions the hooded man added, "Go help with the horses and meet me upstairs. We have to prepare for his arrival."

Boyd held out his mug for another top-off and waited for the trio to leave without sparing a single glance. After it would no longer be suspicious to do so, he stumbled back to his seat beside Piotr–play acting as the drunk the entire way.

"You were right," he said when he sat beside his friend.

"I know I was right," Piotr replied with a grin. Always confident, him, but his ideas lacked flavor—too cautious. "What'd you learn?"

"They're staying here two weeks, and others will begin arriving in a few days. They have rooms upstairs, and also the barrel room as a meeting place. There's only one key to that, so we'll have to improvise," he said with a smile. He was the lock picker and loved tripping the mechanisms of the things. He'd always been good with his hands, tinkering with this or that and somehow lucky with skills requiring a bit of chance.

"Good work," Piotr said, tipping his mug in the air.

"How does it work, then?" Boyd asked. "And how come you couldn't see or hear their entire conversation?"

"I don't know," Piotr frowned. Ever since he'd learned he was fae and not human, he'd changed, but not entirely. He'd always been melancholy or sullen around Tempest, sometimes even sulking mid-month, but learning about his past had sparked new life into the man. It began when their new friend, Alistaria, let him prick his finger on that bush. She'd said it was his birthright as a fae to bleed for it, and promised he'd have some special powers from it as well. She'd promised Markey the same, but he'd refused. Said he didn't need or want magic.

So far Piotr and Boyd had only noticed a few new abilities, and one of those was a knack for seeing ten seconds into the future. A helpful skill for a thief, though they both wished it was longer, or specifically related to horse races, because that's where the real money was found. Piotr could also heal faster after injuries and somehow developed sharper eyesight in the dark. Again, all useful attributes to a thief.

"Don't do it, Boyd," Piotr suddenly warned.

He looked up at his friend with a bit of confusion. "Do what? I ain't planning nothin'. I don't have no ideas, yet."

Just then the most beautiful tavern maid he'd ever seen approached. She was perfectly plump with round rosy cheeks and large arms he could get lost in. His heart fluttered when she approached, and his eyes grew wide with excitement.

"Hel'o, gents," she said with a smile so jolly, dimples emerged as deep as caverns. "What'll ye be havin'?" Her eyes seemed to sparkle with discovery as she noticed Boyd.

That's what women did around him. It wasn't *his* fault, and he never understood it. It was almost like their minds melted into mush when he was around. Piotr was always blaming him though, begging him to avoid their attentions and Boyd tried—especially ignoring the fragile ones. But this buxom young woman was a cut above the others, so wide across he could disappear in fervorous bliss. And her teeth... so perfectly yellow they seemed to match the sun. He didn't mind a few were missing, since that added character to her charm. The mole beside her nose was just as alluring, a masterpiece from the maker who left their signature with three aptly placed hairs in its middle.

"I said no," Piotr warned.

But it was too late. Boyd was smitten, and they *would* be here several days more at least. He just hoped Piotr didn't ruin things by upsetting this tavern keeper like all the rest.

His friend, recognizing the look in his eyes, groaned.

CHAPTER SIX

"The weapons they carried were marvelous – as powerful in our hands as the magic they kept to themselves. Only a select few were lucky to serve in their Kern, and fewer still carried the weapons of gods."
– The Annals of History Book III, Passage 15

The abandoned Deamhan Palace sat foreboding on the hill, high atop the mountain with six spires reaching skyward. These were landing platforms for the Deamhan until recently, and though only a month had passed since unification, the structure had changed dramatically. The walls, once gleaming white and radiant in ancient times, had appeared dull and decayed but stood strong and sturdy the last time Alistaria had visited. They now seemed to crumble before her eyes, and the corruption on the air seemed to shimmer darker than before.

As she and Torian approached, she noticed the forest had sprung up around the hill, lush and sprouting life except for a circular patch directly around the structure. The grounds remained barren and black, and the fog of corruption seemed to swirl in a perfect pattern that matched. She felt ill in her stomach the closer she came.

Torian could sense the change as well. "It doesn't feel right," he said. "It's darker and almost eviler than before."

"Ominous, yes," Alistaria agreed.

"I don't like it."

The young queen swallowed her fears and said, "I don't either, but we *have* to go in."

"I hope we find what you're looking for quickly, so we can travel through the portal with haste."

Alistaria nodded, breathing deep and holding it in to settle her nerves.

"We can't leave it like this—unattended. It's the main passage to Markey's palace in Enatherr, and we have to place guards eventually," he insisted.

She let out her air forcibly. His thoughts reflected hers of late. "We'll have to clean it up first," she said, "and do something about that lingering corruption. But our unification is tenuous, and I don't want this place to become a permanent settlement."

The first spire they tried to land upon proved a dangerous way in. Part of the stairwell had crumbled and fallen away, and the remains of it lay on the floor several stories below. The next one they tried was worn and showed signs of deterioration but proved stable enough to enter. As the roof above them lowered into a narrow approach, they reluctantly touched feet upon the stones. It held, but Alistaria kept her wings ready for flight in case it suddenly disappeared.

Once they reached the ground level, Torian made her remain on the steps while he did a quick search of the throne room.

Alistaria hated being treated like a child. "The war's over. What could possibly lurk in those shadows?"

Torian repeated her words, muttering under his breath but loud enough for Alistaria to hear. "What could possibly lurk in those shadows?" He whirled around with his silver sword held forward, scanning for movement but addressing her. "Shadows lurk in shadows and, in case you forgot about the strangeness in the trees affecting Korl, I don't trust anything that isn't fae in this realm."

She snickered. "What about you then? Aren't you human?"

The look on his face told her all she needed to know, and she instantly regretted her sarcasm.

I keep forgetting he's not like Restarian, she thought. She and her cousin had joked often with each other, poking fun but never taking offense. Torian was more direct about things, and sarcasm often missed. Or was it deeper than that? She wondered, *it's hitting him hard, not being fae.*

"I'm sorry," she said finally, but he had already stormed off the check the side passages. Alistaria stepped onto the marble floor below, suddenly aware of her own loneliness. She watched as Torian left one hallway and crossed to another.

He pointed over his shoulder at the rooms he had just left. "Those are clear," he said gruffly.

"Torian," she said, urging him to turn around, but he ignored her plea as he went about his business of clearing the palace. *I've really hurt him,* she thought. The sad part of it was she truly desired his friendship—yearned for it. Ever since they'd met, she felt a connection, perhaps drawn by his rugged good looks. *Why doesn't he notice me?* she wondered. *Perhaps he doesn't find me attractive,* she thought. She longed to speak with Nastauria, craving her advice and in sudden need of her mother.

She pushed open a heavy door, finding only rubble and the rotted remains of furniture. It reeked of musk but held no books. The next three rooms in this wing were the same, and the next hallway yielded even fewer interesting finds. One had flooded at some point, and whatever had been in there was a total loss for centuries.

"Torian!" she called into the darkness. "Where did you go?"

He answered from across the way. "Over here," he said.

She hurried, momentarily missing a step after slipping on animal bones. The scattered remains were left in piles, ghostly remains of Deamhanen meals. Looking around she found several more and cringed at the way her kinsman had lived. *Like animals,* she thought. She felt a bit of anger at King Girtrán and felt guilty for the luxuries she enjoyed while they suffered. *The reunification may take longer than I feared,* she worried.

She thought again of Maerlin, the sentry. *He warned me of this – tried to explain but I hadn't fully understood.* The sudden change in their lives had been a further reminder of how much culture had truly been stripped away from their memories and hearts.

She found Torian exiting a room just as she was entering. He pushed by, turning his shoulders so they wouldn't touch as he passed. "Your books are in there," he said.

"Where are you going?"

"I've one more room to check," he said dryly.

She watched him stroll off. "What is wrong with you?" she demanded. "I was only joking!" He never even turned to respond and disappeared through a door. Frustrated, she shook her head and went inside the room, lighting it aglow with a ball of fairy spark. It was the library.

Covered with a thick film of disturbed dust, she could tell it had already been searched. But by whom? The clean stone beneath the footprints suggested it had occurred recently—possibly in the past few days. She followed these and found books scattered everywhere. This undertaking would be difficult, far longer than she'd hoped. She wished Torian was helping instead of sulking elsewhere.

Most of what she found were records of trade, though the numbers made no sense and, she wished she could read the language describing the listed goods. Regardless of their meaning, whoever had left these diligently recorded every transaction. Carefully returning each one as she moved down the row of shelves, she commanded her bobbing light to follow.

A particular section drew her attention. It was five rows high, with the middle three entirely empty. The top and bottom were tossed haphazardly, rifled through and left where they'd been found. She examined these closely, finding each a general description of a city. The writing was in the same undecipherable language as before, but the schematics clearly described building plans and what appeared to be a drawing of the palace itself. She shoved the drawings into her satchel, assuming whoever had built the Deamhan Palace had left these behind as well. She stared longingly at the empty shelves, wishing to know what had once filled them and cursing the dusty smudges where books should have been.

A pattern of footprints told of someone's quick departure. Whoever had cleared these shelves shared Alistaria's desire not to tarry and in their haste lost plunder. On the ground she found a discarded tome. It was a simple object with its pages sunk into a deep layer of ancient dust. She bent casually and picked it up, careful not to injure the fragile spine.

As she rose, a figure stood before her, looming with a long spear held outright. Suddenly worried the thieves had returned, Alistaria screamed.

Torian laughed at her fright, casually tossing the weapon in the air and feeling its balance.

She hissed at the vile instrument. "Iron!" she growled.

"I don't think so," he said, holding it closer to her shimmering fairy spark. "It resembles bronze, but seems stronger. Also, it doesn't burn to the touch."

"Iron won't burn you, you're not a Fainne," she said.

He shrugged and continued to study the runes and carvings along the shaft. "You keep bringing that up," he said with unmasked irritation.

The carvings were beautiful, and, from what she could see, depicted a battle. "I'm sorry," she said. "I guess it's a habit, that's all. I was raised to distrust anyone not fae.

"Well, if my being human's a problem, maybe we shouldn't be friends. I'll fight for you, train soldiers for you, but don't expect me to sip tea and play games all night bantering sarcasm like you did with Restarian."

She flinched. She deserved that chide. Changing the subject, she asked of the spear, "Where'd you find it?"

Without turning around, he pointed over his shoulder toward the door. "Just down the hall a bit. I found what appeared to be an old armory. Most of the weapons *were* iron, but they're already rusting – even in this short amount of time. This was the only one useful. It's of a different composition and I like it. Though it's light-weight, it feels stronger even than Fainnen silver. I think I'll keep it..."

Trying his own sarcasm, he added, "With your majesty's permission, of course."

"Sure," she shrugged, ignoring his hurtful tone. "I don't care." But inside she did—not for the spear but for the man. *I really do care for* him, she thought. *But why can't he see me as a girl instead of his queen?*

"We should get going," he said, and turned to leave.

Alistaria clutched the book to her chest and followed.

Torian knew his words had the intended effect. They bit down hard, paying Alistaria back for the way she'd insisted on pointing out he wasn't fae. If only she *knew* how much it galled him to be human. *I'm fae at heart,* he thought, remembering his brief time in Enatherr, and how the absence of wings had forced him into a deep melancholy. But watching the hurt on her face made him wish he hadn't spoken harshly. He was, after all, trying hard not to fall in love with her.

What would she ever want with me, anyways? He mused. *She's the Queen of Fainnotherr, and I'll always be the lowly Skygate sentry to her.*

A sword swung out of the shadows, causing him to jump backward by instinct rather than preparation. Off balance, he staggered out of the way, but that opened up Alistaria to the assassin. The blade hissed downward as she stood frozen with fright. As Torian fell backward, he threw the spear at her attacker, driving it deep between the man's shoulder blades. The man fell immediately.

Just beyond Alistaria, another attacker emerged. Torian shouted, "Behind you!"

She whirled around just in time, using her magic out of necessity instead of planning. The explosion of light temporarily blinded the attacker, and she rushed to get behind Torian. He knelt and retrieved his spear. She stared down at it in his hands, more a piece of art than weapon, despite its razor sharp tip.

"Stay behind me," he whispered to his queen, stepping over the fallen man and squaring off to face the second. By the time Torian set his feet, he regained his eyesight. He could tell right away the man was human instead of fae, having a larger build like he, and eyes of dark chestnut. *His wings are new to him,* Torian thought, *and he won't know how to use them in a fight.* He took advantage of this right away, leaping forward and flying with great speed toward the man. They collided with force, and the assassin crashed into the wall.

Before the assassin could regain his breath, Torian attacked with the spear, lunging forward and stabbing, but the man parried and deflected the tip away. Torian, anticipating the move, shifted his weight. The blunt end of the shaft struck the man's temple, dazing but not neutralizing his ability to fight. Finding they were too close to swing his sword, the assassin punched with the pommel, sending sparks of pain into Torian's chest and knocking away his breath. Still gripping the spear, he put the full weight of his fall into a swing and returned the strike. The smooth metal collided with ribs and cracked several. Torian fell fully atop the man, both now gasping.

Slowly, the fae general tried to stand, using the spear as a crutch as he pulled himself from the ground. The man beneath him found enough room to swing, not at Torian but at the spear, knocking it aside and sending Torian to the floor beside him. The man scrambled to his knees.

"Torian!" Alistaria cried out, turning the assassin's attention toward her.

"Use your magic!" Torian pleaded. But she stood frozen with fear. He could not pull his eyes from her, afraid she'd perish the moment he looked away. His hand searched in the darkness around him, feeling for the spear but finding only dirt and filth.

"Stay back!" Alistaria said with a trembling voice.

She raised her hands and Torian nodded, urging her to use her powers to destroy. He screamed, "Do it! Burn him or something!"

Fire suddenly swirled in the air around her and the man stepped back, expecting her to hurl it in his direction.

Torian felt a fingertip touch metal and pulled his eyes away to grasp the handle of the spear, pausing momentarily as he stared at the tip. The flames swirling in the hallway reflected off the strange weapon, though it seemed to give off a glow of its own.

Alistaria suddenly panicked and her flames abruptly extinguished. Torian heard the man laugh as the room plunged once into darkness.

But not completely. The tip of the spear still carried a tinge of glow as he rolled over and tried to get to his feet. He found himself too far away now, as the man advanced on Alistaria. Her hands were still raised and she was backing away.

"Go," she pleaded. "I don't want to use my powers to kill."

Torian tried to throw the spear but his knee cried out with pain, preventing him from finding balance. He would never be able to hurl it with force. Instead he limped slowly ahead, training the tip forward. Suddenly his leg gave completely out and he fell. Tearing his eyes away from Alistaria, he caught his fall with one hand while still holding the spear with the other.

A burst of flames exploded in the hall, causing him to hide his eyes. Up ahead, the dying human let out a horrific scream as flames consumed his entire body. Lifting his head, Torian peered through the flickering brightness and watched as Alistaria pressed herself against a wall with eyes wide with shock. *She did it*, he marveled, *but she'll have to live with this forever. She'll never forget the screams from her first kill.*

An angry chorus of hissing Ganshee arrived, diving to devour the corpse of the first assassin. Rolling over into a sitting position, Torian waved the tip of his spear and they backed away, lips curled, exposing razor sharp teeth. They growled at the strange metal. He was about to dispatch the disgusting little creatures when a voice boomed from the throne room.

"Leave my children be, Torian, or your soul will become a debt to me."

"Sìth Morkur!" Alistaria exclaimed as the spirit approach.

Torian pulled back the tip of the spear and stood it upright, placing the base of the weapon on the ground.

The Sìth moved to stand between Torian and the Ganshee, and they hungrily feasted on the unburned man. Torian felt bile rise up and looked away, unable to watch as they claimed a soul for their master.

Morkur's cat-like eyes stared at the spear in the general's hands. "Where did you come across that... weapon?" he asked.

"I found it."

"You have no idea what you hold, do you, Torian, son of no one?"

The title stung. *I'm the son of* someone, *surely.* He shrugged and scooted closer to Alistaria, checking her over and ready to protect her if need be. But she was fine, rattled but unscathed, and immediately knelt to mend his wounded leg. He looked at the charred remains of the assassin on the floor, surely proof the queen did not need his protection. *It will always be this way, won't it? Me the simple human who's in constant need of* her *magic to protect* me.

The Ganshee's bellies full, the Sìth turned to leave.

"Won't you claim this one?" Torian asked, pointing at the burnt corpse with the tip of his spear. Both Sìth and Ganshee hissed at the thought, exposing needle sharp teeth and causing Torian to recoil.

The Master of Beasts regained his composure before saying simply, "I cannot." Fading into the shadows, the Sìth departed as mysteriously as he had entered.

"Good work," Torian said to Alistaria, flexing his mended knee.

"It's nothing," she said. "You're mended and should already be full strength. Come, let's cross the portal and meet with Markey. He'll be waiting for us."

"I meant you did good work by killing the assassin. I'm proud of you but also know he's your first kill. Those have a way of sticking with someone."

She frowned. "I don't feel anything about it one way or another," she said truthfully. "To be honest, I don't even know what happened.

I was a coward and flinched—closed my eyes and turned away in fear. In one moment, he lunged with his sword and in the next he was in flames." As they approached the throne room, she grabbed his hand, taking it in hers causing his heart to race hopefully.

"I'm sorry," he said softly. "For the way I acted when we first arrived."

"I'm sorry too," she admitted, "for being insensitive with my jokes."

As they stepped into the ring, the blinding flash left an imprint against his eyelids. He blinked several times on the other side and stepped through to find the throne room had changed since their first visit. Looking around he realized it was no longer even a throne room, but dedicated solely to greeting visitors from Fainnotheria—and not in a welcoming way.

Having departed the Fainnen Ring, he and Alistaria found themselves encircled by another type of ring—a tall wall with smooth and unscalable sides and archer perches from which Storm Guards could rain arrows upon unwanted guests. He felt his skin crawl and the hairs on his neck raise. A squeeze of his hand let him know she shared his shock. Torian longed for her touch the moment she pulled it away.

"Queen Alistaria," a woman's voice greeted them.

A gate on the far side opened, they recognized Markey's wife, Jaana. Despite her own station as queen, she dressed simply with fine materials that didn't boast her newly acquired wealth. She was obviously a wise woman with discernment and knew her people weren't ready for a flashy royal family when facing hardships. She stepped up to Alistaria and greeted her with a warm hug and whispered something in her ear. Both women giggled as she led them away.

"Markey's changed things up," Torian said of the defenses.

"This was actually *my* idea, she said with a smile. I didn't like having a portal to another realm so prominently located in the palace, so I moved the soldier barracks to this level and the throne room and private quarters to the mid-levels. Come," she added. "Markey's waiting."

Torian leaned in close to whisper to Alistaria. "What did she tell you?"

Her smile dropped immediately and she replied, "None of your business."

Chapter Seven

"I truly couldn't have done it without my wife, Jaana. She proved the best ally a king could have, both at court and in the heart. Remember that, child, after we're gone and you're on your own. Find a queen who's your best friend whether she wears a crown or not."
– Journal of King Markey O'Malley, the First of his Name

The assembly gathered in Markey's war room, filling his ears with a litany of complaints and petitions. The bankers wanted permission to call in loans across Enatherr, whereas the farmer's union demanded a stay until crops stabilized—a timeframe which could only be guessed, since no one knew what the growing season would be without Tempest.

A Paige entered and announced the fae visitors had arrived and would be joining the king in short order.

"And not a minute too soon," Conner Liam grumbled. They were late by his reckoning, though Markey disagreed.

"There's nothing untimely by their arrival," he said. "I'm sure Alistaria had reasons for delay. Besides, we're no worse by any extra time she gave us to plan." He gestured at the collection of maps before them, a disorderly pile of disagreeable strategy. Nothing was going smoothly for the man who stumbled into the crown, and he wished he could retire to a quiet life with Jaana and their son Germaine.

"The kingdom's in a state of emergency!" one of the pursers argued loudly. "The crown should cover the loans directly, ensuring solvency of the banks!"

"Preposterous!" the cattle baron representative retorted. "We've no funds to cover feed, and we need ninety days at *least*! You bankers must loosen the strings and provide emergency assistance loans in the meantime!"

"Assistance loans?" the guilded financier balked. "We're not injecting money with no assurance it'll be repaid!"

"If you don't," one of the merchant guildsman cautioned, "commerce will collapse before the end of that time period! Someone, either you bankers or the crown, must put money in the hands of food suppliers or the famine will last more than ninety days!"

All eyes turned suddenly to Markey at mention of the crown. *They mean me,* he grumbled in his mind. *I never wanted this job but here I am solving their problems.* "How much are we estimating the suppliers will need?"

"Six hundred thousand will cover, your highness" the grower's guild representative quickly replied, his estimate obviously inflated.

"That's too high," the king replied. *Your highness,* he thought. *I'm not suited to be their king by any qualification except blood!*

"That figure barely covers seed, plowing, and labor—not to mention irrigation. We're lacking infrastructure!"

"Infrastructure?" Markey roared. He was quickly losing patience with these exploitive windbags. "You've got seed on hand for more than a single planting! All we need to cover is labor and living expenses enough to cover a prolonged growing season and to save the rest for a second go!" He turned to a gray-haired clerk across the table. He thought the scholar's name was Hammond, or something equally ridiculous. What kind of name was that for a historian? "What did you dig up?" he demanded.

"My lord, wheat and corn comprise the most *in demand* staples, and each crop will take longer to grow than any of you are prepared for. But I can't offer a guess until I've estimated water requirements and researched past climate conditions before Tempest, and those records are difficult to find in the archives."

"Venture a guess," Markey demanded.

"I cannot. Not without estimating water requirements and researched…"

"Assume you have perfect water conditions," the king snapped impatiently. "What's the average growing season?"

"For corn or wheat, sire?" the historian asked with a tone of superiority. He was, after all, the only man in the room with answers.

"For both," Markey sighed.

"Corn will be ready to harvest between ninety and one hundred and twenty days, given adequate watering and temperature—but that's assuming we planted the seed at the correct time of year, an impossible assumption given we don't even know what season we're in. If this is spring, then we're fine. If this is fall, then we're wasting seed."

The answer sent the room into an uproar.

"We don't have time to wait four months until harvest! We'll all starve!" replied the grower's guildsman.

Markey raised his hand for quiet and the room complied. "What about wheat? Surely that's a quicker crop!"

The scholar sniffed the air as if he sensed something foul, then answered. "Wheat is much more difficult to estimate, but I figure about six or seven."

Markey interrupted triumphantly. "See?" he said. "Six or seven weeks isn't so bad!"

"Months, your highness. Six or seven months."

The room exploded once more with a cacophony of arguments, and Markey shook his head with defeated exhaustion. While the growers and the bankers were dangerously close to blows, the door opened and Jaana entered in with Alistaria and Torian. The room silenced immediately at the sight of the fae. It didn't help that Torian held a magnificent spear in his hand and wore a sword of Fainnen silver on his side. After an audible gasp, the room simply stared.

"I'm sorry, husband," Jaana explained, "I didn't mean to interrupt, but as you can see our guests have arrived."

"I'm glad you're here," he said to the young queen, and added, "but your arrival isn't well timed with happy tidings. We're gathered to solve food shortages that will last half a year at least, and no one in this room has a solution for starvation."

Alistaria exchanged a quick look with Torian then addressed the room. "The people of Fainnotheria would be happy to donate food. We can set up distribution centers in each of the cities if you like," she said with a warm smile.

One of the men, the representative of the merchant's guild, grunted. "Distribution centers," he said with seething disdain. "You mean occupation zones?"

"Do not insult my guests," Markey warned. His eyes narrowed from the man's insolence.

"He's right," the banker said. "The people won't stand for such wanton access to our cities by these... these..."

"These what?" Markey demanded. "These *allies* against the Shadow Realm?"

"Oh, yes," the banker sighed. "The boogey man monsters the crown asked for money to levy an army against, all the while currying diplomatic ties with these *fae*."

"The Shadow Realm is *very* real," Torian argued. "I've fought against them myself."

"You'd expect me to take the word of a fae warrior?" the banker scoffed. "You don't even have the decency to leave your weapons in the armory when you walk about the palace."

Markey stared intently at the spear in Torian's hand, a strange metal that now reminded him of bronze. It was a far cry from Fainnen silver.

"All of you out," the king commanded. "All except you two." He pointed at General Liam and the pompous historian. Jaana and the fae stepped aside to allow the assemblage to leave, then they moved to take the seats the men had vacated. Alistaria set a heavy book atop the table and Torian leaned his spear against the wall.

Markey took a moment to admire the intricate carvings on the shaft. So did historian Hammond, the king noticed.

"That's remarkable," said the scholar. "Fifth or six century dynasty?"

Torian shrugged and sat down next to Markey. "I don't even know what you mean."

"I mean," said the historian, "What era of Enatherr did your people steal that artifact from?"

"Hammond!" Markey growled. "You'll treat my guests well," he said. "Besides, young Torian here is full blooded human."

"Ah," the scholar said with a smug sniff of the air. "The changeling."

"Our ally," Markey insisted.

"The *ally* who's rubbing of a stone is tying up my days and keeping me up late at night," Hammond muttered.

"The very same," Markey said with an irritated tone.

"What have you learned?" Torian asked hopefully.

"Not much. Your specimen proved poor, and the only word we've been able to make out is, 'fomoire.' That loosely gives us a clue to the origin, since the stone was probably a megalithic capstone to an ancient tomb."

"A tomb?" Markey asked. "If the Draugar can enter our realm through a tomb, I want the entire site excavated at once. Find out how!"

Conner nodded.

"You mentioned *fomoire*," Alistaria said softly. "Weren't those an ancient race of monsters?"

Hammond answered eagerly. "Hardly monsters and mostly humanoid in the tales. The earliest history includes a mention of the Fomorians cast below the earth by the gods."

"So they were real?" Torian asked.

The scholar scoffed. "They were mythological beasts and certainly not real. They would be a waste of time when we should be focused on history." As he talked, Hammond hungrily eyed the book resting on the table. "What other work have you brought me?"

"We recovered this and the spear in the Deamhan Palace," Alistaria explained. "The writing is a language we can't make out, and were actually hoping your people could help. An entire shelf was stolen."

"Stolen? By whom?" Markey was suddenly confused.

"Two humans attacked us, presumably while returning to retrieve this," Alistaria explained. Turning to Hammond she asked, "Can you translate it?"

The historian put on an air of indifference. "I'd love to, but I'm currently consumed by mythological tomes."

Markey lifted the heavy book and dropped it again in front of the scholar. "Make the time, then report your findings directly to me."

Hammond grabbed it eagerly, carefully examining the binding before gently lifting the cover.

To Torian, Markey asked, "The humans at the palace, any idea who sent them?"

"They were Storm Riders."

The king frowned. He'd been worried about this possibility, especially with the Storm Warden and his Searchers on the loose. "Are you certain?"

"I could tell by their gear, despite their armor was restained and all markings sanded off."

Alistaria frowned. "Why would the Storm Warden be after books?"

"Because," Hammond replied, his voice suddenly loud with excitement, "these are the lost annals of the Tuatha de Dannan!"

"Who?" The name was new to Markey. Their legend was never mentioned by Tamee when he grew up in the boarding house.

"Tuatha?" Alistaria turned to Torian. "Doesn't that mean tribe?"

"Less vulgar, I assure you," Hammond replied with a sniff. "Tuatha means people, as in the earliest people of Enatherr."

"Who are they?" Markey asked.

"Who *were* they, you mean?" the scholar grinned, and the king wished he could slap the smugness from his face. "They haven't walked Enatherr for centuries, having completely disappeared long ago. These stories chronicle their history, or legends if you'd rather, since much of their history is speculative."

"Were they important?" Markey asked.

"Important?" Hammond both sniffed and chuckled at the same time, uttering an annoying snort. "They were gods!" With a smile he added, "The very gods who forced your Fomorians below ground, according to mythology."

"I thought you didn't believe in *myths*," Alistaria chided. Before he could respond, she turned to her brother. "Markey, we are at a true disadvantage when it comes to history. We have no one to translate texts and no clues to go off except the tapestries. I'd like to send some scholars to aid this historian and also to transcribe Radviken's journals."

"I don't need assistance," the scholar protested.

At that moment, the door burst open and a laughing Germaine rushed in, surprising everyone in the room. Jaana scooped him up into her arms and turned to shoo the child out. Before she could, the door opened a second time. A short man with a round belly and red beard entered, panting and out of breath from exertion.

"I almost got ye', boy!" His face dropped when he saw the room was occupied. "Sorry," he said. "Ah kin come back later!"

Markey recognized him at once. "Clurich!" he said, happy to see his friend, "You came! Glad you could pull yourself away from the tavern for a day or two!"

The little man waved a piece of paper in the air. "Yah summoned me, lad, suh here I be! Besides, Dierdre runs the tavern without me." Recognizing Torian, he smiled broadly and the two exchanged a handshake. "Yuh lookin' good, lad! Glad to hear yuh made it through just fine!" His eyes settled on the spear leaning against the wall and widened. "What be that?" He motioned as if asking for permission to look closer.

Torian nodded that he could.

The little man picked it up with eager hands, turning it over and admiring the intricate carvings. He said nothing with his mouth, but his eyes betrayed a lustful urge to study it further. Torian just watched with amusement. He'd seen him study his Fainnen silver that way, as well. After a couple of brief grunts of approval, Clurich reluctantly handed the weapon to its owner who returned it to a resting lean against the wall.

The exchange was brief, and Markey waited for his friend to finish before making the rest of the introductions. Jaana, Clurich knew already, and also Germaine. He seemed disinterested in meeting Hammond, but beamed at the chance to meet Alistaria. She blushed at their meeting, giving O'Malley a brief laugh which incited jealousy in Torian.

The king cleared his throat and said, "You arrived just in time, Clurich. Knowing your fondness and understanding of artifacts, I summoned you with purpose. I want you to aid Hammond here with a bit of investigation."

"Oh? What kin' I help ye with, Hammond?"

"I don't need assistance, sir. I was saying just that before you burst into the room." Clurich ignored the protest and whisked the heavy book from the table. With a frown he opened it and went to work deciphering the words within.

"Why, bless me stars," the little man said at once, flipping through the pages.

"Put that down!" the scholar demanded. "Don't tear those!"

"What d'ya be doin' with volume three of the Annals of Tuatha de Dannan History?" With wide eyes he also asked, "And where be the other nineteen?"

Everyone in the room froze except Markey who let out a laugh. "Now you see why I invited him! Hammond, he *will* aid your work." He pointed to the loose papers and the book. "Take those and learn what you can. Clurich speaks and reads more languages than anyone I know and can aid with Alistaria's transcriptions."

Clurich handed the book over to Hammond and moved to reexamine Torian's spear. The little man eyed it questioningly. "First the appearance of the tome, but also this spear," he said as if in deep thought. "Where'd ye find them?"

"The Deamhan Palace," Torian said. "Do you know what it is?"

The little man spun around with sudden disinterest. "Not at all," he said. To Markey he asked, "When would ye like me to work on the research?"

"Go now." The king dismissed the pair with an excited wave. "And make this study your priority." Hammond hugged the tome to his chest with eager excitement and bowed deeply before exiting. After he was gone, Markey nodded to Torian. "Conner here says we've you to thank for keeping our borders safe at night. If it weren't for your Kern, we'd be outmatched and overwhelmed."

"Aye," agreed General Liam. "It's true. We can't keep up with the Draugar spilling over. Their numbers increase nightly."

"We're happy to help, Markey," Torian said, "but your people need to bear more of the load. Two nights ago my group of thirty found only six Riders on a patrol."

The truth met the king in the gut, and he let out a frustrated sigh. "We're in a dire situation here. The Storm Warden took a good number of my Riders and more've defected since. We don't have the horses or time to train replacements and no way to screen their loyalty."

"Then I suggest a new tactic, one that doesn't require horses."

"What do you have in mind?" Conner's interest was piqued, and so was Markey's.

"When our numbers were large, the Kern swarmed the enemy, lighter and more agile in the air than our larger foe. But after King Betarian fell into ambush and lost our most skilled, I've learned to train fighters with no previous experience—and in a shorter amount of time. Our shields are our strength and can face overwhelming odds with a smaller squad."

"Show me," the general said.

"Do you have shield and spear in the armory?"

"We actually have more than we know what to do with. Radviken relied more heavily on Riders."

"Then come. Gather twenty men and I'll show you."

Conner turned to his king who nodded. Torian grabbed his own spear, and the military men hurried from the room. Markey—alone with his wife, son, and Alistaria—leaned into his chair with exhausted relief.

"I hate playing at king," he said honestly. "I'm not cut out for it."

Alistaria agreed. "It's a tough role we play. Only a month ago, I was a root tender, but now I'm making decisions with lives."

"Aye," Markey agreed. "Lives who criticize every step we make and demand more than even a miracle could offer at times." He pointed to the empty chairs and added, "I'm sorry my merchants and bankers didn't appreciate your offer to aid the food shortage. It's just they don't trust anything that isn't fully human these days. I think they'll always prefer Radviken return from the dead over following me."

"They know, then?" the fae queen asked. "You're only half human?"

"No, we've kept that a tight secret," Jaana said, breaking her silence. "But rumors abound. They'll challenge him on it soon."

"I'm sure it's the Warden spreading dissent," Markey agreed. "He'll stop at nothing to take the crown."

"And you're no closer to finding him?"

"I think he's moving east to the Bay of Winds. I've less of a hold over the constables there, but I do have agents on the ground in Midlandis. They have orders to follow him wherever they pick up his scent."

Alistaria raised an eyebrow at this. "Certainly not the boys?"

Markey nodded grimly. "They're all I have, I'm afraid. Plus, it keeps them busy in a *positive* way. They're always more successful when the job's a noble one. Plus, that gift you gave Piotr seems helpful."

"We can only hope," she said. "I gave him the gift of sight so he could keep a better eye on Boyd."

"Alistaria," Jaana said with a gentle interruption, "I have an idea how we can set up food distribution without the people knowing it's from the fae. Would you like to help me make a list of what you can provide, so we can work out the details?"

"Gladly," the queen replied with a smile.

It's good they get along, Markey thought. *Of course, Jaana gets along with everyone.* "It's settled then," he said. "You two set up details and I'll take Germaine to watch Torian and Conner train." He smiled down at his son who took his hand. *Hopefully he'll make a better king than me when his time comes,* he mused.

CHAPTER EIGHT

"Never let a good friend venture too far for too long, and always call them back to reminisce the good ol' days. Occasionally, you should get in trouble trying to relive those days or while making new ones. But always, no matter what, live every moment to the fullest, because that's all you've got when they're gone."
– Boyd

Piotr watched the stairs while Boyd went to work on the lock. While they were both experts in the skill, his partner had a better knack for tripping the mechanism on first try. He didn't mind standing lookout while his friend worked, especially given his new knack for seeing things before they happened. The usefulness of that extra gift would hopefully warn of trouble if it returned early.

At this moment, the Storm Riders were all upstairs in the common area enjoying a meal and strong ale. Piotr had tipped a couple of the girls to give them some extra attention and to keep them there longer. The hard part had been working the tavern keeper into the mix, since he was fiercely loyal to the former king. Boyd assured him he had that covered.

"You sure about this?" Piotr asked Boyd, who stepped back from the door with a triumphant grin and watched it swing inward.

"Absolutely! This idea is the best I've ever had. We'll hear all their plans and they won't be the wiser."

"I don't like it," Piotr protested. The idea, after all, *was* Boyd's. "What if we get trapped down here? We could starve to death and no one would ever find us."

"Relax, Esmerelda knows that if we can't find our way out in twenty-four hours, then she's to come up with a scheme to get us out."

"Esmerelda?"

"Exactly."

"Who's she?"

"That gorgeous goddess of a tavern queen," Boyd explained, "and my future missus."

"The girl you met last night?"

"Yep! That's the one! And oh, what a night it was," he said with a grin.

"What about Lucky?" Piotr asked. "I hate to leave him up there in our room alone. How will he go outside to do his business?"

"Got that covered as well. I put down a pile of those flyers Markey wanted us to post around town, you know, the ones saying he was king now and everything will be alright? Esmerelda said she'd check in on him once in a while, and that she'd give him water and some of those sausages he likes."

"Are you sure you can trust her?" Piotr questioned. "You've only just met her."

"I trust her in ways you can never imagine, my fae friend!"

"Half fae."

"Half fae, full fae, what's it matter? You're special, mate!" After a pause, he added, "I only wish it'd been *me* with the magical lineage. I made a wonderful fae in their realm."

Piotr considered for a moment telling him what Alistaria had suspected. Boyd had manifested strangely in the Fairy Realm. He was odd looking, so much so she thought he may be of luchorpán descent, but asked Piotr not to tell him because she wasn't sure. He had no choice but to agree. Those little round wings were strangely shaped.

He gave his friend a supportive slap on the back and turned to shut the door, locking it behind them. "You *were* a fine looking fae, Boyd. But I think there's something bigger in store for you. Besides, you're my best friend—like my brother even, and you've got skills enough. In fact, yours are better than mine."

"Name one," Boyd said doubtfully.

"You surely can pick the best women, and you certainly *do* have a way with them!" He pulled out a tiny hand cranked drill and put several holes in the top of two empty casks—those waiting to be removed from the tavern at weeks' end. He made sure these were near the back of the pile so the air holes wouldn't be noticed.

"That's not a skill, Piotr." Boyd said as he pried open the tops of the barrels his friend had chosen. Then he tossed a sack of food and water in each.

"No? What would you call it?" Piotr asked, stepping into the one on the left. He leaned over and grabbed the lid with both hands. Boyd did the same with the cask on the right.

"I call it being devilishly handsome," the shorter and stockier man said. "No, my skill is the gift of gab. All I have to do is open my mouth and the women fawn over me and constables let us go." He winked at Piotr and slipped into his barrel, pulling the lid tightly over his head as he did.

The taller thief watched his friend disappear and then did the same. It was dark, but that was to be expected. The only light that shone through was from the holes in the lid. They provided just enough to make out the contents in his satchel. They had plenty of jerky and fruit, and the waterskins were full enough to last three days if need be. The plan *was* a good one, he reckoned. The Storm Riders had already searched the store room and wouldn't suspect there were eavesdroppers hiding among the casks of ale. Boyd had thought everything out ahead of time. They lacked nothing for the job.

"Piotr?" Boyd asked. His voice was muffled by the barrels, and Piotr had to strain to hear him clearly.

"Yes, Boyd?"

"I have to go to the privy."

Oh, thought Piotr. *That's what we forgot.* The plan was Boyd's, after all.

He groaned loudly and was about to push open his barrel and end the entire plan when the store room door opened with a creak.

He paused, holding his breath and waited as sounds of several men entered. They were stuck, and Boyd had *better* hold it.

"You did well obtaining lodging and this meeting place. It's cramped, but will do nicely for the time being." The voice was not familiar to Piotr, and he silently cursed not drilling an extra hole so he could see out the side. "Have you any word from Niamh? I'd hoped she would have returned with the annals by now."

"No, my lord," one of the Riders replied.

He called him lord. Could this be the Storm Warden Markey sent us to find? Piotr thought.

"If she arrives after I've departed, one of you must remain behind with a message. Tell her to meet the rest of us in the Bay of Winds. I've a camp north of the lake, and we'll move our operation there while we search for the artifact."

"What *is* the plan, your highness? With Radviken dead, will you take the throne for yourself once we've found it?"

"If I have to, but that's not preferred. The king was claimed by a Sìth, meaning his soul was taken to another realm. I aim to find which one and recover our true king."

"Is that why Niamh seeks the historical texts?"

"That's part of her mission, the rest is to recover the prince. He's the only known lifeform to have seen the Shadow Realm and return. We need his knowledge and firsthand experience."

"Will he cooperate?" another voice asked.

"He has no choice. Lord Radviken broke him, and he'll do our bidding whether he agrees or not." The man Piotr assumed was the Storm Warden continued, "How many loyalists do we have in the palace?"

"Out of one hundred Riders we know of twenty who support you. But others will change their minds soon. Rider O'Malley is a fledgling and is struggling to protect the realm from the shadow."

"So, he hasn't figured out how the enemy has entered our world?"

"No, my lord."

"Good. Let's exploit that weakness. Continue to send Riders to each passage tomb they can find. Have them break the seal to encourage more shadow to cross through. By the time O'Malley falls, we'll have recovered our king and restored him to power."

Piotr felt his stomach drop at mention of reviving Radviken. Everything their friend Markey had fought for, these evil men were unraveling. He wished he could shift his weight and found he could not. All he could do was listen and wait.

Chapter Nine

"The greatest to challenge the Tuatha de Dannan were brothers, three in number, three of mind, but one in spirit. They killed for sport in the name of balance, wreaking havoc on the lives they spared. Their names spelled destruction."
– The Legends of the Tuatha, Chronicle II, Passage 20

Alistaria found she couldn't stay away after all. She knew what he was doing and where he was, but could no longer keep her promise not to try and watch. After pacing for several minutes and trying to busy herself with other matters of state, she decided to check on Torian's progress. He had been working with his new squad for several days, but was tightlipped on details and she couldn't stand the secrecy. She knew his silence meant one of two things—either it was going really well or the experiment would end with dismal failure. She hurried from her chambers to the Skygate, stepping past the sentries and intending to fly off alone.

"Your highness," a voice called out from behind as she was about to take off. She turned to find Maerlin was one of the fae standing guard.

"What is it?"

"Not that we can order about our queen, but we don't feel you should be travelling the forest unaccompanied."

She rounded. "Am I your prisoner?"

Stoically he answered, "No, ma'am," but General Torian said you're not to leave without an escort, in case you encounter danger."

"Danger?" she demanded. "From whom? We've no enemies in this realm, and even the Ganshee leave us well enough alone. Name one danger I may encounter," she challenged. When he failed to offer any, she grunted. "That's what I thought. I'll come and go as I please, sentry." She leapt off the platform. She had only gone a short way when she realized he had followed. Suddenly alarmed she wheeled in the air. "You'll abandon your post?"

"Not at all, your highness. The general tasked me to your security detail as you requested, and authorized me to follow if you rejected his recommendations to stay behind."

"So he used my own words against me?" She grunted a mixture of amusement and displeasure then added, "So be it." She took off again with lightning speed, aiming to leave him behind. But his broad wings kept up effortlessly behind her. He was both a strong and graceful flyer and would serve well on the Kern someday.

They flew above the lush canopy heading due north toward a rocky mountain range. From this vantage point she marveled at how rapidly the greenery had regrown. Though many of the great trees had already died and fallen to decay and the devouring Ganshees, sprouts could be seen poking up from the forest floor. She felt contentment pass through her body that seemed to finally break her recent stream of constant worry.

This was a good sign and the first glint of hope she had felt since the elders had sent her on the journey to Enatherr. She rose up into the air, higher until she dared not go further. Smiling up at the warm sun overhead, she let the feeling wash over the skin of her face and momentarily forgot the multitude of problems plaguing her people. She even forgot about Maerlin.

He joined her in the sky, hovering and eyeing her with confusion.

"What?" she asked. "You think I'm strange for basking in the sun?"

"No, my queen," he answered with his usual dryness. "I'm wondering what you celebrate. Forgive my saying, but the Fainne have such odd customs, and many of us feel out of place with your constant displays of emotion. Your mood *did* change quite abruptly, just now."

She stayed there a moment, with eyes closed and refusing to turn away from the radiating warmth against her skin. He wouldn't spoil her moment. It felt too good to allow someone else to take. His accusations were... but he wasn't trying to spoil her mood, he was curious. Suddenly she understood. She finally realized what lay beneath the oddness of the Deamhan. They weren't expressive. When she had first recognized their standoffishness, she had assumed they still had disdain for their former enemies, but now she understood.

She opened one eye and asked, "What have you ever celebrated, Maerlin?"

"Your highness?"

"In your entire life, what have you ever rejoiced over or reveled in?"

He paused as if to consider, but said nothing.

Taking his silence as an answer she said, "Neither have we. Our entire lives have been wasted attacking each other or recovering and preparing for the next wave. The result was the destruction of this beautiful place. When I believed myself a Fainne, I never celebrated nor found joy in anything except this forest. At the time believing it was the birthright of my people. I dedicated my life to reversing the Deamhan destruction. Can you imagine my shock when I discovered I wasn't who or what I once believed? I was lost and relieved at the same time. Lost in the sense everything I knew was a lie and relieved knowing I finally had a chance to save it."

"Every moment of *our* lives was wasted on hope, wishing we could obtain a single goal of equality, but not understanding or knowing what that concept even looked like," he said quietly. "Some believed it was instant acceptance and peaceful living beside our enemy, while others believed it was trampling the Fainne under our feet."

"And you? What did you believe?"

"I hoped for an opportunity to make my own way—deciding how and when I do things. I could continue to fight as a warrior, or I could learn to tend roots and restore the world around us. What's important is I would have a choice."

"And now?"

"My choices were narrowed by how I was perceived and made to feel. The root tenders rejected me and most of my kind, so I returned to what I knew. What is comfortable is easier to adjust into. Though I find no joy in what I do, nor who I am, I do a job and put up with the jeers and the slights while waiting to see what direction we'll be led."

His words sobered her thoughts, and she suddenly felt ashamed for reveling in something as simple as the sunlight over the forest canopy. *How dare I celebrate while this Deamhan still suffers.* "I'm sorry," she said. "I'm working on leading you all, but give me time."

"We have," he promised, "and we will always do so. You *are* our queen."

She believed his words then and led him away toward the waiting mountains. The forest fell away at a certain height, forming a green line. Above that, snow caps turned into broad basins. In one of these valleys, they spied explosions of fairy spark bombarding a rock face. She beckoned to Maerlin and they descended on a glide, icy winds whistling against her ears.

She could just make out the shapes of Torian and his squad ahead as twenty mages hovered in a line behind as many soldiers. The warriors were clad in the golden Kern armor and armed with silver spears and shields. The mages, surprisingly, wore crimson robes and also carried shields. *Nice touch,* Alistaria thought, *but I wonder what else he's hiding from me?*

She landed softly on the snow, thankful she had thought to wear moccasins on this particular day. She'd been wearing them more often after injuring her feet badly during her quest into Enatherr. Torian and his crew hadn't seen them approach.

He addressed his squad. "Those holding the wall will need to bend low over their shields while flying close," he explained, "and rest your shield against the edge of your partner on the left. Always lean left. Don't move right or you'll drift apart and create a weakness our enemies could exploit. Let's try again," he ordered, and the line of Kern leapt into the sky as a unit, holding a tight formation just as he described. The mages followed closely behind.

Up ahead another line of Kern hovered above a line of practice targets, each shaped like the scarecrow Alistaria had confronted in Enatherr. She shuddered at the memory and brushed the ghostly tingling of nonexistent Ganshee from her skin.

"Charge!" Torian ordered, and the second line charged the first at blinding speeds. They were not unified like those with shields. As they crashed one by one into the flying formation, Alistaria was shocked to see the line hold. Not a single soldier broke through, and she nodded approval as the attackers were turned downward by the defenders. That's when the mages went to work.

"Firebolts! Loose!" the general commanded, and ten flaming orange and red balls the size of melons shot from the free hands of the hooded squad. These struck the practice dummies which immediately erupted into flames. "Counter right! Swing!" Torian called, and the entire formation swiveled, pushing the attackers easily to the left and opening a full attack from the mages, unimpeded by their comrades. "Ice wall! Loose!" he cried, and a wet wall of ice pellets let loose, crashing into the dummies and dousing the flames. The cold doused the fiery scarecrows so abruptly, icicles were left hanging where the fire had been moments ago.

Alistaria clapped and cheered, causing Torian to spin around suddenly. Some of the mages, whose backs were turned, jumped in fright and sparks flew from one of them wildly. It struck the ground near Maerlin, who merely sidestepped closer to Alistaria. He eyed the spooked magician with cool displeasure, and the young woman flushed with embarrassment.

"Sorry," she muttered.

"Queen Alistaria," Torian said, "I had hoped you wouldn't review our progress just yet."

"You asked to train them privately, General Torian, not hide them completely from me." She eyed her friend with the same stare Nastauria would have given, burning deep into his soul and rooting out any guilt she could find lurking within. "Are they *your* army or mine?" She demanded with an air of command.

"They're yours, but I wasn't ready to present them." He stared down at the steaming spot where the fairy spark had melted the snow. It even scorched black the rock underneath. "They still need some polishing as you can see."

"What I see?" She suddenly beamed widely and turned toward both mages and Kern. "What I see is marvelous! These new tactics will serve our court well, and I'm very proud of each of you! Show me again," she commanded. "I want to see more! What do you call the new formation?"

"Phalanx, my queen." Torian again ran them through their paces, with the Kern formation demonstrating wheels and counter marches which could literally turn an enemy on its flanks as quickly as it attacked or, just as easily, defend their own. The mages were just as fascinating, wielding attacks and defenses with ample effect.

"What happens if someone falls in the phalanx?" she asked.

Torian gave an order and they demonstrated just that. A man fell out, and the formation squeezed tightly to the left, filling in. They landed a few feet ahead of him, and two mages split off to land close to the fallen Kern. One healed while the other continued to do battle from behind the shield wall. Once the injured had risen, he rejoined the phalanx by moving into position on the right-hand side.

Alistaria marveled. "So you can fight both on the ground as well as in the air. Torian, this is the most innovative warfare I've ever seen. You've revolutionized the Kern!"

"I have more ideas," he said, standing taller under her praise.

"Tell me over dinner tonight," she said with a wide grin. "I want to hear all about it." She ignored his look of shock at the private invitation. Turning to the mages and pointing to the golden clad soldiers she asked, "They are the Kern, the most elite of our fighters, but how shall we call you? Our newest class of warrior needs a name, does it not?"

They looked to one another and whispered, then to Torian, who surely was their leader. One of them, a tall and slender man who Alistaria recognized was once a root tender, asked, "What *shall* we be called, General Torian?"

Torian muttered something no one could hear.

"What did you say?" Alistaria asked.

"Tuatha," he said aloud.

That shocked her, for she had not expected the word. "Tribe?" she asked. "Like the Dannan?"

"Yes, but I learned from Clurich it also means family. Just as I was a foundling in the nursery of Fainnotheria, I found brothers and sisters among those I trained and fought alongside. This new group is neither Fainne nor Deamhan, or even Kern or Skygate sentries. But they also aren't root tenders. This new Tuatha changes everything. It's another caste option."

Alistaria smiled warmly and placed a soft hand on Torian's chest. "I like it," she said, and he smiled back. As she turned, she noticed Maerlin's face had changed. He too heard what Torian said, and she knew what he must be thinking. This is what he yearned for— not only purpose, but family. Her stomach twisted as she suddenly thought of Restarian. Her cousin and once best friend was out there somewhere, alone and without family. He had suffered so greatly at the hand of Radviken, and his mind had been broken as well as his body. She had to find him.

Swirling pools of darkness swam in voids where the onlooker's eyes should be. All seeing yet not watching, he sat perched high in the trees above the valley and marveled as the fae trained their wizards. *So they have a new way of fighting,* he pondered. *Let's test them and give them a fright at the same time.* With the slightest incline of his head, ears heard hoof beats in the distance and Dub called them down with his mind. A twitch toward silent paws creeping in the snow brought terror of a different kind. Hopping down from the branch, he connected with a different threat, and a screech in the distance answered his call.

He emerged from the trees to stand on the edge of the clearing— tall and regally clad in his cloak of blackness and shadow swirling around his body, sharply contrasting with the snow and ice atop the light grey of the rocks. His ebony skin rippled with anticipation as he watched the onslaught approaching, and his muscles flexed with impatience. Had anyone noticed him standing there in the open, they would have wondered how he was constant movement yet stood dangerously still.

"Why are you here?" Sìth Morkur asked, stepping from the forest.

"Why are any of us?" the rippling current of darkness replied through unmoving lips.

"If you are here, where are your brothers. Not far? Surely you do not interfere for we are forbidden."

"I am three and three are we," was the solemn reply. "Watch closely, cat, and truly learn about interference."

"You toy dangerously during uncertain times, Dub. The human wields one of their relics."

"Darkness is the opposite of light, Morkur. In shadow, I may toy as I please."

Torian grinned wildly at Alistaria. He had hoped to hold off presenting the Tuatha until after ironing out their capabilities, but her arrival was well timed. Their performance had truly been a sight to witness, and her reaction had filled him with pride. She had never smiled at him in such a way, never displayed so much hope or happiness—and it was contagious. He had to contain himself from trying to hug the queen on the spot.

A not so distant rumble caught his ears and he wheeled around expecting an avalanche. Windswept powder filled the air to the west, kicked up by stampeding hooves. He strained his eyes to find the source, a herd of mountain goat converging on their valley.

"Tuatha," he called, "Kern!" The squads, still in formation came to attention and awaited his command. "To the air or we'll be trampled underfoot!"

Fifty sets of wings stretched outward, fanning and gathering wind for flight. Just as they were about to lift off, ten large mountain cats attacked. Sharp claws scraped against armor as they crashed into the Kern, and powerful jaws snapped at wings. Thankfully all twenty mages rose into the air and they whirled in unison on Torian's command.

What can I order? he suddenly thought, panic muddling instinct. *We can't rain down fire, or we'll injure the Kern.* Instead of focusing the mages on the cats, he turned them to deal with the incoming stampede. "Hold them off!" he cried, and fire erupted immediately, exploding in front of the crazed animals and sending some veering off course. But the main body raced onward, heedless of the fae magic and intent on trampling the fallen Kern.

Those who weren't trapped under the giant cats managed flight and reformed a shield wall. He sent these into a looping arc, gaining momentum. By the time the Kern phalanx descended, they were nothing more than a golden blur to the eye, with shields locked into position and spears pointed forward. They passed over the stampede and through the great cloud of snow, bursting through the fog and trailing icy crystals in their wake.

The full force crashed into the cats with damaging impact. Some fell to spears while the others howled over the cracking of ribs. But shields continued to drive forward, ripping them off the fallen soldiers writhing on the ground. The mages broke off, scanned for a place to land, but found the battle too dangerous for a healing mission. One of them, a young woman named Palathia (the same who earlier nearly sparked Alistaria in her panic) took charge of the red-robed Tuatha.

"Healing squads descend!" she shouted with surprising authority. "Escorts, recover instead of defend and we'll heal them in the air!"

The line of mages complied and raced away in smaller teams, each moving to find a fallen soldier. Those once assigned to watch over and guard the healers, instead gathered fallen Kern into their arms and beat their wings with force, bringing them nearer the healers. They recovered the wounded just in time before the arrival of the stampede, as hundreds of mountain goats sped past underfoot, trampling several great cats and driving off the rest.

Soon the Kern were full strength. Though tender and sore, they quickly rejoined their phalanx formation. The mages moved into a line behind and flew ready, scanning the horizon for more threats.

Torian moved to defend Alistaria. With time to think, he considered the animal's madness and passed those thoughts on to her. "This was no accident," he suggested, "but who could coordinate animals into a deliberate attack?"

She opened her mouth to speak, but eyes rounded with alarm and she screamed instead. Torian spun around just in time to watch a dozen golden eagles descend with talons outstretched.

"Wind!" the general commanded, and all twenty mages flicked their hands. The combined attack proved powerful, blowing the eagles away at the last moment and forcing them to the ground with the sound of wet impact. "Now, fire!" he cried, and feathers singed beneath the mages' fury. Fearing more attacks would come, he ordered the formation to surround Alistaria. "Protect the queen," he ordered, "and return to Fainnotheria!"

Noticeably shaken, Alistaria allowed the circle of shields to form around her. Torian softly whispered. "It'll be okay. We've won the ground. Flee with them!"

But she was frozen in place, staring down at something lying upon the ground. As her eyes adjusted, horror gripped the queen and she pointed to Maerlin. The Skygate sentry lay lifeless in the snow. His body lay trampled upon the icy ground, damaged badly and beyond simple healing. Torian tried to stop her, but she abruptly broke away, racing downward to the valley floor.

"Defend the queen!" he cried, and the phalanx dove, forming around her on the ground. The mages remained in the air, flinging their power from above as the cats renewed their attack. In the distance the goat herd had turned for another approach. A mass of darkness suddenly appeared above the mountaintop, as thousands of leathery wings flew toward them. *Bats,* he realized—enough to block out the sun.

The queen knelt, placing both hands upon the mangled body.

"Hurry," Torian urged.

A strange aura formed around Alistaria as she worked, calling upon the white lily and its gift of resurrection. She also drew upon the healing rose, mending the fallen sentry's body as she restored his life. Maerlin's skin crawled with the movement of bones beneath skin, snapping into place. Soon, his eyes blinked open and the sentry gasped for breath.

"The Shadow Realm!" he cried out. "I've seen it!"

"Go now!" Torian commanded his queen, and she listened, grabbing the soldiers hand and lifting him into the air beside her. The phalanx escort quickly formed, and the assembly wasted no time racing home to Fainnotheria.

Part Two
Darkness and Evil

Chapter Ten

"The brothers rose from the depths of hell, spreading doom in their wake and calling forth unnatural spirits best left on the other side. Darkness preceded Evil, and they tested the way for Violence."
– The Legends of the Tuatha, Chronicle II, Passage 22

Steady rain fell upon the eastern lands, a welcome improvement on the icy gales over the past few weeks. Settled now to a soft windward breeze, the falling water pattered rather than stung the workers. They'd toiled since sunup lightened the clouds, and, though it was midday and the ground was soft, their progress was slower than Rider O'Donnel would have liked. He sat upon horse listening to their complaints, occasionally lodging one of his own.

"Why'd the king order us to dig this place up?" one of the men, usually a farmer but now out of season and eager for pay, asked of the Storm Rider.

"Because he thought we should," O'Donnel said with scorn. A howl in the distance lifted his head as well as the hairs on his arm. They'd been creeping ever closer, and these felt dangerously so. "Look," he said, spitting over the side of his mount, "I don't like it any more than you, but he ordered us to dig up this site. We're to find out where these things are coming from and have to finish before sundown."

The workers said little after that. They all knew what happened after the sun settled behind the mountains. The attacks had been worse of late, with Draugar now reaching the walls of the city.

Guardsmen even reported scratching on the gate and the chattering of hungry teeth on the other side. Of course, none was brave enough to peek out, and everyone was ordered to stay indoors unless in full squads. Only the Storm Riders had faced the monsters in combat, and that gave O'Donnel the recognition he craved. He was a local celebrity now, more revered than the city marshal for his many clashes with the dead. Of course, all the tavern stories about his exploits were begun by him.

"What if it *is* a portal?" one of his team asked. He was a young Rider, a recent recruit named Sean something or another. O'Donnel didn't care what the kid's name was, he had too many to keep up with in his life, and one more was too many.

"Then we die, rookie. It's as plain as that." He shook his head with disgust and watched as the kid paled over with fear. *O'Malley's really scraping the barrel with this lot,* he thought, sending a wad of phlegm over the side.

Another howl in the distance caused him to pull his cloak higher around his shoulders. He wished he could better wrap his entire body against the chill, as a fearsome shudder ran through him as well. *It can't be a hellhound,* he reasoned, *they don't exist.* Of course, just because he'd never seen a hellhound didn't mean they didn't exist. Besides, old stories were often tall tales. Even that fae (Torian was his name, the changeling) hadn't actually seen one. Maybe they really were nothing more than wolves, and not monsters of legend.

Another low-pitched bay met his ear, this one followed by a bark. They were closer, whatever they were, and out during daytime! Even wolves only hunted at night unless disturbed, so no matter what these turned out to be they were maddened for some reason. He noticed the men had ceased their shoveling and stood idly by.

"They're only wolves, men! Get back to work!" he growled.

But they continued to stare down at the hole they'd dug. It was ten strides by ten, the dimensions given by the shard hunter and historian leading the effort. O'Donnel spurred his horse closer for a better look. Beneath their feet they'd uncovered another stone—five by five and perfectly square. It lay directly beneath where the fallen monolith had been found.

"It's just a stone!" he shouted, but they continued to stare as if entranced. "Dig around and lift it up!" he ordered.

The shard hunter, a soft man with a weaselly nose and round spectacles, approached with a bucket of water. Kneeling down he carefully poured it over the stone, revealing a series of markings.

"What's it say?" he demanded of the historian, a rotund little fellow with rosy cheeks and sausage fingers. O'Donnel privately wondered if the man had ever accidently bitten any while scarfing his meals. The man knelt and used a rag to wipe off the extra mud.

"Dother," the man translated.

"That's not a word," O'Donnel said with a grunt.

"It is—fifth century, actually."

"What's it mean, fancy man?"

"It means *evil*."

The Storm Rider laughed, but his revelry was cut short by another howl—this one very close on the next ridge. He commanded, "Well dig it up. I want to get this job finished and return home." Sensing danger, he called the other two Riders over. "Stay close, boys," he whispered, "and keep your eyes peeled."

The stone was heavy and took every worker to lift free of its resting place. At first, refusing to budge, it held in place as if by unseen forces. With a mighty heave, every man strained against the load until it broke free. They managed to lift it high enough air rushed in with a powerful torrent. The workers immediately dropped their tools and fell backward just as the massive rock slammed back into place. Now the seal had broken, and the second effort proved easier. It raised, and the crew slid it to the side with moderate effort, smacking onto the dirt with an audible thud.

O'Donnel was still watching the workers when his nose suddenly detected sulfur on the air. As his nostrils sucked in the brimstone, his ears filled with guttural howls and hysteric barking. He spun around just in time to view a dozen or more sets of fiery orbs floating in the shadowy forest. *Their eyes,* he realized, *are pure fire!* No question remained in his mind over the existence of hellhounds.

The Storm Riders backed into a tight formation, sweating fear and panting sobs of terror as the hounds descended. Beyond the fighters, the workers broke, fleeing into the woods with tools tightly gripped in their hands. These fell one by one as more hounds emerged from the wood, giving chase and drawn by the smell of their terror. They rushed past the Riders to tackle each man, ripping cloth from flesh and flesh from bone, lapping up the steaming red ichor within.

O'Donnel's mistake had been to turn his head to watch the carnage, and was reminded of this by panting against his cheek. The hound's breath reeked of brimstone and hot coals, feeling nearly as warm both against his face. The beast loomed inches away. The Rider didn't move, and prayed the others wouldn't either. Then the rookie broke.

With a whimper, Sean, or whatever his name was, turned and bolted toward the recently excavated tomb. As he disappeared inside, the huge beast grabbed the man on O'Donnel's right, clamping him in its jaws and swinging left and right with a sickening snap of bones. Certain the man was dead, the hound crouched beside the lead Rider and waited.

Soon the others joined the first, circling O'Donnel's squad and crouching low against the underbrush, staring up with those awful eyes from hell. *Why don't they attack?* he thought, but soon had his answer. The rookie backed slowly up the steps, reemerging and quivering with fear. At first the hounds only growled, but when their master emerged after Sean, they moved as if ready to pounce on the young Rider.

The creature who followed was cloaked in garments of solid black that seemed to shimmer against the daylight as if cloaked in dense smoke. Red veins marbled his dark skin, and seemed to flow like freshly emerged lava. Two pools of liquid sulfur swam where his eyes should be, and steam rippled from his smile. A snap of fingers set the hellhounds upon Sean, pulling him to the ground and ripping the boy to pieces. O'Donnel fell to his knees and wept—unwilling to flee but unable to take flight. His sword dropped uselessly to the ground, as the creature loomed.

"I'd forgotten how horrible the rain could feel against my skin, brother."

At first the Rider thought he had spoken to him, but another creature emerged from the forest. This Spirit wore robes of darkness that swirled around him like a mist. His deep ebony skin was flawlessly smooth, lacking the veins of his brother. He looked upon O'Donnel with two swirling voids as empty as they were absent of light.

"I don't know, Dother," the second shade said to the first. "I have missed this realm. The inhabitants are so much fun to torment, and my hounds yearn for more of their flesh."

"Oh, Dub," the first said with a curling smile, revealing teeth forever stained with decay. "You'll again tire of this sport soon enough. We always do." Dother looked around, "Where is Dian?"

Dub replied with a shrug, but added, "We are three..."

"And three are we," answered Dother.

Dub turned to face O'Donnel as if suddenly aware of his presence. "Who is this?"

"Our messenger," Dother said with a smile.

Chapter Eleven

"Nuada wielded a sword unlike any other and before it all would fall with a single blade of light."
– The Legends of the Tuatha, Chronicle II, Passage 20

Alistaria sat across from Torian, watching him chew his lip the way he did when deeply troubled. No one had expected the fight in the mountains, and their actual enemy remained a mystery. The way the animals had attacked in unison was unlike anything they had ever seen. She called together this council to come up with ideas—*any* explanation which could restore reason to the entire affair. So far Erania had the best theory. But the old woman wasn't certain.

"It had to be a Sìth," she explained. "Sìth Morkur is Master of Beasts, and that's what attacked you. Animals. Surely he interfered?"

"I doubt it," Alistaria muttered. She had reread Nastauria's notebook several times, but nothing in the diary suggested the Sìth would choose to do harm unless denied his right to claim a soul. "He was very helpful in taking down Radviken, and seemed a true friend to Nastauria. He seemed to *want* us to recover the Blossom."

"Perhaps our use of the powers in combat offended him," Torian suggested. "We *were* tearing up the valley pretty harshly. We may have offended his connection to nature. Like Erania said, those were *his* beasts who attacked us."

"Could be," Erania agreed, "but legends describe other Sìths—some remain in our realm and some in others, but none of them are bound."

Alistaria agreed. "Sìth Morkur can travel at will between ours and Enatherr. It's easy to assume he's able to travel to the realm of shadows, and perhaps others can as well. I want to know *who* are the others we should fear. All we know of is Morkur." She turned to the elder.

"What's known about Sìths? Anything useful?"

Erania lowered her eyes to the table. "Not much, I'm afraid. Girtrán ordered everything written down be destroyed during his reign."

"So we're entirely dependent upon whatever Markey can dig up." Torian noted. The look on his face reflected his frustration. He wasn't used to fighting enemies he couldn't see.

Erania perked up with a look of caution on her face that leaked curiosity. "You're still working with the humans?"

Alistaria kept secret her agreement to supply food. There'd be time for that later. Leaving out those details, she replied, "We've agreed to exchange information. His scholars are studying the marks Torian found as well as a book we found in the Deamhan Palace. They're comparing it to their history, but so far dismissed much of it as myth."

"And myths are nothing to go off of," Torian added.

"Not entirely," the elder woman said. "Myths are stranger than history and less reliable, but often give clues into the truth. Tell me what you found in the palace and what their scholars have learned."

"We found an ancient library full of mostly useless records from what I could understand—transactions and chronicles of seasons. But several shelves had been plundered." Alistaria went on to tell her about the left behind volume, the men who attacked, and the arrival of the Sìth. "Markey's historian said the book was part of something he called the Annals of Tuatha de Dannan History."

"The Tuatha de Dannan?" Erania's wrinkles deepened and she fell into deep thought. "Something about the name is familiar."

"That's probably because that's what I named my new squad of fighters," Torian explained. "They are the Tuatha."

"No," Erania disagreed. "I've heard it before—before you would have used it. I think they were in a story I once heard about the Deamhan."

Alistaria sat up straighter. "That makes sense, but Hammond said these texts were from ancient people before the Deamhan. These people ruled Fainnotherr far longer than we."

Erania's memory was old, but reliable. "I think I remember the story, and it explains the palace is much older than we once thought." Her gaze fixed on the far wall as she fought to remember the story. "It belonged to the gods," she said quietly.

"You mean the Great Spirit?"

"No," she said, "not as ancient or as powerful as she, but those who came after when her back was turned creating other realms."

"The historian called the Tuatha de Dannan gods, Erania. Please tell us what you remember." Alistaria commanded.

"What I remember is not much. *How* I know is because of my grandmother. She long ago told me a story about a race long past, neither human nor fae nor gnome. Our ancestors called them gods, though they were not spirits. They controlled the original magic—the relics broken apart by the Great One and redistributed, but they also had other relics just as wondrous. Weapons, I think she once said. Weapons and tools that allowed nonmagical beings to wield powers as easily as they. But, like I said, I don't remember much of the story."

The old woman cleared her throat and turned to Torian. "I find it fitting you decided on the name Tuatha for your fighters, because they were the original heroes of legend. Listen now," she said, "and I will tell you of the Tuatha de Dannan."

Before the Deamhan Palace was built, there lay an escarpment of barren rock among the great trees. It was smooth and tall, the perfect foundation for a construction of stone and marble. It overlooked the lush meadows in the valley to the north, marking the northern boundary of the forest and nestled between two rivers fed by weeping falls flowing from high mountains in the North. This place of stone was named the Sliábh an Iarainn, or the Iron Mountain, for the vast amounts of vile metal found beneath and all around. It was here the settlers founded their kingdom.

The people of Dannan were vastly different than the fae living in the trees—for we were very primitive at the time. Without wings, these newcomers more closely resembled the humans beyond the portal. Of course, there was no kingdom of Enatherr during this time, and that race of man lived in caves and had only just began experimenting with planting seed along the river banks. These Dannan were certainly not human in that regard, but the fae never learned from whence these newcomers came. All our ancestors knew was these invaders had the ability to mine the very bane of our bodies and blood—they came for the iron.

King Oberon ruled over the fae during this time, and he approached the Dannan with cautious curiosity. This was before the founding of the Kern, so his soldiers were armed with sharpened sticks and carved stone lashed to wooden handles. They were far from impressive to these people clad in suits made of iron. As soon as he and his entourage arrived, he feared they would be set upon and followed to their home in the trees, but the welcome was surprisingly warm and his gifts well received.

The King of the Dannan was a towering mountain of a man named Nuada. He loomed over the fae, resembling a giant. He was a true colossus—a titan maybe? He explained they had journeyed upriver from the eastern approach after circling the island for thirty days.

"What are you searching for in our lands, which you cannot find in your own?" Oberon asked of the newcomers.

"We have no land, as we are travelers driven from our home by Darkness, Evil, and Violence," was Nuada's reply.

Oberon understood. "All those things are reasons to flee for sure, by are you not certain you haven't brought these plagues upon our land and people as well by your presence?"

Nuada's face abruptly fell serious and full of dire warning. (Oberon later told others he detected a bit of fear behind the giant's confident and jovial eyes.) He leaned in close and said sternly, "I speak not of things or plagues, rather the sons of Aes Sidhe. We disturbed their burial mounds with greedy fervor when we mined, awakening from slumber those who should not be disturbed."

"Who are the Aes Sidhe?" Oberon asked. "Who would slumber under mounds?"

"Not who but *what*, King of the Fae. These spirits awakened from a sleep akin to death, hunger pangs driving their madness and eager to feast upon fear and misery. Their mother is Carmán, the sorceress who once hailed from the enclosed sea but who travelled to our parts in thirst of fresh souls to drink. Our ancestors drove her and her brood underground, but we uncovered the seals and released them upon our society."

Oberon found anger building inside his heart, a strange emotion—one with little usefulness except to muddle the senses. He raged. "Surely, they follow you *here*. We are simple children of the forest with no weapons nor defenses. We have only our magic with which to defend our lives or the trees whose roots we tend. I fear it will not be enough against these spirits you mention.

Nuada considered, for he was a wise and kind benefactor to our people. Since iron was poison to our body and souls, he provided our ancestors with the knowledge to forge silver as strong as their steel. Lighter even. His people were master builders, and soon erected the palace there upon the Sliábh an Iarainn. He taught our people how to build the Skygate, and Fainnotheria became our home.

Erania leaned back in her chair when she had finished, exhausted and unwilling to say more, even if she had more to tell. Alistaria had watched her closely during the telling, and felt sadness at the more noticeable signs of age in the elder. This old woman represented the last of her childhood and family, having presided over both her birth and bleeding for the Blossom. When she was gone, the queen would have no one, having lost both her grandfather and Nastauria, as well as her cousin.

Restarian killed Nastauria, Alistaria remembered. *Cut her down in his rage and took her from me. I must stop worrying over his safety.* Yet she also hoped the healing powers would continue to aid him.

"I'm tired and must rest," Erania said at last. Clearly done talking, she excused herself from the meeting and retired to her quarters.

The young queen watched the elder leave, then turned to gaze upon Torian. He would be her only friend and confidant after Erania passed, and she was beginning to appreciate his presence more and more deeply. Looking at him now she could almost forget he was really a human. *Never trust a human,* Nastauria had once warned, but in the end trusted this one.

Their recent quarrel had greatly troubled her. *I should be thinking of his needs more than mine,* she knew. *He's as Fainne as I,* Alistaria realized. *Neither of us belonged in Fainnotheria, but here we were raised.* Each brought up in the culture and taught the ways they held so dearly important. In reality, they were both changelings swapped for the lives of others taken and hidden away. *Would he ever understand the permanence of love? Could he love another and allow himself to be loved in return?* He caught her staring and she felt her cheeks suddenly blush with embarrassment.

"What?" he asked.

She coughed and sat straighter in her chair. "I was thinking about how so much has changed and how so much more about our pasts was hidden by Girtrán. Do you think the people in Erania's story were real? It's hard to know about the old stories."

He shook his head, appearing nearly as exhausted as Erania. Clearly the events over the past few weeks had been overwhelming for him, rising from Skygate sentry to Fainnen general in a matter of days. His shoulders carried more than his share of the burden.

"I'm not sure," he finally said. "I can't shake this feeling we're running out of time. The three sons she described—do you think one of them could have caused what we faced in the mountains? Despite the cloud of snow, I surely sensed darkness all around."

"I did too," she agreed. "Darkness has been everywhere—in that cloud, in the tree, inside Korl..."

"Yes, especially around the Deamhan Palace."

Alistaria sat up suddenly. "That's what it is," she said.

"What? I don't understand."

"Erania said the palace was built upon a mountain of iron."

"Yes? So? It's underground. It doesn't affect fae until mined."

"No," she agreed, "that's true, but she said the Dannan were there to mine it!"

"For their weapons and tools, yes."

"That means there are tunnels beneath the palace!" She suddenly remembered something else, a scrap of paper she had found in the library and chosen to keep for herself. Alistaria rushed to her satchel and pulled it out—wrinkled and folded but intact. "This is a drawing of the palace as it was originally." She spread it out on the table and Torian leaned in, studying alongside her.

"Look here," he said. "The markings in the margin match the symbols I drew on my shield. Alistaria," he said quietly and with a quiver of fear to his voice—one she'd never heard from a man so brave as he. "Enatherr is exactly like Fainnotherr, except for the subtle differences over time, like the dune sea and lack of great trees."

"Yes, very much so," she agreed

"Nastauria once told us Radviken chose his home of Norgaard as the site for his palace, building it atop the highest hill and upon an older structure. And he insisted he was solely responsible for protecting Enatherr and Fainnotherr from the Shadow Realm. Markey once told me Radviken built his palace atop an existing structure. Do you know what this means?"

She understood immediately. "The Deamhan Palace exists in both realms," she said with a gasp. "Possibly all! But that means Markey's in danger!"

"You must stay here with the elders." Torian urged. "I'll warn Markey and have his scholars study these markings.

She did something that surprised them both. She flung her arms around his neck and kissed him on the mouth. After pulling back, she urged, "Be safe."

Chapter Twelve

*"Never get inside a barrel without drilling an extra hole on the side
to see. You may never need this advice, but believe me it's sound."*
– Piotr

The Storm Warden and his loyal Riders had talked until late into the night. So late, Piotr had somehow managed to doze off inside the barrel. Now awake and unable to stretch or stand, he held perfectly still and listened for movement, hoping they had left the room in order that he and Boyd could soon escape. He tried using Alistaria's gift of sight, focusing on the room how he'd remembered it, and saw a door opening and a woman enter. A few minutes later the creak of hinges announced they'd arrived.

Good, he thought. Boyd's tavern wench came through. *What was her name? Esmerelda?* He was about to speak up, when he noticed she was not alone. The tavern keeper accompanied her. *Certainly he's not on our side?* He wondered. His question was soon answered with the sound of nails hammering into wood. He pressed hard against the lid, but it didn't budge.

"What's the meaning of this?" Boyd demanded from the next barrel.

"Shh!" Esmerelda demanded. "Or you'll ruin our plan! We're getting you out of here, and this is the easiest way!"

"Why the nails?" Boyd asked.

"We've gotta nail them shut so they don't pop open when we roll you through the common room," she explained, and both men relaxed.

Piotr heard a thud and a groan that must have been Boyd tipping over, and then he too was toppled on his side. His head spun as the cask rolled, and soon was clinging to the sides for dear life and against dizziness. He felt like his mind would burst each time he rolled up a step, but eventually heard muffled sounds of revelry as they passed through the tavern. He, like Boyd had complained earlier, had to use the privy and could not wait to be rid of the barrel.

A short time later, they were hefted and presumably loaded upright on a wagon. The bouncing along cobblestones jarred Piotr's teeth, but was better than the stairs had been. *Why are they taking us away from the tavern?* he wondered. Thankfully, the trip wasn't too long, and he breathed a sigh of relief when they finally reached their destination. He knew they'd arrived by the repeated process of the same tipping over, rolling, and hefting as before.

Once he was upright, he heard a pounding on wood. "Boyd!" Esmerelda called. "Are you in this one?"

"I threw up," was the response from within. "And I need a change of drawers," soon followed.

The sound of muffled hammering and prying announced the release of Piotr's friend. Confident he would be freed next, he sat still and let his head settle. But his gift of sight revealed a startling image. Esmerelda was not alone, and the men in the room were not from the tavern. These were strange, brutish fellows, muscled and ready for a fight with clubs hanging from their belts or in their hands. He saw Boyd tumble onto the floor before he actually did. The men immediately surrounded him.

She sold us out, Piotr realized, *but to whom?*

The sound of Boyd hitting the floor was followed by a grunt and a gasp.

"Esmerelda!" he said with surprised hurt in his voice, "What did you do! I thought you loved me!"

She laughed. "Me? Love *you*? You're the sworn enemy of my kind, working your magic on others. You're despicable—a predator feeding on innocent prey."

"I don't understand," Boyd protested.

The sound of club hitting soft flesh caused Piotr to grimace, and he tried to shift his weight. But his own legs, like his friend's, had fallen asleep in the keg. All he could do is listen to the exchange.

"Who are these men, Esmerelda?" Boyd begged between whacks.

"*We* are the League for Humans First," one of them replied.

"That doesn't have much of a ring to it," Boyd said honestly. "How about, *Human Interests Together,* or H.I.T.?" One of the men responded with another whack to his side and the little man groaned. "Okay," he pleaded, "no hitting! How about Humanity United?" Another blow to his shoulder caused him to cry out. "I'm human, so what does your league want with me?" he asked. "Is it because of my friend? He's only half fae, so he's okay, right?"

Esmerelda and the others paused, and Piotr imagined all their eyes on his keg. It wouldn't be long before they opened his cask and beat him in the same way. He braced himself for the scrape of hammer against lid as they worked on his nails, and prayed for the ability to just disappear. *Don't see me,* he begged in his mind, *let me be invisible!* That was possible, wasn't it? Alistaria's gift of sight offered many options. Why couldn't he render himself invisible to enemies?

The lid popped off and fell to the floor with a clatter, and Piotr blinked against the light flooding in. Esmerelda and two thugs stared down into the keg.

"Where'd he go?" one of the thugs asked.

"Must've freed himself before we got inside," Esmerelda said. "Or he was in another barrel and drilled holes in this one to fool us." She pointed to one of the men Piotr couldn't see. "You take two men and track him down at the tavern. He couldn't have gotten far."

The faces hovering above him disappeared, and the thud of club against skin resumed. "Why are you here, leprechaun?" she demanded.

"Lepre... What?" grunted Boyd.

"We know what you are, sprite! You worked your charm on the wrong woman, and now you'll pay. How many more of you are in Enatherr?"

"I don't know what you're talking about!" the little man protested.

"No more lies," she said, "or we'll start breaking bones." To one of the thugs she said, "tie him to a chair and let's start the interrogation for real. Get the finger spreader."

"Finger spreader?" Boyd asked with a shrill break in his voice. "But I'm *human!* I can prove it!"

"How?" the tavern maid asked.

"Ask me how much gold I've got!"

There was a brief pause as Esmerelda and her brutes considered. After a while she asked seriously, "How much gold *have* you got?"

"Not a bit! I'm broke! See? I'm no leprechaun! I've never even seen the end of a rainbo..." His last word ended in a gasp as a blow to his midsection took away his breath.

"Forget the finger spreader," she said to the men, "heat an iron instead."

Piotr could no longer do nothing for his friend and overcame his fear of the clubs. With great care not to make any noise, he pulled himself upright in the keg—swaying and numb while holding his legs steady, all the while willing himself to remain unseen. He tested this once by waving a hand at one of the thugs, then a second time by sending his friend a rude gesture. Neither noticed.

Careful not to tip the entire thing over, he stepped out and crept behind the others. The thugs all faced Boyd, and there were now only three beside Esmerelda.

"Are you part of a network?" she asked of Boyd. "Where are the others? How do you communicate?"

He was now panting for air, more aware and very afraid of what she demanded. "I'm not a leprechaun," was all he could say and answered it several times to each question.

Piotr looked around for something to use against the men. They were not soldiers, so there were no swords or crossbows laying around. Nor were they stupid enough to leave a knife nearby. Each held their club at the ready, eager to pounce whenever Esmerelda tired of Boyd's blubbering. His eyes found a long rod nestled in the hot coals of the fire, the tip not quite aglow as it had only recently been placed in the heat. A careful touch of the handle found it cool enough to grab, and Piotr turned to rescue his friend.

He had no idea if the weapon was also invisible to the goons and worried what would happen next. Neither of the two thieves were fighters, so he had a chance. Except, he wasn't much more skilled than they. Ignoring the queasiness in his stomach, Piotr raised the iron aloft and swung it down with force against the first thug's skull. He fell, just as in the story books.

Esmerelda screamed, and the other men spun around. Boyd continued to mutter and stare at the woman's feet. While the first man lay unmoving on the floor, Piotr sidestepped and stood perfectly still, willing them not to see him and.

"What was that?" one of the men asked.

All eyes returned to Boyd.

"He's working leprechaun magic, that's what!" said another, and raised his club to whack their captive across the temple.

"Wait!" screamed Esmerelda. "We need information from him!"

Piotr swung again as both men looked in her direction and dropped the bigger of the two with a blow across his nose. Esmerelda and the final man watched on with horror as he staggered backward, completely surprised and holding back blood and teeth. The tall thief felt bad for the man as he brought the weapon down once more, this time knocking him to the floor.

"I'm not fighting him alone," the final thug shouted as he tried to leave.

But an invisible strike across his knee sent him to the floor atop his partners. After two more thudding strikes to his head, he fell limp. Esmerelda let out a wild scream of terror that drained the air from her lungs, and she fainted away—lightheaded and collapsing into a heap of her own.

Dropping the veil by hoping he was again visible, Piotr quickly helped Boyd to his feet. "C'mon," he urged. "They'll be waking up soon."

"Am I really a leprechaun, Piotr?" Boyd asked his friend with a worried voice.

"I think so, yes. But we must worry about that later. They're waking up."

Boyd's vision swam into focus as he stared at the unconscious bodies on the floor. "Look what I did with my magic, Piotr!" he said with wide eyes. "I'm a badass leprechaun!"

"Come on," the taller man begged. "We've got to get this news to Markey!"

"We do," agreed Boyd. "But first we've got to go get Lucky from the tavern."

Piotr groaned, but found he couldn't argue this time.

Chapter Thirteen

"Mines ran deep in Sliábh an Iarainn, and in both realms the Dannan dug their vile metal. Ours was not the only realm they affected, and they seemed to exist in two places at once."
– The Legends of the Tuatha, Chronicle I, Passage 6

Torian's Tuatha landed atop Deamhan Palace, quickly forming a perimeter. Kneeling, the general spread the sketch so his officers could see the layout and the areas they would search.

"Some of you already know the place," he said, "you've lived here your entire lives. But we're not looking for anything obvious, and whatever the portals are they'll appear subtle. Look for markings such as these." He pointed to writing in the margins of the page. "Remember, do not try to enter or force open anything closed. We're to identify locations here which may also be present in Enatherr, then take that information to the humans."

He turned his gaze toward a young woman robed in the crimson of the mages. The golden crest and stripes on her sleeve marked her rank as captain. "Today we'll be split into four teams of ten each. I'll lead first division through the armory and library and Captain Palathia will take second division through the old kitchens."

He indicated two other mages, each with a single stripe. "Lieutenants Quinten and Harachen, you each know this palace intimately, so I won't waste your leadership in the upper levels. You will both lead your divisions into the old barracks and dungeons below."

They both saluted.

"Be careful," he warned, scanning the watching faces and saying louder, "and remain vigilant. We don't know what the Shadow Realm is capable of, and this is only a scout mission. Do not engage. If you're attacked, rendezvous in the throne room and be ready to fall back through the Fainnen Ring." After he finished speaking, he nodded to Captain Palathia.

"Second Division," she called, "Fall in on me!"

The other squad leaders did the same, fanning out to descend the spires. Torian turned to his own team. "Stay on me, and keep tight. We can only move three abreast through these halls." Hefting his spear, he paused to stare at the carved design and wished he knew more of its history. Squeezing it tightly, he took in a deep breath, then led them below.

Palathia had been a root tender her entire life, never expecting to fly into battle beside the Kern and certainly not believing she would lead soldiers of her own. When General Torian first approached her, she had laughed. *It was a good joke*, she thought, but then sobered quickly after he explained—mages and soldiers united for a new type of warfare, a concept never attempted, and she found it alluring. Her role, he explained, would be as a combat medic.

But she was more than that now, having grasped his tactics quicker than many of the others. She already had the ability to dual wield powers (both fire and ice) while also healing. The only difficulty she had at first was mastering the fairy spark, and would never forget the time she nearly exploded the queen's guard on the mountain. But that mistake was quickly forgiven, and she rose quickly to the rank of captain—something else she never expected.

Torian had briefed her earlier regarding the kitchens. Though not a likely spot for a mineshaft, the addition was at the far end of the main structure and on the lowest level. They found them just beyond the main hall, a broad series of rooms with wide hearths and tall fireplaces. None had been used in ages, and she wondered what they had been like before falling into decay. This must have been a magnificent fortress in its day, and Palathia could almost imagine its splendor.

But the sense about it was wrong. Gone was the pulsing thrum of the forest, replaced instead by a queasy sense of iron beneath the structure. The metal's effect differed between fae, with some, like Alistaria, feeling its effects to a greater degree. Others seemed to have no ill effects at all in its presence, but one thing about it was certain—it lessened one's ability to use their magic. Palathia dreaded being so close to its source.

"Spread out," she commanded once they had secured each rooms. "Search for anything that could lead into a lower structure or indicate a different time period."

They scoured the area thoroughly, taking their time and examining every crevice, nook, and cranny in the kitchens. The only oddity they found was in what had once served as a pantry.

To the naked eye, the room was perfectly rectangle and unadorned, partially underground to aid food storage. Set down a few steps from the main rooms, they found it cooler. A row of circular indentions ran across the ceiling, and Palathia ran her hand along the groove where the ancients had once hung meat or vegetables for drying. Further inspection found the same ghostly remains along the walls, where wooden shelving had once brimmed with goods. But nothing was out of place enough to suggest a portal to another realm.

She sat down in the middle of the floor with legs crossed—a habit carried over from her days as a root tender. She usually felt more grounded when she was near the roots, but this place had an eerie absence of thrum about it. *It can't only be the iron beneath the earth,* she considered, *but probably also the absence of life.* Thankfully, this spot felt better than any other place in the palace and she could sit and think with a clear mind.

A ruffling of robes announced one of her mages approached, and she inclined her head to see who. It was Ceranth, a former Deamhan recruited by Torian for his promise with sight. "What is it?" she asked. "Anything at all?"

"No, ma'am," he said. "And no word yet from the others."

"Then it must not be here."

"I have an idea," he said timidly.

"Share it then. The best part of the Tuatha is our ability to speak freely. Despite our ranks, we're a team after all."

"We've used our eyes to search, but I've been able to use my gift as well."

She looked up hopefully. "What did your gift reveal?"

"Dust and stone," he said with a smile, "but I want to try again with your help."

"I don't have the gift of sight. How can I be helpful?"

"All the mages respect your grasp of power. With your connection to the morning glory, I was hoping you could amplify my efforts."

"I don't believe that's how it works, Ceranth."

"Only because we've never tried. I have a theory, and don't see the harm in trying. I will work my gift over the room, and you pour power into me. Go slowly at first, increasing until I cannot stand it." He shrugged, "If it doesn't work, at least we've made an attempt."

Palathia had not considered using her gift in that way, no one had. Sure, it worked with root tending, but only when one tender amplified their own power. *This young fae has promise,* she considered. *He's smart and bold—a problem solver.* She motioned for him to sit in front of her on the stone.

"Come," she said. "The ground feels better here, without so much iron as the rest of the palace."

He took his position and worked the gift, spreading out a veil of mist that seemed to seep into the walls, floors, and ceiling. As it did, the composition of each took on a translucent shimmer, revealing spiders and other insects hidden inside crevices all around. In one corner, Palathia was surprised to see a mouse had burrowed deep into a crack she would have assumed too small for the rodent. Its tiny heart pulsed through its transparent skin. But there was no portal or false wall to be seen.

She placed her hands on Ceranth's back, feeling his body thrum with healthy youth. He had a strong pulse. Slowly and carefully she drew from the morning glory, pouring power into the young fae. As she did, the walls completely disappeared, and the nestled insects seemed to now hover above the ground where they hid. They could see the dirt behind the walls, confirming her first thoughts that the pantry was below ground. Beyond that lay ancient layers of sedimentary rock, left behind by some ancient sea as it formed as deposits on the ocean floor. In these she caught glimpses of iron ore, but no vein.

Palathia's eyes focused on the floor beneath them, now invisible as they seemed to float upon air. There was no dirt nor rock below, only a tremendous cavern.

"How do you feel?" she asked. "It seems to be working, but I'm afraid to cause you harm."

With a strained voice, he said, "I'm fine."

She checked his heart, finding his pulse had quickened. Though sitting still, his body reacted as if he ran a race or flew at full speed. "I don't think I should add much more," she cautioned.

"Please," he urged. "I can almost see beneath the floor. It shouldn't be this deep."

She couldn't help but agree, and eased more of her gift into his body. Passages branched away from the cavern, leading away her curiosity in several directions at once. One in particular caught her attention, and both fae gasped at once.

From a crack in the cavern wall a furred beast stared up without eyes, sniffing the air and tasting their presence. The creature was huge, easily fifty times larger than the horses ridden by the humans. Only five hands of thick stone stood between them should it charge, and its clawed talons worked feverishly to complete its tunnel. Though it was blind, Palathia knew this monstrosity could somehow sense their presence. It snapped razor sharp teeth at the stone between them, breaking off shards of rock with each snap. *It can chew its way through,* she suddenly worried, and it did, breaking into the cavern below with an explosion of dirt and stone.

By now Ceranth's blood coursed too quickly through his body, and Palathia feared for his safety. But just as she was about to remove the power flowing between them, she caught a glimpse of something far more hideous than the beast. The face just beyond the creature was that of a Sìth, with skin flowing like molten lava and swirling eyes of yellow. It laughed as it watched the fae, somehow seeing them as clearly as they could see him.

Palathia immediately severed their connection and Ceranth gasped for air against the sudden relief.

The booming voice of the Sìth abruptly echoed throughout the palace so all fae could hear. "Race me to the human realm, fleas, for I have so much evil to unleash!"

"Hurry," she commanded, tapping Ceranth on the shoulder. Screaming toward the kitchens she ordered, "Tuatha! On me!"

Markey O'Malley played quietly with Germaine on the floor, enjoying a break from governing and, for a moment, no longer worrying about his kingdom. He laid out some toy cavalry soldiers and demonstrated how an entire formation could change direction in unison.

"Any decent mount can circle well in its haunches," he explained, "so always make sure yours has a good head and a tight pattern. Otherwise you can't wheel on a movable pivot like this." He moved the toys one by one to show how it was supposed to work. Then he reset them and began again. "A poorly trained horse could disrupt the entire turn. They're smart, but the others on its flank will follow." He moved them again, sending one at an angle and thus splitting the formation into two. "This will kill an entire charge if the enemy exploits the opening. So keep your own head always on a swivel," he instructed.

A messenger interrupted. "General Torian has arrived unannounced, sire. We have him contained within the barrier, but he's demanding you speak with him at once."

"What in the blazes? Let him through! He's our ally for Tempest's sake!"

"Sire, protocol demands we don't. He's with an entire regiment!"

"What do you mean an entire regiment? He agreed never to enter the palace with teams of more than five at a time."

"His total force numbers forty, your highness, and General Liam fears an invasion."

Markey jumped to his feet, calling for his wife. "You two get to the grand hall with the others," he told her, then pushed past the page, hurrying from the room and leaving his wife and son behind. As he dashed up two flights of stairs, he met soldiers gearing up in a foyer. They did not salute or even bow as he rushed past, meaning Conner Liam had ordered them to battle stations. He stumbled once on his robe, but forcibly shed it from his shoulders and left it lying on the stone. He felt odd running through the great hall bare-chested, it was not kingly.

Ahead, two dozen Storm Guard had formed up and stood ready. Beyond them stood Conner Liam, watching through the open doorway. The general turned and held a hand up when his king approached. From the other room Markey could hear angry shouts— an argument of some sort. On the elevated platform, and caught a glimpse of archers with downward trained crossbows.

"Can't let you in, sire!" Conner Liam tried to stop him.

"Move out of the blasted way!"

"He arrived in full force and demands access to our palace. I fear betrayal or some sort of trick."

"Or he has a damned good reason!" Markey shoved his general aside and raced to the top of the wooden rampart.

Below he could make out Torian standing before his soldiers. They were hidden behind shields held in a tight formation, protecting all sides.

"Why are you here with an invasion force, Torian?" O'Malley asked warily.

"We're not invading, we're warning! Let us in now before it gets here!"

"Before what gets here?" the king demanded.

"I don't have time to explain, Markey!"

"Set down your weapons and we'll talk," the king urged.

"We have no time," Torian begged, "the creatures of shadow are coming here!"

"Why would you break protocol?" the king demanded. "Even if something were chasing you, it can't follow through the Fainnen Ring! Now drop your weapons so we can sort this out!"

"Because it's not entering through here!" Torian turned to face his formation and called, "Palathia!" Several shields moved at once, revealing a mage wearing a scarlet robe and holding a shield of her own.

"Yes, sir?" she replied.

"Tell him what you saw!"

"It was terrible," she said. "A burrowing monster, larger than fifty men. Its talons appeared able to dig through solid rock. Its teeth were like those of a reptile, sharp and strong and each the size of a dog."

"Tell him of the other," Torian commanded.

"What *other*?" demanded Markey.

"It was a spirit, sir. Much like the Sìth we know as Morkur, but with swirling eyes of brimstone and cloaked in darkness and shadow. He spoke to me—told me he would race us here."

Markey froze in place. "Conner, what did that Rider report? The survivor from the excavation?"

"He reported a Sìth, with the same type of eyes."

"Blasted! Well, whatever it is, it hasn't reached the palace. Our sighting was only this morning, and miles away from here."

"At least fan out and search the ground levels." Torian pleaded.

"Where? Where's no other portal!"

"I don't know," Torian admitted. "This palace looks different in this realm, so we'll have to search out the spot."

"What do you mean *this palace?* This palace only exists in our realm, and yours has a different building altogether. Torian, you're not making sense, son!"

A symphony of howls suddenly filled the palace—an eerie noise that echoed through passages and stairwells.

"It's here," Torian said. The howls had mixed with barks and brays and grew louder. "We don't have time, Markey!"

O'Malley turned sharply to face General Liam and commanded, "Let them in! Search out the lower levels!"

"But, sire!"

"Now!" he ordered. His shout was answered by a scream and a wail from below.

Conner Liam shouted orders to his men outside the room, and the archers snapped to attention—no longer training their weapons on the fae. The doors to the secure area slowly opened, allowing Torian and his Tuatha to emerge.

He held the diagram up for the king to see. "In our realm, old mine shafts converged in a cavern beneath the kitchens. Northeast quadrant. Based on the size of the Deamhan Palace and the massive rebuild of yours, I think it's just off the center of this structure."

Conner and Markey exchanged an anxious look.

"Bring my armor!" the king shouted, before racing off to join the men gearing up in the next room.

"What is it?" Torian asked the general. "What's wrong with that spot?"

"It's the main hall between the main flight of stairs and the kitchens, but also where we evacuated the women and children after your arrival. His family is down there."

CHAPTER FOURTEEN

"Though they did not simply vanish as many legends suggest, their numbers greatly diminished after many wars against their numerous foes. They ultimately disappeared completely from our world and are thought to reside elsewhere. The wise among us believe they exist within us, having looked elsewhere for bloodlines to continue their own. The evidence of this lies in the gifts they gave to every race."
– The Annals of History Book X, Passage 185

Alistaria eyed Maerlin standing across the room. After Torian departed, the soldier had become her shadow, following or looming in doorways and corners of rooms. She appreciated the gesture but saw no need for protection within her own city. Worse, he hadn't said anything to her since falling in the mountains. He avoided small talk whenever she reached out and kept his hand firmly gripped on his sword hilt whenever someone else was in the room. She also noticed he no longer stood duty at the Skygate. All of this was most certainly Torian's doing.

She turned her attention from Maerlin to Korl. Seated beneath the roots of the Tree of Life, he had chosen to teach just outside the entrance to the Blossom. All around him were the youngest fae, children receiving their first lessons and eager to learn. They stared intently, wide-eyed and taking in every word as he taught the rhythm of the thrum and how to detect the vibration of lifeforce.

She watched him closely. Her heart broke for the teacher, as he was no longer the root tender she remembered. Korl had aged since his accident—physically older and moving slower. It was as if his body leaked lifeforce, something Alistaria did not believe possible. His voice quivered when he spoke, and she even detected a slight stutter. *He's dying,* she knew. *The greatest teacher in centuries, and he'll be gone before his time.* Breaking away, she walked up to Maerlin and stood directly in front of his gaze.

"Let's go," she commanded.

His eyes flickered, locking onto hers, but said nothing. She noticed his jaw was set as if forcing himself silent. *Soldiers always do things like that,* she realized. That's how they cope with the grimness of their duties. If they weren't laughing off pain or fear, they separated from it—pushing emotion aside in an attempt to leave it in another place entirely. Hurt was welcome anywhere but in their minds.

"You're going to argue, but I've decided," she said. "So I'm inviting you with me instead of trying to go alone."

To her surprise he nodded. When she turned, he turned. When her wings grabbed hold of the air and lifted upward, he followed.

The sentries at the Skygate didn't stop her, either. They stepped aside for their queen, opening the massive doors and letting light spill in from above the canopy. Everything was perfect from this vantage point, just as when she and Maerlin had flown northward together. She stood for a moment and let it warm her skin as before, then launched into open sky. Her guardian trailed behind without question.

She circled the perimeter of the city, scanning the floor and searching for anything amiss but finding nothing. New growth had taken hold, and the great trees seemed to flourish. Below, the tenders had moved to a different part of the forest, further away from Fainnotheria and worked diligently without scanning the skies for threats. *The way it* should *be,* she thought with a smile.

It didn't take her long to find the spot they'd worked before—the place where Korl had taken ill. She descended effortlessly, landing softly beside the massive trunk he had tried to heal. To her irritation the burl had grown in size. The entire southern strip of bark now bulged from the ground upward, twisting and contorting as it reached toward the branches above. The sight of it turned her stomach and knotted her gut. Worse, each of the surrounding trees had developed similar ailments.

"I know you've bled for the Blossom, but I want to know. Do you have any connection to it?"

Maerlin shook his head. He did not.

"Can you even feel it" she asked, "just a little or at all? A buzzing or a thrum?"

"I think so," he said quietly. "But I'm not sure."

At least he's speaking now, she thought. "It won't always feel like a heartbeat," she explained, using the words Korl had taught her long ago. "Sometimes it's a ringing in the ears, like feeling the vibrations from a hummingbird's wings—subtle but powerfully consistent."

He shrugged.

She had his attention. Finding a healthy trunk, one untainted by the tumors, Alistaria knelt and placed one hand upon the roots. Her other traced the vertical ridges of swollen bark. "Like this," she said, inviting him to try. To her surprise he did.

Alistaria watched as he mimicked her posture, feeling the exact same places as she. He closed his eyes but shook his head after only lingering a few moments. "Nothing," he said.

"Stay there," she urged. "Keep your eyes closed and stay where you are."

He nodded and closed them tighter.

I'm sorry, friend, she said to the tree, *but he needs your pain.* With a flick of her wrist she sent a dash of fairy spark into the trunk, causing just enough current to shock its lifeforce. It pulsed more rapidly.

Maerlin's eyes shot open with amazement and his mouth opened wide. "I felt that," he said.

"Felt what?" she demanded. "The spark or the thrum."

"The thrum! It was as if the tree's heartbeat was my own. Suddenly rapid and beating against my ears. I could almost... no. Not that."

"What," she asked. "Tell me what you think it was you felt."

"It was almost like the tree gasped before the thrum, like a quick breath of air can set my own pulse beating wildly before battle. Not fear, exactly, but excitement... or surprise."

"And is it there now?" she asked.

He nodded, leaning in close and listening while feeling. A single tear formed in the corner of his eye, holding fast and refusing to fall down his cheek. He smiled broadly with joy at the sensation.

"Now try over here," she said, "on one of these afflicted trees. Describe what you feel."

He knelt and placed his hands the same way as before, leaning in with eyes closed and face determinedly set. He pulled away quickly as if stunned. "What is that?" he asked.

"I don't know, but it's the same thing affecting Korl. Worse, it's spreading to the surrounding trees, and I worry it will do the same inside the city. If I can't heal Korl, then I fear it may spread to the entire court."

"Can you send him away? Isolate him?"

She shook her head gravely. "No. I would never do anything of the sort to one of my people. I might have in the beginning, but I've learned many things since becoming queen. You taught me with this when we spoke above the mountains."

Curious, the sentry asked, "What did you learn from me?"

"This—we're all born to be alive and free, but I can't force everyone to get along. Just like I can't force you to become a root tender or a Skygate sentry. Life is about choosing your own path as you see fit. As long as it doesn't harm others."

"I don't understand."

"At first, I fought Torian by refusing to train tenders to fight alongside the Kern. But now that I've seen their camaraderie—their joy at finding a niche—I've realized people crave freedom to choose, and I don't have any authority over individualism. Just like you, Maerlin."

"What about me? I serve and I'm happy to do so."

"You're not happy. You're not strong enough with the gifts to be a root tender, and you're certainly not happy as a sentry. What is it that you yearn for? What makes you truly happy?"

"I want..." he paused and considered. "I want to be a scholar. I've been listening to you and General Torian talk about the text. I used to walk the halls of the palace and often wandered into that library. I couldn't read the language, but longed to understand what was between those pages. Sometimes I would sit, staring at the rows of shelves and marveling at the possibilities within."

"I can help you with that," she promised.

"How? I'm sworn to protect you here."

"I don't need a bodyguard. I'm safe here, and you're not happy. I'd rather you travel to Enatherr and study under Markey O'Malley's historians. I want you to go to them, study the languages and learn to read them all." She reached a hand into her satchel and drew out a parchment, hastily scribbling a message and then marking it with her seal. "Give this to my brother and he will admit you into his palace. Be my scholar, Maerlin, and return to me happy."

"I don't know how to thank you," he said truly.

"You will in time, once you're my historian."

"I don't mean for this, well, not *only* for this. I don't know how to thank you for saving my life upon the mountain. I died up there, didn't I?"

"You did"

"I know I did, because I saw unexplainable things I can't put into words."

"Then start there," she urged. "Find out everything you can about the Shadow Realm, and record all you know. We may need that knowledge more than anything in the coming war."

"So war is unavoidable?"

"War is the only certainty," she promised. They said their good-byes, and she watched him fly off to the northeast. *The last of my protectors,* she thought with a laugh. *I'll have to learn to defend myself, I guess.*

"That was a kind action on your part," a deep voice said from the forest. She spun to find Sìth Morkur approaching.

"I want him to find his way," she said. "He's lost." A thought suddenly struck her, and she narrowed her eyes. "Are you here to demand a soul in exchange for his?"

"Not this time," the spirit promised.

"Why not? What's different? He died and I revived him. You've every right to demand an exchange from me."

"No. His death was neither natural nor was his soul mine to claim. You had every right to revive him."

"Why this time? Explain."

"I cannot, but you will know the truth of it soon."

"If not to claim a soul, Sìth, tell me why you're here," she demanded.

"Where did you find Areadbhar?" he asked.

"I don't know that name."

"You know not the name, yet young Torian carries the relic. The fact it chose him to wield its magic astounds me. He must be worthier than its previous owners, for it hasn't burned in several millennia."

"You're speaking riddles I don't understand. What did Torian find?"

"Did you not wonder about the fire that consumed the human assassin? Or why my children could not claim him?"

Alistaria frowned, thinking back to the moment in the Deamhan Palace. "I did it," she replied, "though I don't know how."

"No, you were unable to use your power to harm, and the flames you summoned had extinguished."

"But Torian can't... he doesn't have connection to the Blossom, even though he bled for it twice. You're trying to confound me, to trick me into believing his spear holds power, but I won't. Tell me about the mountain valley and the animals. Why did you send them to attack us? They're your subjects, are they not?"

The Sìth laughed a deep and rumbling sound very much like a lion finishing a roar. "It seems, young Torian caught the attention of another Sìth. It is good he found Areadbhar, for he will need it against Dub, Dother, and Dian."

"You said *a* Sìth, but gave me three names. Stop these riddles at once!"

"Darkness, Death, and Violence are one but also three, and attracting one will call forth the others. Be careful where your friend travels, for they seek to test and eventually destroy him."

"Why?" Alistaria asked. "Why will they seek him?"

"Young Torian represents light over their darkness—as proven by his ability to wield Areadbhar. They work to destroy you both, since you will shut out the Shadow Realm."

"Tell me more," she demanded. "We need more if we're to fight them."

"I cannot aid you," he said, "but what you seek is the Annals of Tuatha de Dannan History."

"We know this already," she said with frustration. "What exactly must we find?"

"History," he replied.

"What history?" she demanded.

"All of it," was his answer.

Tired of the Sìth's games, Alistaria got to the point. "How do we defeat them? What must we learn in order to do so?"

"For that information, you will owe me a soul, one I get to name at a later date."

"No," Alistaria protested. "There's been too much killing, and I won't promise you an unnamed soul."

"Not a soul for *you* to name, your majesty." He waved his hand and revealed a vision of Torian walking with his Tuatha in Enatherr. The Sìth focused cat-like eyes on the image. "Your human friend must promise."

"No!" The queen refused.

"I assure you, he will in time give me what I desire." He turned to leave.

"Wait," she begged. "Please tell me of Restarian. Where did he go and who took him?"

Sìth Morkur shrugged. "The prince has sided with the Storm Warden, but you will encounter him soon."

"What will they do with him? *Where* are they taking him?" Alistaria demanded.

The spirit's laugh roared as before. "Why, to the Shadow Realm, of course." As quickly as that, he was gone.

Alistaria wasted no time returning to Fainnotheria. She raced over the canopy, reaching the Skygate and entering before the sentries had fully opened the doors. She stepped inside with a shudder against a sudden chill, shaking off the Sìth and his woeful foreboding. So focused on his words, she even jumped as the massive structure slammed shut behind her. Things were dire, and she needed to speak with Erania at once. She sought the old woman first in her quarters, but found no trace of her there and headed toward the Chamber of Life.

The passage beneath the roots was normally inviting despite its darkness, but, on this passing, it seemed to close in around her. The suffocating feeling overwhelmed Alistaria, teasing shadows everywhere. The chamber itself was entirely wrapped in blackness—the glow stones had extinguished. With a frustrated sigh she cast a ball of fairy bolt, careful not to make it too bright. It bobbed and floated beside her, revealing a horrific and bloody scene.

The elders lay scattered all around, their bodies limp where they lie. Someone had massacred every one.

"No," she begged, closing her eyes and willing the vision to be proven false. Kneeling over Erania, lifeless and cold on the dirt, Alistaria cried. The woman had perished with mouth frozen midscream, and the front of her dress had been singed—a bolt of energy having struck her chest. Scattered all about were the other bodies, each as dead as the old woman. Some were frozen and others were burned, but all of them murdered with magic. So close to the white lily, the queen channeled its resurrective powers.

A voice in the entrance broke her concentration and caused her to turn. "A pity they had to die because of your love for the Deamhan, Banshee Queen."

At first, she couldn't make them out in the shadowy darkness of the tunnel, so she allowed her fairy spark to brighten, bobbing slowly toward the gathering in the entrance. She gasped when she recognized the newcomers. Brechan and Korl stood side by side, flanked by a dozen or more figures. Some wore the golden armor of the Kern while others wore the robes of root tenders, but each had once been Fainne before she united the kingdom.

"I don't understand," she said. "Why did you do this? Why would you *kill* the elders?"

"Because," replied Brechan, "they were loyal to *you*."

She stood quickly, reaching an outstretched hand and ready to hurl a firebolt. But as hard as she tried, the Blossom resisted. She stared down at her empty hand with confusion. It was the same as in the Deamhan Palace. She was not a killer.

"You should have been practicing, Alistaria," said Korl with a dark laugh. "Then you would have known how to wield the gift as a weapon like we do."

Her body instantly convulsed, and she found her limbs unable to move. Brechan controlled her, wrapped in power and choking for air as it squeezed her ribcage. She helplessly watched as he approached the Blossom, picking each bloom one by one.

"I'll have to replant these," he said "and bleed for it once more. I'll strip all Deamhan of the power and gift it instead to every true child of the forest. *All* Fainne blood will feel the connection and know it as a sign of our superiority."

Korl pointed to the bodies of the elders. "How will you explain these deaths to our people?"

"We don't have to," Brechan said, squeezing his hold tighter around Alistaria. "I believe we *all* witnessed her murder the elders over a disagreement, did we not? Our people must know this is what happens when trusting a Deamhan."

With the pluck of the final blossom, Alistaria felt her connection to the gift extinguish.

Chapter Fifteen

"The Fomorian War waged the longest against an enemy from below ground and under water. The Dannan could only ever guess at the origin of the next attack and were eventually surrounded."
– The Legends of the Tuatha, Chronicle III, Passage 3

Restarian was thankful for the cloak Niamh had given to him. It kept his head dry from drizzling rain and kept his white hair from staring eyes. It also hid his crimson eyes, something that surely would have caused alarm among humans. But he was most gracious for the lack of wings in the human realm. He had originally feared they'd be visible to all, but, once they crossed over through the Fainnen Ring, he was finally rid of the useless branches of bone.

They had journeyed through the portal at first light, to where Niamh had left a cart on the human side of the portal. Despite the bumpy roads and dizzying sway atop a wooden seat, they made good time and reached Midlandis before dinner.

"How much further?" he asked Niamh. "I'm tired and my head-ache's returned. I want to rest in a bed tonight, if that's possible."

"Just up ahead," she said. "We'll stay one night and move again by morning."

"Do you have any more of the... medicine?" he asked.

"Go ahead," she muttered, handing over her satchel. The irritation in her voice wasn't aimed at him, for the constant bouncing annoyed them both. "You know where it is and how much to take."

That he did. He'd already grown reliant upon its soothing effects. Despite his body slowly healing on its own, his headache was something he couldn't escape. The throbbing followed him every second of every day, a warning something may still be wrong in his mind. He pulled out the tiny pouch of leaves and noticed Niamh was staring. He pinched some free and placed it between his teeth. "What?" he asked.

"Nothing," she said. "Except for how truly pathetic you are."

"Thanks." He wanted to ignore her, hoping she'd return her attention to the road, but the Searcher continued in a way he had to listen.

"Just so you know, I did find you attractive when we first met," she said.

"Why are you telling me this?" he demanded.

"Some of my flirting was real, and I didn't have to do much playacting to do what Radviken wanted. To... you know, get you to drop your guard and get comfortable."

He lifted crimson eyes to meet hers. "I doubt that's true, you've always despised me." But something in her face caused him to wonder. Their first meeting *had* been pleasant, after all, and he would never forget how her fingers had caressed his neck and shoulders at the time.

"It's true," she said. "I thought you were quite attractive."

"Really?" he asked, feeling his cheeks redden. "Because I actually enjoyed it."

She leaned in a bit and admitted, "I did too."

"Do you regret how you treated me after?" He shivered at the memory of their knives along his wings – *her* knife stripping flesh with careful precision. *Maybe she has remorse,* he thought, *and truly wants to set things right. Maybe her cruelness has been an act all along.* He noticed she was smiling and couldn't help but feel a bit of excitement. His heart beat a little faster at the hopeful thought of her touch once more against his skin.

"Little Scar," she said with a breathy whisper, "I don't regret anything we did that night except for making you so disgustingly ugly." She flicked the nub where his ear had been, then laughed at his reaction. "And you really are...," she added, "... so *ugly*!"

The wheel of the cart suddenly struck a rock and bounced them hard, forcing her to grip the reins tighter and focus entirely on the road ahead. At the same time, the lurch of the wagon jarred his teeth as he chewed, causing him to miss the leaves and bite into his wounded cheek. Flashes of pain shot through his jaw and skull. As he reached his hand instinctively, a sudden sense of vertigo rippled through his head and his eyesight swam. Then all at once the pain was gone, replaced instead by a surge of power. Timidly, he felt the spot once more and discovered the painful cut had mended instantly. The scar was surely there, just as Niamh had promised, but the pain was gone. All but his headache.

At first, he was confused by the surge of feeling. Then he understood the Bláth de Saol was fully in his reach, the connection having returned. But there was more, the healing rose was not alone. *These are the other gifts,* he suddenly realized. *I feel them all!*

The sudden emergence of all blooms could have been Alistaria's doing—a gift granted to free her conscience. *Or,* he wondered, *is this a sign she's been overthrown by those rejecting her rule?* He basked in hopefulness for a moment. A revolution would need a king, and he was the rightful heir of Betarian. Surely, they would seek him out.

He tasted the new thrums, each attuned to an element, but also power itself. There were two additional gifts he couldn't place. *Those must be...* He abruptly realized how wonderful it felt to hold corruption in his heart following all he'd suffered.

Niamh noticed his posture had changed beside her. "What is it, Little Scar?"

"Oh, nothing," he replied. *And yet, everything.* "What town is that," he asked, pointing to the rooftops rising above the trees ahead.

"Midlandis."

"What's here?" he asked, now secretly holding the upper hand. Everything had changed in that instant, and he could scorch Niamh and the two Storm Riders with fire. He considered doing it now, but held back. She had a reason for bringing him along, and he honestly enjoyed the escape from eating rats.

"We're meeting up with the Storm Warden. He has a proposition to offer."

The idea of teaming up with the man repulsed him, but was in a way intriguing, especially if it allowed him to sit upon Fainnotheria's throne. Besides, he may need their assistance if revolutionaries refuse to relinquish control. "What kind of proposition?" he asked.

"That's for him to say, Little Scar," she said, then buttoned her lip tightly.

He tried a different approach. "All you had to do was ask," he said.

She grunted. After a moment she chuckled and he knew he had her attention.

He continued. "If you'd said to me, 'Restarian, come with me from this forsaken hellhole of a palace and return to Enatherr,' I would have come willingly."

"No, you wouldn't," she said.

"Of course I would've. Who *doesn't* relish torture and death at the hands of a beautiful woman?"

Her smile faded quickly and turned into a frown.

There it is, he thought. *She* does *feel guilty for doing this to me, and that's my way in.* "What does he want my help for?" he asked. "Why me?"

"Because you're broken, Little Scar. You're broken and will do anything for King Radviken."

"Radviken's dead," he said. "You told me that yourself."

"I said the Sith took him. *You* said you can still feel a connection to him. No, he's alive and trapped in the Shadow Realm, and you're sworn to aid him."

So that's the plan, he realized. "You want me to journey to the Shadow Realm and somehow retrieve him. Even if I knew how, why would I do that for you or even him?"

"Because he owns you, Little Scar."

Her words quieted his mouth but not his mind. It raced against the tortured memory of Radviken's ministrations. *I despise him,* Restarian told himself, thinking again about Nastauria, his aunt and once a Fainne he respected. *I loved my aunt once, but* she *caused this—all of it—by deceiving grandfather.* He considered the human king once more.

"Radviken revealed Nastauria's treachery to me," he said quietly. "He showed me how she lied to my grandfather and how she sought unity with Clíodhna."

"And if he hadn't?"

I'd be as blind as my people.

"Would you have realized Alistaria meant to take your kingdom?"

"Are you saying the pain... the torture carried meaning?"

"It was meant to strengthen you and still could if you weren't always acting so lowly, like a piece of scum—brooding all the time. It happened and you didn't die... move on."

But I did *die. I slipped into the Shadow Realm several times and he revived me after each.* But there was truth in what she said. As a healer, Restarian had tended many of the battle-wounded Kern. Some of their injuries were brutal, and sometimes warriors who endured horrors emerged stronger for that hardship. But many others felt weaker after even the most minor experiences. Minds were strange, he knew, and reacted differently to pain each time. He felt like his own had broken. He placed another pinch of leaves in his mouth.

"You're saying Radviken did this to me on purpose?" he realized. "To condition me. You're suggesting I should be thankful he broke me down and rebuilt me stronger?"

"I'm saying to stop being a pathetic little loser," she replied as they entered the outer parts of the city.

The leaves had taken full effect on his mind and he felt his body relaxed. He could almost take a nap, were it not for the bumpy ride. He longed for rest, though he knew his thoughts would race all night.

The buildings rose up on both sides of the street, and their cart moved down a narrow road leading to the main gates. People hurried everywhere, crossing into the city in large numbers as if refugees from a storm. They wore urgency on their faces.

"What do they flee?" he asked Niamh.

"Radviken is no longer here to protect them, and they're the ones who will pay for Markey O'Malley's betrayal. The Shadow Realm is spilling into ours, and it's been getting worse each day after that girlfriend of yours stole the Blossom."

As they passed through the gate, Restarian kept his head down, afraid to make eye contact with any humans. He shifted his weight and lowered the hood.

Niamh laughed.

"What?" he demanded.

"Always so pathetic," she said, "But you're probably wise in not letting people see your ugly face."

He whirled in his seat, feeling the magic of the Blossom de Saol raging within his body. He fought the urge to raise his hand and scorch her where she sat. Staying her death, asked instead, "Why are you so cruel?"

She snapped harshly, "Because your weakness disgusts me, Little Scar. You could be so much more if you weren't pathetically childish and naive. You could almost be like *him* if you had confidence."

Her words stung, but there was no denying the truth in her words. Confidence was one trait hoarded by his grandfather and Nastauria—even Alistaria had lorded hers over him. *But no longer,* he promised. *I am different now, and it was Radviken who changed me.*

He focused on the terrified people rushing by. Their urgency driven by fear.

"So Radviken truly was the dam holding it back?" he asked. "He kept both realms safe from the shadow?"

"He was so much more than a dam, Little Scar. Our king... *Lord* Radviken was everything to Enatherr."

The cart pulled to a stop in front of a tavern and Restarian stared blankly while Niamh hopped down. He listened intently to the sounds of revelry within, and the wind carried laughter as the humans drank away their worries. *They're so arrogantly stupid,* he thought. *Sheep hiding their heads instead of fighting back to save their world.* And then another painful thought struck. *Like me, hiding in the Deamhan Palace.* He willed his legs to stand and stepped down to follow Niamh.

She was talking to the Riders. "Don't let those books out of your sight," she said, pointing into the rear of the wagon. "Load them up and bring them inside after we secure our rooms. If he's no longer here, we'll spend one night and head off to the Bay of Winds."

"Why not press on?" one of them asked.

"Because I want a hot bath to wash off the stink of the Fairy Realm." Motioning to Restarian, she said, "Come, Little Scar, you need one more than me."

Like a dog obeying its master, he followed.

"That's them," Piotr said of the scarlet haired woman and three hooded men. They had parked in front of *Nectar of the Gods.* "Those are the other Riders the Storm Warden mentioned."

"That one don't look like a Rider," Boyd said between bites. He was munching on some sausages left over in his satchel. "He's too scrawny."

Piotr looked closer at the man beside Niamh and remembered the conversation they overheard in the barrels. "That's because he's Alistaria's friend, the fae prince she said was tortured and who the warden said this one captured." After a brief pause, he added, "He's the one who killed my mother." Shrugging, he quickly added, "Not that I ever met Nastauria." His words were nonchalant, but he hoped his friend wouldn't recognize the longing to have known her. "Alistaria said he did it because he was confused after the torture."

Boyd narrowed his eyes and sized him up. "I thought she said his wings were skinned. I don't see wings."

"That's because..." Piotr broke off, realizing quickly his friend had joked.

"Well this will be fun," Boyd continued, wiping away a piece of meat stuck to his lip. "Instead of saving only Lucky, we get to rescue a fae prince."

"We're not rescuing him, Boyd. We have to let Alistaria decide his fate, and you and I are no match for Riders. I'm having second thoughts of going in at all now. Niamh *was* a Searcher, after all."

"Yeah? Well she ain't got no magic now, and you do." It had taken a better part of the night to explain how Piotr had freed Boyd from his captors, and the little man was eager for his friend to use it again. "You think you can make me invisible, too?"

"I don't know, but we can try. But even if I can, I don't know how we'll test it."

Boyd dismissed his caution with a wave. "Testing's overrated. I say we just walk in and take on everyone in the place."

Piotr turned, shocked at the idea, and found Boyd smiling broadly and chewing with his mouth open. He was joking again, of course.

The woman called to the Riders, "Don't let those books out of your sight," she said, pointing into the rear of the wagon. "Load them up and bring them inside after we secure our rooms. If he's already left, we'll spend one night and head off to the Bay of Winds."

"Those are them!" Piotr exclaimed with hushed excitement.

"Those are what?" Boyd asked.

"Remember when he said that woman was retrieving the histories?"

"Nope," he took another bite and muttered with a full mouth, "I remember him saying she was retrieving an ass."

"How'd you get that?"

"He said, 'anal,' Piotr. Anal means *ass,* or do I need to draw you a diagram?"

"He said, 'annals,' Boyd, not anal. Annals are a series of books—usually a history."

"Wow... You're so pretentious. Now who's the ass, Piotr? Just because you can read, doesn't mean you get to talk down to me and my miniscule vocabulary."

"But you can read, too! And you have a marvelous vocabulary! You just used the words *pretentious* and *miniscule* in conversation!"

"Then you're an ass for being right all the time," Boyd said with a smile. "C'mon, let's sneak into that tavern and save Lucky." He took a step forward.

"We need the books, too," Piotr insisted, refusing to budge. "And for that we need a better plan."

Boyd hesitated. His magical friend held all the cards now, with his ability to see ahead and hide them in plain sight. He rubbed a bruised rib—a memory of how their last scheme had ended, probably thinking of how much he had trusted Esmerelda against Piotr's advice. "How then?" he asked with a bit of humility.

"You work *your* magic on those Riders, and I'll get Lucky."

"Piotr?"

He sighed. "Yes, Boyd?"

"You know it's not *that* kind of tavern where you can just walk in and get lucky."

Piotr did something he'd never done in his life. Out of frustration he snapped at his lifelong friend. "For Tempest's sake, Boyd! Quit joking and listen to me!"

Boyd's smile dropped and he muttered, "Sorry. I can't help it."

"I know you can't, but you need to focus. You have different magic, and I need you to work it out here with the Riders."

"I don't have magic," Boyd replied with a bit of sadness in his voice. "*You* have magic, and I'm just *me*."

"Esmerelda was right. You're a luchorpán."

"No, I'm not."

"Well, I think you are, and so does Alistaria."

"She does?"

He nodded. "Think about it. You've got an irresistible charm about you, a knack for things. You have natural luck, and right now I need you to work that magic on these men until I return with Lucky. When I do, we're stealing their wagon *and* the books and taking them to Markey."

"What about the prince?"

"I'm drawing the line there. We know where they're taking him, and that'll have to do. Besides, if this works, we'll be in Norgaard by midday and Markey can send a rescue detachment. There's plenty of time before they move on in the morning. You heard her. They're getting rooms."

Boyd had no choice but to agree. "Makes sense when you put it all like that, but where's the fun in the plan?"

"The fun is you get to win over the blokes by the wagon."

"Any way I want?"

Piotr could see the gears working in his friend's mind and smiled. "Any way you can."

CHAPTER SIXTEEN

*"After a father is gone, what legacy remains but his child? Son,
I want you to know I wanted none of this, and so I hold it
only for you. I was always better at destroying than creating,
so know how difficult a job it is that I do. Be better than
me, son. You are my only hope for legacy or redemption."*
– Journal of King Markey O'Malley, the First of his Name

Markey O'Malley crept down the passage, gripping his sword
tightly in his outstretched hand. On his heels followed Conner Liam
and a squad of Storm Guard, each gritting their teeth against inces-
sant howling. They had all endured more than they could stand, but
Markey's need to spill blood pushed him forward. *If they harmed
either of them,* he swore, *I'll go to the Shadow Realm myself and
kill every last specter.* Another scream took away a moment's breath,
followed by wails and sobs. *Those could be Jaana's,* he knew.

A single broad stairway led to the grand hall, a gathering place
converged upon by several passages and descensions. *Just as in the
Deamhan Palace,* he realized. Why had he not recognized the resem-
blance when he first travelled through the Fainnen Ring to petition
Alistaria?

Up ahead, a line of Draugar barred the way. The king bellowed
a charge and broke into a run to meet them—his company followed,
hot on his heels.

"Don't let them flank him!" Conner warned the next line of
soldiers. They had agreed not to over pursue into the room, but
rather to contain the enemy in that space. He watched with dismay

as the king rushed in. A Draugar swung a sword with arcing momentum and O'Malley stepped aside, bringing his own up and into the ribs of the dead man beside him. The monster turned its head as it fell, spewing the foul contents of its lungs into Markey's face. He flinched against the heat then shoved the creature backward into a rushing onslaught. That's when he estimated their count. The broad space was filled with hundreds of Draugar and half as many hounds. Many had already feasted, and the others encircled the women and children gathered within. The king's heart sank as hopes departed.

"Jaana!" he roared into the room, listening and hoping for her safe and sound reply. A strong hand pulled him back just as one of the beasts leapt. Strong jaws narrowly missed his cheek, and the drool it splattered burned hot against his skin. The odor of brimstone overwhelmed Markey's senses, and he nearly retched.

Conner moved in fast, plunging his blade deep into the animal's ribcage.

There was no mistaking the portal. It clung to the air as if a tapestry had torn, and the gash fluttered on the breeze. The edges shimmered slightly but were otherwise no more than a space which shouldn't be. Two worlds existed at once, and Markey viewed the horrors beyond his. More and more Draugars were gathered, running straight for opening.

A mighty roar shook the entire room and dust fell as massive talons dug their way up and over the side of time and space—tearing it wider. Steam and gas bellowed through the slit, as a mighty beast pulled itself up from the realm beyond. The floor shook as it landed firmly on the stones, showering mortar with a shattering impact. Markey couldn't pull his eyes away from the beast—massive and exactly as Palathia had described.

Across the room he heard his name. Though fear gripped him, Markey turned hopefully. There was Jaana, clutching her son as she tried desperately to press into the wall and disappear. In Germaine's outstretched hand was a wooden sword, a testament of the boy's bravery. O'Malley once told his wife that hell wouldn't keep them apart, but that was a lie. Between her and him was that very place, and the King of Enatherr looked on helplessly as the monsters turned toward her.

Torian moved his Kern to form ranks on the left. With O'Malley's force pushed forward, he would have to hold this flank against a line of hellhounds blocking the entrance. He pressed his shield wall against their snapping jaws, biting at the metal shoved hard against their sides. The air around their skin steamed like a cloud of fog around each one. With a start, his eyes shot to the portal, watching as a great beast emerged with a deafening roar.

"Tuatha!" he ordered. "Flames at the ready! Push back these hounds!" The first volley struck home, sending the animals into a frenzy. They slammed into a group of Draugar, ripping through their allies to flee the flames.

Torian finally took a moment to study the beast. He had earlier worried Palathia's description had been embellished, but soon realized she hadn't done it justice. Watching it move, he realized the mage failed to account for its strength. Those jaws could crush solid rock with a single snap—no doubt capable of ripping a horse or man into pieces without effort. Despite its obvious blindness, it scanned the room with an eerie sentience that caused the general's skin to shiver.

How will we fight it? he wondered. *No shield wall could withstand its charge.* As if to prove that point, it chose a line of Markey's men to demonstrate dominance. Men flew in every direction as bones crushed under its massive weight, their groans and screams joining those of the howling dogs from hell.

"Tuatha!" he cried. "Focused fire on the beast! At will!"

His mages complied, and soon a steady stream of flames formed around the monster, now rearing and writhing against their magic. Though hair singed from its back, the skin below remained undamaged.

"Again! With sparks!" Torian commanded, and ten large beams of fairy spark filled the grand hall. The beast recoiled against an explosion of thunder and light. Torian ordered another volley.

Only four sparks flew the second time and murmurs of confusion met his ears. Tearing his eyes from the beast, he turned.

"Try fire!" he called, and they tried. Again, only four mages could manifest any sort of flame.

"We've... we've lost our connection!" Ceranth shouted. "It was there, but now it's suddenly gone!"

"Who lost it?" the general asked. But without scanning the worried faces he knew. Only the former Deamhan were affected. *Alistaria,* he wondered, *what has happened to you?*

He returned his eyes to the beast, just as it charged. With spear aloft he stared down the shaft as the metal seemingly changed in his hands. The carvings shimmered as the beast neared, and the point pulsed with the reflected fire of his mages. Suddenly, he felt movement along his spine as his skin convulsed—not violently, but like a river changing course against a soft shoreline. His muscles moved around the emergence of his wings, unexpected joy in the realm of humans. As the weapon pulsed, Torian caught wind and rose. All at once he understood the weapon was special, and leapt forward to lead the animal away from his Tuatha.

The Draugar and hellhounds watched with confusion as the man rose toward the ceiling, raising their eyes to watch the glowing spear point. It now lit the room like a captured sun. The beast turned as well. As its head moved, so did its body, exposing ribs to the confused line of spears and shields.

"Tuatha! Charge!" Torian screamed into the room, moving with blinding speed of his own.

The beast roared loudly against the glow of his spear, narrowly missing Torian with a snap of its jaws. The metal tip of the weapon entered just below its jawline, piercing the soft skin of a rumbling throat. At the same time, ten spears pierced its side, exposing the supple organs within. The mages joined in, and four streams of flame commanded the blood to boil within. The hulking corpse bellowed steaming shadows of darkness as gases escaped.

Torian ripped his weapon free and turned, hopeful eyes now focused on the more manageable enemies all around.

Markey tried to step forward into the fray, but General Conner Liam's strong grip held him back.

"Let go!" he roared.

"I can't, Markey! You're the king and we can't risk you!"

"I'm a husband and father first, Conner! I've got to get to her!"

"Holy hells," Conner suddenly exclaimed, and Markey joined him in watching as Torian leapt into the air. A fiery spear burned in his hands. Both men gasped as he plunged forward into the beast, felling it with a charge from his squad. While the general stared, the king broke free, racing toward Jaana and Germaine and heedless of Draugar swords. He ignored Conner's worried calls, his family wasn't that far.

But neither were the hellhounds.

Three large beasts abandoned their feast of carnage, tossing aside limp Storm Guards like discarded playthings. They closed the gap in several bounds, and Markey smelled their stench before feeling the heat of their breath. His pulse quickened as he hurried, fearing he'd never outrun the beasts or reach his family in time. As the first jaws snapped at his neck, the king flinched but never faltered. With eyes locked on his wife and child, he continued a mad dash to save them. The creatures were dangerously close and gathering speed when a golden streak crashed into the nearest hound, ripping it away and tripping the others. Torian had saved him.

"Go!" the young man screamed, facing off the beasts.

His family was close now, each staring up at their protector and pleading for rescue. He yearned to cry out, but his lungs could barely draw enough breath and keep his chosen pace. Instead he watched their eyes turn away from his, locking onto a wave of hounds falling upon their helplessness. The king of Enatherr fell to his knees, skidding to a cowardly halt as he could do nothing but watch the gruesome feast.

The first devoured was Germaine, torn apart by the ravenous hounds. Useless to protect the boy, the king had forsaken his legacy and howled his misery into the hall. The cries of Jaana matched his own. Markey looked away with shame, unable to free his legs from their current state of hopelessness. He buried his face as the monsters moved on to the bigger feast, growling and snapping as they fought over his wife's flesh. Tears flowed as the king begged to be taken next, unable to imagine life without his family.

Laughter echoed throughout the hall.

"This was a test, human," the Sìth with brimstone eyes explained. "A test of your fortitude and willingness to submit. Your pathetic display is proof you *will* subjugate this realm. Freely given, your surrender will taste the sweetest."

Markey said nothing, staring blankly at the spirit and thinking only of joining his family in the great beyond. The man who had always fought and protected those weaker than he had failed. Without reason to continue, he blinked helplessly at the Sìth.

Torian squared off against the hellhounds, waving the spear and backing them away from Markey. The arrival of the Sìth caught him completely by surprise. When the spirit spoke, the fae general felt the spear thrum with a pulse of anger and repulsion.

"I see you've discovered the power of Areadbhar," the Sìth said with a hiss. "Time will tell if you wield it with the same effect as Lugh before you."

Another voice entered the hall, and Torian looked up to see a second Sìth had arrived, with darkness swimming as eyes. "We're looking forward to the coming battle, hero," the spirit said. "You've passed both tests put before you, but you're far too weak to face us three."

"Three?" Torian asked.

"We are three," the yellow-eyed spirit replied.

"And three are we," the shadow-eyed Sìth agreed.

Together the pair laughed and sniffed the air as if tasting human defeat. The room abruptly swirled with darkness that filled it wall to wall. Upon it, every surviving human and fae heard cries of wailing anguish or as it seared their skin with wretched foulness. As the final howls of departing hellhounds diminished, the veil lifted and the portal was gone. The remnants of carnage remained.

"We can't remain here," General Liam said to his king, who was now kneeling and broken on the ground, reaching for a tiny wooden sword on the stones. The stains upon it were his son's.

"He protected her. He tried to fight them off," O'Malley said.

"I know, Markey. But we've got to clear this room and form a perimeter."

"I need to stay with their bodies."

"No, you need to lead these men and show them you're king. Fight now, mourn later!" With two hands Conner hoisted the grieving man to his feet, then pushed him toward a group of waiting soldiers. "Get him upstairs to the war room."

"Aye, sir!"

Torian watched the exchange with worry. This could be the end of Markey's rule, and he must find his way back from this grief. "Will he be okay?" he asked Conner.

"I hope so."

Chapter Seventeen

"When thieving, there are many rules so as to remain a respectable profession. Though not all are known publicly, every thief knows not to intentionally leave anything identifiable behind. Of course, if someone in the home or business has personally offended or done you harm, it's fully acceptable to have a little fun at their expense."
— Piotr

Using the gift of sight, Piotr wrapped the shroud of illusion around him. Invisible, he crept into the tavern and up the stairs to the room he'd shared with Boyd. After ensuring no one was looking, he pushed the door open and went inside. Lucky sensed his presence and growled immediately. Dropping the veil, the man knelt beside the dog who whined his approval of being rescued.

"I'm sorry you've been alone, little fella," the thief said honestly. He'd grown on Piotr since their first encounter, and the thief had begun looking past his smellier side.

The little dog whined again, this time with impatience at holding his bladder. Poor thing hadn't been let out all night or morning. He scooped him up into his arms and returned the magical veil, this time rendering them both completely invisible. He was a little surprised to find it had worked. With a grin, he pulled open the door and stepped into the hall. At that moment the redheaded Searcher entered the hall, and Piotr pressed against the wall, narrowly missing a collision.

He waited—willing her to walk past and watching curiously as the fae prince topped the stairs. Niamh found her room and inserted the key, turning once to speak to her companion. "Join us for dinner, Little Scar. And please do bathe first, you reek of fairies and grime."

After she was gone, the hooded figure looked down at the key in his own hand, as if unsure what to do with it. He studied the numbers above the doors, passing by Piotr as he did. He tried the lock of one and it turned. Gaunt hands pulled back his hood, revealing crimson eyes that focused directly on the thief. He studied the air for a moment, then said quietly, "I don't know you. Are you one of them?"

The thief said nothing, only clutched the dog and maintained the illusion as best he could. *Surely, he can't see me,* he thought.

The red-eyed prince leaned in closer. "I *can* see you," he whispered. "Now tell me if you are one of *them*."

"One of who?" Piotr asked quietly.

"Are you a Deamhan? How is it you work the gift of the Blossom in this realm?"

"I'm Fainne, but was left as a changeling in Enatherr," the thief answered.

"I see," Restarian replied. "Then you *are* a friend of Alistaria."

Piotr nodded and Lucky whined. He really needed to get outside to do his business.

"Tell my cousin I'm coming for what's mine by birth, and no Deamhan will be left alive—even her."

Piotr nodded. "You're him, aren't you?"

"Who is it, you think I am?"

"You killed my mother. You killed Nastauria?"

The red-eyed fae staggered backward at this, suddenly off balance and less menacing. It was as if Piotr's question had removed any confidence he held.

The thief drew himself to full height and loomed over him. "You won't harm Alistaria, but I *will* deliver your message. At least then she'll know you'll never be trusted and can move on from worrying about you." He turned to leave, but paused. "True friendship never chooses opposite sides—and neither does family once you've found it.

Whatever you have against the Deamhan is nothing compared to the damage those loyal to Radviken will commit. Find yourself, mate."

Surprising even himself, Piotr walked away with head held high, strolling boldly down the stairs and through the crowded tavern, no longer worried his newfound magic would fail. As he passed the bar, he paused to watch the tavern keeper pouring ale into a mug. His back was turned and the noise in the room was deafening, so he whispered something in Lucky's ear. Setting the dog on the ground he crouched and waited. The animal, suddenly visible but ignored by those reveling in their cups, scurried behind the bar and lifted his leg, exactly where Piotr had hoped—on the leg of the tavern keep. After his business was done, he hurried back to the thief who scooped him up and hurried out the door.

Outside, he found Boyd bent over a dice game with the two Storm Riders. He had turned their backs away from the wagon, and the stout thief held them captivated with a riveting tale about his time aboard a fishing vessel. It was all a lie, of course, he'd never stepped off a pier, but they didn't know.

"It was huge," he said as he tossed the dice, "at least as long as ten men with arms outstretched. The captain put a bounty on its oil, so I hopped into a rowboat and, armed with nothing but a harpoon and sack of raw chicken, rowed out to claim it!"

"I don't understand," one of the men said, "why chicken?"

"Because whales are the chicken of the sea, haven't you heard?"

"I thought that was tuna," the second Rider corrected.

"Who's tellin' the story here?" Boyd demanded. He tossed the dice. "Ha! Double sixes! Hand over your levy!" Both men handed him two silver talents and he handed the dice to the next man and continued. "So anyway, I rowed out to meet it head to head—man to man—and tied the sack of chicken to a rope and tossed it over the side."

"Whales don't eat meat," the first man noted. "They sustain entirely on plankton and other drifting sea scum."

"You'll be sea scum if you don't let me finish my story," Boyd quipped.

The man shrugged and tossed his dice. "Aha! Double sixes!"

"Oh, sorry mate. Double sixes don't win if the person before you tossed 'em first. Levy up, boys."

Both men grumbled, but handed over two more silver talents each.

"So anyways, I tossed the chicken over the side, and the whale came up to have words with me—not real words, I have to say before you interrupt again, but surfaced angry. I tossed raw meat into his domain. Because, like Frank here said, whales eat pinkerton."

"Plankton."

"Right. Plankerton. So, anyways, he surfaced and I picked up the harpoon and reared my arm back to throw. But at that precise time a shark swam up to smell my chicken."

The men listened wide-eyed and did not turn around when the wagon squeaked under the weight of Piotr climbing aboard. Boyd was watching though and knew it was near time to wrap up the story.

"Can I borrow this to tell the next part?" he asked. Without waiting for an answer, he picked up one of the men's swords off the ground. Standing, he hopped onto the back of the wagon and held the sword aloft like a harpoon. "So I reared back, but before I could throw, it the shark grabbed the sack and swam away—pulling my little rowboat out to sea."

"Then what happened?" the Rider named Frank asked. "Did you stick the whale?"

"Of course not," Boyd replied as the horses spurred and the wagon began to move. "This story's the one about the fish who got away!"

The Riders, suddenly realizing they'd been both duped and robbed of money and sword, leapt to their feet. An invisible Piotr snapped the reins and the horses surged forward, dragging the wagon away so quickly Boyd had to sit down in the back. In no time at all they were out of sight, and the Riders were left panting and huffing in the middle of the street.

"Nice story," Piotr said as he reappeared. Lucky sat contented in his lap, watching Boyd with disinterest.

"Thanks." Boyd said with a smile, then frowned, adding, "He'd been up in that room for a while. Did he at least do his business?"

"Of course he did. I've got a leg up on things, don't I?"

"Don't do that," Boyd said sternly.

"Do what?"

"Make jokes."

"Why not? You make jokes all the time, and that one was funny because he lifted his leg."

"Well, you're not as funny as me. You're the straight man in this outfit, the guy who makes everyone else look forward to the jokester. Let's keep it like that, shall we?"

"Of course," Piotr said with a sly smile. "Urine charge."

"Thank you."

Restarian watched the thief stroll away and down the stairs – cloaked in the hydrangea's sight. He had been shocked by the revelation, too shocked to react or he would've drawn his blade. There was still time, he knew, if he ran after him. But the changeling's words had left him stunned. *He is the son of Nastauria and Radviken.* This fae, raised a human, could potentially rule both realms and he just let him walk away.

But what *could* he do about it? He was beaten—broken—and controlled by these humans. *I don't know why I even stay with them,* he considered. But deep down he knew. He had killed Nastauria at Radviken's unspoken request—the man who tortured and flayed his wings had bent him to his bidding. *I tried to hide,* the part of him who yearned to be with his family protested, *I tried to hide myself away where I'd do no harm, but she found me.*

Niamh needs to know, he reasoned, *about the man who was here.* He turned away from the stairwell, moving instead to her room and knocking softly on her door.

"Who is it?" she demanded from within.

"Res... Restarian," he stammered, suddenly wishing he hadn't interrupted her rest.

"What do you want, Little Scar?"

"I... I have news... Information you need to hear."

On the other side of the door, she laughed. "Is that so, Little Scar? Then come in."

He tried the handle and it opened easily, allowing him to step inside. The room was small, adorned with a bed, a mirror, and a place to hang her things. There was also a tub for bathing, full of steaming water that fogged the air above it. Inside of that was Niamh, naked and fully exposed before him. She grinned at his sudden embarrassment, taking cruel pleasure in his abrupt shyness. He averted his eyes and found he had lost the words he meant to say.

"Look at me, Little Scar!" she demanded. "Look upon me and feast your eyes on a meal you'll never touch. Then you'd better have a good reason for interrupting my bath."

At that moment the two Storm Riders entered, both looking away immediately when they realized her state. This time she grabbed a towel and hurriedly covered her body. "What is it!" she screamed.

"Thieves, ma'am. Thieves stole both the wagon and the books."

"How's that possible?"

"I saw one of them," Restarian admitted. "In the hallway, he..." He caught himself before giving away his new ability for sight. *If they knew I was connected to the Blossom they'd... They'd* use *me.*

"Spit it out!"

"He pushed past me, but I recognized him from Radviken's palace. I think he was the fae who plucked the blossoms after I left."

Her eyes shot to the Riders who shrugged. "What did they look like?"

"We only saw the one, but the other was surely there driving the wagon. This one was short and chubby, almost like a luchorpán."

"And he worked his charm on us, for sure!" the other Rider added. "Made us hand over eight talents and then made away with my sword, the books, and the wagon."

"Out!" she screamed at the pair, but to Restarian added, "not you!" They scurried away, slamming the door behind them. Niamh stood from the bath, letting the water drip on the floor as she hastily dried her skin. "Hand me my clothes," she commanded, "those over there."

He lifted a pair of folded trousers and a leather jerkin from the bed, afraid to look at her nakedness directly. Thankfully, she was past trying to embarrass him. "We have to leave tonight," she said, "you and I together. We'll meet up with the Storm Warden and enter the Shadow Realm now, rather than later."

"But what about the books?"

"We don't have time. Markey O'Malley will have them sooner than we could get to Norgaard. We *need* to hurry, Restarian."

Suddenly no longer afraid, he lifted his eyes to stare. She really was quite beautiful, and his mind returned to the sensual caress she had given his shoulders in Radviken's palace. *Perhaps if I'm strong again, I'll earn her respect.* He watched her dress, eying the way she fumbled on her ties and fastened her belt. *She's afraid of something—vulnerable, even. And,* he realized, *she didn't call me 'Little Scar' this time.*

Chapter Eighteen

"The luchorpán magic is not unlike that of man or fae, but the subtle nuance of its workings confounds all. A gnome could be present and then not, and reappear just as quickly. That is the reason myths abound regarding their trickery. They are not to be trusted."
– The Annals of History Book V, Passage 51

Maerlin stepped through the Fainnen Ring, emerging into the human palace. The high palisade rose all around him, but it had been mostly abandoned—unguarded except by a few crossbowmen. They eyed him curiously as he looked questioningly and waited.

"Where are the rest of you?" one of the humans finally called. "When do the reinforcements arrive?"

"Reinforcements? There's only me." He held the note from Alistaria aloft. "I'm here to present this to the king—a letter from my queen.

The crossbowmen nodded, and the wooden gate swung open. "He's with the others in the great hall," the man said, "but the fighting's finished, from what we heard. You'll have to wait here for an escort."

Fighting? Maerlin didn't understand. *Why would there be fighting in the human palace?*

Soon, a young officer arrived with a tattered uniform. From behind a blood splattered face he asked, "Where's the letter? What's it entail?"

"I have to give it directly to the king," Maerlin insisted.

The officer laughed. "That ain't happening. He's in a sorry state, just lost his wife and kid. I'll take you to the general, though. He'll decide if it should go before him."

Maerlin nodded and followed the man through a hall and down several flights. "What happened here?" he asked.

"Damn near half the shadow realm attacked! Apparently they had a portal in the middle of our palace! Ain't none of us are safe now. If it weren't for your general, we'd all be dead now."

"My general?" Torian's here? He'd wondered why there was no sight of the Tuatha at the Deamhan Palace.

"In here," the officer replied, opening a door and escorting him through.

Inside, Maerlin found Torian and Palathia sitting next to the human general and his king. Though Maerlin had never met Markey O'Malley, it was easy to tell the man was downtrodden and without his wits. He stared blankly at the table while the others talked strategy. All but he looked up when the fae entered.

"Maerlin?" Torian was shocked to see him. "What are you doing here?"

Handing over the note, the sentry explained. "She relieved me of my duties and sent me here to aid the research."

The fae general read it over several times before nodding to the human. "This must be why." With a bit of anger, he added, "She was unguarded and vulnerable."

"What are you talking about?" Maerlin demanded. "What happened?"

"While we fought against the Shadow Realm, every Deamhan in our squad suddenly lost connection to the Blossom. I'm afraid something's happened to Alistaria. Either someone else picked the blooms, or she was injured... or worse. Either way, she must've been overthrown."

The words went straight to Maerlin's heart like a dagger, piercing the hope he had felt upon traveling to the realm. "She sent me away, and no one was left to protect her." He turned to leave, "I've got to go back!"

"Wait." Torian was commanding, not asking, and so Maerlin turned. "We'll need to send an army through to save her."

The human general spoke, "We'll stand with you, but before we do, we should at least learn what the historians have figured out by studying that book. Those Sìths weren't like anything else we've come across, and they may strike Fainnotherr next."

"I agree." Torian stood and beckoned for Palathia and Maerlin to follow. The human general led them out, leaving the king alone with his melancholy.

They found the door to the cleric hall ajar when they arrived. Pushing through, they found the carnage had not been contained in the great hall below. A lifeless Hammond lay slumped across the table.

The human general rushed forward.

"Certainly they couldn't reach these levels, General Liam," Torian said.

"No," he replied. "This is murder—a cowardly act from behind." He pointed to where a dagger had plunged deep into the scholar's neck.

A quick search revealed bodies of several more clerics scattered about.

"Clurich isn't among them," a voice said from behind. Everyone turned to find the king had followed.

"He's your friend, Markey. Do you think he could've done this?" Torian asked.

"I hope not, but every single one of them is dead, and he's gone."

"So is that book you brought him," Conner pointed out. "And I don't see the rubbings anywhere."

"I don't understand," Torian said. "Why would Clurich take the artifacts?"

"He's a true luchorpán," Markey admitted. "At first, I looked past it—thought I could trust him, even—but now I see I must've been wrong. I brought this destruction here. Now our hope to learn the truth is gone, and so is my family." He turned to Conner. "I'm no longer fit to be king," he said. "I need to abdicate."

"You'll do nothing of the sort," Conner argued.

"I have to, because I'm about to lead us down a path to extinction."

"How will you do that?" the general asked.

"By hunting these Sìth down."

"You're not alone in that desire, Markey. After what your men witnessed, word will spread that this threat is real and more will join."

"My family, Conner. They're gone."

"Well mourn fast, or wait till this war is over, 'cause we've got bigger problems and you *are* the king."

While they talked, Maerlin pulled Torian aside. "If she's in danger it's because of me. I'm sorry, General. It's my fault."

"Trust me, I know her as well as anyone, maybe even better. She's in danger because she made a choice to send you away, and it's not your fault. We'll rescue her, but we need to know for sure what happened. We have to get inside Fainnotheria, and for that we'll need a Fainne, not *you*." He pointed to the ransacked room. "Your best bet is to piece this mess together and do what she sent you here to do. Become a scholar, and figure out what Clurich knows."

"But I can't read the languages."

"Then start there, but hurry." Turning to Markey, he asked. "Were these *all* your scholars?"

"No. We've got others, but I'll need to bring them in from the field."

"That's your priority, and you need to abandon this palace as soon as possible," Torian advised.

Conner Liam couldn't believe his ears. "Abandon? We're not abandoning this palace!"

"We may have to," Markey agreed. "We're nothing but a waystation between two realms, and we don't know how to close off either one. But this portal *is* in a defensible spot—almost as if Radviken knew it was here and built the palace around it."

Conner argued. "We can establish a perimeter around this area, bring in defenses and hold it until we have more information about what we're up against."

"The scholars must work elsewhere, if you can find a secretive spot," Torian suggested.

Markey nodded. "As a matter of fact, I *do* know a place they can set up shop."

"So do we," a voice said from the doorway. Everyone looked up to find two men, one tall and thin and the other short and stocky. The littler man carried a mangy dog in the crook of his arm. Between the men was a long wooden box. "And I think we can help by providing something for them to read."

"And," the little man added, "we know where the Storm Warden's headed."

"I don't like it," Markey said, shaking his head. They had just gone over every detail gleaned from Piotr and Boyd. "If they find a way to retrieve Radviken from the Shadow Realm, then my claim on this realm is finished."

"So, what do we focus on?" Torian asked. "Seems to me we're split several ways. We must find and aid Alistaria, secure this realm from the Shadow, and stop the Storm Warden from finding his artifacts."

"The third will have to wait. We have the motive, but not the *how* or the specific nature of the artifacts. We need to translate those books the boys brought back."

"So, the plan's the same? I take the Tuatha back through the portal and find Alistaria, while you hold the fort here?"

"That's all we can do—except we must also find Clurich."

"Where do you think he's off to? Back to his tavern?"

"No, I sent Riders there, and there's no trace of him. Diedre wasn't any help, either. She's in custody, but my guess is he moved north."

"What's up north?" Torian asked.

"Nothing but snow, ice, and mountains," Conner Liam tossed in. "But beyond the falls lies the entrance to the luchorpán kingdom."

"So who gets to track him into the mountains?"

Piotr and Boyd both raised their hands.

"No, boys," Markey said, as if anticipating they'd volunteer. "It's not smart to send you both up there, not with those new abilities of Piotr's. Those are a commodity and we need them elsewhere."

Torian perked up, catching on to the plan. "You'll split them up?"

"I don't see any other way. You need a fae to enter Fainnotheria, and Boyd could come in handy now we know he's luchorpán."

Boyd and Piotr shared a shocked look. Piotr turned to O'Malley. "We've... We've never been apart, Markey."

"Don't know if we *can* be apart, Markey," Boyd agreed.

"Don't know if we *should* be apart." Piotr added.

"I'm sorry, boys. I don't see any other way. Conner, you get your team ready to head north with Boyd. Torian, you take Piotr and the Tuatha through the Fainnen Ring." He stood and walked toward the door.

"Where are you going?" Torian asked.

"I'm going to my chambers to cry my eyes out over my wife and child. Then I'm going to wear out my body in the practice yard and probably cry some more. After that, I'll pick myself up and draw up a defense against the Shadow Realm." He paused to swallow after his voice cracked on the words before adding, "Then I'm going to kill some Siths."

Chapter Nineteen

– The Annals of History Book IX, First Passage

The place in which they'd locked her away stank of iron—foul metal so poisonous to the fae, yet wielded in battle by the Deamhan for so long. She would never understand how they tolerated the touch, or lived so close to it in the ground. Gripping the substance must have pushed the lesser of them to near insanity, just as anxiety attacked her now. She yearned to be away from this prison. Wherever it was. The stench of it nauseated Alistaria's belly, which trembled with bile threatening to rise. She stared down at the chains draped coldly against her wrists and ankles but refused to weep.

It had been some time since she'd had any contact with others except by a slot in the door. Once a day it would open, and a dish filled with slop and a waterskin was slid inside. She'd avoided tasting the food the first few days, but soon tired of starvation and dug in each time it was served. But that had proven a mistake, as discomfort and pains soon set in throughout her body. It was laced, for certain, but by what she did not know.

Once or twice Brechan even visited, gloating through the door about the way he'd killed the elders and lording his new position over his captive. He talked about a new council led by Korl and himself, a new type of government without kings or queens—or Deamhan.

She'd die soon, he promised, like Erania. She shuddered at the cruelness in his words and mostly tuned him out. She would never again touch the power of the Blossom, so what did she care what he did to her? Besides, the iron in the room was driving her to madness.

By the time the hallucinations had set in, she embraced the strange visitations as if from friends. Radviken had been the worst, braying on about how they could have ruled both realms together as father and daughter. If she had only accepted his terms. Nastauria was the hardest to endure—begging for forgiveness, and urging her not to seek revenge against Restarian. But then Clíodhna would appear, and Alistaria's two mothers would bicker like two housecats fighting over a saucer of cream. The latter bade her to bring the prince swiftly to justice as an example to others—as if she had authority.

Eventually a new visage had appeared, reclining in the corner of her cell. He was just as he had been along the road to Norgaard, leaning against the wall as he did the fencepost. Long and lean for a hare, with thick dark fur that appeared more like a beard than whiskers beneath his strangely human eyes. He looked like an old man, except with long, ludicrous ears set atop his head. Even his mannerism resembled a beggar on the street, content to lounge, and knowing more than those around him despite keeping silent.

The first time the Puca spoke, she ignored him as a manifestation of her meal. He found humor in that, as well.

"You're not troubled to see me?" he asked.

"Why should I be? I've seen you before, even when you weren't the shade from soured stew."

"Hmm," he agreed with a firm nodding of his head, ears bobbing along and flopping around.

She silently wished she could have proper manifestations. Something with less strangeness—like Torian perhaps. He could be here instead, shirtless and with rippling muscles that offered a different kind of comfort. With a sigh she decided to make do with this one.

"I know you aren't really here," she said. "Why doesn't that make you leave?"

"Because I *am* here. You can touch me if you wish, but I won't do the things you want *Torian* to do instead."

Brief repulsion shuddered through her body, but then she realized he knew her thoughts. "That isn't fair."

"What's not?"

"Reading my mind like that. If you're my delusion, you could at least respect privacy in my thoughts."

"If that's what you desire."

"It is."

After a brief pause, he said, "No, that won't work. Won't work at all."

"Why not?"

"Because I *do* know your mind, and t'would be a lie to act otherwise."

Despite herself, she laughed aloud at this. "So Pucas can't lie?"

"Who said I'm a Puca?"

"Aren't you?"

"Yes, but you said I'm a delusion. You can't have it both ways, Alistaria, daughter of Radviken."

"Don't call me that."

"You prefer *Daughter of Clíodhna?*"

"I prefer solitude and a swift death."

"Neither are in your future, Queen of the Fae."

"I'm not *that* anymore, either."

"Oh, you're still their queen."

She laughed at this too. "I don't *feel* like a queen. I sort of failed in that job." She held up her chains and shook them, rattling her point for the Puca.

"Sometimes the best sign of successful authority is when a faction takes opposition to the changes you impose."

"Sometimes opposition is a sign you're a tyrant."

"Were you taking away liberties or doing harm to a body of people?"

"Well, no. But I *did* force my will upon them."

"Your will being a forced unification of people?"

"Yes."

"Did you take away property from one group to gift to another? A tax maybe? Their homes? Did you spoil the dignity of the majority group and allow the minority to flaunt a new control over it? Or did you cave to the demands of many and further transgress against the few?"

"Well, no. All those would be wrong... and achieve nothing but breed more resentment. I merely made everyone equals."

"I see." His nodding ears bounced in the air as he considered. "And now you think you're opposed by that entire majority?"

"I..." She thought for a moment, considering what she *did* believe. "I don't know. I guess I'm opposed by the loudest minority of that majority—the most vocal."

"Then you're still queen, and will find a way to overturn their revolution."

"I'm not that lucky."

"Alistaria, the fact that I'm here talking to you is a sign that you most certainly *are* that lucky. Pucas are drawn to reward two things—a noble heart and sheer luck."

"I was told you foresaw death and are tricksters."

"As for the first, we take pity on those we like and try to warn them not to dwell on the bad news ahead."

"And the second?"

"Trickster is in our nature, though we do so out of boredom instead of malice. Who doesn't appreciate a harmless prank now and again?"

"So which is this?" she asked.

"Which what?"

"Are you here taking pity on me, warning of bad news ahead, playing a trick, or drawn to the sheer luck I had to wind up imprisoned and dethroned?"

"Sounds ominous when you put it like that."

"Well, you *are* a mythical creature."

"Or a delusion of soured stew."

"Or that." They sat in comfortable silence for a moment, her taking in the words he had said and him studying her. When she spoke again, she asked, "So which is it?"

"I can't tell you." he replied. "My role is *not* to interfere, but to observe and warn."

"So you're a Sìth?"

"That term is dull and without imagination. I am who I am."

"A delusion?"

"So you say."

"If you *are* the stew, what advice would you give?"

His face scrunched in thought as he considered the question. Finally, he shifted his weight and let out a roaring flatulence.

It was repugnant, and she nearly retched at both the sound and smell. "That's disgusting!"

"You never seemed to mind when I did it before," he said. "But you did ask what the stew would say, if it should speak."

She coughed and her eyes watered. When she could finally breathe again, she asked, "Tell me as a Puca, then."

"Face the Shadow Realm and fix what is broken between the realms. Then you'll find strength to repair your own."

"It's that simple then?" she laughed.

"You have everything you need in the texts."

"You mean text. I only have one volume."

"You *had* one volume, but it was stolen. Thankfully, Piotr and Boyd found the luck to steal the rest of the set."

Alistaria shifted her weight. "How do you know these things?"

"You're going to have to fight, Alistaria. You have a big fight on your hands and you will have to get them dirty."

"How?" she demanded.

"I've got to go," he said, suddenly standing, "but I will offer you some luck." With a wave of his hand her shackles fell to the ground and her cell door swung open wide. It surprised her, and she turned toward the swinging iron with a gasp. By the time she looked back, the Puca had gone.

It was really him, she realized, *and not the stew after all.* Rising to her feet she hurried from the cell, looking both ways, then moving carefully down the passage to find her way out.

Part Three
Violence

Chapter Twenty

"Nuada's death came as a surprise to all, shocking proof of his mortality. To us, their vulnerabilities were finally revealed."
– The Legends of the Tuatha, Chronicle III, Passage 3

The Bay of Winds was aptly named – gusty under the full brunt of seasonal shifts. These were cold and unforgiving, keeping the pier side fishing boats from venturing forth. This would cripple the local economy, except for the work provided by a certain benefactor. Only those willing to do his digging knew his secret name. The gathering met lakeside and spread toward the mountains to the north, growing into a tent city almost overnight. The pay was good, the work was hard, and security was provided by Storm Riders—though these withheld loyalties from the new king. It was a perfectly kept secret from authorities, and even those were paid to look the other way.

"What is it?" Restarian asked.

"What's what?" Niamh replied with irritation.

"This place."

"According to the oral legends this was a battlefield, but the texts I found described a gateway existed. Through it, the Tuatha de Dannan locked the Fomoire in the underworld."

"What exactly are you digging for? I thought you had a way into the Shadow Realm."

"We do, Little Scar. But first we seek an artifact that's buried here."

"What is it?"

"I'll tell you when you need to know, now be quiet."

He looked around as they rode, uncomfortable by so many pairs of eyes that may turn toward his strangeness. "What's he like?"

"I told you to be quiet."

"You also told me to have a backbone. What's he like?"

"Who?"

"The Storm Warden."

"He's a man, nothing more... and nothing like Radviken."

"How does Radviken maintain your loyalty?" Restarian demanded.

"I told you, he is our lord. He's the way-finder of balance, and he..." she trailed off.

"He what?"

"Nothing, Little Scar. Now shut your mouth and quit pestering me." She reached a hand into her pack and grabbed the little satchel, thrusting it into his hands. "Here. Chew on this, if it'll shut your mouth."

And it did. Restarian eyed the little purse with excitement, quickly loosening the ties before she changed her mind. He pinched a bit of the medicine from within, and placed it between his cheek and gum—desiring a longer lasting release than usual. He felt the effects almost immediately, leaning back against his seat and staring off at the mountains in the Northeast. He must have dozed, but snapped awake when the wagon came to a stop.

"Wipe your drool, Little Scar. You're disgusting," Niamh said with a wrinkle of her nose.

He dragged his sleeve across his lips and pulled it away, frowning as the green saliva immediately stained the linen. Hopping down, he followed her into a large tent.

"You missed the rendezvous," a man's voice accused from within. "Did you retrieve the annals?"

Restarian entered, ducking through a heavy canvas flap to find Niamh kneeling before the Storm Warden. Her hands were held harmlessly by her side, but he loomed menacingly.

"Lord Nodrick," she said, "we recovered the books, but they were lost... stolen by thieves when we reached the tavern."

"What do you mean, stolen? I sent you on a simple errand, one any Searcher could have completed. Why did you not pursue them?"

"There wasn't time, Storm Warden, and I had already gathered enough information to find the portal."

Restarian laughed from where he stood in the entrance. "You really *don't* know where the portal is? I knew it."

She shot him a quieting glance and continued. "I have enough information and can certainly lead us to the site. It's inside the lower levels of Radviken's palace. As for the thieves, they were O'Malley's men, the same who intervened in the palace and plucked the gems from the vine. We'll get back the tomes as soon as we've rescued our lord."

"Hmm," the warden considered. "We'll see how reliable you are, and if you're not we'll see how strong your favor holds when Radviken is found." He turned to finally acknowledge Restarian. "You found *him* at least. So I take it your trip wasn't a complete and total waste? What does he know? Is he even useful? Will he tell us?"

"Why don't you ask me?" Restarian demanded. "I can speak for myself."

The warden glanced toward Niamh who nodded.

"I want guarantees," Nodrick said, "of your commitment to our cause."

"I'm here, aren't I? As far as my usefulness, I *have* been to the Shadow Realm. I know my way around like the forests of home," Restarian lied.

The warden noticed the silvery blade at the Fae's side. "You left him a weapon?" he asked Niamh. "Are you daft or that certain of his loyalty?"

Niamh answered immediately. "He's loyal enough to Radviken. He must be, since he has no one else," she said. "Besides, he doesn't know how to use it."

"What would motivate you fully?" Nodrick asked.

"To your cause? Once we succeed in rescuing Radviken, I want your commitment to help overthrow Fainnotheria and place me on my rightful throne."

"Do you have loyalists there? Enough to spur revolution?"

Restarian paused. He didn't know, and could only assume. "Of course I do," he lied again, "or I wouldn't be standing here asking for your aid."

"Very well. The matter is settled. But you must atone for the lost tomes, Niamh. You know what needs to be done."

"I do," she said with a grimace, rising to her feet and walking toward the center tent pole. When she reached it, she turned away from the men and with trembling fingers undid the clasps tying her jerkin. She let it fall to the ground and wrapped her arms around the post. Her muscles quivered with anticipation as she waited, her tender flesh prepared to bleed.

Restarian recognized the terror beneath her brave facade. "What is this?" he demanded of the Storm Warden. "What will you do?"

"This is a Storm Rider's punishment for failure of duties. Nodrick grabbed an instrument of torture from a nearby table, grasping a leather wrapped handle with nine braided strands extending from the top. "This tent cannot accommodate a proper lashing, so you will suffer the cat o' nine tails, Niamh. Do you understand?"

"Yes, Storm Warden. Thank you for choosing a private punishment, out of the view of the Riders."

He nodded, "It's your right as a Searcher." He drew his arm back and slapped it forward, snapping the leather tips with a stinging retort.

Restarian flinched at the sound of skin breaking as the crack of the whips echoed. All at once his headache returned, pulsing and ringing while drowning out the second stroke. He turned away, daring not watch as this woman was beaten, but the third lash was worse than the others. As the braids paused midair before another strike, Niamh's blood sprayed across Restarian's cheek, forcing him to turn and face the brutality. Without thinking he drew his sword.

Fainnen silver arced downward, striking the Warden's hand and sending the whip crashing to the floor. The man turned with a mixture of surprise and amusement, reaching for his own blade.

Before he could draw, Restarian made another attack, this time for the neck. He remembered the brief lesson Torian had taught him before, in the forest near the Fainnen Ring. But the prince only realized he had set his feet wrongly after it was too late. His clumsy blow fell harmlessly to the side as Nodrick stepped deftly away, turning his body to dodge what could have been certain death. Restarian attacked again and again, wildly swinging and screaming his anger within the tent.

The Storm Warden laughed, his hand firmly gripping the hilt, but had not drawn. Instead he danced away from each futile attempt at harm. It was game to the master swordsman, who could easily have cut Restarian down.

A blur of movement caused the Fainnen Prince to turn, just in time to feel the crushing impact of Niamh's pommel. The curved stone met his temple and his knees immediately buckled. All around him the tent spun out of focus and the pounding of his brain outpaced his pulse. Blackness came swiftly and swept away his thoughts.

Restarian awoke woozy, lying upon a military cot and unable to lift his throbbing head. The stubborn pulses were as before, dizzying and sharp, but the side of his skull added another dimension of pain. The spot Niamh had struck swelled into a bulbous lump overnight, tender and soft beneath his fingers. When he tried to open his eyes, he saw swirling black spots against the tent's roof above. The pain overwhelmed him, and he turned to retch over the side with rib splitting dry heaves. After he had finished, he sought his connection with the Bláth de Saol.

The comforting thrum was there, softly soothing with healing powers. He drew upon this rhythm and sent it surging through his body, setting right every tiny ache. Once certain he could handle the true test, he placed a hand against his temple and channeled the gift. His skull was fractured, he found, but not badly. The mass of blood around the wound was localized, easily tended and set right. With a snap, bones moved into position and sealed up the tiny cracks within.

Healed and exhausted, he gasped for air and let his body fall limp against the canvas bed. Everything about him should have mended, but the ringing in his ears hummed a different tune—one of worry and anxiety. The headaches should be gone now that connection to the Blossom had been restored, but it seemed now to always remain. Even after this, his greatest effort, he realized something had certainly broken during his torture. He yearned to return his mind to the way it was.

"Did you just heal yourself?" Niamh asked.

He was suddenly aware of company. "Maybe," he muttered with nonchalance.

"Strange how fairies can do that," she said. "I'm envious."

He turned his head and watched as she shifted weight, careful not to rub her wounded flesh against the chair. She wore neither tunic nor leather jerkin, but instead soft cotton. He could see dark strips of her chastisement beneath the white cloth.

"I can help with that," he offered. "I can heal your wounds."

"I need to wear them," she replied, "as my penance for failure."

"Only you didn't fail. You know the location of the portal and will succeed in finding Radviken."

She shrugged, then winced.

"Come here," he demanded, swinging his legs over the side and standing. "Remove your shirt and lie down."

"Well now, Little Scar," she said with an amused grin, "look who suddenly found a voice."

"You'll be worthless in a fight unless those heal quickly, and I'm your only chance for that. Come here and do as I say."

Still wearing her grin, Niamh stood and carefully pulled the shirt over her head. Restarian blushed at the sight of her breasts.

"Oh, come on," she teased, "you've seen plenty of these already, Little Scar." Brushing them slightly against his arm as she passed, her grin grew into a broader smile as he reddened deeper.

Once she was comfortably lying on her belly, he knelt for a closer look. "They're already showing signs of infection," he said, carefully examining the skin around the lines with tender probing. "But thankfully they're not as deep as they appear. I can heal them easily."

"Then stop talking about it and do it," she muttered.

He raised his hands several inches above the wounds and closed his eyes, feeling for the thrum. With her warm body so close to his, he found it louder and easier than before. Her chest softly rose and lowered as she breathed. Fully aware of her half naked form, his body tingled with excitement and his own pulse raced. They became one in that moment, connected hearts beating together. Niamh shifted slightly, a welcoming response to their ethereal union. She was so beautiful, so perfect, but he pushed aside his desire, burying it deep so as not to give in.

He focused instead on her wounds, carefully tending the muscle beneath the broken flesh, then neatly closed the cuts. She moaned softly, not from the pain but with euphoric acceptance. He focused harder on the healing. After he was finished, and she was neatly mended, he ran his fingers along her scars, now raised reminders her skin had once been whole.

"I'm sorry," he said. "I cannot erase the scars, and you'll carry them forever."

At this she rolled over onto her back, taking his hand in hers and bringing it to rest against her bosom. "I guess we both have scars, don't we, Restarian?"

He nodded, very aware of her body beneath his hands. He flushed again at the closeness they shared. He was beyond resisting, and his body responded to her welcoming smile. Niamh nodded, then pulled him closer until their lips met with passion. After he finally leaned back for a much needed breath, he felt her pull his entire body closer. For Restarian, the time they shared was consummation of an unspoken bond—a union of flesh after suffering so much painful loss.

CHAPTER TWENTY-ONE

"Our magic was naturally strong before the Dannan arrival, but their existence in our realms eventually damaged more than we'd feared. Those who coupled with them found each generation weaker, and unable to tend the roots. They even developed tolerance to iron."
– The Annals of History Book IX, First Passage

Alistaria moved carefully down the seemingly endless passage, pushing deeper into the unknown. The cold stone wept moisture and reeked worse of iron. A buzzing bothered her ears, mild at first like the remnants of a too close clap of thunder, but more intense as she moved. Though her heart raced, her mind urged her forward. Despite not knowing what lay ahead, the queen could not return to her cell.

The queen. Was she really a queen? All this time she felt more like she'd only acted at the role, constantly asking herself what Nastauria would do in every situation. How would she compose herself? How would she respond? *She wouldn't have tolerated entrapment at the hands of her enemies.*

The walls seemed to shimmer as she pushed onward, and the anxious flutter grew unbearable. She couldn't proceed, and willed her body to turn around. But the way had disappeared, replaced instead by a dizzying pattern of bricks that seemed to flow and change the course she had come. Where one entrance had been, several offshoots now promised a myriad of chances to lose her way.

This isn't right, she realized. The Puca's magic must have inter-fered—ever the trickster as legends warned. Turning to proceed down the path ahead, she abruptly froze. A mixture of both awe and terror gripped her, realizing the way had changed and no longer resembled the prison corridors. Most importantly, she no longer smelled the iron and the queasiness had passed. Gone also were the musty bricks.

The path ahead sparkled with midnight translucence. Filled with curiosity, she willed her feet forward, testing the glasslike floor that seemed ready to crack beneath her steps. She tapped her knuckles against the cylindrical walls and a resounding thrum replied—so familiar, almost like the Bláth de Saol.

No longer afraid, she stood at full height. *Whatever this is, I will approach with strength,* she promised, mimicking Nastauria's confidence.

A voice boomed ahead. "Your reign failed because you copied her... just as you do now."

"I have her regal bearing, that is all," she replied. "I failed because others were not convinced. Their hatred is dangerous, and I had to force compliance and unity."

"There is no *convincing* others," the mysterious voice cautioned, "so a leader must listen to their opposition and find ways to ease their fears. Otherwise, tyranny prevails and tyrants fall the hardest."

"There are too many to listen to all," she protested, "and their thinking was wrong..."

"And yet their thoughts were their own—made criminal by your edict. That's a difficult position for a law abider—to suddenly find themselves on the side of rebellion. Terror is the chief persuader of one to take up arms. No, Alistaria, you should have listened to each and every protest and given individual freedom a chance to be heard."

"I had to end their hatred."

"There is no collective mind, and attempts to force otherwise will always fail. As for their hatred, suppression is not education, as it snuffs out enlightenment. Open dialogue instead."

The advice made sense, but she was still confused. Why would he choose now to suddenly interfere? "It's you, isn't it?" she asked. "Still the Puca playing tricks?"

The voice did not respond. Up ahead the spirit materialized, this time standing erect on two strong and muscled legs. Everything about the creature had transformed, with the hands and fingers of a man beckoning her forward. Only the ears remained rabbit-like, and the face behind the beard appeared kindly human, softly velveted with fine fur like another she had seen in this form.

"So you *are* a Sìth, like Morkur." Alistaria remarked, to which the spirit only pointed to a short passage and a room on his right.

Moving closer, she peered curiously at the object within. "What is it?"

"You tell me, Queen of the Fae." When he spoke, she knew right away the mysterious voice had not been his.

"More games," she accused. "Tell me so I may continue on and find exit from your labyrinth."

"I told you before, I am bound by balance and cannot divulge to you your destiny. Self-exploration and actualization are your only hope to escape, and no one can provide those but the one seeking wisdom."

With an irritated sigh she stepped forward, examining an object within the room. A perfectly shaped orb, the swirling mass hovered above a golden pedestal. "It looks firm, but it isn't, is it?" she asked.

"Touch it and see," he said, "touch it and *know*."

With a timid hand she reached out and instantly recognized the thrum of lifeforce. Though alarmed, she did not recoil upon realizing just how many lifeforms were connected.

"Tell me what you feel, Alistaria."

"It's the same as when I tend roots or heal flesh. I feel the thrum of lifeforce and the spirit within every fauna and being connected to the Blossom." She let her fingers linger upon the orb, wondering at the sudden warmth and feeling of safety with it against her skin. "How can I feel this here? Are you mimicking the sensation I experienced when connected?"

"Are you not connected now?"

"No. That was severed by Brechan after he killed the elders. He dug it up and replanted the blossoms in a different order. It's his to control."

"And so you're no longer connected?"

"How could I be?" she asked.

"I see." The Puca gazed longingly at the orb, though he made no move to touch it himself. "How did you use it? When you healed?"

"I didn't. The Blossom did the work, since every living thing is tuned to its rhythm—this rhythm. How did you match it so perfectly with this object?"

Ignoring her question, he asked one of his own. "So you never understood the source of the gift?"

"Of course I do. It's the Blossom, and one connects to it by bleeding."

"Who taught you?"

"The elders. It was our living history passed down."

"And they've never faltered before? Never admitted gaps in their knowledge. Never been wrong?"

"Of course they admitted gaps. Erania told me that we know little of our past, much less origins..." She paused, suddenly aware of the paradox in her upbringing. No one truly knew how or why the Blossom worked. *No one except Radviken, it seems.* "When I was in Enatherr during Tempest, I was cut off from the Blossom. How?"

"I cannot answer questions. Only *you* can produce the knowledge you seek."

"That's insane. If I knew the knowledge, I wouldn't be asking."

"All answers come from within," the spirit urged, "but if you are not finding those you seek, I should leave you here. You cannot move on without answers."

"Where is *here*?" she demanded, but he had already turned and retreated further down the corridor. Alistaria hurried, eyes catching his shadow as he turned down another passage. As she came around the corner she skidded to a halt. She had returned to a room very much like the first, once more standing beside an orb.

She approached, eyeing it questioningly. The resonance had changed, now oddly foreign. The strangeness was not altogether unpleasant.

"What is this?" she demanded, but the spirit had already departed, sealing her inside and alone with the object.

Unsure what was expected of her, or how to proceed, Alistaria reached out with trembling fingers and touched its existence. All at once, her mind was transported though her body remained behind.

The dizzying rush plunged her into confusion, but her mind and eyes eventually settled. As they found focus, she made out the two figures nearby. She immediately recognized her friends.

"Piotr!" she shouted. "Boyd!" But they did not turn, unable to hear her cries. She looked down at her body and understood. They were firmly set in this world but she was corporeal—a ghost walking among the living. She watched them with frustrated curiosity.

"I don't like it," Boyd said with a seriousness Alistaria had never imagined possible from him. "We're never to split up! That was the arrangement!"

"What arrangement?" Piotr asked with a chuckle. "I never realized we were bound by a contract."

"Tamee said we shouldn't separate. She said we're to see to each other's safety no matter what."

"Yeah, I remember her saying that, but it was two years ago and a lot's happened since. Markey's king now, and he said this is the only way to save Alistaria."

"I know, but I don't like it," Boyd said with worry. "There's got to be another way."

Piotr stopped packing his satchel with a sigh, then plopped down on the bench next to his friend. "She's probably injured, and needs fae who are still connected to the Blossom. Now that I can do these... these *things*, I can help Torian and his Tuatha retrieve her."

"I can help," the stout little thief said like a pouting child—put out and rendered useless by his lack of skills.

"Boyd," you can't even fly right side up in Fainnotherr. You just kind of bob around uselessly, and that will slow a mission like this down. Besides, you're the only luchorpán we have to go after Clurich."

"I don't know what to do with him if I catch him."

"Talk him into surrendering," Piotr said with a chuckle.

"It doesn't work like that."

"Regardless, you need to find out what else you *can* do. You're not an idiot—you're one of the smartest guys I know."

"Smart? You actually think so?"

"Your ideas are the best."

"They don't always work."

"They don't always work because you don't plan all way through. But they're genius, and somehow you always luck your way out of situations."

"Speaking of luck, where's Lucky?" Boyd suddenly asked.

"I'm sure he's around."

"I haven't seen him all morning, come to think of it. What if he's left us? I can't imagine going north without him."

"He'll turn up."

Alistaria couldn't believe her ears. Torian and Markey were mounting a rescue mission, but were no doubt walking into a trap—bringing her half-brother along. She had to find a way out of this maze and somehow escape her cell. She had to stop them before Korl and Brechan sprung an ambush.

Blinking as their forms flickered and faded, she dizzied and the room tumbled from view. When she came to, she lay upon the floor blinking up at the emerald orb.

Sight, she finally understood. She'd experienced the full measure of the elusive gift of sight.

CHAPTER TWENTY-TWO

"Balor, king of the Fomorians, fell Nuada with balefire, an attack the Sword of Light could not deflect. The battle would have ended there, had Lugh not avenged his king with Areadbhar. His spear glowed brilliantly in battle, sensing the evil within his enemy."
– The Legends of the Tuatha, Chronicle III, Eighth Passage.

Torian scanned the onlookers. Most wore ragged faces, deeply worried over the palace's vulnerability and yearned to cross over to the safety of Fainnotheria. *It wasn't as safe as it once was,* he thought. Something sinister waited on the other side. His team knew the moment the mages lost connection to the Bláth de Saol. But it wasn't every mage whose connection was severed, only the Deamhan.

He looked up one more time, hoping to see his friend whose absence warned of other dangers.

"He's not coming?" he asked General Liam.

"No, last I laid eyes on him, the king was so deep in his cups a bucket of water wouldn't wake him." Conner replied with a hint of disgust.

"I haven't known him long," Torian explained. "Is drunkenness usually a problem with Markey?"

"Let's pray it isn't, although the timing won't help his standing with his men, even if he *is* in mourning. Word's already leaked out he's abandoned them—left them vulnerable to another attack. Your leaving doesn't help, since they all know what you did to kill that beast and having you around helps them breathe easier. Won't you reconsider and stay? I'm sorry I doubted your arrival. You came to warn and not invade, and I know now my doubt was offensive to your kind."

"I must go, but I'll return. If Alistaria's been overturned, they won't keep her alive for long. I need to do what I can to secure her claim to the city."

Conner grasped his hand with a hearty shake. "You were right about those tactics, and we'll continue to train and improve. Hurry back, my friend. Those Siths were only toying with us before, and the next battle will be harder fought."

Torian turned, ensuring the others were ready and locking eyes with Palathia. She'd grown not only as a fighter but also as a leader, and he watched as she moved through the ranks checking both mages and fighters. Neither could guess at what lay on the other side, but only the thief seemed anxious.

"You know what to do if we're ambushed, right?" he asked Piotr.

"What?" He jumped at the sudden question. "Oh yeah, sure. I get to the middle of the formation and stay beside Palathia no matter what."

"How're you at flying? If we have to take off in a hurry, can you keep up with the formation?"

His shaky reply said all Torian needed to know. "I'm... I think I'm steady enough... well, maybe. I only did it that once when we last went through."

"I'm sure you'll do fine. Just stick with Palathia and the other mages. Listen to her and do everything *exactly* as she tells you. Remember to always lean on the person to your left in the phalanx." Torian spied Quinten and Harachen standing in their usual position on the front line. "You two can't be beside each other and need to space out. Since you were once Deamhan, you'll need to ensure you're in contact with a Fainne when we step through... just in case they hexed the portal."

Both lieutenants shifted position in the ranks. He would have to follow that same advice, being full human. With a sigh he moved to the rear and took up position on the far right column. The grip on his spear tightened. With it he was a different kind of weapon—as powerful as an entire phalanx on his own.

"It's time," he told his warriors, and they popped to attention with anticipation. On his command, they stepped in perfect unison toward the portal.

When the first row passed through, the second squad leader bellowed. "Company. Halt!"

A collective gasp from the parapet reached his ears. Releasing from his rank, Torian rushed forward. Both Quinten and Harachen had been left standing in the center, unable to cross. "Spirit, guide us," Torian spat. "You two, move to the rear. We'll try again." He nodded to the second squad leader who swallowed and took charge of his rank.

"Second squad. Forward, march!" the fae ordered, and his line moved into the ring. As the light flashed and then faded, three more soldiers were left staring confused at their general.

"It's okay," he lied. "Move to the rear with the others."

One by one, each squad attempted to travel, and each time Deamhan were left behind. Soon, nearly half his force milled about behind him.

"General Liam will quarter you until we return," he promised them. "Do what you can to aid his troops. You're still soldiers, and there's a fight here as well."

He ordered the final rank forward, leaning firmly against the shoulder to his left. As they stepped into the circle a blinding flash swept away his men but left him standing alone within the circle. Palathia and the Tuatha were on their own.

Palathia quickly joined the waiting ranks, half dragging the thief. They had shifted to cover the missing soldiers, and shields protected all sides. As soon as she arrived, they opened ranks and made room for her team in the middle.

"I want a head count ready for the general," she said. "Sound off!"

Half her mages were left behind.

When the final rank arrived without General Torian, their situation swam into clarity. She was in charge.

After a hard swallow, she said, "I'm taking a look." Two shields shifted position, giving room to raise her head and scan the area. The empty palace betrayed no sign of ambush.

Torian's original plan would have split the Tuatha into two groups while ascending the steep staircases. They would be most vulnerable then, and two ranks would potentially flank any threat lurking on the rooftop. But he devised that plan before half their force was left in Enatherr.

"Listen up," she said, lowering her head. The shields locked into position above. "This will be risky, but we can't ascend those stairs ten wide. We'll have to improvise."

The responsive silence comforted the captain since no one questioned her leadership. Hopefully, her decision she wouldn't get anyone killed.

"When I say to fan out, we'll thin ranks just as before, but will do it a second time until we're two abreast. That will expose the mages, though, so stay alert with your heads on a swivel. Watch for any surprises. When we reach the rooftop, we'll close ranks in the opposite way, with two fanning movements."

A collection of "ayes" signaled understanding.

"Um... excuse me, sir? I mean... ma'am?"

A moment of dread passed over the squad. She'd forgotten about the thief.

"I don't know what any of that means," Piotr said.

"When I give the order to thin ranks, I will step ahead of you and you close behind me. When I order it a second time, let the person to your left do the same. We close ranks the opposite way."

He nodded.

"Are you certain you understand?" she asked.

"I think so," the look on his face said otherwise, but there was no time to repeat. Dangers lurked above.

Once the formation was up and moving, self-doubt crept in. *What if I'm not ready to lead?* she worried. The feeling intensified when they repositioned out to climb the steps.

Palathia kept her mind busy by going over any possible scenario. *What is waiting above? Will it be Kern or mages?* Normally her shield wall would defend against a Kern swarm attack, but with only two men abreast, her team was vulnerable. They neared the top when a thought struck her.

"Potter?"

There was no reply.

"Thief?"

"Oh," he said. "I'm Piotr. *Peet-er*. Not Potter, not Pe-oh-ter. Piotr. Tamee named me after her father, even if she got the spelling wrong. She doesn't write well."

"Whatever," she muttered irritably, she didn't have time for civilians at the moment. "Can you cloak the entire formation?"

"I can try," he said.

After several more steps she again halted the formation. "Um," she said with obvious frustration, "are you trying now?"

"Oh," he said. "I thought you meant when we got to the roof."

Sneers from the squad confirmed the others doubted Piotr's worth, and she wished Torian hadn't insisted on bringing the man. He hadn't trained, didn't know simple facing movements, and couldn't remain in step no matter what. Before they left Enatherr, she had tried to teach him how to stutter-step to get back in pacing, but all that had accomplished was adding an awkward skipping to his gait. After a while she had given up trying to make him a soldier.

"I need you to do it *now*," she explained, "before we reach the top. There may be bad guys trying to kill us—if you're not too busy, would you mind doing it now?"

"Oh, absolutely."

"Well?"

"I think I've done it, but I'm not sure."

"How do we check?"

"Usually I ask Boyd."

Palathia sighed heavily. She would have to take their chances. "Formation," she said, "forward... march."

The final few steps were taken with bated breath by every soldier and mage. If *any* sort of enemy lurked above, it would be nice to have invisibility to give them time to react and reform. As they emerged topside, their fears were realized. Two dozen Kern sat perched and ready, their scouts having already informed them the Tuatha approached. As the first two of her soldiers stepped onto the rooftop, the first squad leader raised a hand to quietly halt the formation.

He stared silently, waiting for indication they were seen. After a few breaths, he turned and flashed another hand signal to Palathia. She replied to continue, and they proceeded without noise onto the rooftop.

When she was certain they were fully through, she softly gave the order to open ranks. As they reformed their lines, the waiting Kern shifted their weight, suddenly aware something was amiss.

"They're here!" one of them shouted, and the golden-clad soldiers lifted into the air.

One of them, an officer Palathia did not recognize, called out, "By order of the new council, you're ordered to stand down. Lift your veil and reveal yourselves immediately, soldiers, so we may ascertain your loyalty to the rightful government of Fainnotheria."

New Council? Rightful government? Palathia briefly considered her next move. "Shield wall," she commanded, then turned to Piotr. "Lift the veil."

All at once the enemy reacted to the sudden appearance of warriors, and muscles flexed with anticipation.

From behind the shield wall, Palathia drew a breath and answered, "I'm Captain Palathia of the Tuatha, and I order you to stand down under the authority of General Torian and Queen Alistaria."

"General Torian is a wanted outlaw—a human without authority over fae. As for Alistaria, the Banshee Queen is currently held by the new council and awaiting trial. All Fainne are urged to surrender now to avoid the same fate. Any who resist, or remain loyal to the Banshees, will be imprisoned and reeducated until deemed ready to return to society."

"On your word as an officer, may I have a moment to confer with my troops?"

"You have two minutes."

"Well," she asked the Tuatha. "What's your answer? Does anyone wish to change sides? Speak now, and go willingly." Then she held her breath and waited.

Thankfully no one defected.

"Quick vote then," she offered. "On my signal, all in favor of a firebolt, say aye. Those who would like to see a blast of power, say ho!" She gave them a moment of laughter—vital to the mood and setting her squad at ease. "Tuatha," she commanded, "vote!"

A ruckus mixture of ayes and hos were lifted into the air above the Deamhan Palace, followed by cheering and more laughter. With a shrug and a smile, she said, "Sounds like a tie, to me." Then louder, she shouted, "Tuatha! *Full* salvo! Fire!"

The commotion that followed struck the waiting Kern, scattering them with a mixture of firebolts and energy blasts. Stone shrapnel flew in every direction as the usurper army flew wildly trying to regroup.

"Kern! Attack!" the enemy officer commanded.

"Brace!" Palathia ordered, then added, "Turtle!" At the last second, the Tuatha ducked to defend against the random onslaught of bashing shields and thrusted spears. But the squad held against the barrage, having trained for this archaic method of attack. With the strength of the Kern to their front, she ordered a shift to the right. Tuatha spears shot out from behind their wall, meeting the weaker attack and dropping many with a single thrust. The enemy fell back to study the wall.

"Salvo!" Palathia commanded, and mages popped up from the middle of the formation. Their fire, spark, and ice pelted the attackers, forcing them higher into the air or cowering on the stones.

With spears at the ready for an offensive thrust, she ordered the charge. The Tuatha ran at full speed in perfect formation (even Piotr managed not to trip anyone up) and crashed headlong into the grounded Kern, killing them instantly.

Palathia was not finished. "Recover!" she ordered, and the formation stepped several paces backward. In the air, the survivors hovered with spears pointed forward and eyes darting toward the safety of retreat.

"Charge!" she ordered, and the shield wall took flight. They rose into the air as a single body, crashing into the enemy and breaking their resolve. Several fled but many more fell to the stone platform below. This gave her time to both breathe and think. Had she enough mages, picking off the stragglers would have been easy. Instead, many escaped her following salvo, returning to Fainnotheria as fast as they could fly to gather reinforcements.

It was messy, but the day was over. She and her squad quickly disarmed and healed the survivors, binding and hiding them away in the forest. While she tried to decide their next move, she smiled along with the grins of victory and relished the pats on her back and congratulatory words. Captain Palathia had won her first battle.

Chapter Twenty-Three

"Luchorpán had always been a troublesome sort, thieving trinkets and treasures and carrying them off into the night. Their horded cache lies hidden deep within the Northern Mountains, beyond the cold and icy lake. Follow the prism to find the entrance, but venture forth only if you wish to perish. What enters their mines will never return."
– The Annals of History Book V, Passage 1

Everything was out of sorts for Boyd, and nothing seemed as it should. Piotr had gone away, passing through the portal while even Torian had stayed behind. That upset him most, since he'd been praying for the opposite. Now his friend could be in danger and he'd never know. They never should have split apart their duo.

Even Lucky had left him. He desperately searched the palace high and low, but found him nowhere. Even the kitchens turned up nothing, which irritated him to no end because finding them was a hassle. Seriously? Who builds a castle and puts the grand hall in the basement with the kitchens at the farthest point away? He was a bit out of breath upon finding them, and even more frustrated at not discovering his pup. Eventually he had to leave him behind.

Now, stuck with a trio of Storm Riders, he stood holding reins and waiting for the ferryman to finish their trip upstream. It was cold, more so than it should be, and it snowed on the far riverbank. But this is where they'd tracked the man who stole from Markey. Over what? A book. It had better be a damned *good* book for all the trouble he'd been through.

"Get ready, men," Murphy, the leader of the Riders, said, "with eyes alert and scanning the shoreline. The ferryman claimed Clurich wasn't alone when he put him on the other side, and claimed he has two companions. Find their trail quickly, so we can make short work of 'em, and get back to the palace."

But the fresh snowfall would make finding their trail impossible, Boyd knew. He was smarter than he looked and far more so then he often put on. But it wouldn't serve any purpose to remind these man. They were seasoned Storm Riders, three of the best Markey could spare.

"Thief," Murphy said with a spat, "try not to get in our way if trouble starts."

Boyd gave him an agreeable smile, then added a rude gesture and outstretched tongue the moment his back was turned. He silently wished again to have Lucky and Piotr along. At least *they* understood him.

The flat-bottomed ferry rocked violently when it put aground, causing everyone to lose their footing a bit. The horse on the other side of the reins whinnied its protest, and Boyd whispered calming words in return. It settled. Animals were good in that way, understanding tone much more easily than humans.

It turned out the trackers were good (better than Boyd expected) for they quickly picked up Clurich's trail. Murphy said something about broken branches at a rider's height. *I would have noticed that,* thought Boyd. It led them northward along the bank, offering no pretense regarding stealth, suggesting instead the murderer focused only on speed. They were in a race to wherever they were headed.

"What is this far north, anyway?" Boyd asked.

Murphy grunted annoyance but replied, "not a whole lot. To be honest, I'm not rightly sure *why* a thief would come this way, unless he really is luchorpán. He won't be able to sell what he stole out here, not in the wilderness."

"Have you ever met a luchorpán?" Boyd asked dryly. This was the conversation he'd been dreading, but figured to get it over with.

"Nope. Not a one. But they say you may have qualities of one, so I figured you know why he's luring us out here."

There it was—the bigotry. The hatred. The mistrust because he was so devilishly handsome.

"First off, there ain't nothing untoward about me," he said angrily. I was born and raised in Crosston all my life. Now, if'in I be a luchorpán, having their powers and what not, it's news to me. If you're worried about my loyalty, just remember—Markey O'Malley may be a brother in arms to you Storm Riders, but he's an actual brother to me! He was there from me first day on earth to now, so get those ideas outta your head!"

Murphy silenced at that, though he never bristled. It may have simply been a question of loyalty to decide where Boyd stood. The conversation ended in that regard, but Boyd took it another direction.

"What'll we do with him once we catch up, if'in he is a luchorpán?" he asked.

"Doesn't matter to me either way, if he is or ain't. What he'll hang as is a criminal. Theft is one thing, but murder's something different altogether." They rode up on a cool spring, not quite frozen over, though it would be within a few hours or another day. "Rest here and water the horses," Murphy commanded. "But don't dally, because I aim to catch him by sun up."

The other men grunted their understanding, and Boyd groaned as he swung off the tall horse. He'd never been much for horseback, preferring instead comfy carts. He handed off the reins and stumbled off into the woods to do his bathroom business.

"Don't wander far," one of the men cautioned.

"I wouldn't dream of it," Boyd muttered. He missed Piotr. Now, there was a real good travelling companion. He wasn't bossy, nor did he treat his friend like he had no value at all. He would trade all three of these Storm Riders for one Piotr.

What if everyone's right, he wondered, *and I am a luchorpán?* The thought wasn't that troubling when he considered. Also, he *did* have a bit of luck about him. Luck. That made him think about Lucky.

As he buttoned up his fly, movement caught his eye. "Guys," he said aloud, but they all three shushed him in unison. "There's something out here," he said.

"You're in the northern forest, there's many things out here," Murphy grumbled. "Come closer to the horses if you're afraid."

The others laughed at that. Boyd hated being laughed at, especially by strangers. Piotr never laughed at him, even when his plans went wrong (which was really the fun part about them) and never teased or called him a dolt.

"What if they sneak up on us?" Boyd asked, eyeing the woods cautiously.

"They're a half a day ahead," Murphy said, "and haven't doubled back. Whatever you see out there is an animal and probably a big one so stick close."

But he could clearly see whatever this was, big was nowhere near an accurate description. Only the smallest of branches rustled, and those only just. He crept closer. Eyes on a particular bunch of ferns. They clung to the memory of warmer days, and had yet to begin their winter shrivel or to give in fully to the snow weighing them down. Beneath those, a single eye stared out of the shadowy darkness.

"You're just a little fella, aren't you?" he whispered so the others wouldn't overhear. "What's got you so afraid?" he asked.

Slowly, so as not to further frighten the critter, he lifted the fronds to see within. Lucky sat shivering with his broken tail, one eye, and mangy fur—though he noticed that ailment had greatly improved over the past few weeks.

"I knew it was you, Lucky! How'd you get here? Have you been following?" he asked. As he reached down to pick up his friend, the dog hurried away, running to a point deeper in the forest before turning as if to wait.

"What is it?" he asked. "What've you got to show me?" He stepped deeper into the night, cautious of what danger they could both be exposing themselves to. "You gotta come along, buddy, it's not safe out here."

Just as he reached the dog, it turned, running deeper into a grove of tall trees. There it sat down, as if smiling up at the thief. An explosion of lightning caused Boyd to look over his shoulder, back the way he'd come. He started to move away, toward the danger and to aid the Riders, but Lucky whined.

"I have to help them," he told the little dog. "That could be an ambush—a magical one nonetheless." Another blast of energy confirmed it was. "But maybe I can just wait here, with you a bit," he decided, suddenly afraid. He wished Piotr was around.

Lucky whined again and run underneath a clump of fallen branches.

Horrific screams of pain suddenly echoed into the night, and Boyd followed his friend into hiding. Hugging the little dog closely, he prayed he would see Piotr, Markey, and Alistaria again—and soon.

Boyd awoke shivering and alone under the light of sunrise. He looked everywhere for Lucky, but there was no trace of the dog nor tracks of his exit in the fresh snow. The best friend he ever had besides Piotr had left him again. Though it caused great pain and heartbreak, he eventually had to give up the search. He also had to check on the Storm Riders.

Nothing remained of the camp, not even the horses. Thankfully, the snow had ceased falling before these had been ridden away, and their tracks led northward the way they had originally planned to travel. Boyd hugged himself against the winter wind and followed. Along the way he considered the possibilities.

The Storm Riders may have survived the ambush, and, not finding Boyd, probably continued on without him. They wouldn't have had time for a thorough search and never wanted him along in the first place. It made sense this is what happened. But a few dozen paces up the trail, he discovered that clearly wasn't the case. Though the black armor and cloaks were mostly covered with snow, he spotted three bodies stacked neatly behind a fallen tree. Murphy was on top. The stakes of his mission rose considerably without the aid of these soldiers and, with a glance over his shoulder, he considered returning home.

I'm only a thief, he considered, *and not a very good one without Piotr along.* Alistaria and Markey wanted that book, and Clurich had it. He checked the sky, it was clear and the air much drier than previous days, so there wouldn't be any more snow any time soon. He could follow the tracks as long as they remained and sneak up on their camp. They would have to rest the horses eventually. With a deep sigh he breathed in the crisp air and made up his mind. He'd find the stupid book.

But he needed a plan (not a daring and bold plan like he usually cooked up) but a sensible and meaningful plan like Piotr was good for. These people, whoever they were, posed danger. He took inventory of what he possessed or had ready at his disposal for the task at hand. Listing them off, he considered their usefulness. *I have a small dagger.* He froze in his tracks.

That's it? He suddenly worried, but pushed his feet onward. That was it. He had a small dagger. *And my wit and charm,* his mind added. A blade and a knack for winning people over would prove useless against magic and swords—maybe even magical swords— unless the wielders were absolute dolts. Surely, he possessed more helpful resources. He thought so long and hard he nearly gave himself a headache, and promptly quit. A dagger and smarts would have to suffice. He stepped into a clearing and nearly onto a pile of burning coals. He froze once more, staring down with sudden worry at a smoldering campfire and a stewpot resting nearby. There was also a sack of potatoes.

A campfire. Whose?

Careful not to make a sound, he scanned the area immediately around the circle of rocks. He found three bedrolls, each occupied with a short and stocky form. Off to the side, he spied four horses neatly tied to a tree. One was the grey mare he'd been riding. Eyes wide with a mixture of amusement and fear, Boyd realized he'd found the people responsible for killing the Storm Riders. And so, he did the only sensible thing he could think of. He pulled out his dagger and pulled up a stump on which to wait. Then he opened the sack of potatoes, lifted the lid from the pot, and started peeling and quartering breakfast. He decided his wits and charm would make the best weapons.

Chapter Twenty-Four

"After killing Balor, Lugh turned his spear loose on the entire race and destroyed their hold on the land. It was decided then, the sword of light should never be wielded by any except its master, and Lugh laid Nuada to rest with Claímh Soluis at his forever side."
– The Legends of the Tuatha, Chronicle III, Ninth Passage.

Restarian awoke to Niamh nestled beside him, her cheek on his shoulder and her emerald eyes staring up at his blood red orbs. Hers were alive with amusement, having watched as he slept, and now lit up as he awoke.

"Good morning, Little Scar," she said soothingly rather than with the cruel intent of their past.

He looked around, the entire tent was cloaked in pitch black and it obviously was not morning. "What time *is* it?" he asked. "It feels long past gloaming."

"It's near matins," she said, nuzzling closer and closing her eyes.

Everything felt right in that moment, and he closed his to relish the feel, absorbing her scent, her touch, and the closeness of it all. This was the life he was born for—to lead his people and live luxuriously with a strong and lovely partner at his side. On this night he was finally a king. Tonight he was a *man*.

Her hand moved downward, caressing his chest and stomach as she made her way toward the part of him she had earlier pleased. He breathed slowly, basking in the loveliness of it all, and anticipating the joy they would share again.

She suddenly gripped him tightly, squeezing with force and causing him to grunt loudly.

"That hurts!" he cried.

Niamh swung her body on top of his, still squeezing his manhood so hard his eyes began to water. Bile rose in his throat and he suddenly felt the need to vomit.

"You lied to me, Little Scar!" she said with wild eyes full of anger. "You have your full powers and used them to heal me! You *hid* them from me, and I want to know why!"

But he was unable to speak for the pain. He tried to wrestle free, but she only gripped him harder, twisting away the pleasurable memories they had shared.

"How long have you had your fairy magic?" she demanded. "Are you in contact with the gems?"

"I don't... I don't know!" he sputtered, finally wrenching her hand free and gasping for air.

Her hands moved like lightning to his chest, digging her nails deep into his skin and dragging them downward. Eight crimson lines formed quickly before she pulled them away, grabbing his throat and squeezing tightly.

"I can still kill you," she snarled. "With or without your powers you belong to Lord Radviken!" Leaning in close enough their lips nearly touched, she added, "and you also belong to *me*." Just as quickly as she had moved to choke him, her hands released, swinging off and planting her feet on the floor. She retrieved her clothing, this time choosing her jerkin, and pulled them on.

Restarian watched, terrified and gasping against the moment as he tried to heal the sensitive parts she had damaged. "It was recent," he tried to explain as she fastened her sword belt. "Just before we reached the inn. I don't know how they returned, but I think it's good they did. I think it means Alistaria has fallen to my loyalists."

"We both know you have *no* loyalists, Little Scar. You're pathetic and your people know it. You're worthless except for providing a good tumble like you did tonight." She drew her sword and held it to his neck. "Why didn't you kill him?" she asked.

"Kill who?" His eyes grew wide with confusion. "The Storm Warden was a better fighter, and I'm horrible with a sword."

"Although true, you're miserable with a blade but that's not who I meant. I'm talking about the thief in the inn. He was invisible, wasn't he? But you saw him with the gift of sight?" She inched her angry steel forward, crimson brimming dangerously on the point of her blade. "Sight was *my* gift, and your girlfriend stole it away. I *know* how it works!"

"I did." he admitted. "I saw him though he was invisible."

"Then why didn't you kill him?" she demanded.

"Because I can't even swing a blade. You're right! I don't know how to fight, nor am I strong enough to have bested him with my hands."

"It's your fault he got away with the annals," she said, pulling the sword away and sheathing it at her side. "I took that beating for your pathetic failure, not mine. Now get up and get dressed. We're going."

"Where?"

"To the dig site. They're moving the tombstone at midnight."

"Niamh," he begged as she turned to leave.

Though she paused by the door, she refused to even turn and make eye contact.

"What about earlier? What we shared was wonderful, but I don't know what it means. What does that make us? I think I'm... I have feelings for you I can't explain."

Though her back was turned, he could imagine the sly smile on her face when she replied, "That was to satisfy my curiosity. I've always wondered if the legends about fae lovers were true, and they weren't. There was nothing memorable about you, Restarian. But you left something behind and now I own you. You *are* my Little Scar and I'll take you whenever it pleases me to reward your loyalty. So ensure you remain so. The gods know I'm your only hope for pleasure, since you're so hideous. No other woman—human nor fae—will ever welcome you into their bed but me.

As she stepped through the tent flap, he urged himself not to shed tears but failed. He hurried to his feet and dressed as she commanded, then rushed to follow his master.

The dig site nestled where the water met the mountain, buried beneath eons of rockslides and worn by time and floods. The bright glow of a full moon lit the workers, revealing men crawling over the cleared debris. They drilled eyelets and tied off ropes with which to heave the rock away. The tombstone was nothing at all like Restarian had expected. For some reason, he'd assumed the workers would be gathered around a simply hewn stone of flat material covering the entrance to a raised mound.

What he found instead amazed him. The excavation crew had carefully cleared the rubble to reveal the single boulder, only recognizable by its smooth facing and oddish color. While most of the cliffside was comprised of jagged sandstone falling away under constant wear, this rounded piece of granite certainly did not belong and had been brought to this location from far away. Its pinkish hue clearly contrasted everything around it. What awed Restarian the most, however, was the sheer size of the rock—ten workers could be stacked atop one another and barely reach the top.

He let out an audible gasp at the effort necessary to dislodge it. Two teams of horses stood hitched and ready, idly waiting for the excavators to finish tying off the load.

"It's massive," he said.

"I know," Niamh replied. "It's beyond reason how the Tuatha de Dannan placed it here, or even from where. There's not another rock like it anywhere on this island, I'm certain."

"These Dannan, they sealed their dead inside?"

"Only one, buried among those they defeated in a great battle near this very spot."

"What is the artifact? How will you know it?"

"It's a tool necessary to protect us on the other side. The old stories mentioned it only briefly, but I found confirmation of its existence in the annals. The last mention of it anywhere was during the telling of this battle, when the Tuatha defeated the Fomorians and drove them beneath the lake where they had emerged."

They were interrupted by the arrival of Nodrick. He was dressed ready for battle, clad in black armor and draped by the intricately woven cloak depicting his station as Storm Warden. Beyond him stood fifty Riders with similar regalia. Each held hands to the weapons resting on their belts. They expected trouble, and each sheath was clearly unclasped and at the ready for a quick draw.

"It's tall enough, for sure, to allow the giants entrance," the warden said to Niamh.

"Aye," she replied, "and broad enough to permit an army of them through." She pointed toward the horses. "Those aren't draft animals. Can they support the load?"

"They are all we could muster without drawing notice of O'Malley's authorities. But worry not, they won't need to pull it far. The foreman expects the stone to roll easily once dislodged—far enough for our Storm Riders to enter two abreast from each side."

"You're sending soldiers first?" Restarian asked. "Surely you don't expect trouble in a tomb?"

"Trouble?" the warden snapped. "There's already been nothing *but* trouble throughout this land, ever since you fae interrupted Radviken's balance." As if on cue, a distant howling far to the south echoed northward, causing the soldiers to shift their weight uncomfortably.

"They're growing closer," Niamh observed.

"Yes, and soon they'll be as much a problem for us as much as they've been for O'Malley. If Claímh Soluis lies within, I may need it to vanquish those vile beasts here, before making our journey into the Shadow Realm."

Restarian turned to Niamh. "What is Claímh Soluis? Is it a weapon?"

"Never mind that, Little Scar. You'll know after Nodrick has it securely in his possession."

Several of the workers shouted, and men scrambled off the massive boulder to get out of the way. Once they were free of the area and any falling debris, whips cracked and the horses took up the slack of their load. The entire process took only a few minutes, and cheering soon erupted to indicate their success. The entrance to the tomb was unsealed and ready for the Storm Warden's approach.

Lanterns bobbed as workers scurried back to their tents, a promise of free ale awaiting the completion of the job they'd worked so hard to achieve. As the civilians moved away, the Storm Riders carried lanterns toward the entrance, forming two lines on either side. Restarian watched as these soldiers wasted no time in entering the tomb, checking for traps and securing the space for their leader to follow. After only a few minutes of waiting, a signal lantern flashed a message.

"It's clear," Niamh translated. "We can enter."

"Good. Let's find the sword and get on with our next plan," Nodrick muttered.

"Sword?" Restarian asked with surprise. "Claímh Soluis is a sword? You already have swords. What's this effort for, just to find one old one?"

"This isn't any ordinary sword," Niamh explained. "Claímh Soluis is the Sword of Light. We need it to defend against the Shadow. Only the weapons of the Tuatha can fatally kill the creatures of that realm. Come along," she commanded, hurrying to catch up to the warden.

The light spilling through the opening only illuminated a small sliver within the entrance, but Restarian realized right away the cavern was large. In the center a bonfire sparked to life, tended by a group of Riders. Several others held lanterns and lit torches to aid in their search. The flickering of these small fires revealed a network of many openings and several small branches off the main passage.

"That's remarkable!" Niamh grabbed a torch, holding it aloft to view three tunnels. She found each carefully carved into the soft sandstone. Above them was an image.

Restarian had to peer closely to make out a face in the lines, but one like none he'd ever seen. It appeared to be an ogre with a large head and a cycloptic eye in the center of the skull. "What is it?" he asked.

"Who," she corrected. "Balor was the king of the Fomorians, a giant among giants who went toe to toe with the Tuatha before his defeat."

"Why would they bury their sword with him?"

"They didn't," Nodrick explained. "Nuada wielded the Sword of Light in the great battle waged outside this cave. The sword could unravel a weaving of any gift by the Blossoms, but did not protect the Tuatha king from Fomorian balefire. Too reliant upon the weapon, he fell to Balor and was enshrined here as well. We must figure out which tunnel leads to his tomb, and we must hurry before O'Malley's lackeys track us. Drunken workers talk, and news will soon get out about our find."

"You're counting on that, aren't you?" the fae prince realized. "Loose lips will inform him you're still in the game, and he'll send an army to fight you, leaving his palace unprotected while you slip in to find the portal."

The warden nodded.

"After you find Radviken, you'll have the sword and also the reputation as the savior who ventured into the Shadow Realm, rescued the king, and saved Enatherr, all the while painting O'Malley as the opponent who allows it to fester. You're setting him while you play the hero."

Nodrick shook his head. "Not me. Lord Radviken deserves that role. His resurrection and return will be celebrated throughout the land."

"And you'll continue your place at his side, but sharing his final gifts—wielding corruption and resurrection as his equal. You'll be a god alongside him and hopefully his heir apparent."

"You're wiser than you look, Prince Restarian. Too bad you're worthless in a fight, or we could find other uses for you."

"Over here!" a voice shouted.

With the bonfire now raging, the entire chamber glowed with an eerie orange flicker. Niamh led them to a place on the opposite side of the cavern, where another carving stood over more tunnels. "It's him. It's Nuada."

"How can you tell?" Restarian asked.

"I saw this image drawn several times in the margins of the annals. I know it's him, and one of these tunnels must lead to his shrine."

"Split up!" The Storm Warden called to the Riders. "Form teams of two and search every tunnel, but do *not* touch either sword or sarcophagus if found. Fan out and cover every inch of these caves. Claímh Soluis *will* be mine."

Chapter Twenty-Five

"They had to replace what was lost. No, stolen is the better word. Either way retribution was paid and the gifts of Saol restored. Only those pure of blood needed not the relics, and that condition had faded into generations."
– The Annals of History Book IX, First Passage

The emerald orb pulsed with a life Alistaria now understood as the gift of sight. It had revealed her friends, but why? *To save them?* she wondered. *Or to help me relax and know help is on the way.* She rose to her feet and decided to try once more. After holding her hand to the sphere for several minutes, she realized it had nothing more to offer. *Why, then, had the spirit shown me this? Why does he insist I use gifts to which I've no connection?*

She considered the gift of healing. *Not entirely healing,* she suddenly realized. With hand against its essence, she had felt a connection of life—all life. Everything had seemed intertwined in that moment, though the Puca had suggested her people demanded independence. *Why would anyone wish to be apart from such a beautiful feeling as that thrum?* She suddenly saw the world as a living organism comprised of all things in every realm. *That thrum is the world's lifeforce, not our own.* How could people remain independent? Shouldn't they be all of one mind? Of one communion?

Independent, she thought, thinking back to her lessons. *Separated. Apart.* Not apart, when living among one another. Even the realms are independent despite the portals connecting them. *Each connected but existing under their own control. Are people the same way?* she wondered. Then she understood. *Our minds are independent, free to choose our own path, but our persons rely upon each other for survival as a species.*

Mind, she wondered. *What does* mind *have to do with any of this?* Mind wasn't sight, for knowing is not the same as seeing. *The great spirit gifted the elements to every realm, so she must have gifted power over them to us all. To balance each realm.*

"Puca!" she called.

"You have answers?" he suddenly asked from the now open doorway.

"I think so, but I also have questions."

"I told you I cannot answer questions without disrupting balance. Tell me what you *know.*"

"Every realm was given a Blossom."

He nodded. "This you already know. Sìth Morkur confirmed so to Nastauria."

"Yes," she strained to remember their names. "Bláth de Saol, Eolas, and Cumhacht. Life, Knowledge, and Power." He nodded again and she continued. "I assume each has eight Blossoms."

"That is not knowing, that is assumption. I cannot answer."

She began again, "It's reasonable she gave each realm control over the same elements, since we are all of substance. The difference in our realms, then, is the role of each in obtaining balance—Life, Knowledge, Power."

"Very good. What else? Surely you know more, or you would not have called for me so soon."

"The fae were granted the gift of body through healing and life, so therefore the humans were granted the gift of mind through knowledge."

"And the luchorpán?"

"I don't know enough of them to figure that out, yet. But I am certain the human gift also involves the mind."

"And here, with this orb? What did you learn?"

"The fae enjoy the gift of sight—to see over long distances, or to obscure and distort objects visible to the eye. The human counterpart must also deal with the mind instead of body. When I traveled just now to Enatherr, I could not touch or move objects. I cannot say for certain, but I believe their gift allows them to do just that. Instead of altering what is seen, they can affect the physical placement of objects with only their minds."

"A useful gift." The spirit nodded and stepped aside. "You may continue to the next orb."

She smiled smugly as she passed, satisfied with her own cleverness and certain she could win this game of his. Of course, once she stepped into the corridor, she realized she did not know the way. A tap on her shoulder revealed a smiling Puca.

"Would you rather I lead you, like I did the other who learned these lessons?"

"Please," she said, suddenly embarrassed at her own overconfidence and followed him down a different branch full of twists and turns. These led to a glowing orb of radiant white light. She recognized it at once. "Resurrection," she said quietly.

"Such a simple word for something as complex as life itself. For what is life, if not existence on a mortal plane?"

"So the other side of it?" she asked. He answered with a gesture to try the orb and see for herself. Touching it revealed her deepest fear—the duality of her existence as both Fainne and Deamhan.

The glow of the room flickered softly at first, then beamed radiantly with such force it glowed pure white with a shimmer she could almost lean against. Through the folds she saw beyond what her eyes could imagine, catching a glimpse of a terrible storm filled with wails and gnashing of teeth. Just as Restarian had described so many weeks ago. Through this orb she could see the Shadow Realm.

"I don't know how to do it," she admitted.

"Your heart will do it for you," the Puca replied.

With eyes brimming with tears she watched two figures standing together. They each turned and smiled before stepping toward the fold she had created between realms.

"Hello, mother," she said to them both.

Nastauria noticed the fold before Clíodhna. With the gentle voice of a friend, she put the grieving mother at ease. "You have the opportunity now, if only briefly."

The Queen of the Banshee lifted sad eyes—red with mourning and full of tears—and gazed in the direction she pointed. "Surely she hasn't discovered its power so soon. Is she as clever as that, to accomplish a passage through?"

"It appears to be a fold, a meeting place which will expire, but come, let me introduce your daughter." The Fainnen princess took the Deamhanen queen's hand in her own and led her gently to a waiting Alistaria.

Their daughter stood beside a golden platform above which floated a brilliantly white orb. Beyond that stood a spirit, wise and watchful in the guise of a Puca. As the two women stepped up to the fold, they found they were unable to step through. Each placed hands upon the rift and smiled at the girl on the other side. Nastauria proudly listened as Alistaria spoke first to Clíodhna.

"You stand together in this realm," she said, "am I to believe you've forgiven her the treachery against you? Are you once again friends?"

Clíodhna smiled, wiping away tears with the back of her hand. "I understand why she did, and Nastauria truly kept both of my babes safe by taking them away. But that does not prevent the sorrow of having never known my children."

"She raised me well," Alistaria said, lifting wet eyes toward the mother she knew, "and treated me like her own. All I ever felt was loved."

"Alistaria," Nastauria said gently, "there is much to warn from this realm. Three brothers of chaos have awakened, and are exploiting passages to the human realm. Soon they will reach yours as well."

The girl's face suddenly lit up. "Can you escape through those?" But the look shared by the two women answered her question. "Why not?" she asked.

"Because if we try, we'll emerge as Draugars. They are the remnants of souls without sentience—unwilling subjects of the dark spirits. They've each gone mad while agonizing over their own sorrows and no longer resemble their former selves."

"Torian has encountered them already. He also mentioned hellhounds have passed through. As for the brothers, we've encountered Dub."

Clíodhna suddenly flinched with fear, pressing her body against the fold and hissing a whispered warning. "Speak not his name in this realm or through the rift. Speak none of them, or you'll welcome the brothers through."

Alistaria visibly shivered at her mother's words.

Nastauria spoke with a warning of her own. "You will only achieve balance once you've recovered the Bláth de Eolas for your brother. He must find it soon and have time to master its gifts before the third brother awakens."

The girl nodded, but then suddenly shook her head. "I cannot, Mother. I failed. A faction overthrew me—killed the elders and trapped me. They stole the Blossom for themselves, and I'm no longer connected."

The fold shimmered and the glowing light of the orb suddenly flickered then dimmed. The rift was closing.

"Alistaria," Clíodhna said gently. "You don't need ...." Suddenly their daughter was gone, and the two woman stared instead across a chasm of wailing souls. "She'll figure it out, Nastauria. She's a clever one. I see that now."

"She is," the Fainnen princess agreed. "So are they all."

The rift closed before she could hear all of Nastauria's words. Falling to her knees, Alistaria sobbed. Finally, free to grieve, she let the sorrow escape on its own. The spirit, unfazed by her display, waited until her sorrow had subsided.

After her wails only rumbled as low sobs, he asked gently and with a hint of sympathy, "What did you learn here?"

"That I do not have the power to enter the Shadow Realm."

"That is correct, child. But with enough practice and the aid of power, you *will* be able to bring them back."

This caused her eyes to raise, puffy and exhausted to meet his emotionless stare. "Even if their souls were paid to Sìth Morkur?"

"Their debt was paid. Can not a debt be paid twice, if given freely?"

A rumbling response came from the main hall. "And given freely, the debt is always the sweetest." Alistaria turned to find the Master of Beasts had joined them.

"You arrived just in time to hear her new lesson, Morkur."

"What have you learned child?"

"The Bláth de Eolas will grant humans the ability to enter the Shadow Realm at will, and the fae will be able to retrieve them."

"Very good," Sìth Morkur said. To Sìth Puca he said, "Then she is ready for the final blossoms."

"Blossoms?"

Alistaria looked around with surprise, finally understanding her surroundings. The smooth cylindrical corridors made sense, as did the branches jutting off randomly to dead end or to host an orb. "Certainly not," she said aloud.

"Yes, child, you are *within* the Bláth de Saol. You stand inside the Blossom of Life."

"Can I bleed on the orbs from here?" she asked. "Is that what I do?"

Both Sìths said nothing as they led her down the corridor to wonder.

Chapter Twenty-Six

A leader is not destined for perfection, nor meet that unrealistic expectation they've placed on themselves. For that matter, neither is a husband nor wife. Leading a nation, like living in bonded marriage or heading a family, is simply about making the best with whatever's at hand. It's also about setting at ease those around you who lean on your wisdom. Mostly though, it's about realizing nothing is ever about just you.
– Journal of King Markey O'Malley, first of his name.

"Get up, you drunken sot!" Torian kicked the bed and ripped the blanket off Markey O'Malley, while Conner Liam doused him with fresh water.

The king sat up dizzily, sputtering and reaching for his blade. Still feeling the effects from the night before, he fell hard onto the floor instead.

"Look at you," Torian said without compassion for the king's condition. "Hardly ready to do battle and represent your people."

Conner threw open the curtains, spilling light into the room.

"My wife and child are dead!" Markey lamented with hand over his eyes, shielding them from the morning. "What would you do if someone you loved were senselessly murdered in cold blood?"

"Certainly not lie around like a coward, drinking away my misery! I'd seek revenge while the rage inside me is hot! Now get up and help us solve the matter at hand."

"Help you solve?" the king demanded. "There's no solving the Shadow Realm, not without the Blossom." He tried to stand, but slipped and fell instead, landing with his back against the nightstand.

"You can't even stand. Maybe those who whisper mutiny against you speak truly. Perhaps we should cut you down now and rid them of your cowardice!"

"Perhaps you should!" O'Malley screamed. "Maybe that's what I *want* is to join them wherever my family is!"

"Then you truly are a coward," Conner said softly. "Only the weak seek death in their misery. It seems the best way for them, but in the end, it selfishly destroys those around them who care the most."

Markey focused on his general, hearing his words and taking them to heart. "I don't know what to do, Conner. What kind of leader am I, with no plan to fight the Shadow?"

"No one has all the answers. That's never been a prerequisite to *any* job leading others."

Torian agreed, adding, "If I've learned anything as a lifelong soldier, it's just that. Your job isn't to solve all the problems, nor was it solely to protect your wife and child. You must be an inspiring leader—someone your followers trust to find answers when there are none. Jaana loved you not only because you kept her safe and alive, but for your ability to help her live! You gave *her* the strength to go on, and that's your job here and now! Rise up, put on your armor, and meet us in the war room. Make sure you're seen along the way by as many of your men as possible." He turned to leave, then added, "And hold your head up the entire way!"

Markey did as Torian advised. He put on his full uniform, even the black cloak that once designated him as a Storm Rider. With head held high, he walked the halls and checked on his men at every station, listening and talking with each. He allowed even their most honest grumbling be heard. This was no time to mourn. This was time to lead.

By the time he reached the war room, Torian and Conner were already inside with heads leaned together over the palace designs.

"How are defenses shaping up?" he asked.

"Not bad," Conner said. "We've effectively sealed off the grand hall where the new portal emerged. We have archers at the ready behind rows of sandbags and improvised shields. We also moved in ballistae which can swivel to provide heavy defense against those larger beasts."

"That's good," he said. "I assume the idea is to eventually build more permanent walls with murder holes for the archers to use?"

Both generals nodded.

"Good work. May I also suggest we move in bear traps and other defenses against the hellhounds and Draugars? I think pools of pitch and oil would slow them down bit and give our marksmen time to line up their shots."

Conner beamed at his old friend. "That's an excellent idea, Markey."

"Look," O'Malley began, "I want to apologize to you both…"

"No need," Torian quickly said. "Kings should never apologize—your presence speaks enough."

"Well then, allow me to thank you both for what you did."

"What exactly did we do, Markey?" Conner asked.

"You screwed my head back on straight. I fell into the hole that only Jaana has ever pulled me out of. It's good to have trusted friends to help keep me in line."

"What of the men?" Torian asked. "Did you set things right with them?"

"Mostly, though I'll need to visit with the night watches. You were right to say what you did, and for that I'm thankful."

"What the devil is this?" Conner Liam leaned over a diagram, examining closely a section of the palace foundation.

"Let me see," Markey commanded, and took the drawing.

"That area there," the general said.

"What is it?" asked Torian.

"Looks like a design flaw," Markey said with a grunt. "With all Radviken's improvements, you'd think he'd have shored up weaknesses."

"Unless," Conner corrected, "it was intentional."

"What do you mean?" O'Malley asked.

"He built a dead man switch into the design." Conner explained. "He designed a way to collapse the entire structure!"

"The portal," Torian realized, "is right beneath that portion of the building. Look, we can all agree that, despite his narcissism, he actually cared about protecting this realm from shadow. He *had* to know the portal was in this very spot."

"It makes sense," Markey said. "He must have had a plan in the event he could no longer contain the portal. Do you think it would've worked? Would a pile of rubble keep out those Sìths and their minions?"

"If it were a pile of rubble the size of this overbuilt palace, it would." Conner took the plans from his king and reexamined the setting of the pillars. "How would he do it, then?"

"He would have assumed he'd lost his powers," Markey said thoughtfully, "so it has to be simple."

"We should search now," Torian said, "in case they attack again."

"We will," Markey said, "and we'll add those bear traps too."

The king let the other men leave first, leaning for a moment against the door before following. He breathed deeply, settling his broken heart and fluttering stomach. For a moment, the breath caught in his throat and almost turned it into a sob. He closed his eyes, picturing Jaana once more huddled with Germaine. He swallowed hard and pushed it from his mind. *I have to put you two aside for now,* he explained to their memories, *but I'll be back somehow to finish my grieving.*

He pulled upon his most regal bearing, and followed the generals down the hall.

Chapter Twenty-Seven

"The worst thing a thief could do is rob another thief. But if you find you must, do it in the most grandiose of fashions."
- Piotr

The shield over Fainnotheria shimmered, restored by the new council to keep Alistaria's supporters at bay. Extra watches also patrolled the Skygate, and the golden flicker of the Kern zipped around outside the magical dome watching for trespassers. Palathia and the others suddenly found themselves watching the city as the Deamhan once viewed it—impenetrable and futile to attempt a raid.

From their perch hidden high in the trees, she sat with Piotr among the branches of the forest canopy. They were cloaked by his gift of sight and invisible to the city defenses.

"I could ferry each Tuatha one or two at a time through that gate," the thief suggested.

"Through the Skygate? It's not as easy as you'd think, plus you'd have to go inside and out so many times those guards would eventually notice. After defeating the ambush at the palace, I wouldn't be surprised if they have someone watching with the gift—able to see through illusion. Besides, time is of the essence, and we don't know how much of it we have. No, we need to get everyone in with as few trips as possible."

"How does the shield thingy work?" he asked. "Can't we just turn it off?"

"Only the elders and a few others know for sure. But I think it had something to do with the power absorbed by the Tree of Life during the centuries the Blossom grew at its base. From what I understand it must be turned on or off by connecting to its roots."

"Yeah, that would be difficult."

They sat in silence for a while, each pondering different ways inside. Finally, after a while, Palathia spoke on a different matter. "I'm sorry," she said.

"For what?"

"I'm sorry I doubted you. I admit I was irritated we were forced to bring you along, but you handled yourself pretty good during the fight. You weren't afraid and actually proved useful... so thank you..."

Piotr chuckled. "It sounds like you're thanking me for not screwing up the entire operation."

"I guess I am in a way," she said with an honest grin. "So you're her son?"

"Nastauria? Yeah. Did you know her? What was she like?"

"Magnificence embodied," she said without delay. "That woman was regal in every sense of the word."

"Well, she wouldn't have liked me, then. There's nothing regal here."

"Surely that's a lie."

"Not at all. In fact, you keep calling me the thief, but I'm literally just that - a common street thief who's actually pretty bad at his job."

"Well, it got you this far. Also, I heard how you saved the day and retrieved the Blossom. Thank you for that."

"That was mostly Boyd..." he broke off, suddenly worried for his best friend.

"Oh, yes," she said with a grin. "The fellow with the funny wings. He's an odd one."

"Alistaria and I think he's part luchorpán, so that kind of explains his oddness. We've never been apart before, so I'm kind of distracted... praying he's fine."

"I'm sure he is."

"I dunno, his crazy schemes have ways of going awry even when all is well. Without me to get him out of trouble, I fear he might not return."

"What do you mean by *going awry*?"

"Well, one time we pulled off a massive heist on the waterfront in the Port of Enat. Really riled the Thief's Guild doing this one—but nearly got pinched in the process."

"What did you steal?"

"Forty cases of the finest wine in Enatherr—the 754 vintage. We were paid to break in and take four cases, but Boyd thought the buyer said forty. We knew it would be tough getting it out, but the night we picked just happened to be the first night of their convention. A party, that is, they just happened to be throwing in that warehouse!"

"Wait... thieves have parties?"

"That's exactly what I said to Boyd, and he apparently knew about it. But anyways, the place was crawling with members of the Thief's Guild. So many, in fact, we couldn't dream of getting even a single case out without them knowing. But we were also worried the buyer wouldn't pay if we didn't bring all forty, and there were *lots* of people drinking that wine!"

"So what did you do?"

"We hid it... hid it right there under their noses—and us with it. They thought it was stolen, so they took every guard off every door and sent them looking for the wine each day. But we knew they'd catch us on the street with it, so we literally camped out right there in the warehouse—eating their delicious food for six days."

"How'd you get it out?"

"Eventually the party ended, and the warehouse was abandoned again. We simply pulled up a cart, loaded it down and covered it with a tarp, then delivered that 754 right to the buyer across town! If Boyd hadn't bragged, they'd never have known, but that's why we can't go back to Port Enat."

She nodded, smiling at his story and yearning for the chance to meet Boyd after this was all over. They seemed like the oddball pair to her, but the sort of oddballs who make everything fun.

Palathia suddenly sat up. "That's what we should do!"

"Steal their wine supply?"

"No! Fool them into thinking they've already been breached, then fly right in after they stop looking for us!"

"How do we do that?" Piotr asked, obviously confused.

"Come on," she said, "we need to ready the others. I'll explain along the way."

Palathia had been correct about the Skygate being a tough entry point. Their hope was to not encounter any sight-gifted fae at the entrance, and to ensure there wasn't, they sent ahead a fake scout to lure away attention. As soon as one of the Tuatha soldiers made their diversion, Piotr waited on the forest floor until all eyes were on the sky. As quickly as he could, he flew up and onto the landing, daring not waste time marveling at the massive structure.

Once he was in, the going was easier, following the directions the captain had laid out and making his way to the second floor, settling upon a balcony. There he waited and watched the sky above the shield. Once he saw Kern again flying their patrols, he knew the scout had escaped without issue and searched for a way down.

The next phase in the plan was trickier, and he had to concentrate not to lose the veil or cause the entire ruse to fall apart. The plan required three illusions. He closed his eyes and thought long and hard about the woman, praying he'd miss no detail. Truth be told this wasn't as difficult as it sounded, since he had spent much of the past day closely studying her features. She was a true beauty by every meaning of the word, and he'd grown quite fond of both her face and their quickly developing friendship.

Soon Palathia stood over the roots, animated and looking around carefully like someone suspicious and up to no good. He hoped she would draw attention from the guards, and soon enough, shouts echoed across the hall and the buzz of wings filled the air. Security raced to stop the intruder. By the time they reached her, however, the image was gone and the shield above no longer shimmered.

It was still there, of course, for he lacked the ability or knowledge to actually remove it. Instead he wove a pattern of light that completely erased the image from below. Just as he'd hoped, the soldiers immediately went searching for the captain. But he did not give them long before sending the image of Palathia flying upward and through the fake gap in the ceiling.

Shouts set in motion a flurry of activity. Several of the most experienced tenders rushed over and placed their hands against the roots, working feverishly to replace the shield above. Here is where he had to focus the hardest. The moment they accidentally deactivated the magic keeping it in place, he flipped his illusion so both the Kern above and the soldiers below would believe it intact. He waited five minutes for all normality to return, then flew upward, out through the open hole, and into the sky.

Waiting was always the most difficult part of anything for Palathia, and she nearly jumped with excitement when she saw Piotr materialize before her. She would have hugged him if it hadn't meant dropping her military bearing and gave him a slap on the shoulder instead.

"It's done?" she asked.

"It's done," he replied with a devilish smile. "They've no idea it's down and won't until I release the illusion. We can proceed whenever you'd like."

"I'm sure they're finished with security sweeps by now, and they *did* see me fly off, right?"

"They did."

"And did you pick out the spots their mages watched from?"

"For the most part, but there's no guarantee. Though few fae were watching the sky, most attention was on the Skygate."

"Then let's proceed." Turning to the squad she asked, "Does everyone know their assignments once we're inside?"

Though heads nodded affirmative, she forced each soldier to recite their role in the mission. Once they were inside and out of their armor, they would break into six teams and search for prisoners, the elders, and Alistaria—the priority being finding and freeing the Deamhan. If they could free and gain access into the armory, they should be able to take the city and hold it. At the very least, they could get to the Blossom, pluck the blooms, and rebury it while holding the Chamber of Life. That would be Piotr's job, Palathia had decided, with him the heir to Nastauria.

It would be temporary, of course, but he protested.

"I don't want that power!" he said.

"You're a third party in all this," she said, urging him to reconsider. "If one of us took the gifts for ourselves, we'd be tempted to keep it without any sort of legitimacy. You're a prince, so to speak, so you'll take it if needed. Besides, you've already plucked them once before."

He cussed, kicked the dirt, then relented, muttering something about this being like another of Boyd's harebrained schemes. But in the end, he suited up and flew with the others under the veil of illusion.

Their approach through the false shield proved easy, and any anxiety had been for naught. They touched down easily on the fourth level, then crept quietly to the living quarters.

"No more shield walls," Palathia said while stowing her gear. "Dress in plain clothes and arm yourselves with daggers and simple weapons you can conceal. Don't draw attention, and act naturally."

The others nodded, then hurried to do the same. Piotr, she noticed, stood quietly in the corner of her apartment.

"What?" she asked.

He shrugged. "I don't have living space here," he said. "I've nothing to change into."

She reached into her trunk and drew out a flax dress as blue as the sky. "This is all I have," she said, giggling as his eyes rounded. "But you're not watching me put it on, so get out of my room."

His cheeks darkened, but he darted out to wait in the corridor. She had to admit, he was awful cute when flustered.

Chapter Twenty-Eight

"The final gift of Saol was not originally wielded by our kind, but became essential to working the relic. Their corruption was a necessity by then, as it tuned our bodies like instruments before the thrum. We became like those we feared."
– The Annals of History Book IX, First Passage

The room glowed less than the others Alistaria had entered, but not for lack of brightness. The orb in the center seemed to draw the light in, devouring the essence and leaving behind a lingering void. Her heart thumped as she approached, anxious to finish this test and hopefully escape the prison and the Spirits as well. Though she had to save her people, all she could focus on now was the shimmering task hovering just beyond her outstretched hand.

As soon as she was close enough to touch the void, the passage slammed shut behind her, locking the queen in alone and without the aid of the Sìth. Though she never heard retreating footsteps, she knew they had gone entirely from the Blossom. *This is something I must do alone,* she knew, and graced the swirling blackness with her fingertips. It spread apart, avoiding their touch as it swirled. She reached further in and it did the same, refusing to make contact with her skin.

Stepping back, Alistaria puzzled. Though she had avoided this gift before, she had always been aware of its existence and recognized the stain within the orb. *I've sensed it, and Radviken used it, why am I denied contact?* She tried again, focusing her mind on the feeling she'd felt in her father's throne room when it swirled all around. The faint thrum of its rhythm could almost be heard. It was there, but lingering in the distance and refusing to accept her touch. *This is the gift most often withheld and never bestowed*, she knew. *I refused to gift it to others, and so did Radviken. We kept it from our people, but why?*

She considered what she knew—the simple, most obvious reason that it was the essence of corruption. To corrupt is to taint, to make unclean or dishonest. To deceive. Girtrán corrupted her people when he cloaked the Banshee under a veil of lies, hiding both their voice and their appearance from their enemies and dooming them to an existence of repulsed hatred. *Except Clíodhna.* Her mother had remained beautiful, just as every Banshee queen before her. *Just like me*, she realized. *I was born under the veil, but remained free of the spell.*

Corruption. She focused on the meaning of the word. It could also be an immoral act or depravity of values. The opposite of virtue is, in itself, a form of corruption, is it not? But virtue is based on culture and upbringing—what is important to some is not virtuous to others, so how can that be corruption? She sat down upon the floor to better think, her back against the pedestal and eyes tightly closed. If only she knew her people's history, she would better understand.

But Clíodhna was not entirely free of the stain, was she? Alistaria thought of the day her birth mother had died. During her entrance into Radviken's chambers she had flown in on the cloud, hovering above the ground as corruption circled her body and held her aloft. *Circled, but not touched.*

Alistaria regretted not giving more thought to the power when she had access. It had always been a vile and disgusting thing in her mind, something to be avoided. Even when she considered using it against Brechan, cloaking him to appear like a Banshee at the Skygate—she had used sight instead. Now, forced to face its true form, she wished she had truly taken time to get to know the gift. *And it is a gift, after all. It has to be.*

This gift was bestowed by the Great Spirit to... *to what?* she wondered. *The Great Spirit never would have given anything meant to harm unless it also held beneficial values.*

In a flash her eyes shot open and Alistaria leapt to her feet, trying once more to touch the orb. Again it swirled around her fingers, refusing to touch her skin and seemingly holding her hand upon a cushion of darkness. *Banshee Queens and their female offspring are free of corruption, so it would not touch Clíodhna. It would linger but never mar her skin like it had her people, just as it refuses to touch me now.*

Frustrated, she dipped both hands into the orb and watched the darkness retreat from each, forming a ball of its substance within—but never touching—her hands. She tried to lift it free but it would not budge.

"Irritating, isn't it?" someone asked from behind. "How it has a mind of its own."

Though she did not recognize the voice, she turned confidently with head held high and refused to appear afraid. The newcomer was fae, withered and wrinkled with hunched shoulders and stooped chest.

"I don't know you," Alistaria said. "What have the Sìth sent you to teach me?"

"You're arrogance marks you as royalty." The elder laughed sadly with a knowing smirk. He looked around for a place to sit, and finding none waved a hand in the air. A crystalline structure rose from the ground and formed a chair with a high back. He eagerly climbed upon it for comfort. "The Puca first granted me entrance, just as he did you. But neither he nor Morkur sent me to do anything. Do you understand what is so special about you they desire to lend aid?"

"Each claims they cannot help me and force me to learn the lessons on my own," she explained. "Did they help you?"

"They never aided me nor did I desire their intervention. No, I've lasted eons without their help—forever alone and forced to learn the secrets of Bláth de Saol just as you." He narrowed his eyes at Alistaria. "What has happened to my people?"

"Your people?" she demanded. "You're a king, then? Who *are* your people? I've never met you among the elders."

When he finally spoke, it was on his terms. "We all bleed for this cursed *gift*," he said, "but only those who planted the gems may stroll its branches or find final respite among the orbs." He pointed a shriveled finger toward the swirling globe of corruption beside her. "I've watched many after me come and go, and they mastered each and every bloom except this one."

"Why is that?" she asked, hoping to prod some hidden knowledge from the stranger.

"Because no one understands it." His smirk turned into a broad smile, revealing gaps where there had once been teeth. Whoever he was, this newcomer was older—twice, possibly—than Erania had been.

It proved too soon to think about the old woman Alistaria had loved like a grandmother, and thoughts of her slain body and those of the elders formed a hard lump in her throat. She looked around for a place to sit, but found none. She waved her hand as he had, but to no avail. Standing awkwardly, she turned to face the orb and gazed once more into its darkness.

"I can't figure it out," she said softly, admitting her limitations. "Why can't I wield it?"

"Because of the curse."

"Yes. Girtrán's curse of the Deamhan. He really fouled things up for us all, didn't he?"

"In some ways, I suppose he did. But in others, I think he was the only fae in centuries who acted selflessly."

"Selfless? How can you call that man *selfless*? He tainted half our people with the mark of bigotry, and his actions created centuries of war! He erased our history by painting it over with hatred and confusion. King Girtrán was an evil man!"

"He wasn't as evil as you say, Alistaria. As a young man, maybe, but he grew wiser in his years and eventually sacrificed himself for all fae."

"Other than the legend of the curse, we know nothing about his story." Then a thought struck her and she looked him over more closely. *Is he from Girtrán's time?* "How do you know these things?" she asked. "Did you know him?"

"I knew him as well as I know myself," he replied. "I know enough to say his decision to hide our history was a mistake—perhaps his greatest—but he did not do so with evil motives. At the time he believed it the only way to promote healing and prevent further war with the humans."

"Tell me what you know," she demanded.

"I hold several millennia of knowledge in my head, but your time cannot be wasted listening to every story. Besides," he said with a shrug, "you've the mystery of corruption to solve if you're to return to Fainnotheria."

"Start with Girtrán, then. Tell me how he corrupted the Deamhan."

"I can give you that one if you wish, but it isn't the story you need. You've already heard the legend."

"What is the correct story, then, the one I need to hear?"

"You need to understand *why* he corrupted the Deamhan."

"I know the reason why. He was angry over their betrayal and the weakness of his father that led to it. The human-luchorpán alliance trapped the Fainne in this realm, then Calug turned on Octavian and sided with the Deamhan to steal the Bláth de Eolas for himself."

"That's some of the story but not all. It says nothing regarding the true nature or origin of the Deamhan."

"I know that as well," Alistaria said, turning away from the orb to meet the ancient one's eyes. "We're all one race."

"So the tapestries have led you to know, and it is true all people share one origin. But the original fae were the Deamhan, until our ancestry was tainted." That smirk had returned, not betraying smugness, but revealing wisdom and knowledge and the pride of being the only one knowing the truth. "You did not expect that answer, did you Alistaria, Queen of the Fae? If you look beyond political boundaries, you will discover true history brings us all together."

"Then why did Girtrán punish them? The war was won and the humans and luchorpán had left. Why did he feel the need to steal the Bláth de Saol and doom his enemies to eternal loathing? Why did he hate the Deamhan so much?"

"Not for all time," the elder corrected, "and it wasn't out of hatred that he dealt punishment."

"What was it, then? What about my people did he despise so much he used this," she pointed to the orb floating before her, "to corrupt and divide two peoples who should otherwise be allies?"

"Have you ever wondered, Queen Alistaria, why two parents with blonde hair can randomly give birth to a raven-headed child? Or why eyes can vary with shades of green, or blue, or...," he gazed deep into hers with lips upturned with that stupid smirk, "or even brown?"

No, she hadn't wondered, and never really cared. She had always assumed her own dull eyes were a result of Radviken's contribution during conception. Looking up, she noticed this fae's eyes were as dark as hers. "Yours are like mine," she remarked. "Are you part human like me?"

"Great Spirit, no," he said with a frown, "certainly not *that*. But we *are* very similar. You and I lack the contribution of *others* who arrived and watered down the true history of the fae."

"Who? Who arrived?"

"Though you have not read them, the answer lies in the books now within your possession. You must escape your imprisonment and learn those answers, Alistaria. The Sìth brought you here for knowledge."

"Will you tell me the story of *why* he corrupted the Deamhan?"

"No, but I will ask you a question, just as your elders did when you first bled for the Blossom."

"Anything. Please, ask me whatever may help me understand."

"Why were you and Clíodhna spared corruption?"

"Because of the curse."

"Not the curse, but a gift."

"I don't understand."

"Try. Sound it out as if you know it to be true."

She thought hard on what she remembered of the legend, how King Girtrán had transformed every living fae in the palace into Banshees. *All, except the queen.* "He promised her... gifted her... beauty."

"No. She was already beautiful."

"He gifted her purity—free from corruption."

"Yes. Why would he do that? What was his promise?"

"That the curse would be lifted..."

"No!" the ancient one shouted. "Not a *curse*!"

"Okay," she revised, "he promised she would have a perfect son to herald the queen who would unite their people." She paused, turning to stare at the orb. "So this corruption... isn't corruption. It's something else?"

No response, only quiet and the thoughts buzzing around in her head.

"Each queen was born without this..." She said, facing the elder. "Oh, but what is it?"

"The reason why Girtrán used it to mark the Deamhan," he explained. "It's a stain of those who do not belong in our realm—the true corruption which descended through bloodlines."

"So I am different by blood than the other Deamhan?" She shook her head, refusing to accept her people were truly tainted. "Were we *ever* united as fae?"

"We were, both your people and mine, until *they* arrived and split our camps into two tribes."

"Tribes," she muttered. *That word has another meaning,* she realized. With eyes wide she exclaimed, "Tuatha!"

"Yes. There were fae who accepted the Tuatha de Dannan into their beds and adopted their culture. Eventually, the differences between fae and the gods became unrecognizable, and the tribes fought over culture. The first wars bickered over which was better— the old ways of the fae or the new ways of the Dannan."

"So which were the Fainne?" Alistaria asked.

"The losers were the Fainne, and we were forced through the portal to reside in the human realm. Our ancestors constructed a wondrous home among the forest—a shining homage to the Great Spirit. But that forest was quickly attacked and cut down by human greed, and the seedlings of the great trees became their boats and homes. So we stole their Bláth de Eolas to preserve our way of life and what was left of the forest. But it wasn't meant for us and imbalance hastened deforestation."

"The dune sea," she marveled. Though she had not seen it herself, Torian had described in detail how different her home looked in Enatherr.

"Yes," the elder agreed. "As our home shrank around us, my father vowed to take back Fainnotheria. He recognized the human gifts could be used as a weapon to rival our rightful Blossom."

Alistaria couldn't believe her ears. "Your father...," she said, "*You* are Girtrán?"

The ancient one nodded solemnly. "I was, until I gave myself completely over to the Bláth de Saol, ensuring it would always serve my people no matter who stole away its power. Even Radviken."

"But I'm not of your people. I'm not Fainne like you! Why are you even speaking to me like an equal?"

"Because you were the gift, Alistaria, both you and your brother. You were each born free of the corruption—pure and worthy of the Blossom's full power, and able to wield it without bloodshed."

"I don't understand."

"*You* were the gift I gave the Banshee queens and to my own people, a promise their lines would someday be free of the remnants of the Tuatha de Dannan."

"But why me? Why *us?*"

He shrugged. "Until a Deamhanen Queen mated with a male other than one of her corrupted followers, you would never have been born. I knew it would someday be an eventuality."

"What's so special about me? Does this mean there's no Dannan blood in my line?"

"Though the Great Spirit gave each race their own Blossom, as well as the ability to draw gifts from them directly, they could only do so as long as their bloodlines remained free of the Dannan stain."

"But they didn't. The Dannan interfered with the fae, and they lost their abilities. How then, did the blossoms continue to work for them?"

"That was also interference by the Dannan. They were master craftsmen, able to create wonderfully magical relics, and some of that knowledge passed down through the Deamhan. They changed the Blossom—made it so they could filter out imperfections in their blood by feeding it to this orb."

"Which is why we have to bleed to use its power," she realized. "But that doesn't explain your actions. Why did you use corruption on the Deamhan, but spare the queen?"

"I knew the queen's bloodline carried very little Dannan blood, and hoped she would someday bear a child who could harness the gifts without bleeding for them. I ensured the queen could redeem her sins through future offspring and offered them a way back into the Fainnen fold."

"Which is why you left her a beauty amongst her people—so she would find them disgusting?" Alistaria abruptly reviled his arrogance. "You *gifted* beauty to her and her daughters so they would be attractive to others? To draw a human who would hopefully lie with them instead?"

"No. She was already beautiful, and her beauty was something I could not bring myself to mar because..." he drifted off, as if unsure whether to proceed or finding the courage to answer. When he finally did, the words shocked Alistaria to her core. "I could not mar my own mother, even if she *had* left my father to marry the Deamhanen king. I would not harm her, despite it was she who handed over the Bláth de Eolas to the Luchorpán King. I also could not bring myself to harm nor murder my half baby sister. So you see, I acted selflessly."

Alistaria felt the room spin as her eyesight suddenly whirled into blackness. When she found her wits enough to open them, both the orb and King Girtrán were nowhere around. Neither were the Sìth. She was once again lying shackled in chains and leaning against cold stone which reeked of iron.

Chapter Twenty-Nine

"The original site of Fainnotheria is not known, lost completely to memories long passed from the realm. The new site became a final effort by the Deamhan to preserve their ways, though even that place was inspired by the Dannan. Their knowledge helped us channel the shield overhead, the final relic created before their last secrets were forgotten."
– The Annals of History Book XIII, Passage 3

Fainnotheria, usually a bustling city with more faces buzzing about than one would have time to inspect, uncharacteristically lacked activity. Though some fae moved around, the numbers were few except for the Kern standing everywhere. On the upper levels, these soldiers wore grim expressions as they moved about the living quarters, waving dousing crystals over the bleeding hands of people herded like the humans move their cattle to slaughter. On the first level, Palathia and Piotr approached a group addressing a gathered assembly.

"I know the restrictions are uncomfortable," a captain told a worried couple, "but things are different now. It will take some time for the temporary council to figure out a new ruler, but we must focus first on security! The Deamhan walk and hide among us, disguised as Fainne and threatening our future."

"But Alistaria lived among us," a citizen complained, "and was the daughter of Nastauria! She was good and meant well!"

"Lies!" the soldier argued. "The Banshee Queen fooled Nastauria into raising her child. The girl was planted among us to sow confusion!"

"Then who leads us?" the woman's question garnered shouts of agreements from others who moved closer for news.

"The council specifically addressed that matter when they arrested that Deamhanen imposter! It was announced all changes during her brief tyranny have been erased by the council, but choosing and putting in place a leader will take time. Until then, they rule as a group."

"But she taught love and acceptance!" another resident argued. "She did nothing to harm Fainnotheria, and instead helped us to see the truth of the Deamhan! We're related, all of us, by blood!"

"More lies!" the captain decried, motioning for several Kern to move beside the resident. "By authority of the council, we may assign you to reeducation for spreading these lies, so be careful with your words!"

"But it's true," another protested, earning nods of approval from the gathering.

"Disperse," the captain ordered, "this is your final warning!"

"Free Alistaria!" someone cried from the back, followed by similar shouts among the group.

"Kill the Banshee Queen!" shouted another off to the side. "Break her neck from the limbs of the Tree of Life!" Soon others joined in until two groups formed, squaring off with the Kern in the middle.

The captain drew a whistle from his belt and blew three short blasts, instantly drawing golden clad warriors from every level. He and those with him drew silvery weapons, training their points at those urging Alistaria's release. "Arrest this group," he commanded, and soon man, woman, and child were beaten, bound, and dragged away.

Beside Palathia, Piotr stiffened and softly gasped. "What is happening?" he asked. "Your city was peaceful before!"

"It seems the city is split," she observed, "and the new council is making it a crime to show compassion for the Deamhan."

Shouts drew her attention, and she watched as several Kern surrounded a family. The father protested as his children were grabbed away from his wife, palms sliced open, and crystals held over their blood. Each glowed brightly, giving them away as Deamhan.

"They're even checking children," Piotr whispered with disgust.

"Why does it glow for them?" she asked.

"What do you mean?"

"Torian told me the crystals glow in the presence of Deamhan blood, but why only for theirs and not ours? Especially when we're so closely related?"

But before Piotr could answer, the father drew a blade and lashed out at the soldiers, knocking one aside and earning a sword to his belly. The wife fell to her knees and keened, mournfully screaming sorrow into the chamber below. The sound sent chills down Palathia's spine. It so perfectly matched the wail of the Banshees. One of the soldiers must have also noticed the similarity and rammed a silencing blade into the woman's chest.

The children, watching with horror as their parents bled out, were scooped and carried away down a main passage. The rest of the crowd dispersed peacefully then, hurrying to their quarters and fleeing the halls.

"They're taking the children to the amphitheater," Palathia suddenly realized. "That must be where they're keeping the Deamhan." Thankfully, others from the Tuatha had noticed the same, and she watched as three of her squad moved to follow the soldiers and crying children.

"We have to find Alistaria," Piotr urged, pulling her away.

The pain of what she'd witnessed grew suffocating, and tears of anger welled in her eyes. *What are we doing?* she wondered. *I don't even know where to find her.*

"You, there!" The pair turned to find a group of Kern walking toward them.

"We're returning to our rooms," Palathia said with a warm smile, wiping tears with the back of her hand.

One of the approaching soldiers pointed toward her palm, unblemished and not bled. "Present your hands, so we know you've been examined."

"Flee," she whispered to Piotr, as an idea suddenly formed in her mind. "Go, but follow after."

"After what?" he asked, face full of confusion.

"Free Alistaria!" she screamed, kicking the sentry and sending him toppling backward. Whirling toward the other, a fireball sprung from her palm and struck the Kern squarely in the chest. She followed up with a blast of ice. She did not wish to kill the men, only to wound them and draw attention.

Beside her, Piotr had not moved.

"Go," she mouthed, the look in her eyes sending him scurrying away.

Piotr had no choice but to run. He sprinted, desperate to get away and shocked by the sudden turn of events. These abrupt catastrophes were expected during jobs with Boyd, but he would have bet against the same from the Tuatha captain. Realizing she hadn't followed, he briefly glanced over his shoulder. She suddenly dropped to the floor and lay motionless with palms up. Then he understood she'd hoped for capture. It was the only way to find the prison cells.

He rounded a pillar and used the gift of sight, disappearing instantly from view. With closed eyes, he waited until the buzz of many wings had passed. Only then did he venture another look toward his friend. They had Palathia on her knees by now and drew a line of blood on her palm. The crystal hovered but failed to light up, causing them to turn for guidance to their captain.

"She's Fainne, but her loyalties are to the criminal," one of them explained.

"Lock her in the cells beside her queen," the officer commanded. "Bind her with iron, but watch closely for trickery, and, if she tries again to channel the Blossom, kill her without a second thought." The captain looked around. "Where's the other one?"

"Hiding nearby."

"Well find him. If she's wielding the Blossom's gift, then so might he. I'll inform the council."

The soldiers nodded then locked heavy shackles around Palathia's wrists and ankles. After draping iron chains around her shoulders, they dragged her off and down a corridor passing near the Kern barracks. *No wonder she didn't know the location of the cells,* Piotr realized. Only the Kern knew what lay down those passages. He waited patiently until they were several paces ahead, then stalked carefully from a safe distance.

He passed row after row of military style barracks, sparsely adorned and tidy. The Kern kept their own armory, and he spotted a single sentry standing by while the armorer polished shields. Neither looked up as he passed. The end of the hall seemed to fall away, and Piotr realized it terminated with downward leading steps into a deeper recess beneath the city. These were of spiral design twisting clockwise—unlike the parapets he'd seen in Enatherr. Those always twisted the other way, to prevent intruders from gaining right handed momentum in a fight. These favored those climbing, instead of descending, and he assumed the depths served as a final rally point if Fainnotheria fell to attackers. Near the bottom, voices met his ears.

"Put this on her," the jailer said. He was another Kern officer, though obviously not happy with his duty. He held a heavy jacket to one of the soldiers, thick with long arms extending several feet. It was the kind Piotr always teased that Boyd needed, since it forced a madman to perpetually hug himself into comfort. But this device was heavily lined with iron plates among the padding. "This will render her powerless until they sever the Bloom's gift," the jailer explained to the others.

Palathia realized their intent and suddenly panicked. Struggling against strong hands, she tried to break free. A heavy blow across her temple cast a slumping silence that both angered and worried Piotr. As their friendship had recently strengthened, so too did his desire to protect this woman. He started forward, then remembered his mission. Palathia would be fine. She had planned her capture, and it was Alistaria he must find. Creeping carefully backward from the holding cell, he set out to find his half-sister.

CHAPTER THIRTY

"Lugh and his brothers did not worry about others finding and wielding Claímh Soluis, even if it fell into the hands of the greatest swordsmen time could produce. If it needed found, and their mission were noble, it would shine forth to dispel shadow and crown its hero king."
– The Legends of the Tuatha, Chronicle III, Ninth Passage.

Restarian followed the bobbing torch. The tunnel snaked around so many times he lost all sense of direction, and claustrophobic doom set his heart aflutter. Darkness suffocated and squeezed whatever was left of his courage. He yearned to be topside, standing among the trees and fauna and staring up at the stars and moon above. The soft glow led the prince down another passage in his mind, thinking of home and Fainnotheria. He missed the trees, especially the great roots and the thrum he would feel during tending. He'd only found loneliness without them, a hopeless state without ambition. He needed the vibrancy of the forest and to feel their...

So deeply lost in his thoughts, he crashed into the back of Niamh. It was the third time he had done so, and she whirled around angrily.

"Watch it, klutz," she growled. "I swear if you do that again, I'll take that stupid nose off your ugly face."

"I'm sorry," he muttered. "It's hard to see and you've got the torch."

"Then pay attention to where I'm holding it," she barked.

"Why'd we stop, anyway?"

"The passage forks, and I'm trying to decide which to take."

"We'll have to split up," Restarian suggested.

"I have the torch, or did you forget?" She waved it in his face to prove her point, forcing him to step backward.

With a shrug, he snapped his fingers and bright flash lit the passage. A bluish glow formed around the fairy spark held in the palm of his hand, revealing his devilish smile of satisfaction.

"We've been walking around with a torch in the dark, and you've been able to do that this entire time?"

"First off, you never asked for my help, seemingly intent on doing things your way. Secondly, I wasn't sure I could, until just now. I poured a little bit of power into it, and voila! Fairy spark!"

"Fine," she said with a huff, "you go right and I'll go left. If you find the tomb call out for me and I'll come find you. I'll do the same if I do first."

He shrugged with satisfaction and smiled smugly as she turned her back. He waited till the bobbing torch disappeared into blackness, then proceeded. He walked with more confidence now that he held the spark, every dip and loose stone visible before him. But there was one downside to the extra light—now he could clearly see the network of spider webs above his head. All around he was surrounded by silvery strands of sticky tinsel, full of egg sacs and surely hiding lurking eyes that watched intently and waiting for the light to wane. A glance over his shoulder caused his stomach to sicken as he found his cloak was now covered with the same. He gagged for a moment, wiping wildly with a panicked hand and hurried into the tunnel.

The end of it terminated with an inscribed stone slab.

He immediately wished Niamh was with him to translate, and called out for her. "Niamh!" he said. "I've found something!"

He waited several minutes, but impatience won out against reason. He examined the stone and found tiny indentions at the top and sides. He squeezed bony fingers behind and pulled, but to no avail. It refused to budge. He stared at the slab, considering every way in which to force compliance. The light of his fairy spark bobbed in his hand, flickering against the lettering and offering a single option.

With a single thrust, he flung the power of the morning glory, closing his eyes in case shrapnel bounced his way. Rock sprayed everywhere, but he ducked and covered his face with bloodied hands. The gravel fell like rain around him, and he coughed and wheezed on the dust all around. When he finally stood to study his handiwork, a gaping hole remained—just wide enough for him to slip inside.

The tomb was simply arranged, with a stone slab set upon a casket of the same rock as the boulder that once blocked the cave. Upon examination he could tell it was indeed a sort of granite, only pinkish and finely formed. With a shove, the stone slid easily from the sarcophagus, revealing a gruesome sight within. The corpse had long since rotted away the tenderest of flesh, and Restarian stared down at the gaping face of a skeleton clad in golden armor. Timidly, he reached out a finger and dusted away eons of filth to better view the intricately carved symbols on the chestplate.

He was surprised to find it finely molded Fainnen Silver. It was much like the golden version worn by the Kern, only thinner and lighter of weight. No doubt also stronger. Thinking of the Kern sent his mind in a tailspin of thoughts—of Betarian. He was a warrior, not a root tender like he, and would have fit nicely into this set. His grandfather, the former king, would have gladly claimed it for himself, taking it as plunder from the tomb. Part of him yearned to do the same.

He studied the laid out warrior, judging his height at about twenty hands from top of crown to sole of boots. His thick bones were strong, not wiry and thin like Restarian's. Whoever this man was, whether Nuada or Balor, he wasn't a true giant. This warrior was merely taller than most fae. Clearing away the dust surrounding the corpse, he was shocked to find the skeletal remains of two massive and once powerful wings. The bony structures caused Restarian to think of his own and shuddered.

He felt along the side of the warrior, finding cold metal beneath the dust of decay. From this he found a sword and a sheath, once connected by leather straps which had long ago turned to powder.

He turned it over and examined the strange carvings on the sheath. It seemed to depict a battle of winged warriors fighting against one-eyed giants. Wrapping his fingers around the grip, he drew it forth.

The sudden explosion of light completely filled the room, as if the sun itself had risen within. Had he not seen it for himself, he would never have believed the Sword of Light held such wondrous magic, and held it aloft with a grin.

"Niamh!" he screamed wildly and with joy. He had found it and would surely be rewarded by his lover. Even Nodrick would approve. "Niamh! Come and see what I've found!"

After several breaths, the light from the sword faded, and he lit a fairy spark in the air to dispel the darkness. The sword felt perfect in his hand—balanced and less awkward than even his father's. But he had no right to wield this weapon, it belonged to the Storm Warden. Giving it over would provide a means of entering Radviken's grace.

The blade at his side suddenly felt heavier, and he thought of his father Justarian. He was no warrior either, only a lowly Skygate sentry until sacrificed by Betarian to Sìth Morkur. Restarian suddenly understood what he must do.

Standing, he removed the belt, and slid off the Fainnen sword. In its place he tied on Claímh Soluis before once more securing the clasp. He placed the sword of his father in the tomb beside the fallen warrior and returned the lid of the coffin—laying to rest his warrior dreams.

Restarian lost his way among the dizzying maze, fumbling around for hours before finally emerging into the main chamber. The bonfire had long burned down to embers, and the rising sun tried to peek around the boulder into the cavern. Niamh waited outside with the Storm Warden, the pair huddled together over a bundle and watching intently as a Rider rolled it out.

"What is it?" Restarian asked. "What did you find?"

"Where've you been?" Niamh demanded. "We could have used your help pulling it out!"

"I was..."

She cut him off with a hand gesture and a shushing sound. The wrapped cloth rolled out, all gathered stared down at a magnificent sword.

"You promise you didn't touch it with your hands?" Nodrick demanded of Niamh. "It never came in contact with your skin?"

"Never. I was careful and took every precaution. I wrapped it in the cloth immediately."

"I don't understand," said Restarian, "how did you find..."

"While you were off doing gods know what, I found the tomb. The path I took ended with an open door into the room. It wasn't as elaborate as we'd hoped, but it held the corpse of an enormous warrior and I found this inside the casket."

Restarian suddenly worried she'd found his Fainnen blade after he'd left it behind. Willing his knees to hold steady, he leaned over for a good look at the weapon resting in its sheath. The knot in his stomach relaxed, and he remembered to breathe. Beautifully carved, it looked very much like the one on his side.

The Storm Warden wasted no time, grasping the handle and drawing the blade for all to see. It was magnificently polished and made of steel that seemed to shine on its own. Only, it didn't. It merely reflected the soft light of the rising sun.

Restarian suddenly knew they had found the wrong blade, for the weapon at his side had shone brilliantly when drawn. He whispered questions to Niamh. "There was no door? The tunnel merely ended with the room?"

"That's right, shh!"

"What was the warrior wearing? What kind of armor?"

"Be quiet! Nodrick is about to speak!"

"But this is important! Tell me about the armor the warrior was wearing!"

"It was steel, now shut up!"

Nodrick spun to face the gathered Storm Riders, holding the blade for all to see. "Today we begin the next phase in retaking our realm! With the Sword of Light in my possession, I am now the most powerful swordsman, and no one can oppose our might! When this blade is wielded in battle, none can defeat the bearer it has chosen to share its bond!

Cheers erupted among the Riders, calls for victory and to depose the usurper named O'Malley. With timid legs, Restarian stepped forward. "My lord," he said with a shaky voice. "You have the wrong blade."

"What are you talking about?" demanded Niamh. "Be quiet you fool!"

Nodrick turned slowly with anger burning in his eyes. In a low voice he growled, "I have the only blade. *The* blade. Do not forget your place, or your small role here will end. With the Sword of Light, I can find Radviken myself. You were always the backup plan."

Restarian stood taller, intent on correcting his earlier mistakes. "But that's not the true Claímh Soluis. I think this is."

He grasped the hilt on his side and drew it forth, holding it aloft. The explosion of light that followed was blinding, forcing everyone watching to look away. All but the fae prince blinked against the spots suddenly swimming in their vision.

"What is this treachery?" Nodrick demanded. "Did you really think you could take it for yourself?"

"No! I brought it out for you!" He lowered the blade, intent on handing it over, but the Storm Warden leapt into an offensive strike.

With jealous murder shining hotly in the man's eyes, Nodrick swung the steel in an arcing motion. Had the prince known anything of sword play, he would have possibly stood a chance against the superior fighter. Instead he closed his eyes and waited to die. Restarian flinched at the last moment, cowering and ducking with his own sword held to block the blow. It wasn't a move any swordsman would have made, for the blow should have slid off, glancing his own blade to the side while his opponent struck home. But when swords collided, they met with a deafening explosion.

A second flash of light accompanied the sound, and shards of steel flew all around. As the fae prince slowly opened his eyes, he witnessed every Storm Rider bowing down in reverence. Blinking away tears he turned to face his attacker, kneeling on the ground and holding a bloody arm filled with shrapnel. His sword of steel had disintegrated.

Dumbfounded, Restarian looked around for someone to explain. *I shouldn't be alive,* he thought. His eyes fell to the sword in his hand, now thrumming with lifeforce and softly glowing in the morning sun. *It's true,* he realized. *This blade cannot be defeated!* He focused then on Nodrick.

The warden's eyes were gone, replaced by shards of steel. More covered his body and he was drenched with his own blood. Restarian looked closer at the man's hand, mangled and dangling useless. *What have I done?* He lifted his eyes to view the others, bowing and murmuring in reverence. Every man stared with awe, whether for him or the sword it did not matter. He wielded it now.

Niamh was with the Riders. Though she did not kneel, her face reflected terror, most likely thinking of the pain and suffering she'd caused him. *You expect to die, don't you?* He *should* kill her, to repay the pain she dealt, but instead focused his anger on the bleeding wretch wailing before him. With a single swing of the blade Restarian removed the warden's head, sending it rolling to her feet.

All eyes remained fixed as he raised the sword into the air. The light of Claímh Soluis warmed every face as it beamed victory over his fallen attacker. The magic of the sword filled his body, and with a flutter, the cloak upon his back moved aside. The bones which once were wings emerged, and he felt them spread out as if muscled and strong, no longer hanging useless. He marveled at how the spider webs from the tunnels now clung, knitted like sinewy flesh and stretched as if eager to catch wind.

Filled with his connection to the sword, he pumped them up and down, lifting his body into the air and hovering above the kneeling army. He was more of a demon, now, than fae—a menacing sight with skeletal wings and eyes that glowed like red fire in the light of the sword. In that moment he chose his path.

"We *will* rescue Radviken," he announced, "and return him to rule over this land. Because of that you will follow *me*. Let none defy us retaking what rightfully belongs to our lord."

Chapter Thirty-One

"Luchorpán magic is fiercely guarded, but it is known they have ability to share with allies. The only literary reference regarding bestowment to a human occurred during the reign of the Tuatha de Dannan. During a battle against Dub, the luchorpán army united with humans. The unified force unexplainably appeared on the flanks of the enemy at precisely the right time to turn the battle. The claims of soldiers included whispers of magically transporting from a spot more than a league away."
– The Annals of History Book V, Passage 30

The stew actually tasted quite good, with bits of rabbit and leeks floating in the mixture. Boyd stirred it until the potatoes floating on the surface were soft and easily cut by his knife. He was getting annoyed by the sleeping campers, realizing they'd actually slept so soundly he could have slit their throats and been done with it all. But that was knowledge he needed then, and now they were close to awakening. Besides, breakfast was ready and he couldn't bear the thought of wasting it.

The first luchorpán stirred, stretching and yawning and blinking surprised eyes at Boyd.

"Good morning," the thief said merrily, "would you be having some stew?"

The little man jumped to his feet, drawing a blade and kicking the others awake. "We've got an intruder!" he screamed till they joined him with weapons drawn. "Which one of you had third watch?" he demanded from behind a thick red beard which hid most of his face. His emerald eyes flashed a bit of red around the edges as his anger flared.

One of the others pointed to a stocky fellow with a round belly. It was full like that of a man who loves his ales. "It was Clurich," he accused, and slipped a string of beads out of his pocket. Each was made from a different gem of vibrant colors in the order of a rainbow. "I'll take care of it," he said.

Boyd acted fast, asking, "Where are your bowls? I'm very hungry, but didn't want to steal and waited on you three to awaken." Squinting up at the sun, he added, "Though I didn't know you'd all be late risers. But it doesn't matter because the potatoes are finally ready!" He pulled the lid from the pot with flair, like a magician revealing a rabbit in a hat. The tasty smell wafted just where he'd hoped—into the nostrils of three hungry luchorpán.

"Who are you?" Clurich demanded. "And what're you doing in our camp?"

"Serving breakfast to answer the second question. As to the first, well," he paused, but not long enough to arouse suspicion. He sipped a bit of stew from the spoon to build suspense while he thought. *Markey would've talked about me and Piotr to Clurich*, he realized. "The name's Murdock Kelly, at your service." The name he chose was an old friend who used to frequent Tamee's when he was a boy. The rapscallion's exploits were legendary both in and outside the brothel.

"Get out," Clurich demanded.

"I would, but may we have breakfast first? I really am starving. Been wandering out here for three days. Can't remember the last time I ate."

"Three days?" the man holding the beads asked.

"Three," replied Boyd with an assertive nod. He hoped it would be long enough to throw them off. Maybe they wouldn't realize he was sent by Markey.

"And what are you looking for in the northern mountains?"

"Please promise not to laugh," he begged. "I'm looking for the luchorpán kingdom. My nanna told me I'm mix blooded, that my maw, gods rest her soul, was bedded by my paw who ran off not long after. She said he was a true luchorpán. That's why I'm up here, looking for my own kind."

"Where's your pack and your food for the trip?" Clurich asked, "Where's your weapon, for that matter? These woods are dangerous."

"Well, I had all that, but three Storm Riders stole my pack about a day and a half ago. I was looking for them when I stumbled upon your camp." He waved his dagger around like a sword, as if demonstrating what he'd meant to do to them if he'd found the Riders instead. "But you fellas ain't them by any stretch, so I made breakfast."

"It does smell good," the man holding the beads admitted.

"And his story seems plausible," Clurich agreed.

"Well, if your blood's good, then today's your lucky day, mate!" the first man said. He nodded to the little man holding the beads. "Douse him, Grainne."

Boyd knew what was coming and had an idea how it would turn out, but held his breath while offering his palm. With a sharp knife, Grainne cut a slice and held the beads aloft. They glowed vibrantly, despite the morning sun had fully risen.

"Congratulations," the first man said, pulling out a handful of bowls from his satchel. "We just happen to be travelin' to a place where like-blooded kinfolk are always welcome."

Boyd let out the breath he held. "Well then, that's something to eat to!"

The luchorpán holding the beads seemed irritated. He protested, "I still wanna check out his story, Osheen!"

The first nodded. "Do what you must, Grainne, but I doubt you'll find followers. I detected no lies from this cousin."

Clurich also appeared to have doubts. He eyed Boyd with deep suspicion but nodded toward Grainne. The little man suddenly blinked out of sight.

"Oh, nice trick!" Boyd exclaimed, assuming he had the same magic as Piotr. "Is he invisible?"

"Not in the least," Osheen explained. "He's gone away travellin'."

"Travellin'?"

"Aye, that's part of luchorpán magic, or didn't you know?"

"I honestly don't," Boyd admitted. "That's why I'm looking for the kingdom. I want to learn everything I can about my kinfolk."

Grainne suddenly popped up in a different spot, made a face as if he'd a new thought, then blinked away once more. A few seconds later he reappeared standing closer to the fire. "He's certainly alone, that's for sure."

"Then sit down and eat," barked Osheen.

Boyd dug a spoon into the stew and gobbled it down. His hunger was the only part of the story he didn't fabricate and had no trouble convincing the three luchorpán he was famished.

Chapter Thirty-Two

"Though they had disappeared in form, the stain of their presence had never departed our realm. The only hope for our progeny is to remove it by selection, or hope it filters itself in time. For us, it is too late."
— The Annals of History Book IX, First Passage

The iron dug deep into the wrists of Alistaria's slumbering form, and their sickening taint had worked into her body. Upon awakening, she leaned to the side and retched, emptying what little contents her stomach had retained. Despite a spinning head, her mind somehow remained focused on the vision she had experienced. Had she really walked within the Blossom, or was it all a dream? Even if her body had never left, the thoughts were remnants of knowledge she might not have discovered on her own.

Everything finally made sense. She would confirm the history of the people with the texts once she was free, but she was certain of the rest. Finally understanding the differences between the fae and human blossoms, Alistaria felt she could master her own with more study. Only the question of corruption remained. If Girtrán had spoken true, she could not wield it no matter how hard she tried. Except... He had been able.

She sat up, pushing aside the sickening aura of iron and its hold on her body. She concentrated on the act Girtrán had performed. If he spoke true, he had not corrupted the Deamhan out of malice, but used it to counter the stain within their bodies. *A stain like that afflicting the Deamhan Palace.* Corruption could be worked, even if it could not be channeled, but *how* remained the question. She would have to figure it out if she were to cleanse the land for good.

The Tempest, she suddenly realized, *was a cleansing event.* In the human realm it had hastened decay and welcomed the Ganshee to feast upon the remnants. *But what's its purpose here? How did Girtrán place this veil over the Deamhan Palace, and why did the Deamhan slumber during its height?* Her mind returned to their conversation—whether it had really occurred or not. *His hope was to purify his* mother *and her offspring.* But what of the rest of what he said?

The stain of the Tuatha de Dannan resided in their descendants. If his mother held the blood of the gods, so did he. Girtrán's mother was Fainne, and therefore so was her son. *So then,* are all fae—sharing blood with a descendance of giants from a faraway place. *No fae is pure of blood, the way we were before they arrived. Except for Markey and me.* Then she remembered his eyes. They were as brown as hers—the only other fae she'd ever met with eyes neither green nor blue. *That detail must hold meaning.*

The Dannan changed the Blossoms, she realized. *These are relics devised to harness power given to the races of fae, human, and luchorpán by the Great Spirit. A power,* she suddenly understood, *the races could not naturally wield without aid of the relics after their blood had mixed with that of the gods.*

"Clíodhna could wield corruption to a small extent," she said aloud, "and she never bled for the Blossom." She could also travel upon the Tempest as if it also gave her sight. *But only when her people slumbered.* That meant, she was pure enough in fae blood not only to birth a child free of the taint, but to also possess limited access to the gifts. *And so was Girtrán, if he could enter the Blossom!*

Alistaria abruptly retched once more, this time at her knowledge instead of the iron. A pure born fae could wield the power of the Bláth de Saol without bleeding for it. All of its gifts, that is, except for corruption which had been changed by the Dannan. For that they must draw from sources around them with Dannan blood. *Or from the iron beneath the palace.* Iron they so greedily mined.

Her mind returned to Tempest and how Radviken had brought it through the portal to balance the perfection of the realm he created with the Blossom. She also thought about Girtrán, how he drew upon it to eventually purge the Banshee Queen of her remaining Dannan blood. She thought about both men and how ancient each had turned without the Blossom to refresh their youth. And then she knew. *Corruption isn't the stain of the Tuatha.* No, it had been one of the original gifts—the blossom changed by the Dannan. *It was originally Time.* Time is the ultimate corruptor.

A storm of Dannan-influenced corruption lingered over the Deamhan Palace, and Radviken had pulled it through the portal for his own benefit, not for that of his people. He craved youth with an arrogance that welcomed the purging winds of the storm, bending it to reverse his aging. When Tempest swept across Enatherr, it drew life from the crops in the field. Life that time had fleetingly granted to plants and animals. The Tempest drew it forth from those as they died and fed it to Radviken, fueling his lust for control over all elements as well as Time. That had been his trade with Sìth Morkur—his ability to draw upon Time itself.

But Time is not to be taken, handled, or harnessed. It can only be borrowed, saved, and used. Alistaria could not wield the corruptive gift of time because she tried to draw upon it like the other blossoms, and also because the stain of the Dannan interacted differently with her. She had to use it just as Clíodhna had, gathering it around her like a veil. Alistaria closed her eyes and concentrated.

Puca, she called, but he did not answer.

"Puca," she said aloud, but he did not reply.

"Sìth Morkur!" she screamed until her temples trembled and her eyes fogged over. After she was finished screaming, she slumped exhausted onto the ground.

"You know the answer," a disembodied voice echoed in her head, "now figure out the question."

"The question...," she muttered... *What is the question?*

She had grown tired of this game, sick from the cat and mouse and felt like a wrung sponge, twisted and squeezed until every drop of knowledge was discovered. "I don't care about the question," she whispered. "I want to go back and put right the realms."

"Good for you," the voice of Girtrán replied. "Now figure out *how*."

She hadn't the strength to respond and fell asleep against the cool stone of the ancient floor.

"Sìth Morkur!" Piotr heard the shout and ran toward it.

The voice was certainly Alistaria's, weakened and hopeless with its plea. Down the hall to his right, several guards laughed and mocked her misery.

Her cries had come from behind an iron door, heavy and impenetrable. He could only rescue her with keys. *What would Boyd do,* he wondered, *if he were here?* The thought of his friend bobbing upside down with tiny wings brought a smile, and he nearly laughed aloud at the trouble he would have also had brought with his plan. Then sadness replaced humor, as he realized his buddy was as far out of reach as Alistaria behind this door. He needed help, a bit of luck, actually.

He turned to head the way he'd come, to examine the guard post and see where they kept the keys, but a low whine caused him to turn. At the end of the hall he saw the impossible, a small dog with mangy spots and a broken tail. As it stared up at Piotr, he could tell it had only a single eye.

"Lucky?" he asked with amazement.

The broken tail wagged in the dog's usually lazy way, then ran off down the other corridor. Piotr rushed to follow.

This can't be, he marveled. *He was lost at Markey's palace. Surely, he can't be here.* But he caught glimpse of the animal twice more, and there was no denying it was Lucky. Piotr followed him around the final turn and nearly ran into a group of three lounging guards. They were tossing dice and complaining loudly about their duty. Forgetting he was invisible, the thief panicked and jumped back into the hall, pressing against the stone and hoping they wouldn't hear the beating of his heart.

The little dog nudged his leg for attention, and no more argument remained that this wasn't Lucky. He stared dumbfounded while the animal pointed his nose toward the guards. The key was in there, it had to be. What other reason could there be for the animal's strange appearance? He shook his head at the little animal, refusing to do what it wanted out of fear.

Lucky let out a *pffft*.

"What was that?" one of the soldiers demanded. "Which one of you broke wind?"

By then then the smell was so obnoxious it was impossible to ignore. The sound of chairs scraping against stone announced the guards would walk his way.

"It wasn't me," one of them argued.

"It had to've been you!" another insisted. They were about to come to blows. If they didn't quiet down, the jailer would come and sort them out.

And there it was.

The Boyd-like idea he needed suddenly popped into his mind. *It's feasible,* he considered, though there was no guarantee it would work. In the end, it was his fondness for his friend's foolery that made him try. He stepped around the corner and spoke with authority.

"What the blazes are you fools doing? Have you forgotten you're on duty?"

All three turned and popped to attention, saluting the illusion surrounding Piotr. "Sorry sir," one of them barked.

"So you gamble while ignoring your duties?" Piotr asked, using the best impression of the man he could. It was difficult, but so far, the men bought it.

"We were just about to make our rounds, sir!" one of the soldiers insisted.

"Hmm," Piotr replied, as unconvinced as the officer would have been. "Give me the keys to the queen's cell. I'm to bring her to the new council."

"Should we accompany, sir?" the brightest of the three asked.

"No need," Piotr replied, "not if it meant interrupting your game!" He picked up the dice and examined them closely. "What's this?" he asked. "Whose are these?"

Two sets of eyes focused on the taller of the three.

"He's been winning tonight, hasn't he?"

"Why, yes!" the pair of losers agreed. "How'd you know?"

He placed them in his pocket and said, "Because they're loaded—weighted on the single so the six will always roll." He moved closer to the taller man and worked his true thief's magic—sleight of hand. His deft fingers quickly transferred the dice to the man's pocket. Stepping back, he accused, "I'll bet he has another *normal* pair in his pocket!"

"I don't sir!" the guard protested, "I swear!"

"Prove it! Empty your pockets onto the table!"

The soldier did, producing not one, but two pairs of dice. A lucky guess turned out to be correct! His partners eyed him angrily as he tried every excuse he could muster.

"I'll not discipline you this time," Piotr said. "I'll trust these men to ensure you never cheat them out of wages again!" He extended his hand, and the shorter of the three men handed over a set of silver keys without taking his eyes from the cheater. "Have your way with him, but don't make too much noise. I'm sending down another prisoner soon."

As quickly as he could, Piotr left them behind, cringing at the thuds, slaps, grunts, and groans now coming from the tiny room and wishing they would take their time. He turned the corner and nearly collided with two more guards escorting a dazed and badly bruised Palathia.

"Sir!" one of the newcomers said with surprise. "But you were just..." He pointed over his shoulder the way they'd come.

Piotr quickly thought for proper excuse. "I forgot something and came to tell you in person instead of waiting for you to finish up and return. I want this one placed in the cell next to the Banshee Queen."

Both guards eyed him suspiciously, then shrugged.

"Well, go on then!" he commanded. "Lead the way."

With strong hands, they turned Palathia around and shoved her in the opposite direction. She staggered, but found her feet and kept walking. After a few turns, they reached the desired cell. Piotr slid the key home and turned, opening the door and holding it while entered and tossed the mage inside.

"That'll be all," he told the soldiers. They were almost to the door and out of his life. Soon he could get on with his mission of freeing both women.

"Who the blazes are you?" a voice demanded from behind.

Piotr turned to find the real jailer staring him down. Thinking quick, he shoved the two guards as they were leaving the cell, slamming the door and shutting them inside. Their cries for help would soon draw more soldiers, so Piotr acted as fast as he could.

He took off running toward the jailer at full speed, not even wavering when the man drew his sword. Just before they crashed into each other, he raised a veil of invisibility and stepped to the side. He hugged the wall as closely as he could, praying the Kern officer wouldn't feel or hear his breathing.

"What in the blazes?" the man demanded, then frantically began to run up and down the corridor looking for Piotr.

As soon as the real jailer rounded the far corner, the thief hurried to Alistaria's cell, slipped in the key, and stepped inside. He shut the door firmly from within. As soon as he did, a thought struck him. He was behind a cell door. Slowly, he glanced down and searched for a keyhole. With a heavy sigh, he mentally kicked himself for being such a fool. There was no place to insert it from the inside.

Just as if Boyd had been along, the mission had ended the worst possible way—with three prisoners, instead of one. From the other side of the door, he heard Lucky barking. It sounded almost like the little dog was laughing.

Chapter Thirty-Three

Dub, Dothur, and Dian were their names, the sons of Carmán, the witch of the surrounded sea. Their blight cursed this island, just as the last, but the Tuatha de Dannan knew these foes. They fought valiantly against Darkness, bravely against Evil, and heroically against Violence. But they could not kill the brothers. The war ended with stalemate, eternal banishment for each side. Woe be any realm to encounter all three without the power of the Tuatha.
— Annals of History Book IX, Passage 40.

"We've been through every inch of this palace," Conner Liam complained. "There's nothing here!"

"It has to be," Markey insisted. "Look at those pillars. It's obvious they're set to collapse."

Torian had been eyeing them, examining every inch so closely his head hurt. "How deep into the mountain are we?" he asked the others.

Conner considered the question carefully, "Several stories, deep enough we're at the river's waterline."

The river. That gave Torian reason to pause. "What could topple an entire palace without magic?"

"A thousand men with pick axes," O'Malley grumbled.

"Too slow," argued Conner.

"And too much effort. Look, this mountain is made of solid rock, right?"

"And iron," the general explained. "These were once mines."

Mines. Just as in Fainnotherr, beneath the Deamhan Palace, Torian thought. "That's it! What happened to the old shafts?"

Markey shrugged. "I'm assuming Radviken had them sealed, especially knowing the portal would open up in this room."

"Not unless he used them for his own device."

"Explain," demanded Conner.

Torian spread out the drawings on the stone. "It's right here. Three passages lead into the hall from these points, each leading to stairwells and the guest quarters above. But the kitchens lay beyond the great hall, which makes sense when providing for a banquet or feast. But the position is horrible, when considering logistics."

"Jaana complained of that often, said they were so far away from the rest of the castle, the servants were riding the dumbwaiters up and down instead of making the walk."

"What are dumbwaiters?"

"Mechanical lifts," explained Conner. "Instead of lugging food and other items up and down stairs, the kitchen was designed to lower from a point up above, and store it in the cellars below."

Torian laid out the map of the surrounding city. A magnificent drawing showed the palace set high upon the hillside, with the river splitting around it to run due west, with another branch tracing south and east. The rest of the city was built on the west and southern sides.

"This makes no sense, either," he said.

"What's that?" asked Markey.

"The biggest problem for every city is the matter of sewage. In Fainnotheria, we let it flow downstream of our water supply, letting nature wash it away. How does it work for Norgaard?"

Conner pointed to the western branch of the river. "It's carried from here, away from the populated areas in the south."

"Okay, that makes sense, but won't work for the palace. We're too far east and on the wrong slope of the hill."

"That may be why Radviken built the privy towers."

"Oh, yes," said Torian, "the chutes Piotr and Boyd climbed."

"Now that you mention it," Conner said, "it *would* have been easier to route water beneath the palace and carry off to the west."

"Unless he had a different use for that flow." Torian accused.

"What are you thinking?" O'Malley demanded.

Torian slammed his finger on the cellars nestled beyond the kitchen. "Water is the strongest force in nature." He drew an imaginary line from his finger northward, toward the western branch of the river. "If a shaft were to exist here, it could lead to flood gates in the north. Water could easily be routed into this hall." He rested his eyes on the pillar closest to the kitchens. "That one," he said. "Would you call that loadbearing?"

"I wouldn't dare call it otherwise," Conner Liam agreed.

"Then we know the how, if we can find the where."

"I don't like it," Markey admitted. "The switch could be in the kitchens, but it's a dead end, and there'd be no escape for the poor sap who pulls the switch. I doubt anyone would be fool enough to commit to the task, especially not Radviken. He was too full of himself to make a sacrifice like that."

"Unless he had a thousand witnesses watch him walk in to martyr himself, but also had a secret way out," Conner suggested.

"Take me to the dumbwaiters," Torian demanded. "Show me how they work."

The mechanism was complex and well designed, but simple to operate. The crank turned both ways, ferrying a platform wide enough for eight servants to stand abreast. If you turned it one direction, the lift descended and vice versa. But nothing was out of the ordinary or appeared to operate a gate.

The cellars themselves were unremarkable, with smooth stone along the northwest wall. The room was neatly stacked with food stores, barrels of flour, salted fish, and wine casks lining the walls. Salted hams hung from the ceiling. Nothing resembled a gate.

"This had to be it," Torian said, defeated.

"We'll keep looking," Markey said. "But we're sitting ducks here and need to get behind the defenses in case the enemy returns."

They had even less time than he thought, as horns sounded in the great hall. The next sound they heard was a deep and mournful howling. Hellhounds had made it through the portal.

"We're trapped in here," Conner growled.

Torian picked up his spear while the other men drew their swords. Only six riders accompanied them, so they were a small force. They formed a shield wall before moving down the long corridor to the hall.

"Trapped! And we didn't find the gate," Conner said. "I think you're right about the layout. A sudden rush of water onto that pillar would surely topple the structure."

"Then we have to find the mechanism," Torian agreed.

"What if it isn't here on the inside, but upstairs?" Markey suddenly asked as they marched.

"Halt!" Torian commanded. "Double time back to the dumbwaiter!"

"What's your plan, boy?" O'Malley asked as they ran.

He pointed a thumb toward the main hall. "To go through there would be certain death. If shadow's spilling through, then we won't make it behind our lines—not with all the traps we laid." Rapid barks and painful howls let them know some had already sprung. "We'll ride the lift up to ground level and quickly search there before joining our force from the rear. But we *must* find the mechanism at all costs."

They climbed aboard, bunching tightly together. Torian turned the crank, and they lifted three stories upward to ground level. Though the climb felt like an eternity, only a few minutes had gone by and they soon found themselves standing on a loading dock. The apparatus here was exactly as it appeared below. Nothing indicated it could lift a gate or open a spillway.

"It has to be here!" Torian complained, having wasted all the time there was to spare.

"We have to get to the battle," Conner urged, "our army is without a general!"

"He's right," Markey said, "we have to attend our troops and help turn the tide. You're welcome to stay and search, but we have to fight." The king and his general trotted off with their soldiers, leaving Torian where he stood.

He had never felt such uncertainty, torn between winning a battle or finding the means to topple the palace and save the realm if the time came. Torian, who always reacted without hesitation, faltered. His grip angrily tightened around Areadbhar, willing it to react how it had done before, but found the spear lifeless and cold.

Choosing to fight, his feet set in motion and carried him swiftly toward the fray. He yearned for wings as he ran toward the entrance to the keep.

His ears picked up the howls coming from within, and the grip of his spear abruptly warmed. He stole a glance at the tip, feeling the fiery glow warm his face. *Both times when danger is present*, he realized. He felt his wings emerge through his tunic, and he beat them against the wind as he ran, slowly rising above the courtyard. Then he sped headlong toward the danger, passing over both Markey and General Liam.

The howls grew louder as he entered the keep, joined by screams of men and growls of unimaginable beasts. His feet never hit the stairs as he descended, gliding toward the chilling sounds of pain and dying. His spear was fully engulfed in the strange fire by the time he arrived. Torian pulled to a stop above the shield wall, scanning the lines for weakness and seeing none. It held, despite the unstoppable force spilling through. This was the full invasion force.

Markey and Conner soon panted up beneath him, eyes growing wide as several ballistae impaled a beast mid charge against the line.

"Your men hold well," Torian said to the king. A group of fifty Draugars were racing to attack the humans' weakest position.

"Aye," Markey agreed, "but move the archers to cover the right flank, Conner!"

Torian turned. "No," he warned, "that's a ruse! Fire on the left!"

Both king and general turned, just as sixteen hellhounds charged the strength of the unit.

"Archers! Fire to port!" Conner cried, and arrows flew into the charging horde. Five fell harmlessly to the stone floor.

Laughter filled the hall.

Torian lifted his eyes from the fallen beasts, focusing on the swirling portal and the two creatures now emerging.

"We are three," one of the newcomers said.

"And three are we," his brother agreed.

Thankfully, there were still only two.

CHAPTER THIRTY-FOUR

"The relics were a wonderful gift to their descendants, but will serve no purpose after she is born. She will remove the stain from both their hearts and bodies, and the Tuatha de Dannan will no longer rule over our realm."
– A note found in the Annals of History Book IX, signed Girtrán I.

The Puca's laughing woke Alistaria. Looking around, she realized she was once more within the Blossom. The orb appeared oddly different with her new perspective and she no longer focused only on its corruptive nature, instead identifying the ebbs and flows of the tidewaters of time. What was once future quickly became past, and the now was simultaneously the future for others. She found she understood the entire concept without confusion.

"That's how you Sìth travel, isn't it?" she asked, and the Puca nodded. "When Morkur carried Markey and Piotr through the portal, he simply chose different places in the pool to dip into. I'm amazed by it, but not sure how our Blossom is affected. I know it has something to do with the Tempest, but that's all. I don't think we can transcend timelines like you can."

"Once again you are correct in finding the knowledge, Alistaria, but you'll need to be certain if you are to again approach the orb."

"The only part I'm confused about is where the Tempest originated. It isn't from the Blossom, but it's certainly controlled by it or Radviken wouldn't have been able to bring it to Enatherr." She pulled herself onto her feet and walked closer to where he stood with eyes reflecting the swirling mass. She frowned. "I have that part wrong, don't I? The Tempest isn't controlled by the Blossom, rather the other way around. The Tempest is a separate entity, something left over from the time of the Tuatha de Dannan."

The Puca said nothing.

"That's it. I don't know where they went, or why, but they had to leave behind something when they did. If their essence is spread among all the fae—enough Girtrán was able to corrupt the Deamhan as Banshees—then what's left in the air around their palace is the source."

Another voice joined them from the entrance to the room. "Use it, then," Girtrán urged. "Use it and free yourself from your prison, then reset the balance between the realms."

She stared back at him with thoughts swirling as violently as the vapors in the orb. *But what if this is all a trick, to expose me to an evil—a darkness—that fells the entire realm? What if this action actually lets the darkness into our realm?*

That's assuming, she could actually manipulate the swirling orb this time.

Alistaria drew in and held a deep breath then let it out very slowly. Her eyes followed the swirling passage of time, then reached out with a single hand. She did not grab for the vapor as before, instead reaching where it was going to be. It flowed into a tiny pool within her cupped palm. Drawing it free, she studied the structure of it more closely and willed it to stretch out with her mind into a line.

"All points of time," she said softly, "in a single strand. Girtrán, you didn't change their appearance, you made the Banshee what we could have been if a single point of history had changed. It wasn't corruption, it was the wrong timeline altogether."

"You are ready to study the books your people have found," the Puca advised. "Recreate the timeline, and learn how to harness and use the power of the Tuatha de Dannan alongside your own."

"But I don't have access to the Blossom, I..." She broke off, recalling her last lesson. "The Blossom has no bearing on me because these powers come naturally without the taint of the Tuatha de Dannan. I should be able to access it from the realm itself!"

She placed the swirling mass of vapor back into the orb and held out her hands with palms facing upward. Two fireballs formed, and she tossed them into the air before creating two more. Juggling these took effort, but she succeeded without dropping a single one. It was as if she could see the place each would land along with the preciseness of its arrival. She abruptly clapped her hands and the fireballs disappeared.

Girtrán nodded his approval and smiled like a kindly grandfather. "Rule over them all," he said to Alistaria. "Love them and be patient, but end the conflict I created out of necessity so you may emerge. Be everything I wasn't, and create a lasting legacy of unity." Then he called for Sìth Morkur, who arrived without delay. "I'm finally ready," the ancient king said, "to fulfill my bargain to you."

"Your soul is given over freely?" the spirit asked.

"Yes, both now, and at the natural end of my lifespan."

With a sigh of obvious relief as he unyoked his heavy burden, Girtrán released his connection to the Bláth de Saol and fell into the Sìth's waiting arms.

Piotr watched as Alistaria peacefully slept. She appeared restful, a sight he wished he could reproduce in himself. But sleep would not bring him the same comfort, not with his anxiety over their predicament. He dared not fall asleep, not now, with soldiers looking for him.

He thought about Boyd, wondering if he was even alive much less doing well without him, and sent up a quick prayer to watch over his friend. They should never have parted, at least not in this situation, he could have used his friend's charm and wit to get out of this cell. But at least he had Lucky. *Where is that dog now, and how did he get here?* he wondered.

Now he was alone and in a fine pickle, lying in the corner and remaining invisible in case the soldiers returned. They knew by now he had a key, and at least one of them would be angry about the beating he took. He was certain they were searching each cell, probably using someone gifted in sight. But at least he had Alistaria's peacefully resting form to look over. Her eyes were open. They stared directly at him and she smiled.

"Hello, Piotr. You came to visit my dreams too?" she asked.

"I wish this *was* a dream," he replied.

She looked around, smelling her chains of iron and grimacing. Iron always seemed to bother her more than anybody else, he noticed. In his short time knowing he was fae, he had wondered why the metal never bothered him except for occasionally feeling ill to the stomach. It seemed to affect the fae in varying degrees, but her the most.

Alistaria stood and brushed off her clothing. "Are you ready to go?" she asked.

"We can't," he said, waving the key in the air. "No locks on this side. Though I may be able to open those." He pointed to her shackles and chains.

She stared down, as if channeling the gifts she'd lost or simply judging the craftsmanship. A black cloud formed around them, swirling and weaving within each link and lock. Abruptly they broke apart and fell to the floor with a rattle, crumbling into reddish powder as they did. Alistaria stretched her back with sudden relief from their shed weight—both physically and emotionally unburdened.

"How did you do that?" Piotr couldn't believe his eyes.

"Come," she urged, "I don't have time to explain now, but I will. Please tell me you didn't come alone." She paused as if only just noticing he was veiled and invisible. "Nice use of your gift, by the way."

"Thanks. No, we have a small team working to free the Deamhan upstairs. The fighting may have already begun."

"Then we certainly have no time to lose." She turned to face the door, examining it as she had the chains."

"Alistaria, Captain Palathia is in the next cell. If you're breaking us out, we must stop and retrieve her as well."

"Who? I don't recall that name."

"Palathia, she's part of Torian's Tuatha."

"Torian? Is he here as well, then? Wait, no, of course not. They would have blocked the portal to both humans as well as Deamhan."

Piotr watched with amazed wonder as the door suddenly crumbled into a heap of the same reddish powder as the chains. "How are you doing that?" he insisted.

"I can wield the final blossom," she said. "I can at last wield them all."

"But how? Does this mean your loyalists have won?"

"No, but I've found I no longer need the Blossom and can tap all powers where they naturally reside."

"I'm sorry," he said with confusion, "I don't understand."

"Things have changed, brother, as you'll soon see. I *will* explain, but first we must hurry."

They stepped into the hall and Piotr quickly turned the key in the door between them and Palathia. He rushed in, but skidded to a halt. The iron around his friend was coated in the misty swirls of corruption and fell away to powder as soon as he arrived. He heaved the beautiful woman to her feet, and she fell into his arms with an embrace.

"Can you heal her?" he asked Alistaria.

"Not here, not surrounded by the iron and so far from the roots. I still need access to those."

Palathia stared wide-eyed at the queen. "Thank you, your majesty."

"I know you," Alistaria realized. "You're the Tuatha who almost fried me atop the mountains. I hope you've found better control of your fairy spark," she said with a grin.

"I did," the captain promised, shyly looking up at a hugging Piotr.

"She's amazing!" Piotr added, planting a kiss on her cheek. "She led the squad and came up with the plan to sneak past the shield..." He stopped midsentence, suddenly blushing as both women exchanged knowing smiles, his crush on Palathia now visible to them both.

Alistaria led the way into the hallway. "Let's get moving," she said, "we need to hurry."

"Stop!" a voice demanded from the end of the hall. Three Kern stood in their way, including the jailer.

Piotr looked over his shoulder and found three more had moved to flank. He immediately raised the veil of invisibility around him and his companions and prepared for whatever came.   " Y o u can't get by us, not with your tricks like before," the jailer claimed. A mage stepped out of the shadows to linger behind the officer. As soon as he emerged, Piotr's veil disappeared in a puff of mist. They were revealed.

"Alistaria," Piotr said, "Torian told me what happened in the Deamhan Palace, and I understand you're not a fighter, but Palathia will need your help if your powers are back."

Her words shocked him when she said, "We don't need to fight, for they're about to let us walk past them all."

By Piotr's expression, Alistaria knew she could never make him understand. Even Palathia seemed unconvinced and stood ready to fight off the Kern soldiers. But the time for fae infighting was over, as she finally held the key to forever ending their strife.

In her earlier attempts at unity, she had missed one crucial element—the inherent nature of people. As individuals they're mostly loving and kind, save a few outliers with evil intent. But, as a whole, they ultimately live their lives in constant fear and often allow their selfish needs to motivate their behavior. That was how tyrants like King Betarian held power over them, by exposing their fear and using it as a bargaining chip for more. He had twisted their resentment and anger toward the Deamhan to fuel his grip over Fainne lives, ultimately seizing their liberties not by force, but by their willful offering.

King Girtrán had proven a different kind of ruler who, after meeting face to face, her opinions of had changed. Though she still disagreed with his actions of creating the Banshees, and he ultimately deserved blame for creating the centuries of fighting that continued thereafter, he knew true unity can only come after strife. There is a reason civilization never emerges on lush tropical islands or in harsh barren climates. Those places are either too easy or too difficult for people to develop sophistication. He was merely the catalyst to prepare the world for what it truly needed, a unified force against the real threat—the Shadow Realm.

When she first took charge of the fae, she had forced them to band together but never gave them motivation to do so. She also offered no relief from their fears and provided no comforting. That mistake opened the ears and minds of Fainnotheria to the whisperings of Brechan and Korl. But now she was stronger than they.

Turning to the jailer, she said simply, "Our quarrel is not with you or your men. Take us to the new council so I may discuss my terms."

The mage standing behind the jailer stepped forward. "Our orders were to kill her if she escaped," he said.

"You'll step into a cell, Banshee," the officer growled in return.

"So I may simply walk out once more and we do this again and again?" She waved her hand in the air, and every cell door and iron fitting suddenly and immediately became dusty piles of rusted powder. "No," she said, "this prison will not hold me, nor do you have the means to do so elsewhere. I will not harm you, nor will my friends. But you will take me to Brechan and Korl."

The mage replied with a firebolt, one aimed directly for Alistaria. She did not step aside, nor did she try and block. She caught it and held it up for all to see before snuffing it between both hands.

"Do it again," she asked the mage politely. "Do it now."

The man blinked eyes wide with sudden fear.

"Go on," the jailer urged.

"I... I cannot!"

"Why not?" the officer demanded.

"Because I... I can't find the..."

"Because I severed his connection to the Bláth de Saol," she explained. Turning to Palathia, she said, "Even yours." And to Piotr she added, "Yours is gone as well."

Palathia stood with mouth agape as she struggled to find her gifts. "They're gone! I... I can't even create a fairy spark!"

"Do you pledge your allegiance to me as your queen?" Alistaria demanded. "Do you recognize me as the queen of all fae?"

"I do! Yes, your majesty!" Palathia swore. She and Piotr knelt immediately before her, and she placed tender hands on each of their shoulders. "Then I bestow upon each of you the full powers of the Blossom, to use in service of Fainnotheria and the true crown. I choose not to kill or use my gifts for violence, but I grant you freedom to exercise your own judgement when dealing with both the Shadow Realm and those who oppose our unified kingdom. Now rise."

"You don't have that kind of power," the jailer accused nervously. "You're bluffing."

But the mage interjected. "Brechan severed her connection to the Blossom. There's no way she could have these gifts, much less to bestow and take them away!"

"My offer is for all fae, Kern or root tender, Fainne, or Deamhan. Whoever wants to follow me will receive the gifts as long as they follow my laws," she said to the soldiers. "Choose your side in the battle to come. Those who stand at my side will wield both the gift and my protection. Any who oppose me will be crushed."

All at once, the three soldiers behind Alistaria knelt, soon followed by the mage and two others. Only the jailer remained standing.

"This is mutiny," he said. "And she's a Banshee!"

Palathia stepped forward. "I don't know how, but I felt something just now, when she restored my powers. She *is* fae. In fact, I believe she's the purest in Fainnotheria. As she said, you are either with us, or destroyed."

"I'll never!" the officer proclaimed.

Alistaria nodded sadly, and fire sprung from Palathia's hands. It burned hotter than any she had ever wielded, and the jailer died without even a scream.

"Come," Alistaria said, "we have a battle to stop."

Chapter Thirty-Five

*"Everything changed in a single instant, the moment
I donned the crown, but still I yearned to be Nastauria
instead of myself and never truly found the queen
within. The day I earned the loyalty of my people
though, was the day I walked among them as myself."*
– Queen Alistaria of Fainnotherr, First of Her Name.

Alistaria emerged into a scene she'd hoped to never see. Fainnotheria had descended into chaos. When the Deamhan rose up against the new council, they did not fight alone. Hundreds of Fainne remained loyal to her ideals and picked up anything they could find to fight off the Kern. The soldiers, duty sworn when they put on the gold, fought valiantly for the new government, whether they accepted their rule or not. Amidst the clanging of Fainnen silver against golden armor, fire, ice, and fairy spark lit up the city. The fierce fighting continued for hours and had split the city in two factions.

"Let us enter first," Palathia urged, flanked by Piotr and the Kern who pledged loyalty in the prisons.

"No, they must see me as confident," Alistaria insisted.

She rose into the air, not by use of her wings, but on a flowing sea of corruption just as Clíodhna had when alive. She hoped the spectacle would catch the attention of the entire room, and it mostly did. The cloud lifted her high, and she ignored the Kern darting back and forth in battle. One by one the soldiers noticed her and dove in to attack. She repelled with a shield now flowing and shimmering around her body.

Abruptly, every mage lost their powers, except for those who accompanied Alistaria into battle. One by one, invisible bonds seized the Kern, plucking them from the air like butterflies held by their wings. They struggled against the swirling corruption, unable to do anything but watch the queen and wait for her to speak. Her aura of corruption now filled the entire space around the great tree, and the fighting ended with all eyes upon her.

"New council!" she shouted in the hall, her voice eerily amplified and echoing throughout the city. "Show yourselves and face your queen."

Several heartbeats passed, but finally Brechan and Korl emerged with several others. Some Alistaria recognized, but others she did not.

"I've severed your connection to the Bláth de Saol," she told them. "You are powerless."

"We'll replant it," Brechan said, holding the gems in a pile in his hands. "I don't know how you recovered your gifts, but as long as I hold these, you cannot take it away from me a second time."

"They're worthless against the true power," she said, filling the air above the tree with shimmering fairy spark. She was finally positioned where all would see and hear. "Korl," she said with true sadness in her voice. "Your betrayal hurt me the most, to know my teacher, the tutor of many root tenders over several generations, had chosen hatred over love and desired to remain living in fear."

Even from her vantage point, she could tell he was very ill and had not recovered from whatever his ailment had been. He appeared ashen and pale, bearing the sickness throughout his body. Alistaria flew downward, lowering herself until she loomed above him as if in authority.

"You do not fear me?" he asked quizzically, lifting a dagger. "I could kill you standing so close."

"I do not fear my friends."

"I'm not your friend," he said. "I don't befriend my enemies."

"Then you're a fool and do not know who your real enemies are." She thrust out her hand and connected with his chest. He tried to pull away, but found his body drawn in by the powerful presence of healing. It held him against her palm, unable to resist as she probed his mind, body, and soul.

Speaking so all could hear, she explained, "I did not understand what had injured the trees and you until now. I could not comprehend because I was limited by the Bláth de Saol—a mere relic modified by a disappearing race as they merged into the fae. But our gift does not come from an artifact, the Blossom is merely a conduit from the real source, the energy binding together three realms. In ours we are connected to the gifts differently than the other races of man or luchorpán. As our gifts differ, so are the maladies facing each. Your wound is from the realm of shadow, but will trouble you no longer."

Korl slumped to the ground the moment she released her palm, breathing deeply and with color returning to his skin.

"I forgive you, Korl, but will not tolerate such insolence should it happen again." She then turned her attention to Brechan, finding him staring up with stark realization. There was no way to defeat the Queen of the Fae. She addressed the people looking on, "We are only strong while united, as weakness and vulnerability come from division. Look around at the dead among you—brothers and sisters slain by each other's hands. Brechan, use the pearl in your hand to resurrect the dead. If you're so great, restore them all. Or, if you choose, raise only those you call Fainne and use them to defeat me once and for all."

He tried. Holding the gem tightly in his hand, he squeezed until blood began to flow. With all his effort, he willed the people to rise. Knowing he'd failed, he doubled down, adding the diamond of power, but still she blocked him.

"Hatred is a sign of weakness, Brechan, and you are pathetically impotent. You are a killer—a murderer. I know it was you who killed the elders, and for that crime you will pay. But sadly, my dungeons lack doors and so I have no room for you in Fainnotheria. But we are also at war with the Shadow Realm, and I cannot trust you to roam in exile while that shadow is at large. We've already lost

Restarian, and I'll not allow my enemies to work together. You will die, but not by my hand."

"I don't understand," he said with a trembling voice.

She pointed at the gemstones in his hands. "Choose one—the method of your choosing shall be your death."

He held up an aquamarine.

Alistaria cringed at his choice, but the sentence would stand. "Hold it to your mouth," she said, "and breathe in what it has to offer. I allow you this one use of the gift, to end your own life."

He wasted no time, lungs immediately choking and coughing as they filled from within. A horrible way to die, drowning, but it allowed him to demonstrate fully his hatred for Alistaria. With his choice, he lived a few moments longer. That boon was all he deserved. After a few minutes, he collapsed on the floor in a puddle of sea water.

"I do not need the pearl," she said to the fae, and one by one the dead began to rise – all except Brechan. Healed and whole, their wounds disappeared and those who had fallen stared with confusion at the hovering queen.

"Each of you may share in this power, one which may not be taken away by stealing a blossom. The only price is loyalty, for I may take it or give it at my discretion. All who wish to share in this power—in all the gifts of the Bláth de Saol—kneel and swear allegiance to your one true queen."

She released her grip on the fighters and waited. One by one, knees touched the ground. Not a single person refused and not a single oath was given falsely. Through a mixture of fear and awe, they swore devotion.

"Now rise," she said, "with hand over heart and recite one more pledge. Repeat after me the solemn oath to a united people, the scorned free from damages and the once offending forgiven. Stand proudly and never kneel again, for the very existence of our people represents brotherly love and sisterhood. The fae must always stand for unity."

Once the oaths were made, she pointed to the sky and the city was freed from the shield. "Now, every Kern and root tender must follow me," she said, "to forge a weapon against a foe far more deserving of our wrath."

The entire assemblage of fighters and healers rose into the air and hovered in the clouds. As they gathered around Alistaria, she drew from their presence the part of the Tuatha de Dannan passed down with each generation.

"Palathia," she said to the captain, "form the Kern into ranks behind me. Ensure they understand what will come next. Behind them, organize every root tender who wishes to fight."

The woman nodded and whisked away to gather the officers.

Piotr looked around, unsure of his role or where to line up with the soldiers. Alistaria watched as he considered joining the noncombatants mulling about the city.

"You'll fly beside me, brother?"

"I don't have much to offer," he said. "I'm truly more human than fae, and I'm no soldier. Truth be told, I'm not much of a thief. Maybe I'm best suited to remain behind."

"You're the son of Nastauria, and grandson of a king. You have a role to play here, even if it hasn't been revealed. As for being fae or human? Enatherr is under assault by the Shadow Realm, and I must help to drive it back. Fly beside me as my brother."

"And then we'll find Boyd?" he asked.

"We will."

"Then let's go."

Chapter Thirty-Six

"Lugh promised Areadbhar to his favorite son, Ibic, born to his luchorpán wife Nás. Her heart heard the moment the King of the Tuatha de Dannan died in battle, and fell into death herself before retrieving the spear for her son. Lugh had many children, each as worthy as the others to bear the weapon, but knowledge of who won the artifact faded with the fog of war."
– The Legends of the Tuatha, Chronicle IV, Twelfth Passage

Torian had no name for the great beasts, though Conner Liam's men had taken to calling them "Rock Crushers," or "Crushers," for short. Though he killed one in their previous fight, the sudden emergence of three at once swelled panic in his heart. They burst from the portal and landed on the stone floor with a furious cloud of debris. Everyone holding the line covered their faces behind shields.

"We've got Crushers!" Conner called, "Ready ballistae! Middle target first!" The large turrets spun at once, aiming toward the steaming hot beast. The smell of brimstone filled the air, and every man looking on continued to shield their eyes as pieces of stone rained down. "Fire!" the general commanded.

Several bolts released at once, most of which hit the mark. The beast fell.

"I'll take the left!" Torian called, and Conner readied his scorpions for another volley.

The fae general swooped down, aiming the tip of his spear at the charging Crusher. It was a scorching blue, hotter than he'd ever seen it glow. Snapping jaws bit at the air as he dove, narrowly missing as he bobbed out of the way. But his point missed, only grazing the animal's neck instead of impaling its heavy skin. The beast reared in pain, as it seemed only a prick was enough to inflict great injury.

Torian darted left and right, avoiding strong jaws, but he was caught too low to get away. He faced it head on. Movement caught his eye and he dared a glance to the floor just as three hellhounds leaped to attack. He turned the spear downward, meeting one in the throat and turning its body as a shield against the others. The impact knocked him to the floor.

He scrambled for his feet, gaining his balance just as the farthest beast crashed undaunted into Conner's shield wall. The line broke, and the beast thrashed among them while limbs and bodies dashed about the room. Hellhounds fell upon these at once.

The heavy twang of ballistae met Torian's ears and he instinctively ducked, his assumption correct that Conner chose to fire upon the beast looming above him. Though it fell, the hellhounds took advantage of his now vulnerable position. He searched them for weakness, but only the one he'd wounded seemed slowed. There was no time to fly, and he faced them with shield and spear.

The heavy blow of Fainnen silver met jawline with a shield smash, rolling into the body of the beast and placing it between him the others. With a ferocious leap he brought the spearhead down into the animal just beyond, dropping it with a heart stab. But he lost his footing on the landing, and the weapon stuck deep. Torian found himself entangled beneath the feet of the hound serving as his shield. He held on tight as the mass of bodies spun.

Try as it may to bite the man trapped against its ribs, Torian's shield lodged deep into its neck and prevented full reach. He prayed the spear would hold—a broken shaft would mean his death. He briefly closed his eyes against images blurring past, and imagined the beast must appear to others like a pup chasing its tail. After several more dizzying turns, the spear wrestled free and so did he. Luckily the hellhound was as disoriented as he.

Torian nearly retched as he found his footing, squaring off to face the wounded hellhound and its staggering ally. He tried to fly, but flashing pain in his left wing informed him of injury. Rendered little more than a human without flight, he searched for a way to defend against their killing blows and willed courage into his legs. The animals lunged with snapping teeth and he braced.

From both sides, steel pressed past his shoulders and locked into place with a resonant clang, and men grunted against the sudden impact of beasts against shields. It took him a moment to understand, but the pincer charge had worked. Torian found himself saved by his own invention. Just as his Tuatha mages could be surrounded and protected by closing in the shield wall, so had the humans under Conner Liam protected him. He eyed the right flank and confirmed it held, the embattled Crusher finally falling to an exhausted ballistae crew. The gaping hole in the line quickly filled in and readied for the next wave. Torian pushed through the ranks to find Conner and Markey O'Malley barking orders from the rear.

"Thank you for saving me twice back there," he said to the human general.

"What I love best about your shield wall," Conner took time to explain, "is the strength of unity and its reliance on the entire formation. I wouldn't have needed to save you if you'd remembered the tactics *you* created."

Markey chimed in, as well. "You're an excellent soldier, Torian, but learn to stick to the plan. Though it worked in the first attack, you can't keep flying off and fighting these creatures separately."

Effectively reprimanded, Torian followed the man's gaze. The two generals of shadow had arrived. They loomed. One with dark swirling pools where his eyes should have been—the other with orbs of brimstone.

"They said they're *three*, when they attacked before," Torian thought aloud.

"Well, I see only two, but even that's two too many," Conner muttered. "They toyed with us before, testing our defenses and gauging how we'd respond. They appeared the moment you charged that Crusher, heads held close in congress and watching your every move just as before."

"It was a trap," Torian realized, "and set for *me* to see if I'd leave the formation again."

"Aye," agreed Markey, "and one you fell into."

"Well, we're holding well against the Draugars, and it appears the hellhounds have pulled back," Torian appraised. "I don't see any more of those Crushers. Why don't we push them back toward the portal?"

"Because of a gut feeling," Conner explained, nodding toward Markey.

Torian watched his friend closely, thankful to see the soldier's mind was fully committed to battle, and that his mourning seemed set aside for time being. "What's your worry?" he asked.

"The way they watched you fight made my skin crawl. They don't command their armies like normal men. Their forces are far more expendable, like pawns on a chess board. They toss them indiscriminately at our swords and spears, caring little how many fall. We don't know their true numbers, and I still feel there's more to come."

"That's because their fallen come back," Torian said. He pointed toward a single Draugar charging the line. His armor was painted with a broad stripe of yellow paint. "I did that. I painted his chestplate after dropping him in battle more than a week ago. I thought then we may be grossly outnumbered and fighting the same beasts each and every night."

"But why are they so focused on testing you?" O'Malley insisted.

"It's the spear," Conner realized. "They called it something before."

"Areadbhar. They called it Areadbhar," Torian recalled. "Sìth Morkur called it the same shortly after I found it. It's certainly special—magical even—but why're they so interested in watching it during battle?"

Their musings were broken by a renewed attack on the right flank. The hellhounds had recommitted, and circled out from around a line of Draugars. With fierce howls they seemed to harken death to their side.

"Here it comes," Markey warned. "They always send the hellhounds just before launching another wave."

They didn't have to wait long. The gate to the shadow realm suddenly surged with a scathing wind full of heat and horrifying screams. Then winged demons burst forth.

Torian's entire body froze, locked in place by a mixture of fear and awe as hundreds of flying creatures flooded through the portal. At first, he thought them huge bats with leathery wings, beating out a pounding *whoosh* as they gathered in the rafters. But their bodies were neither bird nor bat. Their long limbs seemed almost human or fae. Straining his eyes to see in the torchlight, he felt transfixed by an eerie curiosity and found he could not look away.

"Holy Lady of the Loch," Conner Liam profaned, then shouted for the line to hold.

"What are they?" Torian asked. "I can't see them clearly in the dark." A strange sense filled him, believing he had seen these beasts before. He silently wished the light in the room was stronger and thought to have him men stoke the fires.

"General Torian," a voice called from behind the shield wall.

He was about to turn and reply, when a larger, more frightening specter arrived. A large, winged Spirit stepped through and fanned his massive wings, spreading them as a peacock would strut its fanciful feathers for attention. His crimson eyes reflected countless souls destroyed, literal pools of blood churning just as the brimstone and darkness did in those of his brothers. A new sensation shook the fae general and filled Torian with untenable terror. The gasps from the human soldiers reflected they had felt the same fearsome ripple pass through their ranks.

The three Sìths had gathered. The first two looked upon their brother with devilish glee. He, like the others, carried with him a shimmering veil of evil that drifted along as he joined them.

"They are three," Markey O'Malley said without thinking, marveling as Darkness, Death, and Violence stood before them.

"General Torian!" the voice shouted again, this time louder.

He shook himself free from the spell and turned to see who called. Torchlight reflected off familiar faces as Quinten and Harachen stood in the center of the formation with two mages, each with beaming faces and sharing a secret joy. "What is it?" he asked of the Tuatha soldiers. Their fate was as his—trapped in Enatherr and cut away from the Blossom and its gifts—and none of them had a reason to rejoice. *Their message had better be worth their smiles*, he thought.

"Our connection to the Bláth de Saol, sir," Quinten explained, "has returned."

"To all of you? Or just the mages?"

"All of us, sir!"

"Heavens save us!" O'Malley said, overhearing their news. "Light up the room," he commanded. "I want to see what we're facing in the light of day," he said. "To hell with this darkness!"

"Turtle!" O'Malley suddenly ordered, hoping to shield the men's eyes and spare most of them a horrific sight. The formation secured at once beneath the protection of the four-sided wall, leaving open only the center where the fae mages stood with outstretched hands. They channeled the fairy spark into a glowing sun of yellow light.

Torian kept his eyes locked on the scene before him, watching for any reaction from the creatures of shadow. He refused to blink as the light flashed all around, filling the entire palace with brightness. The creatures hovering in the rafters cried out with a screeching howl, higher in pitch than the hounds who joined in with their low bray. Torian fought against a sudden sickness at the hovering sight above.

"Good god," said O'Malley. "They can't be!"

But they were, and Torian finally understood they could no longer fight against this foe.

"Begin the retreat," he urged Conner, "and pray we find a way to close this portal."

The general nodded silently and gave the order. One of these creatures when small were troublesome enough. There was no telling what a full sized Ganshee could do to a man. They gnashed their razor sharp teeth and hissed between howls, ready for a chance to devour the army of humans and fae. But still the brothers held the army of shadow on a leash.

"Why do they toy with us?" O'Malley wondered aloud. "They know we're outnumbered, and cannot defend against them all."

Torian hefted Areadbhar, gripping it tightly as it glowed white hot. He knew why they held back—they feared the spear for some reason. His forearms shook from the fierce vibration of its desire to destroy these creatures. "Quinten," he said, "provide cover as we depart."

The mage nodded to the other three and stood ready to defend as the army stepped backward with shields held all around.

All at once, the hellhounds roared and charged. The Ganshee and Draugar followed.

Fire flew from the hands of the mages, forming a wall between the attacking creatures of shadow and the retreating army.

"Get them outside!" Torian screamed to Conner, then stood with Areadbhar held high and ready for whatever came. "Go now! We can't hold them for long!"

The general nodded, then ordered the retreat. In a single command the entire line reversed, spinning on its heels to face the rear and freedom. "Double time!" he called, and the last line of defense sprinted away.

Chapter Thirty-Seven

"One son of Lugh, both devious and cunning, went on to father the race of man. The purest of heart, however, the fae folk crowned as their king. Through his bloodline redemption is hoped."
– The Legends of the Tuatha, Chronicle IV, Twelfth Passage

Restarian stared at the sword in his hand. It glowed softly as they rode into Norgaard, pulsing with a familiar rhythm he could not place. His eyes had been fixated on the weapon for several minutes without knowing why. Once he understood, he focused even harder, pointedly avoiding looking at the palace upon the hill. Ghostly knives caressed his bony wings until he firmly closed his eyes against the memory. His flesh was not all he shed upon that hill.

"You're going to have to learn to use that," Niamh muttered, not accusingly nor aggressive, but with stern resentment over his sudden rise in position.

She hates me even more, he knew.

"Will you teach me?" he asked.

"If we make it through the portal I will, but you won't need training to defeat the Shadow. The Sword of Light is supposed to repel them, felling all who stand before it."

"Then why do I need to learn?"

"Because there are other weapons against which you'll need skill. That's why Nodrick was supposed to wield it and not *you*."

She was right, as he well knew, but killing the Storm Warden had brought much satisfaction. He had left any regrets he might have held behind at the tomb. "Yeah, well you all follow *me* now, and I'm your only path to Radviken."

"That's the only reason we stand beside you, Little Scar." She hadn't looked at him the entire time since setting off for the capital, but she focused angry eyes when she added, "and Radviken will kill you for what you've done."

"I think not," he said, dismissing her words with a shrug. "I remember him as a lord who *rewarded* boldness. Besides, Nodrick had grown too powerful. He was a threat and would have taken Enatherr for himself if we failed to retrieve Radviken. With the sword, he could have been nearly as strong as his former master."

Her silence suggested she found truth in his words, but stubbornness would never allow the former Searcher to admit so to him, her Little Scar.

Restarian finally lifted his gaze and focused upon the palace. The scene was oddly still, without even a bird flying overhead. It was a beautiful night, lacking clouds in the sky. A bright moon lit the stone walls while his eyes scanned for defenders. He found none—not even a lookout.

"Something's wrong," he said. "I thought you said this O'Malley was a Storm Rider."

"He was one of the best."

"Then where are his defenders? He doesn't know the Storm Warden is dead, but surely expected an attack would come eventually."

Niamh shrugged. "Maybe he dispatched his forces elsewhere—spread them thin fighting against the Shadow leaking into our realm?"

"No. This must be a trap."

A sudden flash of light lit every window of the palace from within.

"What was that?" he demanded.

"I've no idea," she admitted, spurring faster to ride ahead. Restarian gently kicked the ribs of his mount to keep up, though did so with caution. He still hadn't grown accustomed to riding.

Once they reached the main walls of the palace, they each reined their horses and surveyed the scene. Only a few sentries manned the gates. Shouts of alarm carried on the night, and soon dozens of stretcher bearers rushed out of a row of tents in the courtyard, quickly dashing into the keep. Screams of agony escaped into the night before the heavy doors slammed shut behind them.

"There's a battle raging within," Niamh said with shock. "The portal must already be open!"

"But how could they have translated the texts so soon? They've only had them a few days."

"I think it opened from the other side," she whispered, careful not to worry the others as they rode up beside her. With eyes suddenly growing wide with excitement, she lifted her head with a smile. "We should attack now!"

"What about the Shadow?"

"You've got Claímh Soluis, Little Scar. They will fall against you if attempting a challenge."

"So what do you suggest?"

"We charge." Pointing at the gate she added, "We kill those guards, then outflank O'Malley and kill him too. After that we can escape through the portal and retrieve Radviken."

But Restarian lacked convincing. "You're certain they won't challenge Claímh Soluis?"

She nodded. "The Sword of Light is undefeated in battle except by certain weapons."

"Which are those?"

"As yet, they're undiscovered."

The fae prince allowed a smile to betray his budding confidence. Holding the Sword of Light aloft, he felt energy course through his grip as it lit ablaze with the radiance of the sun. "Sound the charge," he said with confidence.

The Riders spurred forward with Niamh in their lead. Restarian followed, barely holding on and trying to keep up. With one hand he gripped the saddle while holding the Sword of Light aloft with his other. He watched as the Riders challenged the sentries, overwhelming their position and rendering them quickly defeated.

"To the keep!" Niamh commanded, and her men answered with a roaring battle cry.

Her men. Restarian knew better than to assume they followed him. He wielded the sword, but would never command their allegiance. He dismounted along with the others and raced toward the palace doors. A portcullis hung low, ready to drop in place. *But not to keep* out *an enemy,* he realized, suddenly piecing it together. The flash of light in the palace. A battle raged within.

"Stop!" he cried, but the Riders kept their pace.

He had to stop them.

"Everyone stop!"

They rushed forward with fury and deaf to his voice. He had no authority and never would.

Five sentries turned slowly in the night, surprised by the sudden arrival of rogue Storm Riders and cut down as quickly as they appeared. Only then did Niamh and the others slow.

"The battle," Restarian panted, "*inside* the palace... It's a trap. It'll be death to go in!"

"We're attacking O'Malley's back," Niamh said. She drew her blade from a guardsman's chest and led the group forward. "But either way, we have to find the portal." Her Riders grunted their agreement and followed her off.

In a fit of rage, he picked up a sword from one of the dead sentries, swinging a wild tantrum against the chains and gears of the portcullis. *I will be in charge,* he screamed in his head, then tossed the sword aside and rushed inside to catch up.

Restarian had only ever seen the upper levels of the palace, and was surprised to learn the great hall was below ground and not on the main level. A long stairwell led them beneath the structure, and sounds of battle echoed the moment they reached the first flight. Eerie howls drifted past his ears, and shouts of men told a tale of defeat. Boots on stone echoed as O'Malley's army suddenly appeared on the landing, cowardly fleeing their enemy.

"That's too many," he whispered to Niamh.

She hesitated, assessing their numbers against her own.

"Up against the wall!" he commanded. "I have the gift of sight!"

"Nodrick is dead," she replied, "and with him our hopes to survive. Each of us would rather die for the memory of Radviken than live under the tyranny of O'Malley!" She abruptly rushed forward with sword held high and the others followed, catching the retreating force by surprise. Each soldier barely had time to lift their heads before they were mowed down by Niamh's Storm Riders.

"Shield wall!" someone finally yelled, and a line formed on the stairs.

Niamh attacked with fury, never letting up despite the sudden wall of steel between her sword and the flesh of her enemies. She never saw the spear until it entered her chest.

"No!" Restarian screamed, raising his hands and channeling fairy spark into the line of men. The electricity rippled through the air as it struck, bouncing from one chestplate to another and dropping O'Malley's front ranks to their knees. Niamh's Storm Riders flinched away from the energy, stepping backward with awe as he took over.

Torian hefted Areadbhar and turned its point toward the pillar. He had to collapse the building, even if it meant trapping himself inside. As soon as Quinten and Harachen dropped their wall of fire, he would order them from the hall. He studied the bricks, searching for any weakness or vulnerability and hoping his spear's magic would be strong enough.

Shouts from the stairs echoed trouble.

"What's happening?" he demanded from Quinten.

"I'm not sure, but they halted retreat on the stairs," he replied. Sounds of clashing steel told the rest of the story. "Not sure how much longer we can channel this barrier, General."

"Hold that firewall," he urged. "O'Malley's under attack from above."

He peeled his eyes from the pillar, focusing instead on the stairs. High up above, a line of nearly one hundred Storm Riders clashed with the main army. Conner seemed to have it under control, but a lone figure on the top flight caused his blood to run cold. The white hair and blood red eyes were enough, but the bony protrusions that once were wings confirmed it was Restarian.

The fae prince raised his hands and sent fairy spark into the front lines, killing several men with a single bolt. Then he drew a sword from his side, raising it high above his shoulder. The air around him shimmered, forming a brilliant light as it glowed from within. Torian clutched Areadbhar as he watched, wondering if the weapons were similar in origin. Worry turned to fear as he watched the light explode into the army. He flinched away from the brilliant flash, but lifted his head in time to watch everyone collapse to their knees with a single slice. As the blade swung, the light wove tighter, extending the blade as it sizzled and steamed through flesh, sinew, and bone.

Death is horrible to watch, especially when it includes friends—good friends, like Markey O'Malley. That's especially true when men and women you've trained with and lived among, fought beside, and laughed with, fall before your eyes in battle. Everyone in Markey's army perished, and Torian choked back tears and bile as he helplessly watched.

Restarian killed without remorse, sheathed the weapon, and knelt down beside a woman. Not just any woman—Radviken's Searcher, the red headed woman who fought so fiercely against him and Markey in the upper levels of this palace. Her blade had trimmed the flesh from the prince's wings, killing him over and over again while her master brought him back for more punishment each time. Though she lay bleeding on the steps, Restarian knelt beside her and placed a lover's kiss upon her lips, healing her wounds and somehow restoring her lifeforce as well.

"What happened?" Niamh asked.

"You died. You all did." Restarian gestured at all the bodies littering the stairs. "But I defeated O'Malley's army with this." He touched the sword at his side. He offered his hand and she took it, then the prince helped her stand beside him.

"Can you raise our men?" she asked.

"There's no time," he replied. Stepping carefully over O'Malley's fallen, they walked hand in hand down the steps. A single soldier stood before him, dressed in the golden armor of the Kern.

"What have you done?" Torian demanded.

Restarian found it difficult to see his face for the dancing shadows made deep by the fire raging behind him. Eerie howls warned of danger beyond the inferno, and the Shadow Realm lay just beyond.

"I'm fulfilling my destiny," he replied, "as King of the Fae. I'll retrieve Radviken and restore his control over Enatherr, then challenge Alistaria for my rightful place."

"It's not yours, Restarian. A lot changed after you hid away like a spineless coward. Alistaria may be Deamhan, but that doesn't mean she isn't fae. She deserves her place as queen and makes a far better ruler than you could ever dream."

In his hands, Torian held a spear, intricately carved and with a glowing tip. He raised it, ready for combat, with wings spread outward to taste the air. This was a surprise as well.

"So you have wings after all? How's that so if you're human?" Restarian asked.

"Just because you lost yours, does it make you less of a fae?" Torian charged forcefully, with fiery spear pointed directly at the prince's chest.

Restarian drew Claímh Soluis, feeling it vibrate as it did before while channeling light. He stepped into a warrior's stance, the same Torian himself had taught him at the edge of their first Fainnen Ring. His own wings spread gloriously, with spidery webs filling the space between bone.

Torian's eyes grew wide at the sight, and Restarian laughed as he rose into the air. He held the sword at the ready, then swung it as he had when killing O'Malley's army. The razor thin stream of light lashed out, narrowly missing the upstart Skygate sentry, sending him veering off course.

"Don't fight him!" Niamh begged.

"Why not? I have the Sword of Light!"

"Because he wields Areadbhar!"

This rattled Restarian, though he did not fully understand her meaning.

Torian returned with another attack, charging shield first with spear point ready to plunge. The glow of it was bright blue and searing hot. The prince tried to move out of the way, stepping clumsily to the side and slicing the blade over his head wildly. The cutting light returned, but had no effect on its target. As it passed harmlessly through, Torian's spear erupted with a fiery discharge and collided squarely into his chest. Though warm, the flame had no effect on him either. Then he remembered Niamh's warning. There were weapons against which his would have no effect. Restarian had no chance but to fight this trained warrior in simple combat.

The tip of Torian's spear was close and so was the shield. Restarian dodged the point but a square blow tossed him aside. As he tumbled down the steps he watched hopefully as Niamh attacked. Her swords danced in a deadly fury, pushing Torian backward and off balance. But his spear provided reach, and soon tipped her leg with a sweeping spin. A line of blood formed beneath her leather armor, skin exposed as it melted away.

Screams from behind caused all three to turn. The wall of fire had failed, and dark shadows descended from the rafters.

Ganshee! he suddenly realized.

More than a dozen charging hellhounds joined the attack, as the two Deamhan holding the firewall disappeared beneath a pile of writhing death. Beyond them stood three Sìth Spirits and an army of Draugars. All but the Spirits advanced.

Restarian found the eyes of the trio oddly entrancing, one pooling darkness, another brimstone, and the other's a deeper shade of crimson than his own. They each wore a smile, and their faces and bodies swam with deeply glowing lines to match their eyes. With sword held aloft, he gathered unsteady legs beneath him. The blade glowed brightly, and the Spirits laughed.

Torian suddenly stood beside him, but showed no intent to do harm.

"Stand with me, until this threat is over," he urged. "Those are the brothers Dub, Dother, and Dian – Darkness, Evil, and Violence. That pillar is rigged somehow to collapse and close the portal, and I need your help to do so."

"I can't.... I *won't*," Restarian replied. "I've a bigger task, and don't care if these creatures destroy Enatherr."

Torian turned with angry eyes, fiercely blue and challenging. He shook the spear and pointed. "If they take Enatherr, then Fainnotherr is next! You must..." His words were cut off with a gasp as Niamh's blade entered his side. He fell to his knees.

"Come," she said, pointing to the portal beyond the brothers. "With the Sword of Light you can cut us a path and get us inside!"

"But your leg!" It was already festered, growing green on the edges where it wasn't too badly charred.

"Is fine, and supports my weight without effort. You can heal me on the other side, but we have to hurry!"

He raised Claímh Soluis, charging it with light, and swung, driving back the hellhounds and scattering Ganshee to the rafters. The line of Draugars split before them and they ran for the shimmering rift, racing headlong into the realm beyond.

Chapter Thirty-Eight

"The Tuatha de Dannan defeated every enemy except the true residents. The Sìth were older to this island than even the fae, humans, or luchorpán combined, and were more persistent in their dealings with the gods. In the end, the Dannan defeated themselves by blending in with their servants and fading away. The Sìth, in celebration of the invaders' decline, divided the realms. The land had always belonged to the Sìth, this place called Hy Brasil."
– The Legends of the Tuatha, Chronicle V, Fortieth Passage

Alistaria stepped through the portal and into Markey's palace, instantly feeling a deep wrongness. No sentries stood on the raised platform, and no archers watched the ring. She assumed they must be deployed elsewhere, most likely fighting against the threat Piotr had described. He claimed the portal emerged in the great hall, and that is where she must take her people.

"Captain Palathia!" she called as she stepped into the welcome area. "Organize everyone as soon as they cross through. Send the Kern ahead with the root tenders second." Everyone on this side paused as an eerie howl echoed through the stone hallways. "Tell them to hurry."

"Where are *you* going?" Piotr demanded.

"I'm going to find Torian."

"Don't go alone! Please, wait for us!" Palathia urged. "It isn't safe."

Alistaria smiled, this woman was truly a strong one, with good instincts and certainly a protector. The fact that Piotr was sweet on her was also a good sign. He had a way of picking good people. "I'll be fine," she promised. "Besides, Markey and General Liam will no doubt have the line secured. I'll stay behind it."

"We'll be there shortly," the captain insisted. "Right behind you with the first wave."

The queen departed, hurrying down the hall and descending several staircases. Each step brought the howling closer to her ears. Once she reached the main level, her gut urged caution. There was no sound of combat—no clashing steel or even the twang of bows.

Her feet skidded to a halt on the second landing. Bodies littered the stairs below. Though most were Markey's soldiers, a few were Torian's Kern. With heart pounding she peered further into the room. Beyond the fallen, two mages held a wall of fire against a terrifying enemy. Hellhounds paced back and forth as if waiting for the barrier to drop, and hundreds of Draugars stood motionless, fixed in place and unmoving without even the rise and fall of their breasts.

If they haven't made it through, then who killed Markey's army? she wondered.

Movement caught her eye in the flickering firelight, as two figures moved. *Restarian.* Her heart broke for him once more, the wretched creature so damaged by Radviken. She hadn't noticed him while bent over the girl, and only recognized him now by the bony wings sprouting from his back. Then she recognized the girl. It was the Searcher who had seduced him with hope, enticing him into the torture that damaged his body and mind. He held her in a lovers embrace, and the energy flowing between their bodies was from the healing blossom.

Then another figure moved, as Torian stepped from the shadows and into the firelight. He called out to Restarian, then charged with his glowing spear. Alistaria stood dumbfounded, too far away to intervene. Whatever their quarrel, Torian meant to kill her cousin, and the prince intended the same. Both weapons glowed brightly then, clashing as two gods fighting in mythological clouds. Until the wall of fire collapsed. When the mages holding the barrier fell, the enemy sprang forth at once. Fae sized Ganshee swept down from the rafters, and hellhounds bound for the two fae lying exhausted on the stone.

Too shocked by the giant Ganshee, Alistaria never saw Torian fall. She watched with sadness as Restarian sprinted with his woman toward the portal. That's when she noticed the brothers—three Spirits observing the chaos they had wrought. They made no attempt to stop Restarian, but keenly watched as his magical sword ripped through scores of their Draugars. Only then did she realize Torian lying injured at the bottom of the steps.

Footsteps pounded as the first wave of Kern arrived. Behind them was a line of root tenders. She hurriedly gave them orders.

"Get between Torian and those beasts, fight and hold them back. The fire seems to work best against the hounds and Ganshee."

"Ganshee?" Palathia asked. "Aren't those more of nuisance than a threat?" But then she saw them rise up from their feast and fly toward Torian. Her hands immediately cast bolts to drive them back, careful not to hit the Kern as they moved into position.

"Piotr," Alistaria commanded, "stay with me. We must attend Torian."

By the time they reached him he was barely conscious, staring up at the Kern but unable to speak or offer commands as their general. She could tell that bothered him more than his injury.

"I'm here, Torian," she said gently, placing her hands against his side. The woman's sword had driven deep, and the organs within were badly damaged. It would have been a slow killing blow had she not arrived when she did.

"The pillar," he muttered.

"Don't speak."

"... Collapses the palace. Must... Close the portal..."

"Stop moving," she urged, "or I can't heal you properly."

"There's a mechanism," he explained, "somewhere here or above to spring the trap. If we don't find it, we can't keep them out."

Piotr leaned in closely. "I can find it, that's what I do is find ways in and out while avoiding traps. What's it look like?"

"I'm not sure, but it I think it's above the kitchens. There's a lift to lower food and stores below, and I believe it's connected to that."

"How does it work?"

"Flood gate..." Torian gasped, suddenly coughing blood. "I think the river breaks the pillar."

Alistaria nodded, and Piotr rushed off, carefully stepping over bodies as he raced up the stairs.

"Now lie back," she urged. "Let me tend to your wounds."

"Alistaria..." he whispered.

"Shh..."

"I love you."

She paused. This man had the worst timing, but she was glad he finally realized it on his own. "Well, then. I'd kiss you... but you're coughing up blood and dying on me, so let's discuss that later."

The last time she'd summoned healing powers on this side of the portal it took great effort, they were weaker and harder to find the thrum. This time, by drawing it directly from her realm, she had no trouble at all. She restored him easily, surprising even herself with the quickness with which they attuned.

I wonder, she thought, turning from Torian to eye the fallen soldiers. There was Markey, cut down with a wound across his neck. She began with him. Leaving her sentry to recover, she eyed her cousin's handiwork. Restarian's weapon had wreaked havoc on every soldier's body and, though some would prove easier to repair than others, many required the rejoining of limbs and sometimes torsos. After a quick glance to ensure the wall of fire held, she poured healing into the King of Enatherr.

"What are you doing?" a voice demanded. "They belong to me."

She did not look up to answer the newcomer. She had expected him. "You and I both know they do not. They died unnaturally, by a weapon intended only for gods."

"Claímh Soluis." Sìth Morkur named it.

"As you say. You cannot claim these souls, nor will your Ganshee devour their flesh." She did not need to look at them to know the tiny sprites hovered behind their master. "What are those other creatures?" she asked of the larger monsters fighting against the Kern. "Are they yours as well, Master of Beasts?"

"I am the master of these two realms, but not where shadow rules. Things there are not natural, as you can tell after meeting the brothers."

"Why do they hold back?" Torian asked, climbing to his feet and gently stretching the muscles where his wound had been. "They toy around when they could easily have defeated us straight away. Why?"

"Every Sith feeds differently. I devour souls, whereby they consume something... far fouler."

"Fear," Torian guessed.

"In a way."

"What then?"

"Darkness, Death, and Violence are all to be feared, but that is not what they consume. Humans and fae are very much alike in many ways, despite their differences. But when exposed to those elements, you destroy yourselves. You fight against each other. You fight against the unfightable—the unseen and uncertainty drives you to madness and they feed upon your response. Despair, terror, anger, and irrational hatred—those fuel their power."

"Freely given it is sweeter," Alistaria remarked, once more quoting the legend. Markey was awake and listening. She moved down the line to restore his soldiers.

The Sith nodded, "Freely given it is *sweetest.*"

"So each time we fight against them, they what? They grow stronger?"

"Beyond your wildest expectation."

"But they *do* kill," Torian pointed out.

"Only to increase the fear."

"Then we cannot fight them. We *must* get our soldiers out and away, Alistaria!"

"Only if Piotr can find the mechanism," she cautioned. "Otherwise we risk freeing them into Enatherr."

"Did you forget everything you learned in the Blossom, young queen?" Sìth Morkur laughed his grumbling growl, then turned to leave. "Or do you fear what you know you must do?"

Alistaria said nothing in return. She knew what she must do and did indeed fear it badly. But she would not grant that morsel to their enemy. "As soon as I get them raised," she said to Torian, "I will get them outside. You take care of my people, and bring them to safety, as well."

"I will," he promised.

"And Torian," she added, "I love you, too."

Chapter Thirty-Nine

"The gods of Hy Brasil are gone, dead or faded with time, but their legacy remains and their relics abound. Keep alive the stories and worry not of a return, but prepare for a second age without the Sith."
– The Legends of the Tuatha, Chronicle V, Forty-First Passage

Piotr rushed outside and made his way to the far end of the courtyard. He had seen the lift before and made haste to the spot. Once there, it was simple to figure out the workings—turn the crank this way to make it go up, and that direction to descend. He found it locked securely in the up position. But that was it, no other moving parts to suggest a dead man switch like Torian described.

Besides, he thought, Radviken wouldn't put such a dangerous device too close to machinery servants used every day. Though it would provide good cover, accidents happen too easily, and manual laborers often enjoy pushing buttons and moving levers they shouldn't. He tried to put himself in the king's shoes, climbing the parapet and wandering to the edge of the wall. The river raged as a torrent against the rocks below.

If I were he, and the palace was evacuated, how would I collapse it? Not as Torian suggested. His plan involved too much risk, to place the entire building's fate on one pillar. An earthquake could level the entire building with a single shake. He tried to remember the last time they'd had one and couldn't, but that didn't mean the risk wasn't there. *No,* he thought. *That's the dummy rigging, the sham or lure.* Why else would he have placed it in such an obvious spot, if not to trick the enemy into following him elsewhere?

He and Boyd had encountered deadfalls before when they dabbled in targeting other thieves. The guild house had them—nearly caught Boyd in one when they stole the casks of 754 wine. No, Radviken would lure the enemy away from the portal, then trigger it in a way they couldn't retreat back through. Sure, he'd collapse the palace, but only to seal them into tomb of rock. If Piotr knew one thing about Radviken, it was the man's endless opinion of himself and his expectation for success. The man was egotistical, self-righteous, and selfish. But he was also wise.

Piotr scanned the rocks, searching for a flood gate or any way to bring water into caves below. Not caves—*mines!* Just as in Fainnotherr, this mountain is made of iron. No doubt, the iron was mined here in Norgaard, and the series of tunnels would run underneath the entire palace. Torian had figured that out, but not the answer to the dead man switch. Radviken wouldn't flee from here, rather, he'd trap his own forces inside while fighting the enemy, then walk away untouched.

He stepped onto the lift, unbuckled the safety latch, and began lowering himself downward. *What am I doing?* he thought. *This is the kind of plan Boyd would try.* But sneaking toward danger is what he and his buddy did best. While he lowered, he wondered what the little guy was doing at that moment with just as much stupidity as this. Knowing Boyd, he'd probably be stealing the book from the clutches of a dragon or rolling in the sheets with the luchorpán King's plumpish wife.

The lift shook as it settled in place, suggesting there were braces underneath, and not solid ground. He scanned the sides of the platform, looking for anything that could release the structure and allow the device to descend further. He found nothing obvious. Stepping off, he studied the base. It was simply decorated with several tiny faces staring back at him. As he peered closer, he realized they looked like Ganshee. He reached out a hand and touched one, feeling the teeth and noseless face. He touched the eyes, and the image moved.

Piotr pulled back his hand like it had been struck, and the carving snapped back into place. Reaching down more boldly, he placed a finger in one of the eyes, pressed, and rotated until it was turned upside down. Only then did he release it, pulling back his finger and praying it would remain in place. It did.

One by one, he rotated the images, turning the tiny faces upside down. After each had been turned, he stepped cautiously onto the platform and turned the crank. The lift shook and shimmied, but lowered easily. *Jackpot!*

The subbasement was literally a cave, rather a series of them, with branches running out in every direction. He chose the path leading directly beneath the great hall. It opened into the mother of all deadfalls, with boulders placed atop tall ramps, and with more passages behind each one. He quickly surmised the water would push the boulders, sending them rolling below, and toppling these pillars. He ran around and removed the safety boards preventing each from rolling prematurely.

Piotr knew time was fleeting, but tried one final passage—the one leading upward beneath the stairs leading to the palace entrance. The entire assembly was hollow beneath the stairs, with flimsy pillars supporting each flight. This was it, the deadfall to trap the enemy forces beneath the rubble. Turning, he ran toward the lift and turned the crank once more, sending the platform up so no one would follow. Then he travelled the only way he could, up a ramp leading to the coast. If he were right, Radviken would have provided for both the demise of his enemy and also his escape.

Torian had little trouble shoring up defenses, backing the Kern slowly up the stairs with a wall of fire between them and the creatures. When they were halfway up, he called to Palathia. "How are your mages holding up?"

"Good so far," she replied. "But this work is exhausting, and I fear we'll rapidly lose control at some point. I'm also worried about the entrance to the palace."

"There's a portcullis, so we should be able to drop it into place," he suggested. "That'll help if you're fully exhausted and can't hold on until Piotr finds the mechanism."

She nodded back her thanks, but the look on her face troubled Torian deeply. The woman, just like all her mages, were painted with a weariness that made him think of Quinten and Harachen—collapsed by fatigue. Their bodies were unrecoverable. Thinking of the men who *were* restored, he glanced over his shoulder just in time to see Markey O'Malley and Conner Liam exit the top of the stairs. The survival of those two men ensured a glimmer of hope for Enatherr.

Alistaria watched as Markey emerged.

"Set the line up here," he shouted to his general. "But not so close we fall into the hole if the thief succeeds."

"I'd rather be closer," Conner argued, "in case any escape."

"Let's hope he's quick about it, then." Markey turned to Alistaria just as she wrapped him in a hug. Surprised, he asked, "What's that for?"

"It's for Jaana and Germaine. I'm sorry you lost them. They were beautiful souls, and Jaana was a wonderful woman."

"Well, sometimes the creator is nothing more than an ass who enjoys watching his favorite creations die."

"I doubt that's the case," she said hopefully, "and I'm sure their deaths had purpose. I can't bear believing in a creator who only lives to kill us off."

"Well, if their deaths held purpose, then the creator is sicker than we thought for killing innocent and sweet things like them."

"Look," she said, "there's Torian."

The line of mages had made it to the top of the stairs, and Torian had run to get started on the portcullis. But, as Palathia and her team rushed out, he struggled with the controls.

"It's jammed!" he shouted. Conner rushed over to inspect.

"No, it's been sabotaged. Look here, someone hacked up the gears, and now they're immovable."

"Palathia!" Torian called. "Hold that barrier! The portcullis won't engage!"

"We'll try," she promised, but the look on her face screamed doubt.

Alistaria stepped up beside her. "I'll take over if yours fails," she assured the captain. She looked to the east and saw the glimmer of sunlight beginning to rise above the mountains. Though she had never heard of the Shadow Realm attacking during daytime, this night was far from over. Still, she allowed her gaze to linger while she thought about other things. Things like Sìth Morkur.

Did you forget everything you learned in the Blossom, young queen? He had asked on the steps. *Or do you fear what you know you must do?*

Of course she was afraid. She was terrified to work that vile corruption. It nauseated her to even consider touching it again, but she knew she must. She had drawn a lot of it already—first after taking the oaths from her people when she had drawn from them the stain of the Tuatha de Dannan coursing their blood. She took more from the Deamhan Palace, absorbing from its iron tainted ground. It sickened her to hold it in and yearned to release the substance, but it wasn't time—until time suddenly ran out.

Captain Palathia and her mages suddenly collapsed in the courtyard. They were beyond exhausted, and the barrier had fallen as soon as they fainted. Before Alistaria could even throw up a fireball, the enemy poured through the gate. The Ganshee came first, flying low against the ground and then spreading into a hellish formation searching for soldiers to devour. They dove quickly and often, but the shield wall held.

Next came the hellhounds and the Draugars. Alistaria never had a good count of them before, but there seemed to be more than before—as if a constant stream had begun pouring through the portal as soon as the second barrier went up. Too late to contain them, the Queen of the Fae raised her arms into the air, and a murky shadow rippled slowly away from her body.

The corruption would not touch her body as she released her invisible hold, but it raised her off the ground all the same. She hovered upon the swirling clouds, working darkness and spinning it into something larger—something more magnificent. Six of the Ganshee dove in to stop her ministrations, but were caught up into the vortex as soon as they neared. These, she knew, would be dealt with later.

She flew higher and higher as the storm grew into a raging torrent. Rain and ice fell within, and thunderbolts flared out in every direction. Soon it enveloped the entire courtyard.

Through the storm she looked directly at Torian and Conner Liam. "Move the line," she said, "beyond the outer walls. Get everyone free!"

Both men nodded and complied, fighting off the beasts as they ran.

The Tempest drove many of the shadow beasts into the palace for cover, but most were swept up. There was no escaping her storm—much fiercer than Radviken's had been—and the power rejuvenated Alistaria by ripping away all doubts and previous worries. She understood now Radviken's arrogance. Once you've controlled the Tempest and fed upon its corruptive power, one truly became like a god—or, she suddenly realized, like the Tuatha de Dannan.

There was no stopping it now, and she set it free to intensify and ravage all of Enatherr—to purge the land and set right the growing season upon which its people had grown accustomed. They needed the storm now and, surprisingly, so did she. With a final push, she drove the last of the shadow creatures into the palace.

Piotr followed the passage and found it much deeper than expected, climbing higher in elevation for some time before leveling out. At the top he found a room. In the center, he found a wheel. He laughed at how simple it was—turn the wheel and open the flood gates. Though the act was easy, the timing was not. He had no idea if Alistaria, Torian, and the others were free. If he turned it now, he may kill them all. On the other hand, if they had escaped and held the enemy at bay, they may be pleading with him to hurry.

He had no idea what to do, and so he closed his eyes and wished Boyd were there. "Little buddy," he said, "I miss you something fierce and could really use your help right now. I'm nothing without you by my side—only Piotr. But together, we're Piotr and Boyd. I *need* one of your harebrained schemes right about now. I wish you could tell me what to do!"

"So you admit I have the best ideas?" his friend replied.

Piotr opened his eyes with amazement, setting them upon Boyd sitting in the corner and chewing on a sausage. "How?" he demanded.

His stocky little friend held up a string of beads and book. "With this," he said. Then he frowned, set down the book, and raised the beads. "Well, with these. They're like the gems on the fairy blossom thingy, except some are strange. Apparently, if I'm holding this, I have powers just like Alistaria, only slightly different."

"Is that the book that Markey sent you to get?"

"Yep! It's the anal!"

"Annal."

"Whatever. Anyways, I asked the beads to take me to you, closed my eyes, and it worked—showing up just when you needed me, apparently. Now say it again, how great are my ideas?"

"They're the best, Boyd."

"Thought so, and so are you. Now, what do you need help with?"

"I have to turn this wheel to collapse the palace, and I have to time it when Alistaria and the others aren't trapped inside."

Boyd scrunched up his nose as if smelling something tart. "That's a *horrible* plan, Piotr."

"Yeah, well you weren't around to come up with anything better."

"No, I reckon I wasn't. Okay," Boyd said. He scooped up the book, held up the beads, and closed his eyes, "I'll be right back."

In a blink, Boyd was gone. A dozen blinks later, he was back and soaking wet. He wasn't happy about that part. He also wasn't carrying the book.

"Poofed right into a raging Tempest, I did! That really is rude not to warn a fella he's gonna get soaked, Boyd."

"I didn't know."

"Nope, didn't figure you did. Anyways, they're all free and begging you to *spin the damned wheel and please get on with it*, to be exact. Oh, and I gave Alistaria her anal, so you don't have to worry about that." Without waiting for an answer he shrugged and held up the beads. "Love you, brother, but I've got to get back."

"Back where?"

"Luchorpár. I love it there, but don't worry, I'm coming back. I'm just scouting ahead to get the lay of the land." He wiggled the beads. "And need to get these back into a certain pocket before someone finds they're missing." He suddenly frowned as if remembering something. "Piotr? I don't think Lucky's a dog."

"Why not?"

"Well, I saw him at the oddest time, like he showed up just to help me out with a problem I had."

"Yeah, he did the same for me, too—in the oddest of places."

"Yep. I think he's more than a dog."

"What do you think he is, Boyd?"

"I haven't worked that out yet, but just don't think he's a dog." Then he wiggled his fingers and poofed away into thin air.

Piotr shook his head, let out a laugh, and turned the wheel. He could hear the rushing of water in the caves, and was briefly worried he'd be trapped. But as the wheel turned, the wall opened before him. Outside, where the sun should have been shining and the birds chirping, he stepped into a raging Tempest, the most ferocious he'd ever seen, and frowned when he realized he'd have to walk back the entire way in a storm.

By the time he reached the ridge, he heard a rumble and the ground beneath him shook violently. He hurried along and rounded the top, just in time to watch the palace collapse into a heaping pile of rubble. It filled the pit perfectly, trapping whatever remained inside and burying the portal completely. Boyd was wrong. It was a good plan... a *great* plan, after all.

Chapter Forty

"The Tempest was the key as it lessened the Dannan hold on the island, and worked strongly against the Shadow Realm. It seems I was wrong about their presence in our world, and realize now there is usefulness in everyone. But I've a feeling we've only scratched the surface in restoring our history, with books to read and new experiences to share. For starters, I must restore what was stolen from the humans."
– Queen Alistaria of Fainnotherr, First of Her Name.

In a boarding house in Crosston, Alistaria sat around the kitchen table with Torian, Markey, Piotr, and Palathia. The last two were holding hands under the table and hoping no one would notice. But that was okay since she did the same thing with Torian. The door burst open and Tamee barged in, trailed by Maerlin and his armful of books. He laid them on the table and smiled at the others.

"Well," the queen of the fae asked her friend, "what did you find out?"

"Fascinating things!" the sentry turned scholar beamed. "Inside these books is the entire history of Fainnotherr, beginning with the arrival of the Tuatha de Dannan! They give us the meaning of every bloom on every Blossom and even why they were created in the first place! You see," he explained with excitement, "once they started mating with the fae, luchorpán, and humans, those bloodlines could no longer work their magic! So they adapted the Blossoms to filter out their influence!"

"That follows what I learned," Alistaria agreed. "What else?"

"So much more," he said.

"Wait," Torian interrupted. "Humans really had magic? I thought we had it only because of the Bláth de Eolas."

"You did, but it went the way of the fae." Maerlin replied. "Once you retrieve the Bláth de Eolas, you'll be able to wield it again after bleeding and filtering out any Dannan in your blood."

"What of ways to defeat the brothers? They never climbed the stairs, and I'm assuming they passed through the portal. I expect we'll see them again," Torian said.

"The annals did indeed mention the brothers, several times actually. The Tuatha de Dannan are the ones who defeated and banished them the first time. Though it didn't specifically explain how, there were many clues. I need to dig some more, but hopefully can piece it all together."

"What of Restarian's sword?" Alistaria asked. "Sìth Morkur had a name for it."

Maerlin pulled out a volume and carefully opened it to a bookmarked page. "Right here," he said. "Claímh Soluis. It belonged to Nuada, the first king of the Dannan."

"It's powerful," Torian said, painfully remembering the way he'd cut down an entire army with a single swing.

"Yes, but so is Areadbhar. Your spear once belonged to Lugh."

"Who was he?" Torian asked, sitting up taller and listening intently.

"He was another king of the Dannan, the balancer of truth and law and order. It is said the spear detects treachery as well as evil presence."

"That explains why it lit up around Restarian." Torian muttered.

Alistaria said nothing, but the way everyone avoided looking at her revealed much. They all feared she would continue to search out goodness in her cousin. Though she never saw him slay Markey's army, the result was the same either way. He had turned—chosen a life with Niamh and Radviken over reconciliation with her and Fainnotheria.

"I need to get back," she said finally. Thinking of home had reminded her. "There's so much to do." She glanced out the window to find the Tempest waning. That was good, since part of her worried she had built it so powerful it would never end.

Markey followed her eyes and read her thoughts. "You did good, bringing it back. This will help keep out the shadow, though I fear the brothers will continue to try our realm. But at least we can plant dependable crops and the starvation period will end in a couple of days." His eyes betrayed a sadness of his own, suggesting that some sad things would continue—in his case the time for mourning.

Tamee walked over and wrapped him in a motherly hug. "I know you loved them, Markey, and they died knowing it just as well."

He wiped them with the back of his hand. "I should have done more to avenge them."

"You'll get your chance," Torian promised, "but first we must retrieve for you the Bláth de Eolas."

For that they would need Boyd, and all eyes turned to Piotr who shrugged. "I haven't seen him since he brought the book and told me you were out."

"Well, as soon as he shows up, we'll put together a plan with his help."

"Oh, you don't want him coming up with a plan," Piotr said with a laugh. "His have a high rate of failure."

"Yeah?" Markey said with a grunt. "But in this case, Boyd's the only hope we've got." He looked around. "By the way? What happened to Lucky? This is usually where that stinky little dog would have something to add."

Alistaria knew, but kept that bit of knowledge to herself. All she said was, "I'm sure he'll turn up when we need him most." Then she winked to the Puca reclining in the corner as a hare, invisible to all but her.

Thank you for reading *Howling Shadow*. If you enjoyed my story, please leave a kind review so that others may find it. For updates about my writing and where I'll appear in person, please sign up for my newsletter at *tbphillips.com*.

Books by T.B. Phillips are found most places books are sold or by visiting *andalonstudios.com*

Chilling Tales
Ferryman (October 2022)
Don't Pay the Ferryman (Expected June 2023)

Corrupted Realms
Wailing Tempest (May 2021)
Howling Shadow (September 2021)

Andalon Saga

Andalon Origins
Andalon Project (April 2022)
Andalon Paradox (Epected Winter 2022)

Dreamers of Andalon
Andalon Awakens (June 2019)
Andalon Arises (July 2020)
Andalon Attacks (December 2020)

Children of Andalon
Andalon Legacy (September 2022)